Sue MacKay lives with her husband in New Zealand's beautiful Marlborough Sounds, with the water at her doorstep and the birds and the trees at her back door. It is the perfect setting to indulge her passions of entertaining friends by cooking them sumptuous meals, drinking fabulous wine, going for hill walks or kayaking around the bay—and, of course, writing stories.

Louisa Heaton lives on Hayling Island, Hampshire, with her husband, four children and a small zoo. She has worked in various roles in the health industry— most recently four years as a Community First Responder, answering 999 calls. When not writing, Louisa enjoys other creative pursuits, including reading, quilting and patchwork—usually instead of the things she ought to be doing!

Karin Baine lives in Northern Ireland with her husband, two sons, and her out-of-control notebook collection. Her mother and her grandmother's vast collection of books inspired her love of reading and her dream of becoming a Mills & Boon author. Now she can tell people she has a *proper* job! You can follow Karin on Twitter, @karinbaine1, or visit her website for the latest news—karinbaine.com

D1331387

000003012146

Tempted By The Single Doc

SUE MacKAY
LOUISA HEATON
KARIN BAINE

MILLS & BOON

First Published in Great Britain 2019
by Mills & Boon, an imprint of HarperCollins*Publishers*
1 London Bridge Street, London, SE1 9GF

TEMPTED BY THE SINGLE DOC © 2019 Harlequin Books S. A.

Breaking All Their Rules © 2016 Sue MacKay
One Life-Changing Night © 2016 Louisa Heaton
The Doctor's Forbidden Fling © 2016 Karin Baine

ISBN: 978-0-263-27665-7

0719

MIX
Paper from
responsible sources
FSC™ C007454

This book is produced from independently certified FSC™
paper to ensure responsible forest management.

For more information visit: www.harpercollins.co.uk/green

Printed and bound in Spain
by CPI, Barcelona

BREAKING
ALL THEIR RULES

SUE MacKAY

Dear Lyn, I am going to miss your laugh and
those good times we yakked in your sewing room.
Thank you for dragging me out to find my other
passions that I'd forgotten all about until I met you.
You read every book and this one is definitely for you.

CHAPTER ONE

OLIVIA COATES-CLARK STRAIGHTENED up and indicated to a nurse to wipe her forehead in an attempt to get rid of an annoying tickle that had been irritating her for some minutes. 'Is it me, or is Theatre hotter than usual this morning?'

'I haven't noticed,' Kay, the anaesthetist, answered as she kept an eye on the monitors in front of her. 'Sure you're not stressing about tonight, Olivia?'

'Me? Stress?' Olivia grimaced behind her mask. She was a control freak; of course she stressed. 'Okay, let's get this second implant inserted so we can bring our girl round.'

'So everything's good to go for the gala fundraiser?' Kay persisted.

'Fingers crossed,' Olivia muttered, refusing to think about what could go wrong. Her list of requirements and tasks was complete, neat little ticks beside every job and supplier and by the name of every attendee, including the seeing eye dog coming.

'I bumped into Zac yesterday. He's looking forward to catching up with everyone.' Kay's forced nonchalance didn't fool her.

'I'm sure everyone feels the same.' The anaesthetist *had* hit on the reason for Olivia feeling unnaturally hot. Zachary Wright. Just knowing he'd be at the function she'd spent weeks organising made her toes curl with unwanted anticipation. Not to mention the alien nervousness. 'Zac,' she sighed into her mask. The one man she'd never been able to delete from her mind. And, boy, had she tried.

'You need more mopping?' the nurse asked.

'No, thanks.' That particular irritation had gone, and she'd ignore the other—Zac—by concentrating on supervising the plastic surgery registrar opposite her as he placed the tissue expander beneath the pocket under Anna Seddon's pectoralis major muscle on the left side of her chest wall.

The registrar had supported Olivia as she'd done the first insertion of an expander on the right side, watching every move she made, listening to every word she said, as though his life depended on it. Which it did. One mistake and she'd be on him like a ton of bricks. So far he was doing an excellent job of the second breast implant. 'Remember to make sure this one's placed exactly the same as the first one. No woman is going to thank you for lopsided breasts.' This might only be the first stage in a series of surgeries to reconstruct Anna's breasts but it had to be done well. There was no other way.

The guy didn't look up as he said, 'I get it. This is as much about appearances and confidence as preventing cancer.'

'Making a person feel better about themselves is our job description.' Her career had evolved along a path of repairing people who'd had misadventures or deforming surgeries. But she didn't knock those specialists working to make people happier in less traumatic circumstances. Everyone was entitled to feel good about themselves, for whatever reasons; to hide behind a perfect facade if they needed to.

For Olivia, looking her absolute best was imperative: a confident shield that hid the messy, messed-up teenager from the critical world waiting to pounce. Making the most of her appearance hadn't been about attracting males and friends since she was twelve and the night her father had left home for the last time, taking his clothes and car, and her heart. Leaving her to deal with her mother's problems alone.

Kay glanced down at the table. 'This isn't the first time I've seen a perfectly healthy woman deliberately have her breasts removed, but I still can't get my head round it. I don't know if I'd have the guts to have the procedure done if I didn't already have cancer.'

Olivia understood all too well, but... 'If you'd lost your grandmother and one sister to the disease, and your mother had had breast cancer you might think differently.' Bad luck came in all forms.

'I'd do whatever it took to be around to watch my kids grow up,' one of the nurses said.

'You're right, and so would I.' Kay shivered. 'Still, it's a huge decision. You'd want your man on side, for sure.'

'Anna's husband's been brilliant. I'd go so far as to call him a hero. He's backing her all the way.' A hero? If she wasn't in Theatre she'd have to ask herself what she was on. Heroes were found in romance stories, not real life—not often anyhow, and not in her real life. Not that she'd ever let one in if one was on offer.

As Olivia swabbed the incision a clear picture of Zac spilled into her mind, sent a tremor down her arm, had her imagining his scent. *Oh, get over yourself.* Zac wasn't her hero. Wasn't her *anything.* Hadn't been since she'd walked away from their affair eighteen months ago. But—she sighed again—what would've happened if she'd found the courage to push the affair beyond the sex and into a relationship where they talked and shared and had been there for each other? Eventually Zac would've left her. At least by getting in first she'd saved herself from being hurt. Tonight she'd see quite a bit of him, which didn't sit easily with her. The day his registration for the gala had arrived in her inbox she'd rung him for a donation for the fundraising auction. Since then she hadn't been able to erase him from her mind. *Come on. He's always been lurking in the back of your head, reminding you how good you were together.*

'So there are good guys out there.' Kay's tone was acerbic.

Zac might be one of the good guys. She hadn't hung round long enough to find out. She'd got too intense about him too quickly and pulling the plug on their fling had been all about staying in control and not setting herself up to be abandoned. Going through that at twelve had been bad enough; to happen again when she was an adult would be ridiculous. So she'd run. Cowardly for sure, but the only way to look out for herself. And now she had an op to finish and a gala to start. 'Let's get this tidied up and the saline started.' She had places to be and hopefully not many things to do.

An hour later she was beginning to wish she'd stayed in Theatre for the rest of the day. The number of texts on her phone gave the first warning that not everything was going to plan at the hotel where the gala evening would be held; that her list was in serious disarray.

As she ran for her car, the deluge that all but drowned her and destroyed her carefully styled hair, which she'd spent the evening before having coloured and tidied, was the second warning. At least her thick woollen coat had saved her silk blouse from ruin. But rain had not been on her schedule, which put her further out of sorts. *Everything* about tonight had to be perfect.

Slamming the car door, she glared out at the black sky through the wet windscreen. 'Get a move on. I want you gone before my show starts tonight.'

The third suggestion that things were turning belly up was immediate and infuriating. One turn of the ignition key and the flat clicking sound told a story of its own. The battery was kaput. Because? Olivia slapped the dashboard with her palm. The lights had been left on. There was no one to blame except herself.

Olivia knew the exact moment Zac walked through the entrance of the plush hotel, and it had nothing to do with the sudden change in noise as the doors opened, letting in sounds of rain and car horns. She might've been facing the receptionist but she knew. Her skin prickled, her belly tightened, and the air around her snapped. Worse, she forgot whatever it was she'd been talking about to the young woman on the other side of the polished oak counter.

So nothing had changed. He still rattled her chain, made her feel hot and sexy and out of control—and he hadn't even said a word to her. Probably hadn't recognised her back view.

'Hello, Olivia. It's been a while.'

That particular husky, sexy voice belonged to only one man. 'Since what, Zac?' she asked, as she lifted her head and turned to face him, fighting the adrenaline rush threatening to turn her into a blithering wreck. This was why she'd left him. Zac undermined her self-control. How had she found the strength to walk away? Not that there'd been anything more to their relationship than sex. Nothing that should be making her blood fizz and her heart dance a tango just because he stood a few feet from her. No way did she want to jump his bones within seconds of seeing him. She shouldn't want to at all. But no denying it—she did. Urgently.

Black-coffee-coloured eyes bored into her, jolting her deep inside. 'Since we last spent the night together, enjoying each other's company.'

'Go for the jugular, why don't you?' she gasped, knowing how wrong it was to even wish he'd give her a hug and say he'd missed her.

Zac instantly looked contrite. 'Sorry, Olivia. I didn't mean to upset you.'

'You didn't,' she lied. Behind her physical reaction her heart was sitting up, like it had something to say. Like what? Not going there. 'The bedroom scene was the grounds of our relationship.' That last night she'd got up at three in the morning, said she couldn't do it any more, and had walked out without explaining why. To tell him her fears would've meant exposing herself, and that was something she never did.

'So? How's things? Keeping busy?' Inane, safe, and so not what she really wanted to ask. *Got a new woman in your life? Do you ever miss me? Even a teeny, weeny bit? Or are you grateful I pulled the plug when I did?* Right now all her muscles felt like they were reaching for him, wanting him touching them, rubbing them, turning her on even more. Had she done the right thing in leaving? Of course she had. Rule number one: stay in control. She'd been losing it back then. Fast.

Zac had the audacity to laugh. 'What? You haven't kept tabs on me?' His grin was lazy, and wide, and cut into her with the sexiness of it. There was no animosity there whatsoever, just a deliberate, self-mocking gleam in his beautiful eyes. He was as good as her at hiding emotions.

Shaking her head at him, Olivia leaned back, her hands pressed against the counter at her sides, the designer-jeans-clad legs Zac had sworn were the best he'd ever had anything to do with posed so that one was in front of the other and bent slightly at the knee, tightening the already tight, annoyingly damp denim over her not-so-well-toned thigh. 'My turn to apologise. I haven't kept up with any gossip.'

'Dull as dishwater, that's my life.' Unfortunately that twinkle she'd always melted for was very apparent, belying his statement.

'Right.' She rolled her eyes at him, unable to imagine Zac not being involved in and with people, especially feminine, good-looking, sexy people. Was she jealous? Couldn't be. She'd done the dumping, not him. But Zac with another woman? Pain lodged in the region of her heart.

'Never could fool you.' It was inordinately satisfying to see his gaze drop to the line on the front of her thigh where the mulberry three-quarter-length coat cut across her jeans. Even more gratifying when his tongue lapped that grin, which rapidly started fading. And downright exciting to see Zachary blink not once but twice.

She didn't need exciting in her life right now, and Zac and exciting were one and the same. 'I keep to myself a lot these days too,' she muttered, not really sure what she was talking about any more with the distracting package standing right in front of her.

'Now I'm shocked.' The grin was back in place,

lion-like in its power to knock her off her feet and set her quaking.

'Why? It's not as though I've ever been a social butterfly.'

'There's never been anything butterfly-like about you, Olivia.'

Confidence oozed from Zac that didn't bode well for the coming evening when they'd be in the same crowd, the same venue. At the same table. Of all the things she'd organised she should've been able to arrange that he sat on the opposite side of the room. It had proved impossible as they were the only two people attending the gala who were on their own. All the others were in pairs.

'You're saying I'm not a flapper?' They were toying with each other. Reality slammed into her, made her gasp aloud. They'd teased each other mercilessly the first night they'd gone to bed together, and had never stopped. Well, she was stopping now. Time to put distance between them. She needed to get on with what she was supposed to be doing. 'I've got a lot to do so I'll see you later. I hope you have a great evening.'

Disappointment flicked through his eyes, quickly followed by something much like hurt but couldn't be. Not hurt. She hadn't done anything more than push him aside, though that'd probably spiked his pride. He had a reputation of loving and leaving.

It had taken the death of a small child in Theatre to throw them into each other's arms for the first time. Desperate to obliterate the anguished parents from her mind, Olivia had found temporary comfort with Zac. She'd also found sex like she'd never known before. How they'd spent years rubbing shoulders at med school and not felt anything for each other until that day was one of life's mysteries. From then on all it took had been one look and they'd be tearing each other's clothes off, falling into bed, onto the couch, over the table. They'd done little talking and a lot of action.

Tonight, if they were stuck together for any length of time, she'd talk and keep her hands to herself. That had been the plan, but so far it wasn't working out. Not that she'd touched Zac yet. Yet? With her mouth watering and her fingers twitching, it would take very little to change that. She had to get serious and focus on what had to be done. 'I'll leave you to check in.' Her voice was pitched high—definitely no control going on there.

'I'm not checking in.'

She should've remembered that. She knew all the names of the people who'd elected to stay the night here instead of driving home afterwards. 'Do you live nearby?'

'Over the road.'

'In that amazing apartment building designed to look like a cruise ship, overlooking the super yachts and high-end restaurants?' Oh, wow. He had done all right for himself. Of course, he came from a moneyed background, but she recalled him saying he'd paid his own way through med school. She had never told him she also came from money or that her mother had used it to bribe her to keep her onside until she was old enough to work out that hiding bottles of alcohol from her father wasn't a joke at all.

'Are you staying here?' he asked casually, making her wonder if he might have plans to pay her a visit if she was.

'Yes.' The house she'd bought last summer was less than twenty minutes away in upmarket Parnell. 'I'm going to be busy here right up to kick-off, and going home to get ready for the evening would use up time I might not have if things go wrong.' Which plenty had done already. She looked over at the receptionist, suddenly remembering she'd been in the middle of another conversation before Zac had walked up. 'Can you let me know when Dr Brookes and his family check in, please?'

The girl nodded. 'Certainly, Dr Coates-Clark.'

'I'll be in the banquet room,' Olivia told the girl needlessly. The hotel staff had her cell number, but right now she wasn't doing so well on remembering anything she should. Better get a grip before the evening got under way.

Zac shrugged those impressive shoulders that she'd kissed many times. 'I'll give you a hand.'

'Thanks, but that won't be necessary. I'm getting everything sorted.' As much as having someone to help her would be a benefit, Zac would probably get her into a bigger pickle just by being in the same room. Turning on her heel, Olivia headed to the elevator that'd take her up to the room where tonight's dinner, auction, and dance would be held. The evening was due to get under way in a little over three hours and she wanted to check that everything was in place and see if the flowers had finally arrived. Something about bad weather causing a shortage of flowers at the markets that morning had been the harried florist's excuse. But bad weather didn't explain why the place name cards were yet to arrive from the copy centre.

Unbelievable how she'd softened on the inside when she'd first looked at Zac, despite the heat and turmoil he instantly ramped up within her. Like she'd missed him. But she hadn't known Zac beyond work and bed so not a lot to miss apart from that mind-blowing sex.

Odd she felt there was more to him she wanted to learn about when she hadn't been interested before. Not interested? Of course she had been. That's what had frightened her into ending the affair.

A large palm pressed the button to summon the elevator. 'It's out there on the surgeons' loop that you need some help with running the auction tonight. I'm stepping up. Starting now.' Zac looked down his long straight nose at her, his mouth firm, his gaze determined. 'No argument.'

Why would he want to do that? It meant being in her company for hours. She'd have sworn he would've planned on keeping well away from her, and that the last five minutes had been five too many in her company. 'Thanks, but no thanks, Zac. I've got it covered.' Second lie in minutes. She doubted she could spend too much time with him without dredging up all the reasons why she'd been a fool to drop him—instead of remembering why it had been a very sane move. No one was going to walk away from her ever again.

She made the mistake of looking at Zac and her tongue instantly felt too big for her mouth. Zac was so good looking, his face a work of art, designed to send any female who came near him into a lather. Including her. Olivia closed her eyes briefly, but his face followed her, seared on the insides of her eyelids. Zachary Wright. If ever there was a man she might fall for, it was Zac. That was a big 'if'. Painful lessons growing up were a harsh reminder that there was only one person who'd look out for her—herself.

But one touch and Zac had always been able to do anything he liked with her. Not that he'd taken advantage in a bad way. He wasn't that kind of man. See? She did know something about him. Hopefully he hadn't known how close she'd come to being totally his, as in willing to do absolutely anything to keep him.

'You all right?' He touched her upper arm, and despite her layers of clothing the heat she associated with him shot through her, consumed her.

'F-fine,' was all Olivia could manage as she stared at him, pushing down hard on the urge to touch him back, to run her hand over his cheek, and to feel that stubble beginning to darken his chin.

Taking her elbow, Zac propelled her forward, into the elevator. 'Third floor?'

'Yes,' she croaked. *Go away, leave me alone, take your sexy body and those eyes that were always my undoing, and take a flying leap off a tall building. I don't need this heat and need crawling along my veins. Go away.*

'I'm not going anywhere for the rest of the day, so get used to the idea, Olivia.'

Ouch. Had she said that out loud? What else had she put out there? One glance at him and she relaxed. He hadn't heard anything about jumping off a building. But she couldn't relax fully until tonight was put to bed.

Olivia groaned. 'Bed' was so not a safe word when she was around this man. It brought all sorts of images screaming into her head. Images she refused to see or acknowledge. They were her past, not her future. Or her present.

CHAPTER TWO

WHO'S TAKEN ALL the air out of this box? Zac stared around the elevator car, looking for a culprit. His eyes latched onto Olivia. He had his answer. It was *her* fault he couldn't breathe, couldn't keep his heart beating in a normal, steady rhythm. Olivia Coates-Clark. CC for short. CC *was* short. Delicate looking—not delicate of mind. Tiny, yet big on personality. Filled out in all the right places—as he well knew. Fiery when pushed too far, sweet when everything was going her way. An itch.

An itch he would never scratch again. He absolutely had to ignore it.

She'd dumped *him*. Hard and fast. Slapped at his pride. *He* did the leaving, when he was good and ready, not the other way round. He should've been grateful, was grateful. Having more than his usual three or four dates with Olivia had got him starting to look out for her. On the rare unguarded moments when something like deep pain had crept into her gaze he'd wanted to protect her; and that was plain dumb. Given his past, that made him a danger to her. He hurt people; did not protect them. He also didn't feel like having his heart cut and cauterised again when she learned of his inadequacies. No, thanks.

Hang on. Had she found out? Was that why Olivia

had pulled the plug on their affair? Because she'd found him to be flawed? No. She still looked at him as she always had—hot and hungry, not disgusted or aloof.

Breathing was impossible. Not only was Olivia using up the oxygen, she was filling the resulting vacuum with the scent of flowers and fruit and everything he remembered about her. *Hell, let me out of this thing. Fast.* He took a step towards the doors, stopped, glanced at the control panel. They were moving between floors. *Get a hold of yourself.*

Yeah, sure. This is what Olivia always did to him. Tipped him upside down with a look, sent his brain to the dump with a finger touch, and cranked up his libido so fast and high just by being in the same air as him. Exactly what was happening now. His crotch was tight, achingly tight. As was his gut. Nothing new there. Eighteen months without setting eyes on her, with only once talking on the phone about the auction, and he was back to square one. Back to lusting after her. Unbelievable. How could a grown man with a successful career as an orthopaedic surgeon, presumably an intelligent and sane man dedicated to remaining uninvolved with women, lose all control because of this one?

Olivia Coates-Clark. She was why he felt three sheets to the wind—and he hadn't touched a drop of alcohol all week. He'd been too busy with scheduled surgeries and two emergencies involving major operations to have any time to enjoy a drink and take in the ever-changing view from his apartment living room. But within minutes of being with CC he felt as though he'd downed a whole bottle of whiskey. This was shaping up to be a big night in a way he didn't need.

A phone buzzed discreetly. As nothing vibrated on

his hip it had to be Olivia's. He listened with interest as she answered, totally unabashed about eavesdropping.

'Olivia Coates-Clark speaking.' Her gaze scanned the ceiling as she listened to her caller. Then, 'Thank you so much. Your efforts are really appreciated.' Her finger flicked across the screen and the phone was shoved back into her pocket. 'One problem sorted.' She smiled directly at him.

'Had a few?' he asked, trying to ignore the jolt of need banging into his groin as his gaze locked on those lush lips.

'I guess it would be too much to expect arranging something as big as this has become to go off without some hitches. It hasn't been too bad, though.' Had she just crossed her fingers?

'Whose idea was it to raise money for Andy Brookes? Yours?'

Olivia nodded, and her copper-blonde hair brushed her cheek, adding further to his physical discomfort. 'I'll put my hand up, but from the moment I started talking to surgeons at Auckland Surgical Hospital it went viral. Everyone wants to be a part of supporting Andy. I imagine tonight's going to raise a fair whack of dosh. People have been unbelievably generous with offering art, holidays, and other amazing things to auction.' She smiled again, her mouth curving softly, reminding him of how he used to like lying beside her in his bed, watching her as she dozed after sex. All sweet and cute, and vastly different from the tigress who could sex him into oblivion. 'Thank you for your generous gift,' she was saying.

He'd put in a weekend for a family of four on his luxury yacht, with all the bells and whistles, and he'd be at the helm. 'Andy was the most popular guy in our senior registrar years. He never failed to help someone out when they were down.'

'You forget the practical jokes.' Again she smiled, making those full lips impossible to ignore.

So he didn't; studied them instead. Covered in a deep pink sheen, he could almost feel them on his skin as she kissed his neck just below his ear, or touched his chest, his belly, his... He groaned inwardly and leaned away from her, concentrating on having a polite conversation with his ex-lover. 'I have vivid memories of some of the things Andy did to various people.' He sighed as he tried to ease his need. Memories. There were far too many of Olivia stacked up in his mind. He should've heeded them and replied no to the invitation to join his colleagues tonight. He could've said he was doing the laundry or cleaning his car. But he'd wanted—make that needed—to get her out of his system once and for all, and had thought joining her tonight would be the ticket. Now he'd like nothing more than the gala to be over so he could head across the road to his quiet, cold apartment and forget Olivia.

'Have you met Andy's wife?'

'Kitty was at a conference with Andy that we attended in Christchurch last year.' *The conference you were supposed to speak at and cancelled the day after you walked out of my life.*

Olivia must've recalled that too because a shadow fell over those big eyes, darkening the hyacinth blue shade to the colour of ashes. Why did he always think of flowers when he was around her?

'I had an emergency. At home.' She spoke softly, warily.

'You lived on your own.' She didn't have kids. Not

that he knew of. Hell, he didn't even know if she had siblings.

'My mother was unwell.' She straightened her already straight spine and said, 'Andy was going places back then. Hard to believe he's now facing the fight of his life to remain alive, instead of continuing his work with paraplegics.'

What had been the problem with her mother? If he asked he doubted she'd tell him, and if she did then he'd know things about her that would make him feel connected with her. The last thing he wanted. Feeling responsible for her was not on his agenda. So, 'Andy's got a chance if he has the radical treatment they're offering him in California.'

'It must be hard for Kitty too.'

'Unimaginable.' Zac took a step closer to CC, ready to hug away that sadness glittering out at him. Sadness for their friend? Or her mother? Something had disturbed her cool facade.

Zac understood confronting situations that threatened to destroy a person. He'd been eighteen when the accident had happened that had left his brother, Mark, a paraplegic. Two years older than Mark, he was supposed to have been the sensible one. *Try being sensible with an out-of-control, aggressive younger brother intent on riling him beyond reason.* Nearly twenty years later the guilt could still swamp Zac, despite Mark having got on with his life, albeit a different one from what he'd intended before the accident.

The guilt was crippling. Being ostracised by his family because he'd been driving the car when it had slammed over the wall into the sea was as gutting. That's what put the shields over his heart. If his parents couldn't love him, who could? If he wasn't to be trusted to be responsible then he had no right to think any woman would be safe with him. Or any children he might have. So he had to keep from letting anyone near enough to undermine his determination to remain single, even when it went against all he believed in.

Olivia shuffled sideways, putting space between them. 'Here's hoping we raise a fortune tonight.'

Zac swallowed his disappointment, tried to find it in himself to be grateful Olivia had the sense to keep their relationship on an impersonal footing. It didn't come easily. He'd prefer to hug her, which wouldn't have helped either of them get past this tension that had gripped them from the instant he'd sauntered into the hotel. He wanted her, and suspected—no, he knew—she wanted him just as much. The one thing they'd been very good at had been reading each other's sexual needs. There hadn't been much else. Shallow maybe, but that's how they'd liked it. Their lives had been busy enough with work and study. Their careers had been taking off, leaving little time for much else.

But right now hugging Olivia would be wonderful. Why? He had no idea, but being this close to her he felt alive in a way he hadn't for months. Eighteen months, to be exact. This feeling wasn't about sex—though no denying he'd struggle to refuse if it was offered—but more about friendship and closeness. No, not closeness. That would be dangerous. He hauled the armour back in place over his heart. One evening and the itch would be gone.

The elevator doors slid open quietly. Zac straightened from leaning against the wall, held his hand out to indicate to Olivia go first. 'After you.'

Following her, his gaze was firmly set on the backs of those wonderful legs and the sexy knee-length black boots highlighting them to perfection. Was it wrong to long for what they used to have? Probably not, but needing the closeness with her? That was different from anything he'd experienced, made him vulnerable. Earlier, seeing Olivia standing in Reception, looking like she had everything in hand, he'd felt the biggest lurch of his heart since the day his world had imploded as that car had sunk into the sea and his brother had screamed at him, 'I hate you.'

'Zac.' Olivia stopped, waited for him to come alongside her.

That slim neck he remembered so well was exposed where her coat fell open at her shoulders. 'CC.' If he used the nickname he might stop wanting something he couldn't have. This woman had already shown she could toss him aside as and when it suited her.

He watched as the tightness at the corners of her mouth softened into another heart-wrenching smile. 'Funny, I haven't been called CC for a while. I used to like having a nickname. More than anything else it made me feel I belonged to our group.'

'You never felt you belonged? Olivia, without you we wouldn't have had so many social excursions or parties. You held our year together.' She'd worked hard at organising fun times for them, sometimes taking hours away from her studies and having to make up for it with all-night sessions at her desk. But to feel she hadn't been an integral part of the group? How had he missed that?

Her smile turned wry. 'I've always taken charge. That way I'm not left out, and I get to call the shots. No one's going to ignore the leader, are they?'

His heart lurched again, this time for the little girl blinking out from those eyes staring at some spot behind him. He certainly didn't know this Olivia. 'I guess you're right.' With his family he'd learned what it felt like to be on the outside, looking in, but at university he'd made sure no one had seen that guy by working hard at friendships. A lot like Olivia apparently. Everyone at med school had adored her. She could be extroverted and fun, crazy at times, but never out of control. It was like she'd walked a tightrope between letting go completely and keeping a dampener on her feelings.

Except in bed—with him.

Damn, he'd like nothing more than to take Olivia to bed again. But it wouldn't happen. Too many consequences for both of them. The vulnerability in Olivia's eyes, her face, told him he could hurt her badly without even trying. That blew him apart. He wanted to protect her, not unravel her. *He cared about her.*

Trying to get away from Zac and her monumental error, Olivia rushed through the magnificent double doors opening into the banquet room now decorated in blue and white ribbons, table linen, chair covers. Since when did she go about telling people about her insecurities? Not even Zac—especially not Zac—had heard the faintest hint of how she didn't trust people not to trash her. She did things like this fundraiser so that people thought the best of her. That was the underlying reason she could not fail, would not have tonight be less than perfect. The same reason everything she did was done to her absolute best and then some. She must not be found lacking. Or stupid. Or needy.

Coming to a sudden halt, Olivia stared around the function room, which had been made enormous by sliding back a temporary wall. The sky-blue shade of Andy's favourite Auckland rugby team dominated. In the corner countless buckets of blue and white irises had finally been delivered and were waiting for the florist to arrange them in the clear glass bowls that were to go in the centre of each table. Everything was coming together as she'd planned it.

She was aware of Zac even before he said, 'Looking fantastic.'

Zac. Those few minutes in the elevator had been torture. Her nostrils had taken in his spicy aftershave, while her body had leaned towards his without any input from her brain. When he'd looked like he'd been about to hug her she'd at least had the good sense to move away, even when internally she'd been crying out to have those strong arms wound around her. Now she stamped a big smile on her face and acknowledged, 'It is.' Too bad if the smile didn't reach her eyes; hopefully Zac wouldn't notice.

'You're not happy about something.' He locked that formidable gaze onto her. 'Give.'

Once again she'd got it wrong when it came to second-guessing him. 'The florist's running late, the wineglasses haven't been set out, the band assured me they'd be set up by four and...' she glanced at her watch '...it's now three twenty-five.' *And you're distracting me badly. I want you. In my bed. Making out like we used to. Actually, I'd settle for that hug.*

'We can do this. Tell me what you want done first.' His eyes lightened with amusement, as if he'd read her mind.

He probably had. How well did she know him? Really? They hadn't been big on swapping notes on family or growing up or the things they were passionate about. Only the bedroom stuff. Shoving her phone at him, she said, 'Try the band. Their number's in there. Eziboys.'

'You've got the Eziboys coming to this shindig?'

Admiration gleamed out at her. 'What did you have to do? Bribe them with free plastic surgery for the rest of their lives?'

With a light punch to his bicep she allowed, 'One of them went to school with Andy's younger brother. They want to help the family.'

'Not your formidable charm, then?' He grinned a full-blown Zachary Wright grin, one that was famous for dropping women to their knees in a begging position.

Click, click. Her knees locked and she stayed upright. Just. 'Phone them, please.' Begging didn't count if she remained standing. Anyway, she wanted the band at the moment, not sex with this hunk in front of her looking like he'd stepped off the cover of a surfing magazine. Another lie.

Zac was already scrolling through her contact list. 'Got a dance card? I want the first one with you. And the second, third, and fourth. Oh, I know, I'll put those in your diary for tonight.'

Dance card, my butt. How out of date could he get? 'You'll be inundated with offers.' Did he really want to dance with her? She'd never survive. What little control she might exercise on her need would sink without trace if he so much as held her in his arms, let alone danced with her. Anyway, he wasn't making sense. He'd been peed off when she dumped him, so he wouldn't want to get close to her on the dance floor. Or did he have other plans? Plans that involved payback? Tease and tempt her, then say bye-bye?

As Zac put the phone to his ear he shook his head. 'If you didn't want dancing tonight you should've gone to the retirement village to find a group of old guys with their tin whistles to play for us.'

'I enjoy dancing.' *Just don't intend doing it with you.*

'I didn't know that. Looking forward to it. Looks like your florist has arrived.' He nodded in the direction of the doors, then went back to the phone. 'Jake, is that you, man? How're you doing?'

Olivia stared at Zac. He knew Jake Hamblin, the band's lead guitarist? That could be good for getting the band to actually turn up. Zac was full of surprises. Hadn't he said something about the florist too? Spinning around, she came face-to-face with a neat and tidy woman dressed in black tailored trousers and an angora jersey under her jacket. Nothing flower-like about her. 'You're the florist? I'm Olivia Coates-Clark.'

The woman nodded, sent Zac a grin. 'That's me. I see the flowers finally turned up. Show me exactly where you want these arrangements and I'll get on with it.'

Zac was handing the phone back to Olivia. 'How's things, Mrs Flower?' That really was her name. 'Your hip still working fine?'

'You were the surgeon. What do you think?'

Zac's laughter was loud and deep, and sent pangs of want kicking up a storm in Olivia's stomach. 'Good answer,' he said.

So he knew this woman too. Probably used her for sending beautiful flowers to all his women. Ouch. He'd sent her flowers when she'd dumped him. A stunning, colourful bouquet of peonies, not thorns or black roses, as well he might've.

'Do we have a band?' she asked in her best let's-get-on-with-things voice.

'Filling the service elevator with gear as we speak,' Zac said. 'What's next? Want those buckets of flowers moved somewhere?'

The band was on its way; the flowers were about

to be fixed. Olivia shook her head in amazement. Two more ticks on her mental list of outstanding things to get finished. Things just happened around Zac. Somehow it had all got easier with him here. 'We need two long tables up against that far wall for the auction. The hotel liaison officer went to find them an hour ago.' She needed to display the gifts that'd been donated.

'Not a problem.' Did he have to sound so relaxed?

The clock was ticking. That long soak she'd planned on in the big tub in her room upstairs before putting on her new dress, also from the shop where she'd got her coat, might just be a possibility. 'Easy for you to say,' she snapped.

Zac took her arm and led her across to where the florist was already wiring irises into clever bunches that were going to look exquisite. 'You explain where you want everything and try to relax. We'll get this baby up and running on time. That's a promise.'

'I am relaxed.'

'About as relaxed as a mouse facing down a cat. A big cat.' He grinned and strolled away before she could come up with a suitable rejoinder.

Very unlike her. She always had an answer to smart-ass comments. Watching Zac's casual saunter, she noted the way those wide shoulders filled his leather jacket to perfection. Her tongue moistened her lips. No wonder she wasn't thinking clearly—the distractions were huge and all came in one package. Zachary Wright.

CHAPTER THREE

AN HOUR LATER, Zac handed Olivia a champagne flute filled with bubbly heaven. 'Here, get that into you. It might help you unwind.'

'I can't drink now. I've got to finish in here, then get myself ready.' Her taste buds curled up in annoyance at being deprived of their favourite taste. But she had a big night ahead of her so having a drink before it had even begun was not a good idea.

With the proffered glass Zac nudged her hand—which seemed to have a life of its own as it reached towards him. 'One small drink will relax you, Olivia.' He wrapped her fingers around the cool stem. 'Go on.' There was a dare in his eyes as he raised his own glass to his lips.

Zac knew she never turned down a dare. But she'd have to. Tonight's success rested on her being one hundred and ten per cent on her game. Her mother had taught her well—go easy on the alcohol or make a fool of herself. Not going to happen tonight when everyone's eyes would be on her.

Zac's throat worked as he tasted the champagne. Appreciation lit up his eyes. His tongue licked his bottom lip.

And Olivia melted; deep inside where she'd stored all

her Zac memories there was a pool of hot, simmering need. The glass clinked against her teeth as the divine liquid spilled across her tongue. And while her shoulders lightened, tension of a different kind wound into a ball in her tummy and down to her core. 'Delicious,' she whispered. Zac or the wine?

He nodded. 'Yes, Olivia, it is. Now, take that glass upstairs to your room and have a soak in the hot tub before getting all glammed up. I'll see to anything else that needs to be done here before I go across to change.'

She went from relaxed to controlled in an instant. 'No. Thank you. I need to check on those flowers and—'

'All sorted.' From the table he handed her an iris that been tidied and then tied with a light blue ribbon. 'Take this up with you.'

Even as she hesitated, her hand was again accepting his gift. What was it with her limbs that they took no notice of her brain? 'My favourite flower.'

'That particular shade matches your eyes perfectly.'

'Wedgwood. That's the variety's name.' She stared at it, seeing things that had absolutely nothing to do with this weekend. Or Zac. All to do with her past.

When she made to hand it back he took her hand and held it between them, his fingers firm. His thumb caressed the inside of her wrist. 'Who does it remind you of?' Very perceptive of him.

How had she walked away from this man? She must've been incredibly strong that day, or very stupid. 'My father used to grow irises.' Before he'd left because he'd been unable to cope with his wife's drunken antics. *And I could? I was only twelve, Dad.*

Tugging free from Zac's hand, she stepped back a pace. 'Why are you helping me?' He hadn't decided to target her for sex, had he? Or was that her ego taking a hit? Zac never had trouble getting a woman; he didn't need her. Even if what they'd had between them had been off the planet.

Zac's eyes held something suspiciously like sympathy. She hated that. She didn't need it, had finally learned how to deal with her mother by controlling her own emotions, not her mother's antics. The same tactic kept men at a distance. Except for Zac, she'd managed very well. When she'd shocked herself one day by realising she cared about him more than she should she'd immediately called the whole thing off. No one would ever leave her again. No one could ever accuse her of being a slow learner.

'I'm here because you needed help.' Zac tapped the back of her hand to get her attention. 'I'm alone, as in no partner, so doing stuff behind the scenes isn't going to get anyone's back up. I figured you'd be pleased, not trying to get rid of me.'

I've already done that once.

The words hung in the air between them, as though she'd said them out loud. She hadn't, but her cheeks heated, as if she was blushing. Not something she was known for. 'I'm sorry for being an ungrateful cow.' She sipped from her glass while she gathered her scattered brain cells into one unit. 'It's great you're here. I'd still be trying to persuade that florist into doing things my way if you hadn't worked your magic on her.' She'd felt a tad ill at the ease with which he'd managed to convince the florist that her way was right. 'You also got that kid behind the bar to arrange the glasses in a much more spectacular pyramid than he'd intended.'

'While you charmed the floor manager into putting a dog basket in the corner for the seeing eye dog. It's against all the rules apparently.' Zac's smile was beautiful when he wasn't trying to win a favour. Too damned gorgeous for his own good. And hers.

'A blind person is allowed to take their dog anywhere.'

'But not necessarily have a bed for the night in the banquet room.' That smile just got bigger and better, and ripped through her like a storm unleashed.

She needed to get away before she did something as stupid as suggesting he give her a massage before she got dressed for the night. Zac's hands used to be dynamite when he worked on her muscles. He'd done a massage course sometime during his surgical training and was more than happy to share his ability with anyone needing a muscle or two unknotted. He'd done a lot more than that with her at times, but tonight she'd settle for a regular massage to get the strain and ache out of her shoulders.

Another lie. She gulped her drink, but forgot to savour the taste as the bubbles crossed her tongue. Lying wasn't something she normally did, not even to herself, as far as she knew.

'Here.' Zac held the champagne bottle in front of her, and leaned in to top up her glass. 'Take that up to your room.'

'You're repeating yourself.'

'Didn't think you'd got the message the first time.' Taking her elbow, he began marching her towards the elevators where he pressed the up button, and when the doors whooshed open he nudged her in. 'See you at pre-dinner drinkies.'

'I'll be down well before six.' As the doors closed quietly Oliva drew in his scent and along with it a whole heap more memories. The night ahead was stretching out ever further. She'd tried again to change the seat-ing arrangement at the tables, but couldn't without up-setting someone else. She sighed. Have to swallow that one and hope she'd be too busy to sit down.

Olivia tapped the toe of her boot until the elevator eased to a halt on her floor. Surprisingly she had nearly an hour to herself, thanks to Zac's help. Plenty of time to wrestle into submission the strong emotions she'd never expected to feel for him again. Then she could carry on as planned: friendly yet aloof. So far her ap-proach had been a big fail.

Inside her room she began shedding clothes as she headed for the bathroom and the tub she wanted full, steaming and bubbling.

After turning the taps on full, she poured in a hefty dose of bubble bath and shucked out of the rest of her clothes. Removing her make-up, she saw a goofy smile and happier eyes in the mirror than she'd seen in a very long time.

Hey, be careful.

Why was she excited? She didn't want another affair with the man. It had been hard enough walking away from the first one; to do that again would kill her. Even though their affair had had little to do with anything other than sex, she'd stumbled through the following weeks trying to get back on track. It had her wondering for the millionth time how her father had walked out on her and her mother without a backward glance. He'd had more to lose, yet every communication from him—not many—had come through a lawyer. No birthday cards, Christmas phone calls. Nothing. Her dad had vanished from her life. And that was that.

Slipping into the warm water and feeling the bubbles tickle her chin eased every last knot of tension from her taut body. Sure, it'd make a comeback, but for the next twenty minutes she'd enjoy the lightness now in her muscles, her tummy, her everywhere. That might help with facing Zac tonight.

Olivia knew she had to be on her best form because their friends wouldn't be able to refrain from watching her and Zac, looking for any hints of dissension or, worse, any sign they might be interested in each other again. Not a chance, folks.

Lying back, her eyes drifted shut and she watched the movie crossing her mind. Zac looking good enough to devour in one sitting. That well-honed body still moved like a panther's, wary yet smooth, the same as the expression in his eyes. Unbelievable how much she'd missed that body. Missed everything about Zac. There'd been the odd occasion they'd shared a meal, because when anyone had had as much exercise as they'd had together they'd got hungry and what had gone best with after-match lethargy had been great food. Ordered in from some of Auckland's best restaurants, of course. The only way to go.

What she'd never seen in his eyes before was that concern that had shown when he'd moved her towards the elevator. Concern for her well-being, and then there had been the flower, the champagne—which had shown he'd remembered she only drank wine, and then usually this nectar. Yes, she pampered herself, but there was no one else to. Except her mother, and she got her fair share of being looked after.

Was it possible Zac had missed her an incy-wincy bit? She'd never ask. That would be like setting a match to petrol. Anyway, he'd never admit it, even if it came close to being true.

Hah, like you'd admit it either.

* * *

Zac prowled the small crowd pouring into the banquet room, and for the tenth time glanced at his watch. Six o'clock had been and gone twenty minutes ago and there was no sign of Olivia. So unlike her. If anything, she'd have been back down here, ready to get things cranking up, almost an hour before it was supposed to start.

'Hey, Zac, good to see you.' Paul Entwhistle stepped in front of him. 'How have you been?'

'Paul.' Zac shook his old mentor's hand. 'I'm doing fine. What about you? Still creating merry hell down there at Waikato?' The older man had taken over as director of the orthopaedic unit two years ago, citing family reasons for leaving the successful private practice he'd set up here in Auckland.

Paul gave him an easy smile. 'I've semiretired to spend more time with the family. What about you? I couldn't believe it when I heard you and Olivia had parted. Thought you'd never be able to untangle yourselves long enough to go in different directions.'

Zac swallowed a flare of annoyance. This was only the first of what he had no doubt would be many digs tonight about his past with Olivia. 'Aren't we full of surprises, then?' Instantly he wished his words back. Paul had been a friend to him as well as teaching him complex surgical procedures that he now used regularly. The man certainly didn't deserve his temper. He tried again. 'There was so much going on at the time something had to give.'

That was one way of looking at it. He knew from friends that Olivia ran with the crowd these days and never with another man. He didn't get it. She'd been fun, and always hungry for a good time. But apparently not since *them*. Did that make him responsible for her change? Had he done something he was completely unaware of to cause her to dump him and become a solo act? He'd always been honest in that he'd had no intention of having anything more than a fling with her. She'd been of the same sentiment. Neither of them had been interested in commitment. Yet it still sucked big time that she'd pulled out. He hadn't thought he could feel so vulnerable. Why would he? He'd spent his life guarding against that.

'I get that, but never thought it would be your relationship that would stop.' Paul unwittingly repeated Zac's thoughts as he looked around the room. 'Where is Olivia anyway?'

Twenty-five past six. 'I have no idea. I'll give her a call.' Walking away to find somewhere quieter, he dialled her cell. Yes, he still had her numbers, just never used them. Deleting them should've been simple, but he hadn't been able to, even when he'd been angry with her for walking away.

'Hey, Zac, I fell asleep.' So she still had him on caller ID. Interesting. 'Is everything okay? I'll be right down.' Olivia sounded breathless.

He knew the breathless version, had heard it often as they'd made love. 'Breathe deep and count to ten. Everything's going according to your plan.'

'Yes, but I need to be there, welcoming everyone. Oh, damn.' He heard a clatter in the background. 'Damn, damn, triple damn.'

'Olivia, are you all right?'

'I knocked my glass off the side of the tub. Now there are shards of glass all over the floor.'

'Call Housekeeping.'

'Haven't got time. I'm meant to be down there before everyone arrives, not after, as though I don't care.' Panic mixed with anger reached his ear. 'How could I be so stupid as to fall asleep in the tub?'

'Listen to me.' Zac stared up at the high ceiling, trying hard not to visualise *that* picture. Olivia in a hot tub with soapy bubbles framing her pert chin, covering her full breasts. *Aw, shucks.*

'I worked every hour there was to get this gala happening and I'm tired, but I only had to hang on for a few more hours.' She was on a roll, and Zac knew it would take a bomb to shut her up.

He delivered. 'I'm coming up to help you get ready.' Like Olivia would let him in. She hated being out of control over any damned thing and would be wound up tighter than a gnat's backside.

'You can't come up here,' she spluttered. 'I'm not dressed.'

So his words *had* hit the bull's-eye. She'd heard him. He found himself smiling, and not just externally. Warmth was expanding, turning him all gooey. Bonkers. This was all wrong.

Zac told her, 'Take your time getting ready, then make a grand entrance. Everyone will be here and you can wow them as you walk to the podium to make the opening announcements.'

There was utter silence at the other end of the phone. No more spluttering. No glasses smashing on the tiled floor. Not even Olivia breathing. Then his smile spread into a grin. He could almost hear her mind working.

'Love it,' she said, and hung up on him.

Zac slid his phone back in the pocket of his evening suit trousers. He guessed he'd see her shortly. Heading back into the room, he hesitated as the elevator doors opened. Seeing the pale, thin man who stepped out, he crossed over to shake his hand. 'Hey, Andy, great to see you.' The guy looked dreadful. Leukaemia was making short work of his health.

'Isn't this something? I couldn't believe it when Olivia told me how many people were coming and all the amazing things that have been donated for the auction.' Andy wiped a hand down his face. 'Enough to make a bloke cry.'

'Can't have that, man.' Zac dredged up a grin for him, feeling a lump rising in his own throat. 'You'll have all the females copying you.'

Andy laughed, surprising Zac. 'Damn right there. What sort of dinner party would that be? They'd be handing round tissues, not champagne.'

'Guess you're off the drink at the moment.' Zac glanced behind, and saw Kitty and their three small boys waiting calmly. 'Great to see you.' He wrapped the woman in his arms and when he felt her shivering he knew it was from trepidation about tonight. 'You're doing fine,' he said quietly, so only she heard.

Kitty nodded. 'Thanks to CC. She's arranged a table for us and the boys, a babysitter for when it's time to send the little tykes to our suite, and basically anything we could possibly want.'

'That's our CC.' *Damn you, Olivia. A man could fall in love with you—if he hadn't locked his heart in a cage. You've done the most amazing and generous thing, arranging this evening.* 'Come on, I'll show you to your table.' Andy looked ready to collapse and they hadn't started.

It took time to move through the throng of people wishing the family all the best for the auction. Zac knew everyone meant well and most were shocked at Andy's appearance, but he wanted to snarl at them to back off and give the man time to settle at his table. He held onto his sudden burst of temper, wondering where it had come from in the first place.

As he finally pulled out a chair for Kitty a collective gasp went up around the large room. Olivia had arrived. He hadn't seen her but he knew. She had that effect on people, on him. Like lightning she zapped the atmosphere, flashed that dazzling smile left, right and centre. Everyone felt her pull; fell under her spell. Which was why they were here, and why many had willingly donated such spectacular gifts for the auction. She was the reason these same people would soon be putting their hands in their pockets and paying the earth for those things. Sure, this was all about Andy, a man everyone liked and respected, but it was Olivia who'd got them all together.

Looking towards the podium, Zac thought he'd died and gone to heaven. Never, ever, in those crazy weeks he and Olivia had been getting down and dirty had he seen her look like she did right this moment. If he had he'd have hauled her back to his bedroom that last night and tied her to the bed so she couldn't dump him. He'd have taken a punt on her not breaking his heart even when it was obvious she would've. Stunning didn't begin to describe her. And that dress? Had to be illegal. Didn't it? She shouldn't be allowed to wear it in public. It appeared painted on, except for where the soft, weightless fabric floated across her thighs. Everywhere her body was highlighted with the gold material shimmering over her luscious curves.

And he'd thought he could handle this evening, being around Olivia. He hadn't a hope in Hades. Not one.

CHAPTER FOUR

'WELCOME, EVERYONE, TO what is going to be a wonderful night.' Olivia stood behind the podium, the mic in her hand, and let some of the tension slide across her lips on a low breath. She'd done it. Andy and his family were here, the colleagues who'd said they'd come were here, and the noise level already spoke of people having fun. Phew.

Zac's here. So? She knew that already.

Olivia could see him standing by Andy, staring over at her, his mouth hanging a little loosely. He looked stunned. What had put that expression on his face? Not her, surely? She stepped out from behind the podium, shifted her hips so that her dress shimmied over her thighs, and watched Zac. Forget stunned. Try knocked out. She bet a whole team of cheerleaders could be leaping up and down naked in front of him right now and he wouldn't notice. His gaze was intense and totally fixed on her. Or, rather, on her thighs.

Despite being like nothing else she'd worn since she'd been a teen, she'd loved this dress from the moment she'd seen it; now she thought it was the best outfit ever created. That sex thing she and Zac had once had going? It was still there, alive and well, already fired up and ready to burn.

Then the silence reached her and she stared around at the gathering of friends and colleagues, the reason she was standing up here finally returning to her bemused brain. She was supposed to be wowing them, not getting slam-dunked by Zac's comatose expression. Slapping her forehead in front of everyone wasn't a good idea, but she did it anyway. 'Sorry, everyone, I forgot where I was for a moment. Thought I was back at med school and about to give you all a demo on how to drink beer while standing on my head.' Like she'd ever done anything close.

But it got her a laugh and she could relax. As long as she didn't look in Zac's direction she should be able to continue with her brief outline of how the evening would unfold.

'I hope you've all got your bank managers' phone numbers handy because we are going to have the auction of all auctions. It will be loads of fun, but just to get you loosened up there are limitless numbers of champagne flutes filled with the best drop of nectar doing the rounds of the room. Stop any of those handsome young men carrying trays and help yourself.'

She paused, and immediately her eyes sought Zac. He hadn't moved, still stood watching her, but at least he'd stopped looking like a possum caught in headlights. His eyes were hooded now, hiding whatever had been eating him, and that delicious mouth had tightened a little. Then he winked, slowly with a nod at the room in general.

She got the message. *Get on with it. Everyone's waiting for you.*

Again she looked around the room filled with people she knew, admired and in a lot of cases really liked. 'Just to keep us all well behaved and lasting the distance, there will be platters of canapés arriving over the next hour. We will have the auction before dinner so take a look at all the wonderful gifts set out on the tables over by the entrance. Most importantly, enjoy yourselves, but not until I've kept hotel management happy by telling you what to do in case of fire, earthquake, or the need to use a bathroom.'

After giving those details, she wrapped up. 'Let's have a darned good time. If there's anything that you feel you're missing out on talk to…' she looked around the room and of course her gaze fell on Zac '…Zachary Wright. He's volunteered to help with any problems and we'd hate to see him sitting around with nothing to do, wouldn't we?' She grinned over at the man who'd got her stomach in a riot. Not only her stomach, she conceded, while trying to ignore the smug smile coming back at her. Not easy to do when her heart rate was erratic. The noise levels were rising fast as she stepped away from the podium to go in search of a distraction that didn't begin with a Z.

Paul Entwhistle stepped in front of her. 'Olivia, you're a marvel, girl. There's as many people here as you'd find at Eden Park watching an international rugby match.' He wrapped her into a bear hug. 'Well done.'

'Still prone to exaggerating, I see.' She laughed as she extricated herself. 'Are you going to be bidding at the auction? There are some wonderful prizes—if I can call them that.'

'I've got my eye on one or two.' There was a cunning glint in Paul's eyes.

'What?'

Paul went with a complete change of subject. 'I see you still like to give Zac a bit of stick. It saddened me when you two broke up. Thought you had what it took.'

Her stomach sucked in against her backbone. *Not in this lifetime, we don't.* But even as she thought it her eyes were tracking the crowd for a dark head. Not hard to find when Zac towered above most people, even the tall ones. He was heading in her direction, an amused tilt to his mouth. 'I beg to differ,' she told Paul. 'Neither of us are the settling-down type.' *If only that weren't true.* 'Now, if you'll excuse me…'

'I think you're wrong.' Paul glanced in the direction she'd seen Zac. The cunning expression had changed to something more whimsical, which didn't make her feel any more comfortable.

'I need to circulate.' *Before Zac reaches us.* 'I'm sure Zac will be happy to chat with you.'

'Thanks a bundle, Olivia,' Zac breathed into her ear.

Too late. She plastered on a smile and faced him, wondering why just talking to him got her all in a twist. 'Thought you'd be pleased. You're flying solo, remember?'

He actually laughed. 'Touché.'

Paul was watching them with interest. She really needed to stop this; whatever the man was thinking didn't have a part in the evening's plans.

'I have to see the auctioneer about a few details,' Olivia put out there, and began walking away.

'Are we going to be holding up the various items as they're auctioned?' Zac was right beside her.

She was regretting giving in to his offer of help—if she had actually given in. He hadn't exactly left it open to negotiation. 'I'm doing it.'

'Then we're doing it.' His hand on her arm brought her to a stop. When he turned her to face him his eyes were full of genuine concern. For her? Or did he think she was going to make a mess of the evening? 'I know you've done everything so far and by rights this is your show, but I'd like to help. And I'm not the only one. Andy's been a good mate to a lot of people.'

'That's a valid point.' Didn't mean she'd hand over the reins, though. When she set out to do something she did the whole thing, from first phone call to seeing the last couple leave at the end of the night. That would give her a deep sense of accomplishment, something she never achieved with trying to keep her mother on the straight and narrow.

Zac's bowed upper lip curved into a heart-squeezing smile. 'Let's grab a drink and go talk to your auctioneer.'

For some reason Zac made her feel desirable on a different level from the hot need she usually found in his gaze. That was there, burning low and deep, but right now she could have curled up on a couch with him and just chatted about things. Not something they'd ever done before. Had never wanted to do. Shaking her head, she gave him a return smile. 'I'll stick to water until I've packed up this baby.'

Without looking away from her, he raised his hand and suddenly there was a waiter with a tray of full glasses standing beside them. Zac lifted two flutes of sparkling water and handed her one. Tapping his glass against hers, he gave her another of those to-die-for smiles. 'To making a load of money for our friend.'

'Lots and lots.' She sipped the water, and tried not to sneeze when bubbles somehow went up her nose. The bubbles won, and she bent her head to brazen out the sneezes.

Her glass was gently removed from her hand as Zac's firm, warm hand touched her between her shoulder blades, warm skin on warm skin, softly rubbing until she regained control. Straightening up, she reached for her glass and locked eyes with Zac. 'Th-thanks,' she stuttered.

How could she speak clearly with so much laughter and fun beaming out at her from a pair of eyes the shade of her first coffee of the day? Those eyes had always got her attention, had had her melting with one glance. For some strange reason tonight they had her fantasising about other, homier things. Like that couch and talking, or sharing a meal over the table in her kitchen, or going for a stroll along the beach. *A bit cosy, Olivia. What happened to forgoing doing things like that with someone special?* 'You ever think of settling down?' she asked, before she'd thought the question through.

His expression instantly became guarded. 'Thought about it? Yes. Followed through? No.'

Oh. Disappointment flared, which didn't make sense when she never intended putting her size five shoes under someone's bed. Not permanently anyway. 'That's sad.' For Zac. He'd make a wonderful husband and father.

'Not at all. I'm happy.' So why the sadness lurking in the back of those dark eyes?

'You sound very sure.' Her blood slowed as her heart slipped up on its pumping habit. Strange that here, surrounded by friends and colleagues, Zac was admitting to not wanting happy-ever-after.

'I am,' he muttered, as he took her elbow and led them in the direction of the auction table and the man standing behind it. 'Just as I'm sure I'm enjoying playing catch-up with you.'

Okay. Hadn't seen that coming. 'We could've done that any time.' What? Since when? She'd been ruthless in avoiding Zac, turning down invitations to any functions she'd thought he might be attending. The air in her lungs trickled out over her bottom lip. Now he stood beside her she couldn't keep her eyes off him. He warmed her through and through, touching her deeply, like a close friend. Except friends didn't do what they'd done, and sex-crazed lovers like they'd been didn't sit around discussing fashion or trips to the supermarket. But she told him anyway. 'I've sort of settled, bought a nineteen-twenties villa in Parnell that I'm slowly doing up.' *My own house, all mine.*

Zac's eyes widened. 'Are you working the do-up yourself?'

'I've got a very good builder for most of it, while I do the painting and wallpapering. Seems I've got a bit of a flair for home decorating.' She felt a glow of pride when she thought of her new kitchen and dining alcove.

'Go, you.'

'Hi, Olivia.' The auctioneer, Gary, held out his hand. 'You've got an amazing array of donations. We should be able to pull off a major coup.'

'That's the plan.' Shaking Gary's hand, she introduced Zac. 'Anything we can do for you?'

'You can take a break and leave this to me and my partner over there. He's come along to help.' Gary nodded at a man sorting through the donations and placing numbers under each one. 'Just keep our glasses full and we'll be happy.'

Zac's hand was back on her elbow. 'Come on, let's mingle.'

She could do that on her own. Yet she went with him as if that was the most important thing she had to do tonight.

Zac groaned inwardly. He should be running for the exit and not looking back. Standing beside Olivia as she charmed everyone within sight was sending him bonkers with need. Every time she moved even a single muscle he'd swear he inhaled her scent. She moved almost nonstop, even when standing in one spot, her face alive, with those lips constantly forming belly-tightening smiles while her eyes sparkled. Her free hand flipped up and down, then out between her and her audience, and back in against her gorgeous body, expressive at every turn.

While one of his hands was shoved deep into his pocket to keep from touching her, the other gripped a glass tight. His feet were glued to the carpet, and his face hopefully impassive. Letting anyone, especially CC, know what he was thinking and feeling would be catastrophic. He'd never hear the end of it from Paul either. The guy stood with them, his gaze flitting between him and Olivia with a crafty glint that made Zac uncomfortable.

A waiter was approaching with a tray laden with glasses. Zac drained his sparkling water and replaced it with champagne. To hell with not drinking. He needed something stronger than H2O, bubbles or not. 'Thanks.' He nodded at the waiter, which was a waste of time.

The guy was too busy gaping at Olivia, the tray on his outstretched fingers getting quite a tilt. 'Ma'am,' the young man croaked.

Totally understanding the poor guy's reaction, Zac tapped the tray. 'Hey, buddy, watch those glasses.'

Olivia swapped her empty glass for a full one, nodded at the waiter, and looked around the room as she gulped a mouthful of water.

Zac saw some of the tension in her neck ease off a notch. Being a perfectionist, CC didn't do relaxing very well, and tonight she was coiled tighter than a snake about to strike.

'Time to start the auction,' Olivia said in a sudden gap of the conversation. 'I think everyone must be here by now.'

'Good idea,' Paul said. 'Make the most of this amazing atmosphere.' He nodded at the crowd talking and laughing.

'Why don't we hold up the articles being auctioned while Gary's man deals with the financial side?' Zac led the way through the throng to the podium.

Olivia nodded, picked up the mic. 'Okay, everyone, can I have your attention?'

Nope. Not happening. If anything, the noise level seemed to increase. Zac reached for the mic, touching the back of her hand as he did so. Soft, warm, different Olivia. His mouth dried. It wasn't too late. He could still run away. And then what? Spend the night thinking about Olivia and coming up with a hundred questions about her?

Clearing his throat, he spoke loudly and clearly into the mic. 'Quiet, please.' The conversations petered out as everyone turned to face him. He wanted to crack a joke but doubted he could pull it off with this tight band strangling his throat. If only Olivia would move away and let him breathe. Finally he started talking and slowly got his voice back to normal. 'We are about to start the auction so take a seat. Gary is our auctioneer and we want him to be able see each and every one of you, so even if you scratch your knee he can take it as a bid.'

As the bidding got under way Olivia's tension climbed back up. 'Relax,' he told her. 'This is going to be amazing, you'll see.'

She turned worried eyes on him. 'How can you be so certain? What if we barely raise enough money to get Andy a one-way ticket to the States?' Her teeth nibbled her bottom lip.

Olivia didn't do nibbling. Taking her hand in his, he squeezed gently. 'I believe in you, that's how.'

Her eyes widened, her chin tipped forward. 'Truly?' she squeaked.

'Truly.' He did. He realised that through the years they'd been training to become surgeons he mightn't have noticed how sexy she was but he had known of her determination never to fail. Perhaps he hadn't learned much more about her during their affair but this was still Olivia, the same woman who'd qualified as an excellent plastic surgeon. Only now he saw how much she cared for their friends. Olivia was a big marshmallow, really, and he liked marshmallows.

'Thanks.'

'Olivia? So do all the people in this room. That's why they're here.'

He felt a responding squeeze where her hand was wound around his. 'You say the nicest things,' she whispered, before pulling free and turning to face the now-quiet room.

She'd been flip in her tone and yet it didn't bother him. That was Olivia covering her real feelings. He was beginning to see she was an expert at doing that. Come to think about it, she'd always shut him up with a kiss whenever he'd started to talk about anything personal. What was she hiding? Who was Olivia Coates-Clark? The real CC?

As Zac picked up the envelope to be auctioned, which contained a week in a timeshare bure in Fiji, he knew he was getting into trouble. Forget quietening the itch. Now he had to fight the need to get to know all about Olivia, right from when she'd lost her first tooth to what her idea was of a dream holiday.

The bidding was fast and furious, with plenty of people vying to buy the first offering. In the end Paul outbid everyone, paying enough to send a dozen folks to Fiji rather than the two that the deal covered.

'That's auctions for you,' Zac whispered to Olivia as at last she began smiling.

'It's not about what they're bidding for, is it?'

'Nope. It's all about the man sitting at that table with his wife and kids, looking like hell and pretending otherwise.' Andy looked shocked, actually. Probably because of the ridiculous amount Paul had bid.

Olivia nudged him. 'We're not a bad bunch, are we?'

'Apart from opinionated, hardworking, and overly comfortable with our lot, you mean?' He grinned at her.

'I'd like to think more along the lines of caring, hardworking, and overly focused on helping others.' She grinned back.

His stomach clenched. That grin, that mouth…oh, man. *I've missed her so much.* Not just the sex. He'd liked being with her too, even if only while they'd ridden the elevator to the apartment she'd rented then, and before they'd fallen into bed.

'What are we auctioning next?' he growled, needing to get back on an even keel.

'The weekend on your luxury yacht. If you're at the helm that should attract a lot of female bidders.' Her grin only grew.

'The ladies here are all taken.' *Except you.* Zac sighed when one of the partners in the surgical practice where he worked bought the weekend excursion.

The man wasn't easy to get along with, and now he'd have to spend two days holed up in a yacht with him and his whole family.

'You're being uncharitable,' Olivia whispered beside his ear.

'I didn't say a word.'

'There was a brief wincing and tightening of your mouth when the hammer hit the podium.' She laughed. 'That man paid a small fortune for the pleasure of going sailing with you.'

'He did, and I'll make sure he has a fantastic time.'

Gary had the crowd in the palm of his hand now, and the bidding went through the roof for everything from a painting of a seagull hovering over a beach to a meal at a restaurant down at the Viaduct Harbour.

Zac watched Olivia every time the gavel hit the podium. Her eyes were getting brighter and brighter. 'We're killing it,' she whispered at one point.

'Says the woman who was worried this wouldn't work,' he retorted. The more she smiled the more she relaxed, and the more beautiful she was. Zac felt his heart soften even further towards her. So he sucked in his stomach and hardened himself against her. Mentally, that was.

'That's me. Control freak with no control over the outcome of the auction. Of course I was going to be concerned.'

Was that why she'd ended their affair? So she could keep control and not wait until he decided to call it quits? Since the morning he'd woken to hear Olivia say she was walking away from their affair he'd felt bruised and let down. He hadn't known why, except it had reminded him of the day his family had cut him off. But with Olivia he'd had nothing to feel guilty about.

'That's it, folks. We've sold everything,' Gary called out.

Olivia crossed to stand behind the podium, a piece of paper in her hand, tears in her eyes. 'You're an amazing group of people. This auction went way beyond even my dreams.' She read out the amount they'd raised and had to wait a long time for the applause to die down. 'You are all so generous it's humbling.'

Zac glanced across to Andy's table, and felt emotion tug at his heart. Kitty was crying and Andy slashed his arm across his face as he slowly stood up. Carefully negotiating his way around tables to reach Olivia, Andy gave her a long hug before gripping Zac's shoulder.

'Hey.' Zac could think of nothing else to say. The success of the auction said everything that needed to be said about the love he felt for this man.

Taking the mic, Andy stumbled to the podium. 'What can I say? Olivia's right. You're awesome.' His voice cracked. 'Tonight means so much to Kitty and me, and our boys. You have given us a chance.' He stopped and looked down. Everyone waited quietly until he raised his head and said, 'CC, I can't thank you enough. I know so many people contributed to tonight and I thank each and every one of them, but without you, CC, none of this would've happened.'

Zac clapped and instantly everyone leapt to their feet to join him. He reached for Olivia's hand and raised it high. 'Our CC.'

Tears were streaming down her cheeks. 'Stop it,' she hissed. 'You're embarrassing me.'

Zac retrieved the mic from Andy and when the clapping died down said, 'In case you missed that, CC says we're embarrassing her. When did that ever happen?'

Laughter and more clapping broke out. Olivia shook her head at him. 'You'll keep.'

There was the problem. He shouldn't want to be kept for Olivia. Or any woman. He wouldn't be able to deliver what she wanted, needed.

CHAPTER FIVE

'DID YOU JUST YAWN?' Zac asked as they danced to the Eziboys' music.

Olivia shook her head. 'Just doing mouth stretches.' Did there have to be a smile in his eyes? It was devastating in its intensity. Made her happy to be with him, when she shouldn't be. Exhaustion had returned as dessert had come to an end, yet somehow she'd still found the energy to shake her hips to the beat of the music.

Zac's eyes widened, and the tip of his tongue appeared at the corner of his delectable mouth. 'Right,' he drawled.

She mentally slapped her head. Mouth stretches. She used to trail kisses all over his body, starting below his ear and tracking down, down, down. The memories were vivid now, in full technicolour, and heating up her cheeks. Hopefully he wouldn't notice her heightened colour in the semidarkness of the dance floor.

It would take very little to fall in against that wide chest and let him be her strength for a while. She'd never known what it was like to let someone be strong for her. If she ever loosened up enough to try it, Zac might be her man.

How had she managed to leave him that morning? Fear. Always a powerful motivator. For her it had been fear of losing control, of never knowing which way was up. As an adult she had no intention of reliving the turbulent life she'd known growing up. Not for anyone.

'Feel like taking a break, having a drink?' Zac asked.

Definitely. Anything to put some space between them. 'Good idea.' She immediately turned for their table.

Waving at a waiter, Zac pulled out a chair. 'Take the weight off.'

When he sat down beside her his chair was way too close, but she was reluctant to make a show of moving away. Anyway, she didn't have the strength to resist him at the moment. Glancing at her watch, she sighed. The band was booked for at least another hour. Sneaking off to her room and that huge comfortable-looking bed was not yet an option.

The champagne was cool and delicious. 'Perfect.' She settled further into her chair. 'You keep dancing, if you want. I don't need babysitting.'

Zac chuckled. 'Dancing has never been one of my favourite pastimes.'

'But you're good at it. You've got the moves.' *Ouch.* Shouldn't have said that.

That devastating smile returned briefly. 'I'd say thanks except you seemed to nearly fall asleep while we were shaking our hips.'

'I can't believe how tired I am. Probably won't go to sleep for hours when I finally make it to my room. My muscles feel like they're pulled tighter than a tourniquet.'

'What you need is a few days away somewhere where no one can reach you to talk about work, or fundraising, or anything more stressful than what you'd like for dinner.' Zac sipped his drink. 'When did you last take time off?'

She thought about it. Glanced at him. Remembered. 'It was a while ago.'

'A little over eighteen months ago maybe?'

'Maybe.' Zac had booked three nights at a retreat on Waiheke Island. They'd only managed one night before he'd returned home after his brother had been admitted to hospital with a collapsed lung.

While accepting he had to go, Olivia had been disappointed he'd not returned to the resort later. She sometimes wondered—if they'd had the whole time together would they have got to know each other a little better outside the bedroom?

'I might as well have stayed with you,' Zac muttered, as if reading her mind.

Olivia's stomach flipped. 'What? Your family needed you.' So had she, but not as much.

'No, they didn't.'

'But they phoned you.'

He shook his head. 'My grandfather called to let me know about Mark. Not my parents.'

She wanted to say that made sense if his parents had rushed to be with his brother, but something in his eyes stopped her, told her she was wrong. 'You don't get along—'

'Mind if I join you both for a moment?' Paul plonked himself down without waiting for an answer.

Relief flicked across Zac's face. 'Can I get you a drink, Paul?'

'No, thanks. I won't take up much of your time.' Leaning back in the chair, he studied first Zac then her so thoroughly she began to think she had chocolate mousse on her chin.

The band stopped for a short break and most people were making their way to the tables. And Paul still wasn't saying anything. She ran her fingers across her chin, came up clean. She glanced at Zac, who shrugged his shoulders.

Finally, Paul pulled an envelope from the inside pocket of his jacket and Olivia instantly recognised it as an item that had been auctioned earlier. A trip somewhere. There'd been a few trips auctioned tonight but she thought Paul's one had been to Fiji.

As he laid the envelope on the table between her and Zac she felt a flutter of trepidation in her stomach. She couldn't keep her eyes off that large white envelope or the finger tapping it, as though it was beating out her fate.

'This is for the two of you. Five nights at Tokoriki Island Resort on the west side of Fiji's mainland.'

No. No, please, no. Tell me Paul didn't say that. I can't go anywhere with Zac, and certainly not somewhere as intimate as a resort in Fiji.

Olivia slowly raised her gaze to Zac and saw him looking as stunned as she felt. 'It's kind of you, Paul, but I have to say no.'

'Zac? What do you think?' Paul looked a little smug.

It didn't matter what Zac thought. She wasn't going.

A few days far away from everything and everyone with only Zac for company held a certain appeal. White beaches, warm sea, palm trees bending in the breeze, and... And Zac.

'It's a no from me too. Thank you, though.'

Paul wasn't easily fobbed off. 'Think before rejecting my offer out of hand, both of you.'

Olivia shook her head. One evening with Zac had her

in a state of longing and wonder. She would never cope with being stuck on a tiny island with him for a week.

'What's this about?' Zac asked in a surprisingly level tone, his eyes fixed on the man issuing the challenge.

'Look at you. You're exhausted. I know you haven't had a break all year. You need a holiday. So does Olivia. Why not someplace exotic? This timeshare bure is on an island catering for approximately twenty couples at any one time. No children allowed. All meals provided, massages as well.' Paul smiled.

Any other time she'd be drooling at the thought of going. But never with the man sitting beside her, looking as perplexed as she felt.

'It sounds wonderful, but you're expecting Zac and me to go together?' Olivia shook her head. *Not going to happen.* Looking at Zac, she could see the lines at the edges of his mouth. He *was* tired. It had taken Paul pointing it out for her to notice.

'You have two weeks to choose between, both in July, so you'll need to get your heads together quickly.'

Which part of 'I'm not going' doesn't Paul understand? 'July's two weeks away. I can't just pack my bag and leave my patients in the lurch.'

'Neither can I,' Zac growled.

Paul hadn't finished. 'I'll cover for you, Zac, and I'm sure we can find someone to pick up the reins in your department for five days, CC.'

'You still haven't said why you're doing this. Us needing a holiday doesn't cover such generosity.' Zac sipped his drink, a thoughtful expression on his handsome face.

An expression that worried Olivia. He'd better not be considering this crazy idea. She snapped, 'It doesn't matter why. It's not going to happen.' Knowing how ungrateful that sounded, and yet annoyed that Paul thought he could manipulate them, she added, 'It's a lovely offer, Paul, but I'm turning you down.'

The moment the words left her mouth she was regretting the lost opportunity. A holiday would be fabulous right now. Keeping up her usual number of patients and working on this gala fundraiser had finally caught up with her. Throw in her mum's latest crisis, and heading offshore to somewhere she'd be pampered sounded better and better. A sideways glance at Zac and she couldn't deny that going away with him didn't have appeal. Her head snapped up. *She was not going anywhere with Zac.*

Someone coughed. 'I'll cover for you, Olivia.' A colleague at Auckland Surgical Hospital sat on the other side of the table, looking completely relaxed about the whole scenario. 'You know you've been wanting to get away for a while now. The timing couldn't be better. Leave it another couple of months and I'll be on maternity leave.'

Thanks a million. You obviously haven't heard the whole conversation, especially the bit about Zac going too. But as Olivia glared at the woman she felt herself wavering. This might be working out too easily, but did that mean she shouldn't be considering it? Should she be grabbing that envelope and rushing home to pack, or was it wiser to continue refusing Paul's kindness?

Zac was watching her with something akin to an annoying challenge in his eyes. 'What about it, CC? It could be fun.'

'It could be a nightmare.' How would she remain aloof when they were sharing accommodation on an island with very few people around for distraction? How would she be able to control herself with that hot bod so close for days on end?

Pulling her gaze from that infuriating taunt in Zac's eyes, she looked around the now-crowded table and found everyone watching, waiting for her answer, almost as though they were all challenging her.

You never turn down a dare, remember?

She'd never had one quite like this, though. She could not go on holiday with the man she'd had to walk away from once already. Not when he'd got her in a tangle of emotions within minutes of turning up in the hotel earlier that afternoon. She'd never survive with her heart and her brain functioning normally if she spent five days and nights in the same space as Zac.

You'd have a lot of great sex.

Not necessarily. They could avoid that. It wasn't as though they were going *together*-together, right?

Tell that to someone who'll believe you.

The little gremlin that had flattened her car battery and made her fall asleep in the hot tub now had her saying, 'It would have to be the first week of July.'

Zac shoved his hands deep into his trouser pockets as he strolled along the Viaduct beside Olivia. At one-thirty in the morning, in the middle of winter, they were the only ones crazy enough to be out here, but he knew he wouldn't be able to sleep. Why the hell had he agreed to go to Fiji? His brain had to be fried from too many hours in Olivia's company. No other explanation popped up. Accepting he wanted time out with her went against everything he strived for. His hands clenched at his sides. What if he liked Olivia even more by the end of the trip? He liked her too much already. Her beauty, her wit, her sense of fun, and her concern for others. He'd pushed her to go away to a place that was all about romance. Romance. A subject he knew nothing about. And didn't want to. That would be like rubbing salt into the wound.

Olivia would be regretting her acceptance of Paul's generous gift. But she would never back down. Not now that others had heard her accept.

Zac sighed unhappily. He was as bad as Olivia. Paul had challenged them both, and he'd fallen for it. Given in to the emotions that had been battering him since he'd arrived at the hotel. To have spent his entire adult life avoiding commitment only to find himself well and truly hooked didn't bear thinking about.

A gust of rain-laden wind slapped them. Olivia pulled her jacket tight across her breasts and folded her arms under them. Her face looked pinched—from cold or from anger at herself for agreeing, he wasn't sure.

Taking her elbow, Zac turned them around. She was shivering. 'Come on. We'll go to my apartment. The weather's about to dump a load of wet stuff and getting soaked doesn't appeal.'

'I should go back to the hotel.' She didn't sound convinced.

'We need to talk about what we've got ourselves into.' Then he might feel happier. Might. 'I've got wine in the chiller. Or there's tea, if you'd prefer.' He also had a huge bed, but doubted he'd get a hug for mentioning that.

'Why didn't you tell Paul no?' she asked when they were in the elevator, heading up to his apartment.

Initially he had. 'Maybe I want to go.'

'Do you? Really?'

While I'm standing here breathing in the floral scent that's you, yes, really. When I see that uncertainty flick through your eyes, yes, I want to spend time with you. When I think about actually scratching my itch, defi-

nitely, yes, but if I remember why I have to move on from you, then a resounding no.

The elevator shook to a halt and the doors glided open. He took her elbow again. 'The idea of going to Fiji, it's growing on me.' His parent's fortieth wedding anniversary was in the first week of July and they were having a party to beat all parties at one of Auckland's top restaurants. Of course he wanted to celebrate with them. Of course he was not invited. 'Yep, getting away has appeal.' He tried to ignore the surprised look on her face and opened the door to his penthouse. 'After you.'

Olivia slipped past him, and walked through to the lounge with its floor-to-ceiling glass wall that allowed an extensive view of Auckland Harbour, the bridge, and closer in the wharves with a collection of large and small sea craft tied up.

He followed, stood next to her, stared out seeing nothing. Why did Olivia unsettle him when no other woman ever had?

'I've never been to the islands,' she said, without looking his way. 'Haven't been anywhere since I was ten, and then it was to Australia with my parents. Mum hates flying.'

'Makes for an uncomfortable trip, I imagine. You haven't inherited that fear?'

Her head moved slowly from side to side. 'Not at all. In fact, I'd like to learn to fly one day.'

'What's holding you back?' It wouldn't be lack of brains or money.

'I have a feeling it would become a passion and what with work and doing up my house there isn't enough spare time to spend hours in the air.' Her reflection in the window showed she was nibbling her lip again.

He didn't like it when she did that. It indicated distress, and he didn't want her to feel distressed. 'Ever thought of cutting back a few hours so you can do some of the things you like?'

Olivia finally looked at him. 'I spent so much time training and working my way to the top that I think I've forgotten there's a whole world out there waiting to be explored, whether through travel or doing things like learning to fly.'

'You're right.' Apart from going sailing whenever he could get a weekend away, he spent most of his time working. 'You said you're enjoying doing up your house. I bought this apartment because the idea of renovations and painting and all the things required to turn a house into a home seemed too huge. It's not a job for one weekend, is it?'

'No, it's a project. But, then, most things I've ever done have been projects.' She frowned. 'That's how I stay in control. Take the house. Next month is bathroom month. The builder's going to gut it and then everything I've chosen goes in and I get to go shopping for all the little bits and pieces, matching the towels with the tile colour, the fittings with the rest of the house.'

Sounded too organised for him. He liked a little disorder, certainly didn't have perfectly matched towels or even dinner sets. Not that he'd gone to the second-hand shop for anything, but he hadn't been hell-bent on getting everything looking like a show home. 'What was last month?'

'My bedroom.' She turned away, and her voice was low as she told him, 'It's cream and rose pink. Very girlie, but I wasn't allowed that when I was growing up so I'm having it now.'

Wow, she'd just mentioned her childhood twice in a short amount of time. Very briefly, sure, but there it was. She hadn't been allowed to pick the colours for her room. Not a big deal maybe, but it could mean there was nothing she'd been allowed to choose. 'I've never seen you wear pink.'

'Rose pink.' Her smile was unexpectedly shy. 'There's a difference. And, no, I can't imagine what patients would think if their surgeon turned up dressed in pink.'

'They'd probably love it.' Taking a step back before he walked into that smile filling him with a longing for something special, he brought everything back to reality. 'Tea or champagne?'

'Have you got camomile?' Her smile had widened into that of a cheeky girl.

He told her, 'Yes, I have,' and laughed at her surprise. 'My mother drinks it.' *On the rare times she's visited.*

'For some reason I didn't think you were close.' She followed him to the kitchen, where she perched on a bar stool at the counter. Crossing her legs showed off a length of thigh where that golden creation that was supposedly a dress rode high.

'We're not.' Mum at least tried to accept he was still her son, while Dad… Forget it.

'You mentioned one brother.' Was that longing in her voice? Hard to tell from her face.

'Mark. He's married with two kids. I only get to see them at Christmas and birthdays.'

Olivia picked at an invisible spot on the counter. 'That's incredibly sad.'

'Yep.' He made himself busy getting mugs from the cupboard and teabags from the pantry.

She lifted her head and locked her blue eyes on him, suddenly back to being in control. 'Think I'll head back to the hotel. I don't really want tea. Or anything.' She slipped off the stool and turned towards the doorway. 'Good night, Zac.'

With little thought he reached for her, caught her wrist and gently tugged her close. With a finger under her chin he tilted her head back so he could gaze down into her eyes. And felt his head spinning with wanting her.

Olivia's eyes widened and her chin rose further as her mouth opened slightly.

Zac was lost. Any resistance or logical thinking disappeared as he leaned closer to place his mouth over hers. As he tasted her, the heat and need he'd kept tamped down most of the night exploded into a rainbow of hot colours. Olivia. She was in his arms, her mouth on his, her tongue dancing with his. Olivia.

Slim arms wound around his neck, pulling his body closer to hers. He felt her rise onto tiptoe, knew the moment when her hips pressed against his obvious desire. Those breasts he'd been fantasising about all night flattened against his chest, turning him into a molten pool of need. His hands spread around her waist to lift her onto the stool, where she immediately wrapped her legs around his thighs.

This is what I've missed so damned much. We are fire on fire. Feeding each other. Consuming the oxygen.

She tasted wonderful, bringing more erotic memories back to him. Making new ones.

Lifting his mouth, he began trailing kisses over her jaw, down her neckline, on towards her deep cleavage. When she whimpered he continued while lifting his gaze to her face, where he recognised the same fiery awakening racing along his veins.

Her fingers kneaded his scalp as she pushed her breasts higher to give him more access with his tongue.

She wasn't wearing a bra. Of course she wasn't. That dress had clung to every curve and outlined her shape perfectly; including her breasts, those peaks now hard against his mouth and hand.

Zac growled as he licked her, tasted her skin, her nipple. A gentle bite had her arching her back and tipping her head so that her hair fell like a waterfall behind her. And he lost himself, tasting, touching, rubbing.

'It's been so long,' she murmured in a low voice that spelt sex. Her hands fumbled with the buttons of his shirt, finally pushed it open, and then her palms were on his skin, smoothing and teasing as only Olivia could do.

The memories that he'd lived on for all those long months apart rapidly became reality. He hadn't enhanced any of them. This was how it had been between them. Then his belt was loose, the zip being tugged downward, and… *Oh, hell.* Her soft hand was wrapped around him, sliding down, up, and down again. *Oh, hell.* There was nothing quite like making out with this woman. She knew the buttons to push, remembered what he most enjoyed, and if she wasn't careful would have him coming long before he'd pleasured her.

That wasn't happening. Zac wrapped his arms around her and carried her quickly down the hall to his bedroom and the super-king-sized bed she had yet to try out. Toeing his shoes off, he knelt on the bed and leaned forward with Olivia still in his arms so that he was covering her before she could move. 'Your turn.'

'I'm ready,' she croaked.

'I haven't touched you yet.' But, then, often he hadn't had to. All part of that explosiveness that had been them.

'Don't, if you want this to last more than the next three seconds.'

Now, there was a challenge. Pushing her dress up over her thighs, Zac slipped down to find her core with his tongue. The moment he tasted her she jolted like she'd been zapped with an electrical current.

Her hands gripped his head, holding him there. Not that he'd been going anywhere else until he had her rocking against him.

'Zac!' she cried when he licked her. 'Zachary…' As he pushed a finger inside.

Her hips lifted, her fingers pressed into his scalp, and she was crying out his name. Over and over as her body convulsed under him.

Reaching for the top drawer of his bedside table, he grabbed a condom and tore the packet open with his teeth. A small, warm hand whipped the condom from his fingers. 'Let me.'

Then he was lying on his back, unsure how she'd managed to flip him so effortlessly. She straddled his thighs and, achingly slowly, slid the condom onto his erection.

Placing his hands on her waist, he lifted her over him and lowered her to cover him, took him inside to her moist, hot centre.

'Zac!' She screamed his name.

He hadn't forgotten she was a screamer but it still hit him hard, stirred him and had him pushing further into her.

It was never going to take long, he was that hot for her, had been wanting this from the moment he'd seen her leaning against that counter in the hotel reception. When she put her hand behind to squeeze him he was gone. Over. Finished. One final thrust and Olivia cried out and fell over his chest, gasping for air, her skin slick with sweat and her body trembling against his.

As she lay sprawled across him, he spread his hands across her back, stared up at the barely illuminated ceiling and smiled. Everything was in place in his world. Olivia was in his bed. They'd shared the mind-blowing sex he knew only with her. Everything was perfect. His itch was being appeased.

Or would be when they did it again, just as soon as he got his breath back.

CHAPTER SIX

ZAC HAD NO idea what the time was when he rolled over and reached out for Olivia, only to come up empty-handed. 'Olivia?' He sat up and stared around. His heart thumped hard. Not again.

'I'm here.' Her voice came from the en suite bathroom.

Phew. He dropped back. Something clattered in the hand basin, and Olivia swore. 'You okay in there?' he called.

Silence.

'Olivia? Are you all right?' His gut started to tighten.

'I'm making sure I can walk past the hotel receptionist without looking like I've been…um, doing what I've been doing.'

'You're heading over the road?' Now he was on full alert. Swinging his legs over the side of the bed, he stood. 'What's wrong with staying the rest of the night? You and I don't usually settle for once.'

'Don't do this, Zac.' She stepped into the room, but kept her distance. 'We've got to stop before we get carried away.'

As the cold reality of her words hit him he pulled his head back, glared down at her. 'Why? We are willing, consenting adults, not two teenagers who have to go home to Mum and Dad looking guilty.' Hopefully she didn't hear the anger her rejection made him feel. Again. And the pain because she was right.

'I'm sorry.' Her eyes were brimming with tears. 'I shouldn't have got so carried away.'

A gut-buster, that statement. 'We got carried away, sweetheart. We.' He shoved a hand through his hair, trying to figure out what had happened to cause her to haul on the brakes. He should be grateful. He'd hoped to sooth his need, not crank it wide-open. How wrong could a bloke be?

'Exactly. We didn't stop to think about what we were doing. Not for a moment.' Her back was straight, her shoulders tight, but her chin wobbled as she said, 'Which is why I can't go to Fiji with you.'

'You're changing your mind?' Of course she was. For some reason he didn't feel happy. He'd enjoyed being with her tonight. It had been like finding something precious after a long search. He could barely look at her and not reach for her again. She might've put the brakes on but it would take a tank of icy water to cool his ardour and return his out-of-whack heart rate to normal.

In the doorway she hesitated, turned around to look at him, sorrow leaking out of those baby blues. 'Yes, Zac, I am. Going on holiday together would only exacerbate the situation. I can't have another affair with you. It's too casual, and anything more is impossible for me.'

He stood rooted to the floor, unable to ignore the sharp pain her statement caused yet knowing she was stronger than him. The itch had gone beyond scratchy, was now an open wound that needed healing. Olivia was the cure but, as she'd so clearly pointed out, that wasn't about to happen.

Moments later his main door clicked shut, presumably behind her, and still he stood transfixed. For a moment earlier on, when they'd been sated with sex, he thought he'd found that untouchable thing he'd been looking for in his dreams and pushing away when he was wide-awake. Hell, he'd felt as though he'd connected with Olivia in a way he'd never connected with another human being in his life. Sure, they'd had sex without any preamble, as they'd always done, but there'd been more depth to their liaison. He'd made love to the woman of his dreams. Literally.

Which made Olivia heading back to her hotel room absolutely right. Unlike him, she had a handle on their situation. Where was his gratitude?

Zac's phone vibrated its way across the bedside table. 'Hello?' Had Olivia had a change of heart?

'It's North Shore Emergency Unit, Dr Wright. We've got a situation.'

Not Olivia. Guess it wasn't his night. 'Tell me,' he sighed.

'A bus full of rowers returning to Whangarei went off the road an hour out of the city. There are many casualties so we're ringing round everyone. Can you come in?'

'On my way.' It wasn't as though he'd been sleeping. A certain woman had taken up residence in his skull, refusing to let him drop off to sleep even when his body was craving rest.

'Kelly Devlin, nineteen-year-old rower, fractured tibia,' the ED registrar told Zac within moments of him striding into the chaotic department.

Zac studied the X-rays on the light box. 'She needs a rod insertion,' he decided, and went to talk to his patient.

Kelly glared at him. 'I'm a national rowing champion, Doctor. I can't have a broken leg.'

Zac's heart went out to her. 'You have. I'm sorry.'

'Does that mean the end of my career?'

'First I'll explain what I'm going to do to help you.' He sat on the edge of her bed. 'I've seen the X-rays and your left tibia is fractured in two places. To allow the bone to heal without too much added stress I'm going to put a titanium rod down the centre of the bone. There will be screws to hold it in place while you heal.' He kept the details scant. He knew from experience that too much information at this stage usually confused the patient and added to their distress.

'Will I be competitive again?' the girl demanded.

'That will take a lot of work on your part, but I don't see why not.' When disbelief stared him in the eye, he added, 'You're a champion rower so you know what it's like to work your butt off to get where you want to be. This will be harder. Your muscles will need strengthening and the bone will require time to knit.' He hoped he wasn't misleading Kelly. 'You may have to compensate in some way for the damaged leg, but we won't know for sure until further down the track.'

Tears slid down her cheeks. 'You're honest, but I don't have to like what you're telling me. It's going to be painful for a while, isn't it?'

'You'll have painkillers.' Bone pain. Not good. 'A physiotherapist will have you working on that leg when I think you're ready.'

'When are you operating?'

'As soon as I get things sorted a nurse will come and get you ready for Theatre.' He stood up. 'I'll see you in there. Have your family been told about the accident?'

'Mum and Dad are on their way from Whangarei,

but I don't want to wait. If I've had surgery before they arrive it'll be easier on them.' She shifted on the bed and cried out as pain jagged her.

'Take it easy. Try to stay as still as possible. You'll soon be given a pre-anaesthetic drug that will make you feel drowsy and dull your senses a little.' Zac nodded at the nurse on the other side of the bed. 'I'll talk to the anaesthetist now, get everything under way.'

As he headed out of the ED to arrange everything Zac rubbed the back of his neck. What a night.

'Morning, everyone. Sorry I'm late. Forgot to set my alarm.' Olivia slid into the only vacant chair at the table in the hotel dining room where she was having a late brunch with Andy and his family, Maxine and Brent Sutherland, who were Andy's close friends, and Zac.

'Have a late night?' Zac asked.

She scowled at him. 'Something like that.'

He told her, 'I've been in surgery.'

'Already? Were you on call?' He'd have mentioned it, wouldn't he?

'A bus went over the bank near Waiwera. The hospital needed orthopaedic surgeons in a hurry.'

'Why was a bus travelling through the night?' she asked.

'Taking rowers home from the nationals down south.'

'Coffee or tea?' A waitress hovered with the brunch menu.

'We've all ordered,' Zac informed her.

'The kitchen will make sure your meal comes out with the others,' the waitress said. 'Drink?'

Yes, yes, yes. Give me a moment. Olivia took the proffered menu. 'A pot of English Breakfast tea, thank you.'

A quick read of the list of tasty dishes on offer. 'Pancakes with bacon and banana, and lots of maple syrup.'

When she turned to find Zac watching her with a soft smile on those adorable lips she snapped, 'What?'

'Pancakes and syrup? I thought you'd be a muesli and fruit girl.'

She was. Always. But this morning her usually strict control over her diet had gone the same place any control seemed to go when Zac was around—out west somewhere beyond the hills. 'Thought I'd spoil myself.' She looked around the table at her friends. Zac's friends too, don't forget. 'Did everyone enjoy last night?'

'You have to ask?' Maxine asked with a grin. 'The band kept playing until one and only stopped because the hotel management asked them to.'

'The dinner was amazing,' Brent added.

Olivia looked at the boys sitting quietly opposite her. 'Did you all have fun too?'

'Yeah. But Mum made us go to our room early. I liked dancing,' the oldest said.

'Your mum's mean.' Andy grinned tiredly. Now that the excitement of the night before had worn off he looked as though he had little energy left.

'It's part of the job description,' Zac added.

'That was a generous gift from Paul,' Maxine chipped in. 'I'm assuming you're both going to take it up. I mean, who wouldn't go to a luxury island in Fiji, all expenses paid? I know I would.'

'Does everyone know?' Olivia shivered. No way would she go after how things had played out last night in Zac's apartment. Nearly a week sharing a bure with Zac would make a joke of her self-control. Remaining impervious to Zac's charm would be impossible. As she'd already proved. 'I don't think I'll be going.'

Unfortunately her eyes drifted to the right and locked with Zac's.

'If that's what you want.'

She wasn't sure about it being what she wanted, but she knew it was how it had to be for her sanity. Amidst exclamations from just about everyone else at the table Olivia told Zac quietly, for his ears only, 'It's for the best.'

'Yours, or mine?' Why the disappointment? Surely he hadn't thought they'd be having a five-day sex fest? Though, if she was being truthful with herself, he had good reason to think that, given how quickly they'd leapt into each other's arms last night.

'Ours.' A picture of blue sea and coconut palms crossed her mind. Going to Fiji would be marvellous. That lump at the bottom of her stomach was her disappointment. It was a great opportunity and she was reneging on it.

'Last night you accepted.' Zac's words arrowed to the core of her concern.

'I did.' She'd be letting Paul down after he'd done something so generous. She wasn't used to people doing things like that for her. She had a feeling she'd also let Zac down. Would he want to go alone? Or could he take someone else with him? Jealousy raised its ugly head. She didn't want Zac going to the tropical island with another woman. If he was going she wanted to be the one at his side. In his arms. Gulp. *Make up your mind. What do you want with Zac?*

She wanted Zac in her life. But to follow up on that would be dangerous. What if they did get close; moved in together? How long would that last? When her mother acted once too often with the mess Olivia was used to dealing with, would Zac walk? If she had a month like she'd had in February, when she'd had so much work she'd all but lived in the hospital for four weeks, would he begrudge the time he didn't have with her and leave? There'd only been one man in her life she'd loved unconditionally—her father—and he'd deserted her. She doubted her ability to cope with anyone else doing that to her.

Her tea arrived and she concentrated on pouring, tried hard to ignore the dilemma going on in her head.

But Zac didn't seem to have any problem continuing the conversation. 'I take it this is because of what happened in my apartment?' He leaned closer so only she could hear him.

Unfortunately his movement brought that heady smell that defined him closer to her nostrils. There was no avoiding the scent, or the challenge in his eyes. 'We wouldn't be able to go the distance without touching each other.'

'Is that what you want?' Disbelief darkened his eyes, deepened his voice. Who could blame him? Last night she hadn't mucked around about getting into the sack with him. He asked, 'Seriously?

No, she wanted to spend the whole time in bed with him. That was the problem. 'It's what I need.'

Zac sat back, leaning away from her, his gaze fixed on her as though he hoped to see inside her skull and read her mind. 'I should be glad you're saying no, but there's one fabulous holiday going begging. Until Paul pointed it out I hadn't realised how much I could do with a break. Fiji would be perfect.'

Olivia said, 'You can still go.'

'Not much fun alone,' he said softly.

'Apply the pressure, why don't you?'

'Yep.'

'Not happening,' she muttered. Lifting her cup, Olivia tried to concentrate on what the others were talking about. When the meals arrived she joined in the conversation, relieved that the subject of Fiji had been dropped. But all the while that picture of the sea and coconut palms remained at the forefront of her mind, with Zac firmly in the middle.

Her phone rang just as everyone was getting up from the table to go their separate ways.

'Olivia, it's Hugo. I'm sorry to disturb your weekend when I said I'd cover for you, but I'm concerned about Anna Seddon.'

Alarm made her voice sharp. 'What's up?' Anna was a healthy woman who shouldn't be having any post-op complications.

'Medically she's fine. Her obs couldn't be better, she slept well until four this morning. But she's having a meltdown about the operation. I've tried talking to her but I'm a mere male and have no idea what it's like to have my breasts removed.' Hugo sighed. 'She's right, of course.'

'Of all the people I've done that procedure for I'd never have thought Anna would break up about it. She's been so pragmatic.' Olivia echoed Hugo's sigh. 'Is her husband with her?'

'Yes, and looking lost. She keeps yelling at him to go away. He doesn't know how to help her either.'

And I can? She had to try. She'd told Anna she'd be there for her throughout this difficult time, and she had meant it. 'I'll come over now.' She dropped her phone into her handbag and turned to face everyone. 'Thanks for the catch-up, guys. I've got to go.'

Maxine stepped up to give her a hug. 'Don't take

so long next time. I want to hear all the details about your trip to Fiji.'

'There won't be any. I'm not going.' She tried to free herself from Maxine's arms and failed.

'Go. It would be good for you.'

Maxine dropped her arms to her sides and Olivia stepped back.

'You might be surprised.'

Olivia couldn't help herself: she glanced across at the man in question. His familiar face snatched at her heart. Talking animatedly with the others, he appeared relaxed and comfortable in his own skin. Then he looked over at her and winked. Caught. He'd been aware of her scrutiny all along. Like they were in tune with each other, which was nonsense. They'd never been like that. Except when it came to sex. But there was nothing sexual about that wink. It had been more a 'Hey, girl' gesture. Friendly and caring, not deep and loving or hot and demanding. But it had been...? Nice? Yes, nice.

Turning back to Maxine, she said, 'I'd better run. A patient needs me.'

'You have to be somewhere in a hurry?' Zac strode alongside her as she raced for the lobby and the elevators, keen to get away before anyone else brought up the subject of that trip away with Zac.

'The hospital. I did a double mastectomy and implant yesterday morning and apparently my patient is losing it big time this morning.'

'That's a biggie for any woman to deal with.'

'She's been so brave all the way through discussions about the operation and what size implants she'd like. She's dealt with her family's history of breast cancer matter-of-factly, and accepted she didn't have a lot of choice if she wanted longevity. Guess it had to catch up with her some time.'

'Has she got good support from her family?' Zac asked as he pressed the up button for the elevator.

'Yes, very good.' Olivia drew a breath. Only yesterday she'd been saying to the Theatre staff how Anna's husband was a hero in her book. Yep, and she'd had thoughts about the man next to her being a hero too.

'You want me to get your car out of the basement? Save you some minutes?'

She stared at Zac. 'I forgot. I need to order a taxi. My car's in the hospital car park with a flat battery. I didn't have time to phone a service man yesterday.' She made to head for the concierge only to be stopped by Zac's hand on her arm.

'I'll be waiting in my car out the front when you're ready.' He nudged her forward into the elevator. 'It'll only take a couple of minutes to get it.'

But I don't want to sit in a car with you, breathing your smell, feeling your heat, wishing I could go away with you. 'A taxi will be fine.' She was talking to the closing doors, Zac already halfway across the lobby. She'd lost that round. There'd been determination in the set of his shoulders and the length of his quick strides taking him out of the hotel. He'd be ready for her the moment she emerged from the revolving door of the hotel.

Nice.

Leaning back against the wall, Olivia smiled despite her misgivings. She'd have to come up with a better word than 'nice'. Zac was more than nice, and his gestures were kind and caring. All good, all sounding bland for a man who was anything but. 'Hot' used to be her word for him and, yes, he was still that.

But now? Now he was a mixed bag of emotions and characteristics she hadn't taken the time to notice before. This Zac was intriguing. She wanted to know more about him. Hell, she wanted to know everything.

As the elevator pinged at her floor she knew she had to walk away from him, because the more she learned about Zac the harder it became to remain aloof. Her emotions were getting involved, putting her heart in turmoil, and that was a no-go zone.

CHAPTER SEVEN

'I AM SO SORRY.' Anna Seddon sniffed, and snatched up a handful of tissues to blow her nose. 'I know it's your weekend off. Hugo shouldn't have called you.'

Olivia sat on the edge of the bed and shook her head at her patient. 'It's not a problem. I'd have been annoyed if he hadn't. What started this off? What's distressed you this morning?'

'I took a look under the gown and saw where my breasts used to be. It's horrible there. The new ones don't look right even wrapped in bandages. I know you said to wait, but I had to see.' Anna slashed at fresh tears spilling down her cheeks. 'Nothing looks normal. The implants are different, ugly, not me, and the scars are bright red. I shouldn't have done this. I should've taken a chance I wouldn't get cancer.'

Olivia waited until Anna ran out of steam, then took her hand. 'You've had a shock. No amount of explaining could've prepared you.' Which was why she asked patients to wait until she was there before they looked at the results of their surgery. 'Remember, I said that your breast implants were going to look and feel strange. They're not natural, like your real breasts were, and we have yet to bring them up to full size. This will take time as we can't pump them full of saline instantly. It's a gradual process, giving your skin time to stretch and accommodate the implants.'

'You told me that, but I saw them and freaked out,' Anna whispered. 'You must think I'm a total head case.'

'Not at all. You've just had your breasts removed when as far as we know there's nothing wrong with them. You're not dealing with the fear of knowing you've already got cancer. Instead, breast cancer is a real possibility for you, so you're working ahead of things. Of course it's a shock and very different from other situations.'

'I know you went over this more than once. I thought I understood how I'd feel, and that the fact I was doing it to be there for my kids and Duncan would override every other emotion. I was wrong.' At the mention of her husband tears began pouring down her face again.

'You're a woman, first and foremost. Our breasts help define us. When we're young we can't wait for them to start growing and then it's what size will they be? Will they be sexy? They're also about nurturing our babies. You've done something very brave. Don't ever think you're not as feminine as you were before yesterday because you are. You've got a lovely figure, a pretty face and a heart of gold. Not to mention a family who adores you. Especially that husband of yours.'

A shadow of a smile lightened Anna's mouth through the deluge of tears. 'Duncan's something, isn't he?'

'He's a hero.' There, she'd said it again. What was it with her that she kept coming up with that word? It wasn't as though she believed in heroes. *But you want to. You want one of your own.*

'You think?' Anna asked, a twinkle slowly lightening her sad eyes and easing her tears.

'I know.' She stood up. 'In fact, there's a hero out

in the waiting room. I'll go tell him you're busting to see him.'

'What will he say when he sees my false breasts?' There was a hitch in Anna's voice and fear in her eyes.

'I bet he tells you he loves you.' Lucky woman. *What was it like to have a man to love you, to say those precious three words to you?* Olivia had never known and wondered if she ever would. It must be the most precious thing—love, unconditional and everlasting. When she walked into the waiting room she found Zac talking rugby to Anna Seddon's husband as though he'd known him for ever.

Her heart did a funny little jig. Zac. Sexy Zac was doing nothing more than yakking to a stranger who was trying to cope with his wife's unenviable situation, and yet he looked…like everything she'd thought she might want in a man, in her man. Her hero.

Get out of here. Where had that come from? Yeah, sure, yesterday when she'd called Duncan a hero it had been Zac's face flitting across her mind, but Zac? Hero? Why would she even think that? What had he done for her to think so?

She'd dumped him and he'd sent her beautiful flowers.

He'd driven her here this morning and taken her keys to get her car battery sorted.

He'd turned up to help yesterday afternoon when everything had been turning to custard.

He'd never once been rude to her, or made fun of her need to keep herself to herself, or told her to stop being so much in control of just about everything she touched.

Did any or all of those things make a man a hero? Didn't heroes slay dragons? She still had dragons, but Zac didn't know about them because she'd never shown that weakness to him. It wasn't as though he could make everything right for her, even if he was aware of her screwed-up family life.

'CC, you're daydreaming.' Zac was smiling at her, his head at an angle that suggested he wanted to know exactly what was on her mind.

Thank goodness she wasn't the type to blush. The absolute last thing Zac needed to know was what she'd been thinking. 'I don't daydream.'

'Then you're missing out on a lot of fun.'

'How's Anna?' There was a load of worry in Duncan's short question.

'Wanting to see her man.' Olivia moved closer. 'She's got past that little meltdown but, Duncan, you need to be prepared for more episodes. I'm not saying Anna's going to fall apart on you long term, but she's facing reality now, whereas before surgery it was still an unknown. It's scary for her.' She continued, 'She's afraid you won't be able to cope when you see her breasts. It's natural to feel that way, but it's how you handle the situation that's going to make the difference.'

'I'll tell you this for nothing. I don't care about scars and a change in her shape. I love that woman and think she's the bravest person I've ever met.' Duncan touched the corner of one eye with a forefinger.

'I think Anna's a lucky woman.' Olivia swallowed the sudden lump in her throat. 'Go tell her exactly what you just said.'

'She's not going to throw her water bottle at me or tell me to go away for ever?' Duncan was deadly serious.

'I doubt it, unless it's because you've taken so long to get along to her room since I said I was coming to find you.' Anna shouldn't have thrown anything—it would hurt her wounds and might pull some stitches. Something to check up on when she examined her later. She hadn't wanted to have Anna expose herself for an exam when she'd been so upset, and had figured that as all the obs were fine it didn't matter if they waited before doing that.

Dropping into the seat Duncan had vacated, she stared at the toes of her boots. And yawned.

Zac chuckled. 'Want to grab a coffee while we wait for the battery man? He's about twenty minutes away and we could both do with something to keep us awake.'

'Hospital coffee will be a comedown after that fabulous brunch.'

'Nothing like a reality check.'

Reality. Of course. 'You don't need to hang around. You've got a perfectly good vehicle downstairs. I can visit patients while I wait.'

'You don't want to share crap coffee with me?' His grin set butterflies flapping in her tummy. 'Anyway, the guy's got my number, not yours.'

'I hate it when you gloat.' She laughed tiredly. 'Disgusting coffee it is.' Along with great company. All in all, not a bad way to continue her morning.

Olivia's bubble burst quickly.

Zac directed her to a corner table as far away as possible from the few staff and visitors using the cafeteria, ordered long blacks for them both, and dropped onto the chair opposite her. 'I've talked to my practice manager so she can arrange for my days off when we go to Fiji. The hospital roster is easy to fix, with Paul offering to cover for me.'

The man didn't muck about. He must've been on the phone the moment she'd clambered out of his four-wheel drive in the hospital garage; ordering a battery, sorting his week off.

She sighed. 'I thought I said I wasn't going.' He had to be deaf as well as organised.

'You did.'

'So you *are* planning on going alone.'

'Nope.' Zac leaned back as a girl placed two over-full coffee cups on the table and took away their order number. 'I want you to come with me.'

So do I. 'No.'

Those eyes that matched the coffee in colour locked onto her. 'Are you telling *me* no? Or yourself, Olivia?'

'We'd probably end up hating each other.'

'Somehow I don't think so.' Shock widened his eyes. So he hadn't thought it through. 'But we won't know if we don't try.'

What was this about? Zac had made it clear he'd only been interested in sex last time round. Her hands were back in her lap, her fingers aching with the tightness of her grip. 'Is this so you can then walk away with no regrets? Did I finish it too soon last time?'

Now his gaze dropped away. He leaned far back and draped one arm over the top of the chair next to him. His eyes cruised the cafeteria before returning to her, a guarded expression covering his face. 'I've learned more about you in the last twenty-four hours than I ever did in those eight weeks last year.'

'Then you're probably up to speed and there's nothing more to find out.'

Zac stared at her. 'You're selling yourself short.'

To hell with the coffee. Pushing up from the table, she aimed for a moderate tone. 'No, I am not. What you see is what you get, and as for Fiji, you get nothing. I'm not going.' *But I want to. Really, really want to.*

Of course he followed her. He was persistent if nothing else. Unlike last time. 'Rethink that, Olivia. We don't have to live in each other's pockets while we're there, but it would be fun to lie in the sun together, to share a meal under the stars.'

The problem was that if she lay on the beach in her bikini beside Zac in his swimming shorts they would end up having sex. Not that doing so didn't appeal. Of course it did. Her mouth watered, thinking about it. But she'd made up her mind the day she'd walked out on him that they weren't going anywhere with their relationship because she couldn't afford to get her heart broken. Neither had she wanted to break his—if it was even up for grabs.

Zac pulled his phone from his pocket and read a message. 'Your battery's nearly here.'

'Good. Thanks for arranging it.' She didn't know why she felt small and mean, only knew she was floundering, fighting between going with him on that trip and staying away from temptation. She was looking out for herself, something she'd always done. Her mother had never put her daughter before herself, never would. She gasped. That meant she was the same as her mother. Putting her determination to remain alone before anyone, anything else. *But... But I'm doing it for a good reason. Dad left Mum because she'd worn him down, tossed his love back in his face again and again. I'm not doing that to a man I might fall in love with.*

A hand on her elbow directed her to the elevator. Seemed that Zac was always taking her to the lift. 'Five days of sunshine and no patients. Sounds wonderful to me.'

Ain't that the truth?

At least Olivia hadn't questioned why he was so adamant they should go to Fiji together. He should be grateful she was refusing to go, but the thought of being alone when he should be celebrating with his family grated. A distraction was needed and Olivia would certainly be that.

But, more than that, it was time to start changing from being reactive to his family's attitude to becoming proactive in sorting out what he wanted for his future— starting with taking time off from his heavy work schedule to have some fun. Hell. When was the last time he'd done that? Nothing came to mind except the hours he'd snatched to be with Olivia eighteen months ago.

The sound of squealing tyres filled the basement garage as they exited the elevator on the way to the outside car park. The smell of burning rubber filled his nostrils. 'What the hell?'

A nearly new, upmarket car raced past them. At the end of the lane it spun left, the rear wheels sliding out of control. Just when impact with parked vehicles seemed imminent the driver got the car under control.

Zac pushed Olivia back against the now closed elevator doors, tugged his phone from his pocket to call Security, and cursed. There was no signal down here. 'The driver looked very young. How'd he get in?'

The garage and car park were reserved for medical personnel and accessed with a swipe card. The car flew past them again as Zac looked around for a wall phone. Spying one by the stairwell door, he changed direction, only to spin around when he heard an almighty thump, followed by a metallic crashing sound. Then ominous silence.

'He's hit someone and then slammed into a vehicle!' Olivia began running in the direction of the crashed car.

Zac raced alongside her. 'We need someone down here, taking charge of that kid.' A boy looking about fifteen staggered out of the car, looking shocked and bewildered.

'Where did she come from?' he squawked as they reached him.

Zac's hands clenched as he saw a woman in blue scrubs sprawled across the concrete, a pool of blood already beginning to form by her head. 'What the hell were you doing?' Zac shouted at the kid as he dropped down to his knees beside the unmoving woman.

'Hey, steady.' Olivia reached across from the other side of the woman to grip his arm. Shaking her head at him, she said, 'This nurse needs our undivided attention.'

'You're right,' he ground through gritted teeth. 'Kid, get on that phone by the elevator and get help down here fast.'

Without a word the youth was gone, and Zac could only hope he was running for the phone.

Zac felt for a pulse, and sighed with relief.

Olivia was carefully feeling the nurse's head. 'Amelia, can you hear me?'

A low groan was the only answer she got.

'Amelia, you've been in an accident. There are two doctors with you and we're going to check your injuries.'

'How much do you think she's heard?' Zac wondered aloud.

Olivia shrugged. 'We can't be sure anything we say registers.'

'You know her?' Zac noted the odd angle of the

nurse's legs and checked for bleeding in case a blood vessel had been torn. 'No major swelling indicating internal bleeding.'

'I can read,' Olivia muttered.

The name badge. Duh. Left his brain behind this morning, had he? With gentle movements he began assessing her hips and thighs for fractures. 'Broken femur for starters. This knee has taken a thump too.' His fingers worked over the kneecap. 'Smashed, I'd say.'

Their patient groaned again and lifted an arm a small way off the ground.

Zac quickly caught her, and gently pressed her arm down by her side. 'Amelia, try not to move.'

One eye opened, shut again.

'At least she's responding,' he said.

'Oh, my God. What's happened?' A man loomed over them.

Zac told him, 'An out-of-control car hit her.'

The newcomer said, 'I'm in Admin, but I can get help if you tell me what you need.'

'Get us the emergency equipment and a bed. I told the driver to ring upstairs but you're part of this hospital, you'll know exactly who to speak to,' Zac told him. Who knew if the boy had done as he'd said or taken a hike before everyone turned up and started pointing fingers?

Olivia was speaking quietly. 'We've got a soft cranial injury, probably from impacting with the concrete. Left ear's torn.'

Zac added to the list of injuries. 'At least her chest appears to have dodged a bullet.' His fingers were gently working over Amelia's ribs. 'The car would've hit her in the lower body.' What had that kid been thinking, doing wheelies in here? He hadn't looked old enough to know how to drive. *Who are you to ask? You were eighteen and still got it wrong.*

'On my way.' The admin man nodded at the vehicle parked with its nose caught in the side panel of a sedan. 'That the car? It's Maxine Sutherland's.'

Olivia's head shot up, horror in her eyes, but all she said was, 'Can you run? This woman needs urgent help.'

With the man gone, Zac said, 'Maxine must've left the car unlocked, unless…' Had it been Maxine and Brent's son driving? Shock rocked through Zac. No parent ever wanted to deal with something like this. He knew. He'd done it to his brother and parents, with dire consequences. They'd never forgiven him, blaming him for not looking out for his younger brother. Like they'd ever been there for either of their sons. But every time Zac saw his brother and that blasted wheelchair the guilt crunched his insides. Zac's remorse would never go away, and was stronger than anything anyone else could lay on him.

'Zac? You okay?' A gentle hand touched his cheek.

His chest rose as he dragged in a lungful of air. 'Yes.' *No.* Now wasn't the time to explain. If ever there was a right time. He tried to straighten Amelia's right leg. 'Her knee is also dislocated.' He had to know. 'Do you think the kid is Maxine and Brent's boy?'

Distress blinked out at him from Olivia's hyacinth eyes. 'No. Couldn't be.' Her bottom lip trembled even as the truth pushed aside her automatic denial. 'How dreadful for them if he is.'

'He was in here, and only card holders have access.'

They were interrupted by the sound of people running and an emergency trolley laden with everything they needed being pushed at a fast pace between the cars. Guess the kid had fronted up for help.

As Olivia explained to the ED staff what had happened and her assessment of Amelia's injuries, the anger Zac had put on the back burner roared to life. 'That boy really has made a mess of things for her.' Zac was equally worried for the lad. *His* life had changed for ever. 'Where is he, anyway?'

'Probably safer away from you.' Olivia came to stand beside him and reached for his hand. 'Calm down, Zac. You're not helping an already tricky situation. I know he's done wrong but let's leave that to others while we help with the medical side of things.'

The last thing Zac wanted was Olivia telling him what to do. It took a moment for it to register in the red haze of his brain that he had an excuse to put distance between them. 'The battery guy. I'll go and wait for him at the gate.' He needed to get away from what had happened before he blew a gasket. Amelia was getting all the attention she needed from Olivia and the ED doctor, while his attitude wasn't helping anyone. He stomped off before Olivia could say anything more.

But not before he saw the shock in those beautiful eyes. Yes, he had his secrets, just as he suspected she had hers. Secrets neither of them wanted to share. His definitely held him back from having a complete and fulfilling life. Was it the same with Olivia? Could that be why she'd walked out on their affair? She hadn't wanted to keep going in case they grew close?

There was nothing for it. They had to take that trip. Time together, talking, relaxing, getting to know each other on a whole new level, was becoming imperative.

Which really meant he should sign up for every orthopaedic surgery coming up at his clinic for the next six months.

CHAPTER EIGHT

OLIVIA POURED BOILING water over the tea leaves. Earl Grey Blue Star. 'Bliss.' She sniffed the air.

Every bone in her body ached with weariness. Her head pounded, her muscles drooped, and it felt as if there was grit in her eyes. The long soak in a very hot shower probably hadn't woken her up at all. Seven o'clock on Saturday night and she couldn't wait to crawl into bed. How pathetic could she get?

Her stomach was crying out to be fed. She hadn't eaten since brunch—the incident in the hospital garage and the resulting investigation by the traffic police had taken up a lot of the day. The pizza she'd ordered would arrive at the front door within the hour. She licked her lips in anticipation and tasted tea.

Her sitting room felt cosy, and lounging in pyjamas and a baggy sweatshirt in front of the fire she'd lit earlier felt decadent. A rare treat to be so sloppily dressed, and she'd die if anyone but the pizza delivery girl saw her in this state.

Right now a holiday would be perfect. *There's one on offer.* Had she been too hasty turning it down? *Not going to think about it.*

Picking up the remote, she turned on the TV, volume low, and flicked through the channels. Nothing interested her, not even the spunky guy showing how to swing a golf club. Not that sport of any kind interested her. It required energy she didn't like expending getting sweaty.

At the moment the most energetic she wanted to be was lying on a beach, getting a tan. Fiji would do that every time. She sighed. Fiji with Zac? What was wrong with her? She should be grabbing those tickets and packing her bag.

The doorbell rang loud in the quiet house. Someone out there must be looking out for her because that pizza was early. She went to get her dinner.

'Hi, Olivia. I hope you don't mind me dropping by.'

'Zac.' Her stomach growled while her heart lifted.

'Is that a good "Zac", or a go away "Zac"?'

'Take your pick.' She stepped back, opening the door wide.

Zac walked in quickly, as though afraid she'd change her mind.

She probably would've if she'd had the energy to think about the consequences of letting him into her home. 'Along here.' She led him into the sitting room.

When his gaze landed on her tea he asked, 'Got anything stronger? Scotch on the rocks?' He sank onto the couch and stared into the fire.

'Sure.' That was one spirit she did have, kept for her delightful elderly neighbour who liked an occasional tipple when he dropped in after a lonely day at home.

Returning with a glass, ice and whisky, Olivia placed everything on the coffee table she'd spent weeks sanding and varnishing to make it beautiful. Taking her mug to the other end of the couch, she sat with her feet tucked under her bottom and flicked glances at her visitor. Something was going on. He'd been furious when

Amelia had been knocked down by that car. No, as he'd told her angrily, it had been the boy who'd banged the car into Amelia. The car was not at fault. Couldn't argue with that.

His anger had been more than she'd have expected, but there hadn't been an opportunity to talk to him about it. When they'd realised it might've been their colleagues' son doing wheelies in the garage Zac had turned pale and charged outside to let the battery guy into the car park. Later she'd seen him standing beside her car, hands on hips, staring up at the rain-laden sky, impervious to everything going on around her. When he'd joined her and the police, he'd gained some control over his emotions but hadn't been able to look her in the eye. After they'd finished telling the cops what little they'd seen Zac had been quick to drive away, leaving her none the wiser about what had been going on. Now here he was, looking badly in need of some quiet time and a big hug.

She'd give him the quiet time by waiting until he was ready to talk, but she'd hold back on the hug in case she'd read him wrong and he took it as more than she intended.

Zac reached for the bottle, slopped more whisky into the glass, and leaned back, his head on the top of the couch, his eyes closed.

It was far too tempting. Placing her glass on the coffee table, she leaned over, pulled him against her, and wrapped her arms right around him. Zac didn't resist, instead shuffling closer to lay his head on her breast.

She was starting to get pins and needles in one leg by the time Zac moved to sit up. Broaching the subject she thought was bothering him, she said, 'Amelia's going to be a mess for a while.'

'That boy will be a mess for the rest of his life.'

'It's going to take patience and counselling, yes, but his parents will be there for him all the way. He'll make it. Hopefully he learned a huge lesson today.' Though what the kid had been thinking, taking the car for a spin in a packed garage, was beyond her.

Zac leaned forward, his elbows on his knees, the glass between his hands turning back and forth. 'You don't know what you're talking about. I do.'

Olivia leaned closer to place her hand on his thigh, her shoulder against his upper arm. 'Tell me.'

She said it so quietly that at first she didn't think he'd heard, but as she was about to repeat herself he said, 'I've been there.'

'Oh, Zac.' Her heart broke for the sadness and despair in those words.

'My brother's in a wheelchair. Because of me.'

She closed her eyes. The pain in Zac's face was too much. He hurt big-time. The load of guilt he carried must crush him at times. Tonight was one of those times. Today's event had brought back the memories in full colour. She opened her eyes and tried to eyeball him. 'Zac, I'm sorry.'

'Don't give me any platitudes, CC. I couldn't stand that.'

'You've heard them all before, huh?'

'Every last one.' He stared into his glass, the liquid golden in the light thrown by the fire. 'I prefer honesty and you've never given me anything else so please don't change tonight. No "Mark's doing fine, it's okay". No "You're forgiven so get on with your life as though it didn't happen".' The warning was issued softly, which made it all the more real.

What the heck was she supposed to say if he didn't

want to talk about it? Or did he want to say what had happened to cause his brother's injuries but couldn't get the words out? Had he changed his mind about telling her anything more? Her mind was a jumble of questions and emotions. She wanted to help him, but Zac wasn't one to ask for help. Or was that what he'd done by turning up on her doorstep?

The doorbell ringing was a welcome interruption while she tried to work out where to go with this. Grabbing the money she'd put out earlier, she went to get dinner.

Zac stood up as she returned to the sitting room. 'I'll head away and leave you in peace.'

'You're welcome to share this. I never eat more than half.' Though tonight she might've, considering the state her stomach was in. 'Sit down, Zac. I'll get some napkins and plates.'

'You want anything stronger than tea to drink?'

Was that a *Yes, I'll stay*? 'No, thanks.'

'You're cautious with your drinks, aren't you?' Zac smiled half-heartedly. 'Afraid of making an idiot of yourself?'

'Absolutely.' Rejoining him on the couch, she sighed. 'Life when I was younger was chaotic and messy. I learned to be rigid in my dealings with my mum, school, everything. Too controlled maybe, but that's how I manage.'

Taking her hand, Zac locked eyes with hers. 'Yet you're completely off the radar when it comes to sex.'

She spluttered over the mouthful she'd just bitten off her pizza.

Zac wiped her mouth with his napkin. 'I wasn't complaining.' The smile he gave her was tender, turning her inside out.

'Maybe sex is my one outlet,' she managed, holding back from explaining it hadn't been like that with the few other men she'd slept with.

He was very quiet for a few minutes, then blew her away with, 'Would you come to Fiji with me if we agreed to no sex for the whole trip?'

'What?' she asked.

'Think you—we—can do that?'

Talk about a challenge she couldn't resist. Especially as she was struggling to keep refusing to go in the first place. And now that she'd heard more about what made Zac tick she wanted to spend more time with him.

Zac grimaced. The need to go away with Olivia just got stronger and stronger, no matter how often he told himself he was making a mistake. When he'd told her about Mark he'd very nearly continued with the whole sordid story of how his life had changed for ever but a modicum of common sense had prevailed. Fear of seeing disgust in her eyes had locked his tongue to the roof of his mouth.

But if only she'd agree to go to that resort island with him. Go and have some good, honest fun. Even if she agreed to the bizarre suggestion he'd just put out there, he'd be happy. He wouldn't mind someone to talk to, to relax with.

He saw Olivia open her mouth, heard her say as though in slow motion, 'I'll go. I won't change my mind again. I'm sorry I've been vacillating.'

Excitement zipped through him, temporarily drowning out the horrors of that morning's disaster. They were going to spend time together without the pressures of work; with time to talk, to be themselves, and maybe learn more about each other. 'Good.'

'That's it?' She laughed, a tinkling sound that lightened his mood.

'Yes.' Relief softened him. 'You know what? I think it'll be great. Just the two of us.'

Olivia smiled.

It was a big, soft smile that caused him to take a risk. 'I was driving Dad's car.' Swallowing hard, he continued. 'It was late. We'd been out all day at the rugby, and stopped at a friend's on the way home.' His gut churned. 'Mark was being a pain in the arse, winding me up as only he knew how, and when we drove away from that house he said one thing too many and I lost it. Slammed my foot on the accelerator. The car spun into the stone wall along the waterfront and flipped into the water. Mark's back was broken.' That was all there was to it.

Her expression showed no condemnation. 'How awful for your family. Especially you. You've taken the blame ever since, right?'

Air huffed out of his lungs. 'Of course. I *was* at fault. I lost my temper.' *Damn, but it still hurt so badly.* If he never made another mistake in his life it wouldn't be good enough.

'You haven't forgiven yourself. Does your brother blame you?' When he nodded once, she continued. 'What about your parents? Surely they don't?'

He went for broke. 'My parents put me in charge of my brother from very early on. They were both busy with their careers as CEOs of big businesses. We were the children to be trotted out at functions or for family photos, and they were proud of us as long as we didn't stuff up. Which I did—monumentally.' At least now she'd understand why he wasn't looking for a woman to love and settle down with, that he'd always fly solo.

One holiday in Fiji being the exception. 'Of course they haven't forgiven me. I was in charge of Mark that night.'

Olivia wanted to cry for him. How could parents do that? Then again, her father had left her with Mum, hadn't he? Zac shouldn't, mustn't take all the blame, but he'd obviously made a lifelong habit of shouldering it. 'So you and Mark don't get along even now?'

'Hardly.' His mouth flattened. 'He's a successful architect, which is something to be grateful for.'

'More than something. It says he's moved on, hasn't let his spinal injury hold him back.' If only she could remove Zac's pain. But there was only one person who could do that. Zac.

'My parents pretty much disowned me after the accident.' Zac's face was bleak. 'I continued living with them for the rest of that year but it was as though I was a stranger. Come the last day of school I was gone. I got a job in a supermarket and went to live with my grandfather. Dad gave me a generous allowance but I turned him down and paid my university fees myself. I never went back home.'

And she'd thought her life had been bad. No wonder she and Zac both balked at commitment. 'That's harsh.' Actually, it was lousy. How could any parent do that? Did Zac think if he moved on, let himself stop feeling guilt, then he'd be setting himself up for another fall? Zac was a very responsible person. That had been abundantly clear when they'd been training to become surgeons. Had that come from this accident? Or had he always been a responsible person who'd made one mistake? Now she understood his outburst over the boy who'd knocked down Amelia that morning. 'I'm glad you have your grandfather.'

He cocked an eyebrow at her. 'So am I. Except he died last Christmas.' That sadness had returned to his eyes, tightened his face, more deeply, more strongly than ever.

Olivia wanted to banish it—if only for a few hours. And she only knew one way. They weren't in Fiji yet. Standing up, she put her hand out to him. 'Come with me.'

His hand was warm and firm as his fingers laced through hers. He didn't say a word as she led him down the hall to her bedroom. Or when she began unbuttoning his shirt.

Running her hands over that wide expanse of muscular chest, her blood began to thrum along her veins. Her lips surrounded his nipple, her tongue caressed slowly. Then Zac's hands were lifting her head so he could kiss her.

A long, slow kiss that had none of the urgent fire of any of their previous kisses and all the quietness of giving and sharing. It was heady stuff.

'Olivia,' Zac groaned against her mouth.

Without breaking the kiss, she pushed his shirt off his shoulders and down his arms, then found the stud and zip of his jeans. When Zac moved to lift her top she took his hands and placed them at his sides, and continued removing his jeans.

When she had him naked she gently shoved him backwards to sprawl across her bed. Her tummy quivered at the beautiful sight. His well-honed muscles accentuated his masculinity. Slowly she raised her top, exposing her bra-covered breasts. Next she slid her hands under the waistband of her shapeless trackies and began pushing them, oh, so slowly down to her hips, her thighs, her knees.

Zac's gaze followed her actions, his eyes kissing her skin. Shivers of excitement touched all the exposed places of her body. Standing in her panties and bra, she suddenly felt uncomfortable. What was she doing? Then Zac's tongue lapped his bottom lip and she relaxed. It wasn't as though he hadn't seen her naked, and while she mightn't be a strip dancer she could undress seductively.

Zac put his hands behind his head and kept watching her.

Placing one foot on the bed, she undid her bra and let it fall into her hands to be twirled across the room.

Zac's eyes widened and his tongue did another lick of his lips.

With one forefinger she began lowering her panties, never taking her eyes off his. She saw when they widened, when his chest began rising and falling faster, when his erection strained tight. Swinging a leg over his body, she hovered above him, moving so that her centre barely touched the tip of his shaft.

'Oh, sweetheart, let me touch you.' Those firm hands she craved on her skin covered her breasts, lifting them, caressing and gently squeezing them. His thumbs teased her nipples into hard, tight peaks.

Heat spread throughout her body like a slow burn, sending lazy flames of desire to every corner, warming her skin, drying her mouth. She began to lower herself over him, taking him deep inside.

Zac moved his hands to her buttocks, and he held her still. 'Not yet.'

Suddenly Olivia was on her back with Zac above her, kissing every inch of her heated skin, drowning her in need and longing. Taking his time to work down her body. They'd never made love like this.

This felt like lovemaking; not hot, frantic sex.

And when Zac moved over her, claimed her, they moved in unison, a slow rhythm that built and built till finally they reached a crescendo that stole the breath out of her lungs and sent her spinning out of control.

Olivia woke slowly. A heavy weight lay over her waist. Zac's arm. His breaths were soft on the back of her neck. His knees tucked in behind hers, and his stomach pushed against her lower back. Wow. This was amazing. Comfortable and cosy, warm and sexy. But mostly wonderful. Something she'd never experienced before. She snuggled nearer, closing her eyes to absorb every sensation moving through her. Warmth from that splayed hand on her stomach, from those thigh muscles behind her.

'Morning, beautiful,' Zac whispered against her neck.

'Wow,' she said. Hard to believe what she'd been missing out on. A small laugh escaped her. Slipping her fingers through Zac's on her stomach, she admitted, 'I've never had a man stay the night.'

Warm lips laid a soft kiss on her shoulder. 'Glad I'm the chosen one.' Another kiss. 'It's not something I normally do either.'

It was as though her whole body smiled. She and Zac had slept together, as in 'closed their eyes and gone to sleep' slept. She'd heard women talk about how good it was to sleep, spooned with their partner, and had thought they were exaggerating. Now she got it.

Careful. This was starting to feel like a relationship, as in not just about sex. Olivia tensed. Really? Damn. Just when she was beginning to enjoy things reality raised its annoying head to remind her she knew nothing about a good, solid, loving relationship between a man and a woman. Neither did Zac.

'Hey, relax. I'm not going to bite.' Zac's voice sounded sleep-laden.

No, but was he going to hurt her? Not today, or next month maybe, but eventually would he realise he didn't want to spend time with her, and walk? She had to protect herself. Wriggling free, she sat up. 'I'm going to take a shower.'

Zac reached for her, pulled her down. 'Come here. Let's stay tucked up for a little longer.'

'But…'

'Do you have to be somewhere in a hurry?' he asked reasonably.

'No.' Neither could she deny that lying in Zac's strong arms gave her a sense of belonging. Something that had been missing most of her life. Tension began tripping up her spine. Not good. Belonging went hand in hand with a serious relationship. Squeezing her eyes shut tight, she worked at banishing the negative feeling. She'd make the most of this moment; give herself something to remember later.

'I can't believe that in less than two weeks we'll be lying under palm trees.' Excitement warmed Olivia as she talked to Zac on the phone the following Thursday night. 'I'm going on holiday.'

'Says the woman who went out of her way to avoid it.' Zac's laughter rolled down the phone.

'Yeah, well, I'm glad I came to my senses. A holiday is definitely what I need. How are you getting on with sorting your surgical list?'

'Not too bad. Because Paul's taking over my private list I haven't had to change too many appointments.

Most patients I've talked to have been understanding about the change.'

Olivia grimaced. 'I wish mine were as accepting. There've been a few tears and tantrums, but I think I've got it sorted. I'll be working some long days leading up to our departure and will be busier than rush hour on the motorway.'

'Wonderful,' he groaned. 'Are you going to sleep the whole time we're away?'

'Absolutely not.' Somehow she doubted she'd sleep much at all, knowing Zac was in the same room and out of bounds. Why had he suggested that? Getting to know each other was one thing, but seriously? No sex? This would be a very interesting holiday. 'I'm going shopping for bikinis at the weekend.'

'Can I come?'

'I don't think so.' She grinned. That so wasn't happening.

'What if I waited outside the shop and took you to lunch afterwards?'

'What sort of lunch?'

'You'd have to wait and see.' Zac laughed again.

'Sorry, not happening.'

'So where do you go shopping for beach gear in the middle of winter?'

'My favourite fashion shop has an accessories section all year round. Apparently bikinis are holiday accessories. Who'd have thought it? But, then, I haven't owned a bikini in more years than I care to count.' Or gone on a holiday.

'Don't you go to the beach?' Zac asked.

'Going to the beach is a family thing, or a teen group party.' Which had been the last time she'd gone with a crowd.

'I think it's time you started getting out there and living, CC. All work and no play is not healthy.'

'Didn't you tell me how little you do outside work?' They were a right messed-up pair. 'We'll make up for it in Fiji.'

'Can't wait.' A sigh filtered down the line. 'I mean that. You have no idea how much I'm looking forward to this now that it's real.'

'Oh, but I do. After at first refusing to accept the trip, I now find I'm often daydreaming about being on the beach or swimming with the fishes. I don't remember being this excited about anything since... Well, I don't remember.'

'We are going to have a blast.' Now he was sounding like an excited schoolboy.

'Sure are.'

Another voice interrupted the moment. 'Olivia, sweetheart, where's the tonic water?' Her mother's wheedling voice grated more than usual.

'Zac, I've got to go. Talk to you again.'

'Something up? Your tone changed. Is your mother there?' He missed nothing, damn him.

'Yes, she is.' Sometimes her mother could be demanding and unrelenting in her quest for whatever today's greatest need was, and other times she'd be all sweetness and light. 'I've got to go.'

'Hey, I'm here for you.' The excitement had gone, replaced with concern. 'We can still have that lunch.'

'I'm good, Zac. Truly.'

'Olivia, tonic water. Where have you hidden it?' Mum stood in front of her, her eyes bloodshot and her tomato-red lipstick smudged on her upper lip.

'Talk to me, CC.' Zac was in her ear.

'It's complicated.' And ugly.

'Try me,' he persisted.

'Not now, Zac.' Her mother was in her face. 'Talk later. Bye.' Olivia pressed the off button, dug deep for patience. No surprise. She was all out of it. 'There's no tonic in this house.' There hadn't been any gin either until her mother had arrived with a bottle an hour ago.

'Darling, that's no way to treat your mother.'

Air hissed over Olivia's lips. 'Keeping an endless supply of gin and tonic isn't either.' She rubbed her thumbs over her eyes. 'You said there was something you wanted to talk about.'

'I think I should sell the house. It's time to move on with my life. But you're going to say no to anything I suggest.' Petulant as well.

Being one of the trustees for her mother's property and banking details came with its own set of difficulties. But if left to her own resources her mother would've gone broke long ago. 'Mum, we've discussed this so often I can't believe you'd bring the subject up again.'

'You are so unfair. About everything.'

Yep, a right old cold fish with a bank account tighter than a fish's backside. That's me. 'Where would you live if you sold? Another house? Or an apartment somewhere?'

'I could move in with you. There're more rooms here than you know what to do with.'

That was never going to happen.

Never say never.

Olivia shuddered. She did love her mother, but for sanity's sake preferred to keep her at a distance. To share the same house day in, day out would send her climbing the harbour bridge and leaping off.

CHAPTER NINE

'TOKORIKI.' THE HELICOPTER pilot pointed to an island ahead of them.

Olivia gasped. 'Oh, wow, it's tiny.'

Zac grinned. 'Perfect. You won't be able to get away from me.'

She elbowed him. 'Want to spend the night outside in a hammock? Alone?'

Zac just laughed. Damn it. 'A night in a hammock would be a novelty. I wonder if there's room for two.'

She did an exaggerated eye roll. 'Not to mention mosquitoes.'

Zac stared down at the bright blue sea as the pilot brought the helicopter around to line up with the landing pad on the resort's lawn. 'Isn't it stunning?'

Olivia leaned over Zac to get a good look at the island. 'Pretty as a picture.'

'Yes.' Zac's head was right beside hers, his scent tickling her nostrils.

Pulling sideways so that she no longer touched him, she tried to ignore the buzz of excitement fizzing along her veins. Not easy in the confined space with the smell of aftershave and hot-blooded male teasing her. How was she going to remain immune to him when they'd be sharing a bure? The photos on the internet had been a reality check, like a dousing under cold water. The one large room containing an enormous bed towards the back and lounge furniture at the front looked so romantic and had set her heart racing—and that had been back at home. Couples didn't come here to sleep in separate beds. Not unless they were Zac and her.

The helicopter touched down with a bump and Olivia snapped open the clasp on her safety belt. A big, strapping Fijian man opened the door and held out his hand to help her out. Feet firmly on the ground, she looked around and was greeted by two young girls.

'*Bula,*' they said in unison, before placing leis made of pink and yellow hibiscus flowers around her and Zac's necks.

'*Bula,*' she replied.

Zac took her hand. 'Welcome to paradise.'

The bure was gorgeous, made from dark wood and covered with thatch. Wide doors and large open windows let the sea breeze through. An overhead fan spun slowly. A perfect spot for a couple to enjoy themselves and each other. Even with the sex ban? A second shower stall, outside and without a roof, made her smile. 'All the better to stargaze.'

'Come here.' Zac still held her hand and now he tugged her over the lawn to stand on the beach twenty metres from what was to be their home for five nights.

'It's going to be dark shortly,' she sighed. The day had sped by getting here.

'Let's pop the cork on that bottle of champagne I saw in an ice bucket on the coffee table. We can sit out on our front porch and pretend we do this every night after a hard day at work.'

Olivia started walking backwards so she could watch Zac. 'You're as excited as a kid on his first holiday, aren't you?' His eyes shone, his mouth the most relaxed she could ever remember it.

'I reckon. This is like my first holiday, only way better.'

'We've barely started.' She stopped so that his next step brought him right up close. Close enough to lean in and kiss that happy mouth, which she did. But when his hands spanned her waist she reluctantly pulled back. 'Sorry, I shouldn't have done that.'

'Did the rule state no kissing?' He was shaking his head at her, his smile only increasing. Was nothing going to mar his enjoyment? 'I must've missed that.'

'Maybe you didn't put it in.' She hoped not. Kissing Zac was too much fun not to be able to do it whenever she wanted. But then there'd be consequences. Looking around for something else to talk about, she spied two hammocks slung between nearby trees. 'There's your bed. You even get a choice.'

'I am not spending my nights slapping at the mozzies, thank you very much.' Zac caught her hand, laced his fingers through hers, then swung their joined hands up to his lips and kissed her knuckles.

Careful. That might start a fire I can't put out. And we have rules. She slipped her hand out of Zac's. 'Where's that champagne?'

He tried not to look disappointed, but she saw it and felt a heel. He'd only been having fun, and she *had* instigated the kiss.

Inside, Zac picked up the card leaning against the bucket in which the ice was rapidly turning to liquid. 'Compliments of Andy and Kitty. They say thanks for the gala night and hope we have a wonderful time.'

'That's lovely. It's not as though they haven't got enough to think about at the moment.'

Minutes later they sat in front of their bure and watched the sun turning the sky red and yellow. 'That's an abrupt change from day to night,' Zac commented.

'Guess that's the tropics for you. Hard to believe we left winter behind.' The warm, heavy air made her clothes stick to her skin. She wouldn't be wearing much for the next few days.

'What's your favourite season?' Zac asked.

'Summer, followed by summer. I hate being cold.'

'Yet you bought an old villa that must be freezing in winter. Though, come to think of it, I didn't notice a chill when I was there.'

'First thing I did was improve the insulation in the roof and some of the walls. Then I had that firebox installed to replace the open fire. There's also a heat pump in the hall.'

Zac chuckled. 'I bought a very modern apartment and you went for the opposite.'

'I love old villas. There's something magical about them. Yes, they come with loads of problems, but get them sorted and there's an amazing home waiting to be loved.' She sipped her champagne. 'There's history in the boards. When I bought the place the vendors passed on to me a book written about the family who originally built it. The man had been an excise officer and his wife a nurse in the First World War.'

'So you're a history buff.'

'Only when it comes to my property, but it's neat knowing about the original owners.' She laughed softly. 'It was also a surprise finding I enjoy working on the redecorating. In spring I'm going to start putting in a garden to grow a few salad vegetables.'

'I saw your pot plants in your hallway. Just go to the markets. That way you won't starve.'

'Thanks, pal.' He was right. She always forgot to water the plants until they were drooping over the edges of their pots.

'You grew up in Auckland, right?'

She nodded. 'Remuera.' One of Auckland's most sought-after areas, where many of the city's wealthy lived. On a street where fences were metres high, hiding a multitude of sins. 'I went to a private school for girls, played the cello and joined the debating team.' That was after the in-crowd had worked their number on her because her mother had followed her around dressed in identical outfits to hers, trying to look way younger than she was.

'Was your childhood home another old house?'

She blinked, got back on track. Her mother wasn't welcome on this holiday. 'Yes. A massive, six-bedroom edifice with half an acre of gardens, a tennis court and a swimming pool.'

'You played tennis?' He didn't hide his astonishment.

'Me run around chasing a ball to bang it back over a net? Not likely.'

They were getting close to things she didn't want to talk about when she was sitting in paradise. 'I can't wait to go snorkelling amongst the fishes.'

Zac went with her change as easily as butter melted on warm toast. 'We should take a boat trip to Treasure Island and the marine reserve where the best array of fish is supposed to be.'

Zac had done some research before they'd left Auckland. She hadn't had the time. 'Five days might not be enough.'

How was he going to cope with not getting up close and naked? Zac grimaced. This magical setting was work-

ing mischief on his libido. What had he been thinking when he'd come up with that brainwave? Hadn't
been thinking, that was the trouble. Now his body was
screaming out for Olivia's, and he had no one to blame
but himself.

'Want a top-up?' was the only lame excuse he could
come up with in a hurry for getting out of the cane
chair and putting some air between them for a moment.

'Of course.' When she handed him her glass she
seemed to take desperate measures to prevent her fingers touching his.

Phew. Damn. Hell. He dragged his hand down over
his hair. Less than an hour and he was a cot case. Cer-
tifiable. Had he been so desperate to come here with
Olivia he'd have bargained with the devil if it had meant
she'd agree? Seems like it. Didn't make any sense,
though.

Back on the porch he passed over a full glass. 'Drink
up. That ice bucket is now a water receptacle and the
fridge is warmer than my toaster on full.'

'Do we get dinner brought over? I'm kind of relaxed
and comfortable now.'

*And I'm in need of space and people around to break
the grip you have on me. I am so not ready to spend
all evening alone with you when I can't touch you.* 'I'm
thinking dining on the restaurant deck with candles
under those palm trees would be special.'

'I guess you're right.' When Olivia yawned there was
nothing ladylike about her.

He grinned. 'That's it? No argument?' Then she must
be very tired.

'If I stay here I'll be asleep by seven, and probably awake again by midnight.' Her throat worked as
she swallowed.

'CC? You all right?'

Olivia stood up and took a step to the edge of the porch. 'Yeah,' she huffed out over the lawn. 'Good and dandy.' Her voice sounded anything but.

Moving quietly, Zac stepped up beside her, rubbed his shoulder lightly against hers. Gave her a moment to regroup her thoughts. But *his* brain wasn't quiet as it tossed up questions about this sudden mood swing. Was Olivia regretting the trip already? His stomach plummeted. Please, not that. No matter what happened after they left the island, he wanted this time with Olivia. Wanted them to have fun and be relaxed, to enjoy each other's company. He felt rather than heard her soft sigh. A gentle lifting of her shoulder against his.

'I'm afraid.'

Or that's what he thought she'd whispered. Olivia afraid? Of what? Him? The urge rose to rant at her, to tell her he'd never hurt her. But reason caught him in time. If she'd ever believed he'd hurt her she wouldn't have come near him, certainly wouldn't be on this island with him. 'Want to talk about it?'

'No.' She spoke to the dark space in front of them. Then after a minute, in a stronger tone, 'Let's go eat.' Back in control of her emotions.

Which bugged the hell out of Zac. How was he supposed to get behind the walls she put up when she kept doing this? He wanted to shake her, shake out her story, then begin to help her move past whatever locked her up so tight. But one look at that jutting chin said that now wasn't the moment. Though when would be the right time was a mystery to him. Olivia had made self-control an art form.

The only place he'd seen her enjoy herself completely, without thought for anything else, was in the sack. Light-bulb moment. Because when she'd finished she could, and did, put on her corporate-style clothes again and the control they represented.

For which he should be glad, but wasn't.

A vision of Olivia in track pants and a sweatshirt. That night she'd started making love to him and it had been as different from any other time as north was to south. Slow and tender, giving and sharing.

For him it had been a game changer. Waking up in her bed in the morning had been a first. Lying tucked up against her back, his arm over her waist, holding her close, had been another first, and absolutely wonderful, like nothing he'd experienced before. So wonderful he'd settle for cuddling Olivia all night to wake up like that again.

Okay, he'd try, but it wouldn't be easy. But he'd try really hard. *Hard is the wrong word, buddy.*

'You plan on daydreaming all night?' the woman causing these thoughts called from the door.

'Why is it called daydreaming when I'm doing it at night?'

As they strolled along the lantern-lit path Zac found himself wondering for the first time ever if he was wrong to stick to his guns and deliberately deny himself a future that involved a beautiful, loving woman and maybe equally beautiful and loving children.

No, he couldn't be wrong. How else did he justify keeping Olivia at arm's length?

Later, Olivia slid beneath the bedcovers and tucked the sheet under her neck like a prissy girl from the convent.

Zac laughed. Long and loud. His eyes twinkled and his gorgeous mouth looked good enough to devour.

'It's not that funny.' She tried not to laugh too, and only succeeded in making hysterical squawking noises instead.

'Yeah, it is, when you think what we've got up to in beds before.'

That dampened down her mirth. 'You want to change the rules.'

'Damn right I do. I'd be lying if I said otherwise.' He came and sat on the edge of the bed, on his side; no sign of laughter in his face now. 'But I'm enjoying our time together. It's like nothing we've ever done before and it's…' He waved his hand in the air between them. 'Does fun sound boring?'

'Fun is good.'

'I want to get to learn more about you, what makes you tick, the things that you'd choose to do first if time was running out. Hell, I want to know everything about you. Before the gala night I didn't know anything about you despite having spent many hours in your company.'

Wow. Really? Of course, he didn't know what he was asking for. 'We trained together. You can't do that without learning some things.' But she was ducking for cover, and that wasn't fair. 'Doctor things, I guess. Like how much you care about your patients, how intelligent you are, oh, and how pig-headed you can be.'

'Thanks a bunch.' Zac smiled. 'Okay, random question. Do you still play the cello?' He leaned back against the headboard and stretched his legs all the way down the bed.

She laughed. 'No way. I sold my cello to buy an amazing pair of leather boots that were the envy of every girl at school.' Which was why she'd wanted them. Now she bought the most amazing pairs of boots any time because she could, and loved them without needing any acknowledgement from others.

'I bet you were good at music.'

'Try very average on a good day. I think the music teacher only persisted with my lessons because he needed a cello in the school orchestra and no one else wanted to be hauling such a large instrument on and off the bus.'

'Why are you doing that?'

'What?'

'Putting yourself down again. You're a highly skilled surgeon, yet right now you're sounding like you don't believe in yourself.'

'I'm not perfect, can't excel at everything I do. For example, the pot plants in my house. But I am honest.' Most of the time.

Zac reached for her hand and held it between both of his. 'I know.'

Warm fuzzies uncurled inside her. It would be all too easy to lean her head against his chest and pretend they were a couple, a real couple with a history and a future that involved more than bedroom antics. The couple that woke up in the morning in each other's arms.

Pulling her hand free, she shuffled further down the bed. 'Time to get some sleep. Sunrise is early around these parts.' As if she'd fall asleep with Zac barely inches away from her. Those pillows she'd stuffed down the middle as a barrier were a joke, and would take two seconds to get shot of. She could only hope his mental barrier was stronger. Hers was weakening.

'Good night, Olivia.' Zac leaned over and dropped the softest, sweetest kiss of her life on her forehead. 'I'll sit out on the porch for a while.'

If he was cross at her abrupt withdrawal he wasn't

showing it. But, then, he was good at hiding his feelings behind a smile or laughter. This time the smile was stretched a little too tight, and his eyes held a tinge of sadness.

'Zac,' she called as he reached the door leading outside. 'Thanks.'

His eyebrow rose in query. 'For?'

'Being you, caring and understanding.'

Understanding? Zac growled under his breath. *Newsflash, CC, I don't understand a thing. Whatever's going on between us is a complete mystery. What I want is no longer clear. I feel like I'm walking in deep mud and every now and then stepping onto a dry patch. A brief moment of hope before sliding back into the mire.*

His right foot pushed against the ground to set the hammock swinging. Stretched full length, he linked his hands together behind his head. The dark sky twinkled with so many stars it was as though a kid had lit up a whole pack of sparklers. The hammock was unbelievably comfortable. So far the mosquitoes hadn't found him. Hopefully when they did, he'd put enough insect repellent on what little skin was exposed to deter them.

His heart was back in the bure, lying next to Olivia. His mind was seeing the despair and fear that sometimes altered her expression and briefly filled those eyes that usually reminded him of flowers. Whatever had caused her grief, she wasn't prepared to talk about it. Yet.

Come on. Why should she choose to bare her soul to him?

Because they were connected. They mightn't have known it before but the threads were becoming more obvious by the day. They both had issues holding them back from getting into a serious relationship. What Olivia's troubles were he had no idea, but they were there. He recognised his own stock standard coping mechanisms in her now that he'd started looking for them.

He wanted to hold her, protect her for ever.

Kind of strange for a guy who had no plans to commit to settling down. Yet all the reasons for why he shouldn't were slipping away, one by one dropping off the edge, leaving him exposed and cautious yet strangely ready to try for the rainbow.

Was Olivia the pot of gold at the end of his rainbow?

No. There wasn't any rainbow. The hardest lesson of his life had been that night of the accident when he'd learned his parents didn't love him unconditionally. Didn't love him enough to support and help him through the trauma of what he'd done. Sometimes he wondered if they'd loved him and Mark at all; as in deep, for ever, parent kind of love. Their careers had been their priority, taking all their time and concentration, with nothing left over for their sons. *Why did they have children?* They clearly hadn't wanted to be with their sons. Zac had asked his grandfather about it on numerous occasions but Grampy hadn't been able to come up with a satisfactory answer. Not one he was prepared to tell his grandson anyway.

Zac swallowed the usual bile that came from thinking about his parents. Coming from a dysfunctional family, the odds were he'd be bad at parenting too. Another reason not to settle down with a wonderful woman and contemplate the picket-fence scenario.

Zac's sigh was long and slow. Around him everything had gone quiet, and lights were being turned off. With nothing to do after dinner most people would be settled in their bures. He pushed with his foot again, swinging the hammock high, sighing as the movement slowed and the arc became less and less. Beyond the edge of the lawn the waves rolled up the sand, then pulled away, rolled in, pulled away.

'Zac, come inside.'

Someone was shaking his arm gently.

'Come on. Wake up. You're getting wet from the dew.'

Hauling his eyelids up, he saw her leaning over him, her long hair framing her face. 'Olivia.' His Olivia.

'The one and only.' She tugged at him. 'You can't spend the whole night out here.'

Swinging his legs over the side, he awkwardly pushed out of the hammock. 'What time is it?'

'One o'clock.' She took his hand and led him inside to that damned bed with its row of pillows down the middle.

Zac shucked out of his shirt and trousers, jerked the bedcover back and threw the pillows on the floor. Dropping into bed, he reached for Olivia where she now lay on her side, facing him. 'Roll over,' he whispered. 'I want to hold you all night.'

If only it were that easy.

CHAPTER TEN

AT THE END of the next day Zac stretched his legs out and laced his fingers behind his head. He would not think about night number two and lying beside Olivia again. Nope, he'd have a drink and watch the sunset. 'Come on, woman, bring me that beer you promised.'

'Sack the last slave, did you?'

'Hell, no. She's good for bed gymnastics.' So much for not thinking about bed.

'For that you're going to have to wait. Or, novel idea, get your own drink.' Olivia laughed. 'I'm changing out of my bikini.'

Phew. Those two narrow strips of red fabric had kept his head in a spin all day. Had had him swimming in the sea four times, and in the pool once. Then there'd been the cold shower half an hour ago. He'd even taken a kayak out to paddle around the island. Anything to keep busy and the need strumming through his veins under control. Huh. As if. One look at Olivia and his blood was boiling and his crotch tightening. This sex ban would be his undoing. Who knew what state he'd be in by the time he got back to Auckland? Ruined for ever, probably.

'Here.'

An icy bottle appeared before his eyes. 'Thank you,

and whoever's responsible for these things.' Then he made the mistake of looking at Olivia and pressed the bottom of the bottle over his manhood. The bikini would've been preferable.

'You're staring.' She sank onto the deckchair beside him. 'You don't like my dress?'

While the skimpy piece of floral material did cover more of that exquisite body than the bikini had, the way the fabric draped was plain punishing. Mouth-watering, muscle-tightening, hormone-fizzing, blood-heating cruel. 'You call that a dress?' he hissed over dry lips.

She laughed, low and sexy. 'Well, it's not a T-shirt.'

How in hell was he to sit here drinking beer and not choke? Then he had to take her to dinner where every male on the island was going to gag, and their women would beat them around the head. 'You're a danger to mankind.'

'I'll change before dinner. Put a T-shirt on.'

'Does that come with trousers?' The beer was cold in his over-hot mouth; cool as it slid past the lump in his throat. One bottle wasn't enough. Holding out his empty one, he growled in a mock bossy tone, 'Another one, as soon as possible.' His eyes were fixed on the horizon, glazed over for all he could see. His imagination was so busy dealing with pictures of Olivia's hot bod and that handkerchief that was apparently a dress, nothing else about him seemed to be in good working order. Except the one muscle he wasn't allowed to use.

'Here you go, sir.' A bottle held around the neck by slim fingers waved in front of his face.

He was going insane. Had to be. Grabbing the bottle, he raised it to his lips and gulped. *Do something. Talk about anything, just get your brain working.* Glancing around, he came up with, 'So you're not into spiders.'

Olivia shuddered. 'Not at all, but until today I thought one the size of my thumbnail was a problem. But those things hanging over the path in webs wider than our bed?' Another shudder. 'Ugh. You were my hero, clearing those monsters out of the way.'

Our bed? This wasn't helping. He tried again. 'The outlook from the top of the hill showed how small the island is.' Not exactly scintillating conversation. 'It's hard to imagine living on such a tiny spot in the ocean. I'd go stir-crazy if this was home for me.'

'I guess if you're born here it's what you're used to.'

'Have you ever thought how lucky we are just because of where we were born?' Deep, Zac, boy. And diverting. 'Imagine how different our lives would be if we'd been born in the Sahara, or on the Indian continent.'

'I'd have five kids and look ready to retire, except that wouldn't be an option.' Olivia grinned. 'You're right. It does come down to luck.'

'I'm going to give that fishing a crack tomorrow. Donny—he's the gardener—is lending me a hand line.'

The guy had strolled up to him as he'd watched the local men work the sudden rush of fish churning up the water at the shoreline and told him, 'Trevally chase the Pacific sardines into the beach in a feeding frenzy. It happens about twice a day at this time of year.'

'Do the men catch many?' Zac had asked.

'Good days and bad days. No one relies on trevallies as a regular supply of food for the family.'

'I've never seen anyone use a hand line and no rod. The skin on those men's hands must be tough.' Zac had introduced himself and before he'd known it he'd had a fishing date for tomorrow. 'I haven't fished since I was a kid and Grampy took me out.'

Olivia was chuckling. 'This I have to see. The immaculate surgeon getting his hands stinky from fish.'

'I'm taking that as a positive sign. You obviously think I'll catch one.'

'And if you do? What will you do with it?'

He hadn't thought that far ahead. 'Ask the chef to cook it for us? Other people must've caught fish and taken them to the kitchen.'

'Talking of kitchens, shall we stroll across to the outdoor lounge for a cocktail before dinner? I've never had one but this seems the place to give it a try.'

'Good idea.' Hopefully there'd be some diversions from that dress. 'You'll get one of those tacky little umbrellas to keep as a souvenir.' He grinned.

'Thought I'd start with a mimosa.' She returned his grin.

'Start? Are we in for a session?'

She shook her head, that shiny mane sliding over her shoulders. 'You want me off my face and losing my mind?'

If it meant forgetting their promise—then, yes. But if he was being a gentleman—then, no.

'I've caught one,' Zac shouted triumphantly early the next morning as he wound the hand line in as fast as possible.

'What? A sardine?' Olivia teased. She'd strolled down the beach to join him, after opting for a leisurely start to the day by reading in bed after Donny had knocked on the door to tell Zac the fish were running.

'A damned big trevally,' Zac scowled. 'This nylon's hard on the hands.'

'Toughen up. You don't see the locals complaining.' Looking along the beach, she could see two Fijian men also winding in taut lines. 'You've got to get in the water and use your foot to scoop the fish up onto the sand.'

'Glad I've got an expert telling me what to do.' He started walking backwards up the beach, hauling his catch out of the water. 'Look at that beauty.'

Trying not to laugh, she bent down to admire Zac's fish. 'Should keep a toddler from starving.'

'Any time you want to go read your book again feel free. This is man stuff. Where's Donny?'

'Donny,' Olivia called to the man standing further up the beach. 'Zac's caught something.'

As he wandered close Donny nodded. 'Not bad for a first time.'

'I guess that means I'm going to release it back into the water.' Zac sighed, and carefully removed the hook.

'Wait, photo opportunity.' Olivia snapped a quick shot as Zac ignored the camera.

'Wait till I get a proper fish.' He held the fish in the water until it swam away, then threw the line as far beyond the churning water as possible so he could draw the hook through the seething trevally.

Olivia sat down, her elbows on her knees, and watched him. Never had she seen him so relaxed. He was concentrating so much he didn't notice her snap a couple more photos. This holiday was showing her a different Zac. She particularly liked the one who'd tossed those pillows aside to hold her against him while they'd tried to go to sleep.

The climate had done a line on them, spoiling that hug, though probably saving her from having to haul the brakes on the raw need that had begun filling her. The humidity had made her skin slick and her body uncomfortably hot in a way that had had nothing to do with sex. They'd rolled apart after twenty minutes. Unbelievably, she'd fallen into a deep sleep not long after. Had to be because she'd felt so secure with this Zac who could take a night off the passion. She'd never spent a night just sleeping with a man. That spoke of intimacies too close for comfort, yet now she craved it with Zac more than anything.

A shudder ripped through her, disturbing in its intensity. Was she seriously in danger of falling for him? Unlikely. She only had to think of her parents' marriage to knock those ideas into place.

Zac tossed a fist in the air. 'Got another one.'

Olivia jumped up and went to stand beside him, eager to enjoy the moment and drop the past for a while. If only it was that easy to dump for ever.

Zac was focused intently on getting his catch on shore. 'Want fish for breakfast?'

'Breakfast of any kind would be good.'

Zac wound furiously. 'This one's definitely bigger than the last baby.'

'That's a good trevally,' Donny agreed minutes later.

'Will the chef cook it for me?' Zac asked.

'Yes, or my wife could use it to make you a traditional Fijian meal to have at our house tonight.'

'Really? Your family would join us?' When Donny nodded, he continued, 'That would be fantastic.'

Olivia asked, 'What do we bring?'

'Nothing. We eat at five thirty because our grandson goes to bed early.'

'You have a grandchild living with you? Bet you love that.'

'His mother's our daughter. She does the massages in the spa.'

Olivia smiled. 'Then I'll meet her this afternoon. I'm booked in for a full body massage at two o'clock.'

Zac laughed. 'Think she'll be better than me?'

She looked away to hide the sudden flush creeping up her cheeks. 'No comment.'

Donny and his wife, Lauan, greeted Olivia and Zac warmly, welcoming them into the small thatch bungalow crowded with relatives. It felt as if half the island's population was there. The fish hadn't been that big, Olivia thought as she sat down on the woven flax mat in front of a larger one with plates stacked at one end.

Zac was soon chatting with the men and Olivia tried to look around without appearing nosey. Apart from her, all the other females were seated behind the circle enclosing that mat. 'Lauan,' she said quietly. 'I can sit with you.'

Lauan shook her head. 'You're a visitor.'

Yes, but I'd love to be with the women. Unfortunately it would be rude to protest. 'I've been looking forward to coming here all day. How do you cook the fish?'

'I wrap it in banana leaves to steam over the open fire. There is coconut milk added, and potatoes. Thank your husband for the fish.'

Husband? To the locals they probably did appear to be a married couple. 'I will.'

Lauan squatted beside her. 'I've also made a chicken stew with carrots, potatoes, and broccoli.' She rolled her eyes softly. 'Too many people for one fish. But they all wanted to meet you.'

Thinking of the scrawny chickens she'd seen pecking around the base of the trees behind the resort, Olivia wondered if one chook would go any further than the fish. All part of the adventure. 'I'm happy to meet you all.' She nodded to the women.

Two of them disappeared into another room and

soon large plates of steaming food were being placed on the mat.

'That smells delicious,' Olivia said.

'Doesn't it,' Zac agreed. Leaning closer, he asked, 'You okay?'

'Absolutely. I'm glad you caught that sucker, or we might never have had this opportunity.' She took the plate of food handed to her and looked for cutlery, feeling silly when there wasn't any. When in Fiji do as the Fijians do. But as she placed a piece of fish in her mouth a fork appeared in front of her.

'For you.'

Zac got one too. 'Thanks, but I'll use my fingers.'

The food was simple and tasty, the vegetables so fresh they must've been picked only hours ago. 'Sometimes I think we forget the pleasure of plain food.' Olivia noticed a child peeking around at her from behind Donny.

'Hello. What's your name?'

The child ducked back.

Remembering Donny's earlier conversation on the beach, she asked Lauan, 'Your grandson?'

'Yes. Josaia. He's shy.'

'I hope he comes over to say hello while we're here.'

'After dinner.'

But it seemed Josaia couldn't wait to take another peek, and Olivia winked at him.

When he winked back she felt she'd won a prize. Her mouth widened into a smile and she was rewarded with one in return. When dinner was finished she did get to see the boy properly when he came close to pick up the empty plates at his grandmother's bidding. Olivia's heart rolled. One of his arms was stiff and awkward, and his left cheek marred by terrible scarring.

Josaia knew she'd seen and his smile vanished as he twisted his head away from her. When he reached out for her plate she picked it up and placed it in his hand. 'Thank you,' she said. 'Where do you go to school?'

Donny was watching her guardedly. 'The kids go to the mainland for school.'

That didn't answer her specific question but she knew when to mind her own business.

Josaia disappeared with his load of plates, and she suspected she wouldn't be seeing him again tonight.

Donny tugged his shoulders back. 'He doesn't go to school because other children tease him. I try to teach him, but he's missing out on so much.'

What had happened to cause that disfiguring scar? She felt sure he hadn't seen a plastic surgeon. That wound had been too crudely sutured. Maybe she could help in some way. But was it her place to ask? It might be better coming from Zac. Man-to-man stuff. Leaning sideways, she gave him a wee nudge and got the slightest of nods.

He asked, 'Did Josaia have an accident here on the island?'

The older man nodded, his eyes so sad Olivia felt her heart slow. *He's broken-hearted for his grandson.* 'Last year Josaia was swimming with a group of his mates when a tourist joined them, asking about the fish and where he should go to try out his spear gun.'

Zac asked softly, 'Josaia was shot with a spear gun?'

Olivia stifled a gasp. *Josaia is lucky to be alive.* She slipped her hand between Zac's arm and his side, wrapped her fingers around his elbow.

Zac continued in the same low, calm voice. 'Where was Josaia treated?'

'On the mainland. In the hospital. It's a good hospital, but no one knew what to do for my grandson. I begged the doctors send him to Australia or New Zealand. They said it wasn't possible, and Josaia would be all right once they stitched him up and set his broken bones.' Tears streamed down the proud man's face. 'I begged them to rethink. He's only seven.'

'There's nothing wrong with him.' Lauan's voice was sharp and angry. 'But you'd think he was a leper from the way boys who used to be his friends laugh at him now.'

'That's so hard for anyone, but especially a child.'

'He was always so popular until the accident.' Donny stared at a spot on the dining mat. 'His mother works hard to raise money to take him away for help. His father works in Australia to make money.'

'When was the last time Josaia saw his dad?' Olivia asked, her heart thudding.

'Christmas.'

Seven months ago. What sort of life was that for a young boy? Not to have his dad there had to be hard. Olivia knew about that. She wanted to slap the floor and say she'd see that Josaia got whatever he needed and as soon as possible, but despite the urgent need to help this boy she held her tongue. She'd talk this through with Zac first.

Zac knew Olivia was barely holding herself together for the remainder of their time with Donny's family. He could see the sadness in her face, feel the need for her to do something to rectify what had happened with Josaia. But most of all he understood how much she was struggling to hold it all in so that she didn't make rash promises she mightn't be able keep and thereby hurt the family further.

The meal was over early by their standards. As they walked away from their hosts Zac draped an arm over Olivia's shoulders. 'I'd like a drink.'

'I could go a cup of tea.'

'We can discuss what you're desperate to do for Josaia.'

'That poor kid. I bet the worst part of the whole deal is the way his old friends are now treating him. Children are cruel.' She shuddered.

'Insecurities, jealousy, wanting to be popular with the in-crowd. Anything and everything. Even plain old nastiness.' The sudden tension in her fingers suggested she'd had her share of being on the outside. But of course. She'd said she'd worked hard to be liked and be a part of the group at med school. 'This is why you want to help Josaia? Apart from the medical point of view?'

They'd reached the outdoor lounge at the main building by the time she answered. 'That boy is surrounded by people who love him, but they're all adults. There don't appear to be any children in his life. At first I thought that was because it was the end of the day and everyone would be at home, except when we walked to Donny's house there were kids playing behind the huts.'

'Then we saw his face and heard the despair in his grandparents' voices.'

'You're onto it.'

Zac pulled out a chair for Olivia at an outside table. 'What are you having?'

A wicked twinkle lit up her eyes, banishing that sadness for a boy she'd barely met. 'You know what? Forget tea. Make that a cocktail.' She looked around. 'Where's a menu?'

'What about PS I...' His voice trailed off at the realisation of what he'd been about to say. It was only the name of a drink, but the import of the words he hadn't finished were slowly sinking in, one by one, adding up to a frightening whole.

'Zac? What's up? Are you all right?'

The concern in her tone wound around him, added to his confusion. Had he really been going to say 'PS I love you'? Shaking his head, he sank onto a chair, putting a gap between them. But her eyes followed, as did that floral scent she wore. Or was that the smell of the frangipani growing a metre away?

'Zac.' Her eyes widened. 'You're worrying me.'

'I'm fine.' *Really? This palpitating heart thing is fine? The knot in your gut is A-okay? The sweat on your palms due to the humidity?* 'Sorry. There's a cocktail made with amaretto, Kahlúa, and Irish cream that's perfect for after dinner. Very creamy and sweet, like a dessert, which you've missed out on tonight.' *Blah, blah, blah.* Shoving up onto his feet, he asked, 'Will that do?' Ordering drinks would give him the space he needed right now.

'Sounds good.' Olivia nodded, looking perplexed. As well she should. Did she know she was with a lunatic?

Moving through the tables full of happy diners, Zac tried to ignore the questions battering his brain. He'd been enjoying getting to know Olivia better, happy being with her, wanted more time together. So why the hell hadn't he ever considered he might be falling for her?

Because love spelt commitment. *Commitment isn't the problem.* No. It wasn't. *It's the responsibility.* That went with any relationship, whether the other person was his best friend, his lover, or his brother. He loved Mark, had done from the day his tiny, wriggly body had been placed in his arms. Yet he'd still managed to screw up in a very big way, changing Mark's life for ever.

'Yes, sir. What would you like?'

Zac shook his head and stared across the bar at the woman waiting patiently for him to tell her what drinks he wanted. 'A whisky on the rocks. Make it a double. And do you know a cocktail called PS I Love You?'

She frowned. 'Not sure, but we've got a book describing most cocktails.'

When Zac told her the ingredients she smiled. 'We call it Love on the Wind. I'll bring the drinks across to you.'

He wasn't ready to return to Olivia. 'I'll have that whisky now.' And ordered a second to take with him.

Olivia watched him placing her glass on the table, returning to his seat. He waited for her to ask why he'd taken so long, and was grateful when she didn't.

'Where do we start with Josaia's case? Talk to his family, or go to the mainland to check out the hospital and see if I can do a surgery there?'

'Why not take him back to Auckland for the operation? If there's going to be one. You've only seen that horrendous scar from across the room in dim light. There might be nothing you can do.'

She sipped her Love on the Wind—he would not think of it as PS I Love You—and smiled. Her tongue did a lap of her lips. 'That's amazing.'

So was the way his heart squeezed and his insides softened. Of course his libido sat up to attention. That was a given around this woman. What was extraordinary was that she didn't know about this new effect she was having on him. He'd have sworn there were signs written all over his face. 'Glad you like it. About Josaia and what to do first.' He had to talk, about anything except them, and talk lots.

Olivia said, 'Operating back home might be preferable so we get the best people on side for Josaia. It's going to involve huge expense for the family, though. Hospital costs, accommodation, flights, and other incidentals I can't think of right now.'

'I doubt there's a lot of spare money in that household.' He locked his eyes on hers. 'You're going to throw in your time for free.'

'Of course.'

'I want to look at that shoulder. There might be something I can do there.' See, he could move on from those other thoughts that had swamped his brain. 'First we'll talk to Donny. If he's willing to take this further, we'll decide how to go about it.'

Olivia's hand covered his, and her fingers curled around his. 'We have a plan.'

'You like plans, don't you?'

'They keep me centred.'

So what was her plan for the rest of the night? It wouldn't be what he hoped for. She'd be keeping to the other plan. Zac drained his glass, trying not to bemoan the fact he'd set the rule in the first place.

CHAPTER ELEVEN

THE ARRAY OF fish in every colour imaginable stole Olivia's breath away when she sank beneath the sea's surface off Treasure Island. She automatically reached out for Zac's hand and tugged him down beside her. 'Unbelievable,' she spluttered in her mouthpiece, even though he couldn't hear her.

When Zac looked her way she saw the same amazement in his face. When he started stroking through the water, heading further out from the shore, she followed. She'd never seen anything like this. When Zac paused she swam up beside him to lean in against his body. Skin to skin underwater. Delicious and exciting. And then there were the fish. One big, fat, enjoyable picture.

Olivia kicked her flippers slowly so as not to disturb the dainty creatures too much and followed a group of yellow and blue fish. Then a larger orange one swam through the middle, scattering the others. Yellow and blue fish. Orange fish. She grinned. Very technicolour. Down here it was like a moving painting: sharp colours, delicate manoeuvres, majestic shapes—and innocence. As though these creatures had no enemies. Which was probably far from the truth, though at least they were safe from mankind. This was a sanctuary, and the results were stunning. The numbers and varieties of fish were unbelievable.

'That's magic down there.' Zac echoed her thoughts when they finally crawled out of the water and flopped onto the sand.

'I've been missing out on so much by not travelling.' She lay on her back, arms and legs spread in the sun. 'It's one of those things on my to-do-one-day list. Think it's time to make that a do-it-now list.'

'Shame your mother hated flying.'

'Didn't matter.' Olivia sat up and started brushing off the sand, which was scratchy on her skin. 'Dad left when I was twelve.'

'That's tough.'

She swallowed hard. 'Mum was—is—an alcoholic.' Swallow. She couldn't look at Zac. 'As in often totally crazy, uncontrollable, off-the-rails alcoholic. Dad ran out of patience.'

'How the hell did you cope?' Zac's hand covered hers.

'Not sure I did, really.' Spill the rest. 'I tried becoming a part of the school in-crowd so that I could forget what went on at home. Failed big-time because of Mum. Everyone knew what she was.'

'Where did the cello fit in?' Zac was giving her breathing space.

'When I didn't make it as an in-person I went for the nerd brigade.' She huffed out a tight laugh. 'That probably saved me, considering where some of the girls I'd desperately wanted to befriend ended up while I was at med school.'

'Why medicine?'

She shrugged. 'No idea. It was just something I

wanted to do. As a little girl my dolls were always covered in plasters and bandages.'

'At least you'd have been sure of your choice, then.'

'You weren't?'

Zac grimaced. 'I started university intending to become an engineer.'

'What changed your mind?'

'Seeing my brother going through rehab and getting no end of help from doctors along the way made me think I'd be happier doing medicine.'

'Your parents didn't sway you?'

'Put it this way, Dad's an engineer at the top of his game, being the CEO for one of the country's largest steelworks.'

'You wanted to follow him into the business?'

'No, I wanted to gain acknowledgement that I was his son.'

Reaching for his hand, Olivia said, 'That's the wrong reason to choose a career.'

'I was desperate.'

She shuddered. 'I understand.' Seemed she wasn't the only one with difficult parents. 'Being an only child, I was never really treated as a kid even before Dad left.' Not wanting to spoil a wonderful day with talk of her childhood, she said, 'Let's go eat lunch by the pool. All that fish-gazing has made me hungry.'

Zac scrambled to his feet and held out his hand, hauling her upright with one easy, fluid movement. 'I could murder a beer. Think I've swallowed a litre of salt water.'

'Yuk.' Around at the front of the resort Olivia dived into the pool, eager to get rid of the salt and sand on her skin. When she hauled herself up over the side Zac was sitting at a nearby table, beer in hand, and his gaze fixed on her. Suddenly her bikini felt non-existent. A pool attendant handed her a towel and she quickly dried off before pulling on a sleeveless shirt and shorts and joining Zac under the coconut palms. 'Food and water, I think.'

Zac pushed a bottle and glass towards her. 'Sparkling water, as requested.'

Turning her hand over, she slipped her fingers between his and enjoyed the moment. This was something she hadn't known before. She had never spent time just holding a man's hand without sex being the ultimate goal. Unbelievable how wonderful it felt. Full of promise without any expectations.

A group of children was leaping into the deep end of the pool, splashing half the contents over the side while shrieking their heads off.

'They're fun but I'm glad glad we're not staying here on Treasure Island when Tokoriki is a no-go zone for kids,' Zac commented. 'I don't mean anything nasty by that, but as a childless adult I don't really want to share my rare break with other people's offspring.'

'I get it.' She took a risk. 'You think you'll ever have children? Once you find a life partner, I mean.'

Zac's eyes widened, and his mouth alternated between a smile and a grimace. 'Now, there's a loaded question. Or two.'

'It wasn't meant as such.' *Wasn't it?* 'Just wondering if you were planning on having a family and a house in the burbs.' Geez, what would she answer if he turned the question back at her?

The level in his beer glass dropped as he drank and stared at the kids in the pool. 'You know what? I'd love to have children of my own.' The surprise in his voice told her plenty.

'Isn't that a natural thing for most people to want?'

'Yeah, but after Mark's accident I decided I wasn't having a family. Too easy to hurt them.' Again he raised his glass to his lips and sipped the beer thoughtfully. 'I think I've been wrong. I do want children.' His head jerked backwards as though he couldn't quite get his mind around this revelation.

Little Zacs. Olivia let the breath that had stalled in her lungs dribble over her lips, and tried to ignore the band of longing winding around her heart. *Pick me for their mother.* She spluttered and almost spat water down her shirt. Where had that little gem come from? Having children meant getting married and *that* would never happen. 'Where's that waitress? I want to order lunch.'

Zac shook his head and looked around. He must've spotted someone who could help because he raised a hand and waved, before doing what she'd hoped he wouldn't. 'What about you? Obviously you'd want more than one child if you felt you'd missed out not having a sibling.'

She went for her standard reply, not prepared to reveal her deep but well-hidden longing that she barely acknowledged to herself. 'I've worked too hard to get where I am with my career to be taking time out for babies. Women I've talked to say that has set them back on the career pathway, and I'm not prepared to do that.'

Zac watched her, while behind those eyes she knew his brain would be working overtime. 'I don't buy it. That's the press-release version. What's the real story behind answering the same question you threw at me?'

He had a valid point. She hadn't minded asking him where he was headed on the subject of family, so she should be able to take it in return. Except she couldn't. They'd moved beyond the couple that used to have crazy sex all the time with no stopping for conversations. Now there was more between them they were learning about each other and she definitely liked the man she was getting to know. More than liked. But to reveal everything about her sorry upbringing was going too far. From years of learning to shut up those memories, they were now firmly locked away and she doubted the words were there. 'I—'

'Excuse me.' The waitress chose to arrive right then.

Phew. Not a reprieve but a few minutes to consider how to get around this without upsetting Zac and the easy way that had grown between them. Because *that* was important. She did not want to lose any ground they'd gained.

'Another water?' Zac asked.

'Yes, and I'll have the red snapper with salad.'

The waitress hadn't even turned away before Zac was saying, 'There's a question on the table, CC.'

Might as well get this over. 'I got Mum's undivided attention. She put all her love onto me. Except it was conditional and ugly.' Her sigh was bitter and very out of place in such a wonderful setting. 'Parenting takes special people and I'm not one of them.'

'Am I allowed to argue that point with you?' His voice was soft, gentle, almost a caress that said, *I'm here for you.*

'Afraid not. It's pointless.'

His mouth tightened. She'd hurt him.

Reaching for his hand, she said, 'I need to drop this, Zac. Seriously. I'm sorry if you think I don't trust you enough to talk about it. It's me I don't trust. My judgement about everything that happened in my family is warped and I'm just not ready to dissect it. I probably never will be, okay?'

His chin dipped in acknowledgement, though his eyes said he was still there for her if she changed her mind.

Squeezing those strong fingers that were curled around her hand, Olivia asked, 'Can we relax and make the most of sitting next to a sparkling pool on a tropical island? Leave the other stuff out of the picture?' She'd get down on her knees if that would help.

Zac leaned forward and placed his lips on her mouth. 'Yes,' he breathed as he kissed her.

As far as kisses went this one was tame, but it wound through her like a silky ribbon, touching, comforting, telling her that she wasn't alone with those deep fears any more. Had this Zac always been there? Should she have scratched the surface of him right back at the beginning, on that very first night they'd fallen into his bed, exhausted after making out in his lounge and still eager for more? No, she didn't think so. They would never have revealed anything about themselves back then. Talking hadn't fit the mix of what had made their affair so exciting. 'Thank you,' she murmured into his kiss.

They were interrupted with cutlery being placed on the table and the waitress asking if she could get them anything else while they waited for their meals.

'No, thanks.' Zac sat back, a smile tipping that gorgeous mouth upwards. His eyes locked on Olivia's. 'We've got everything we need.'

'The trevally are here,' Olivia called from the edge of the lawn in front of their bure an hour after they returned to Tokoriki.

Zac grabbed the fishing line and raced down to the

beach, calling at Olivia as he passed her, 'Watch this. I'm going to catch dinner.'

'You sure you weren't a caveman in a previous life?' She laughed.

'Weren't we all?' He unravelled the line and threw it as far as possible.

'I don't know. This whole "me man, me like hunting-gathering thing"—it's like men are born that way. I prefer going to a supermarket.'

Winding the line in as Donny had taught him, he grinned. 'The urge lurks below the skin, waiting for opportunities to show our women what wonderful providers and protectors we are.'

'So when women fish or hunt, what are they proving?'

'You've just flipped the argument. If I said that women are trying to prove they're as good as us I'd get my head knocked off, right?'

'I'll go and get my club.'

'Before you do, I admit that there are females who love all that outdoor activity as much as their menfolk, and some of them are very good at shooting deer or pig and catching a fish.'

A soft punch was delivered to his bicep. Olivia nodded along the beach. 'The score so far is locals three, visitor none.'

Zac tapped his chest with his fist. 'She wounds so easily.' He loved it when she was being cheeky and not considering every word before uttering it.

'If you can feel anything on the end of your line it's probably a pebble. There's your hook.' She peered at the water's edge, her grin wicked, making his toes curl with longing.

'This time.' He hurled the line out once more and began winding it back in.

'I don't think so,' Olivia said beside him.

'How do you know?'

Throw it out, bring it in. There was a timeless rhythm to this and, yes, he was enjoying fishing with the men.

'You've got another pebble.'

It took a second but he finally remembered where he was and what he was doing. 'This time,' he assured the disbelieving woman.

'Hey, Donny,' Olivia called. 'Zac's last fish must've been beginner's luck.'

Glancing over his shoulder, Zac nodded to the Fijian. 'Donny, don't listen to a word she says. I've got this.'

He was relieved the man had shown up. He and Olivia had agreed this might be the best place to talk to Donny about Josaia. Olivia had also suggested that he do the talking at first, man to man, so to speak.

Zac heard Olivia say, 'Hello, Josaia,' and his disappointment rose. They could not talk about surgery in front of the boy. Damn.

But Olivia had her ways. 'Josaia, can you help me find a shell to take home? One of those small conches would be good.' She waited for Josaia's reply, looking at him as she would any other child.

'I know where the best shells are.' He spoke hesitantly, as though expecting Olivia to withdraw from him any second.

'Cool. Let's go. Hopefully, by the time we get back Zac will have finally caught a fish.'

'Granddad catches them all the time.' Josaia bounced along beside Olivia, looking up at her so often he tripped over his own feet.

Donny watched them walk away. 'She's kind.'

'She is. She's also genuine.'

'I can see that. So can Josaia. He wouldn't have gone with her otherwise. He's learned to be wary of people's empty gestures.' Sadness lined Donny's statement.

Flicking the line out again, Zac said without preamble, 'You know we're doctors?'

'I wondered. Neither of you flinched when you saw Josaia, like you're used to seeing disfiguring scars.'

Zac was relieved. He'd thought he might've shown his feelings for the kid's predicament far too much. 'Olivia's a plastic surgeon.'

Donny turned to stare after his grandson again. 'What about you? Do you work in the same field?'

'I'm an orthopaedic surgeon.'

The man spun around to stare at him. 'Are you pulling my leg? Because if you are and my grandson learns…' He spluttered to a stop, unable to voice his anger.

Placing a hand on Donny's arm, Zac said, 'I am speaking the truth. We want to help Josaia.'

Donny gasped a few deep breaths, rubbed his forearm across his face. 'We don't have enough money. That's why our son-in-law works in Australia. He's trying to save for an operation for Josaia but…' Donny shook his head.

The line was getting into a tangle since Zac had stopped winding. Concentrating on sorting it out, he told the proud man, 'Let's start at the beginning and work from there. If it's okay with you, we'd like to look at Josaia's injuries and request copies of his medical records.'

His statement was met with silence. Could he have approached Donny differently? Might as well lay it all out. If he'd got it wrong then he had nothing to lose. 'We think it's probably best if Josaia has surgery in Auckland, where both of us practise.'

'You make it sound so easy.'

'I do know a thing or two about the New Zealand health system.'

Donny gripped Zac's hand. 'Thank you. I am glad you caught that trevally. It has brought my family much good luck.'

Zac grinned. 'Maybe that's why I haven't caught one today. There's only so much luck out there and we've used up our share for a while.'

Once Donny had talked with his wife and daughter, and explained everything to Josaia, he brought the lad to the bure.

'At the time of the accident we were told by a visiting doctor that plastic surgery would make the scar less visible and the lumps could be removed.'

'Has Josaia seen anyone else about this?'

'There aren't any plastic surgeons in Fiji. But, please, you can look today. Josaia likes you, he won't be a problem.'

'He found me a shell to take home.' She'd treasure it, as long as she could take it through quarantine at Auckland Airport. 'Hey, Josaia, can I touch your cheek?'

The boy nodded solemnly.

The muscle was tight and knobbly under her fingers. 'Open your mouth wide,' she instructed Josaia. Inside there was further scarring. 'I can do something to improve this.' She stepped back to allow Zac space.

'Josaia, show me how far you can move your arm,' Zac instructed.

Donny talked as his grandson moved his arm back and forth. 'It's tight. He can't move it far. Tendons were severed by the arrow of the gun and sewn back together shorter than before.'

'Will you make me better?' Josaia asked them, his eyes wide with hope.

Olivia answered, 'Would you like us to try?'

He nodded. 'Yes, please.'

'You would have to go to hospital again.'

'Will it hurt?'

Zac nodded. 'Yes, I'm sorry, but we'll give you something to stop most of the pain.'

Donny spoke quietly. 'I would like to accept your help, but how do we pay for this?'

Olivia wanted to wrap him in her arms and say *Don't worry, everything will be all right*, except she didn't want to trample on this family's pride. So she dodged some of the question. 'If we go ahead, would it be all right with you if we did the operations as a gift to Josaia?'

Donny blinked, ran a hand over his face. 'Why would you do that?'

'Part of what I like about being a doctor is helping people, giving them second chances, and Josaia deserves one.' Goodness, she'd be crying next.

Zac must've sensed her problem because he leaned closer so that his arm touched hers, and told Donny, 'Children shouldn't be disadvantaged because of someone else's mistake.'

'What can I say?' Donny asked in such a strangled voice Olivia smiled.

'You gave us a beautiful meal in your home. You might think there's no comparison but being welcomed into your house, meeting all your family, sharing that dinner with you was an experience we'll both remember for ever.' Now a tear did leak from the corner of Olivia's eye and trek down her face.

Donny reached for her hands, gripped them tight. 'Thank you so much. It's been hard, you know, watching my Josaia turn into a quiet, withdrawn version of himself. I will ring his father and tell him the good news. He'll be so happy.'

No pressure.

CHAPTER TWELVE

'THERE'S A BAND playing tonight,' Zac called from the outdoor shower box, where he was towelling himself dry.

'What sort of band?' Olivia asked from the bathroom, where she was apparently putting on her face.

Why she did that when her skin was clear and her face naturally beautiful he did not understand. But he knew not to say a word. 'It's a surprise.'

'Which means you have no idea.' She chuckled.

That sound, relaxed and happy, did things to him. Made him wish for more with Olivia: for a future, to be able to wake up every morning with her lying beside him, if not tangled around him. To know she'd be there for him, day in day out, and that he'd have her back all the time would be amazing. Right. Not that he didn't have her back already, but sometimes he didn't know what he was protecting her from.

'Something like that,' he agreed, as he wrapped the towel around his waist and headed into the main room. 'Anything from locals to visiting rock stars. I heard a whisper about two guys and their guitars.'

Olivia leaned around the corner, her hair swinging over her arm, her face lit up with a big smile. 'That narrows the options.'

'Better than bongo drums at any rate.'

She just laughed and disappeared back into the bathroom.

If only they weren't going to dinner but staying here, checking out that enormous bed for what it was intended. He was done playing Mr Nice Guy on the far side. While wonderful, the spooning hadn't been enough, more a teaser of what could have been. Pulling on a shirt, he sighed. One more night. Tomorrow they would fly out of here in a float plane, headed for the airport. This had been a fabulous few days. Continuing to get to know each other seemed the way forward.

'I heard that there's going to be lobster on the menu tonight.' Olivia bounced into the room, her hands busy slipping earrings into her lobes.

His hands faltered, stopped, buttons ignored. 'You look stunning.'

The red dress she'd somehow squeezed into accentuated all those lovely curves to perfection.

'You think?' She spun around on her tiptoes. 'Not my usual style.'

Her cleavage had never been so—so... His mouth dried. The back of the dress—there wasn't any. Nothing worth mentioning anyway. Was it really a dress when there was hardly any more fabric than in the blue and lime-green bikini she'd lounged around in all day? The hemline barely made it onto her thighs. 'So not you.'

Her smile dipped. 'Should I change?'

Zac's heart stopped. He stepped across the gap between them, caught her hands in his, and tugged her close. Not so close that they were touching. Then they'd never go to dinner. But close enough that he could breathe in her scent. 'I have never seen you look so, so beautiful. Ravishing. And before you go thinking you're not beautiful all the time, you absolutely are. I'm going to order you more dresses like that.'

'You say the nicest things.' Her smile was back. 'I've always wanted to go all out and wear something like this but don't often have the courage. That creation I wore on the night of the gala was the first in a long time. You make me feel it's okay, so for a moment there I got a bit worried.'

'I'm a bloke. Clear and concise speech isn't one of my strong points.' He dropped her hands. He needed to finish dressing if they were ever going to head to the restaurant.

But one button done up and Olivia was laughing at him. 'Let me.' She undid the button, realigned his shirt front and started over. Her fingers were light as they worked down his shirt. Over his chest. Down to his abs—which were sucking in on themselves and just about touching his spine.

Zac gritted his teeth, and his hands clenched at his sides. She was killing him. Cell by damned cell.

'Relax,' she said in a low, throaty growl.

Oh, right. Sure. Easy as. He took an unsteady step back and snatched up his trousers from the bed, and muttered, 'Relax, she says.'

Olivia did wicked without even trying. Her mouth curved into a sumptuous smile, her eyes widened with promise as she slapped her hands on those slim hips. 'How soon can you get me those new dresses? I never knew wearing something so simple could have this effect on a man.' Her eyes widened even further, her smile grew bigger. 'Not just any man either.'

'There is nothing simple about you or your damned dress.'

'Damned dress, huh?' Her gaze cruised down his

body, pausing at his obvious reaction to that piece of fabric that was in danger of being torn off her. 'This is our last night.'

Squeezing his eyes shut, he counted to ten, slowly. Nothing changed. He continued to twenty. His blood still pulsed throughout his body, heating every cell it touched. Finally he drew a shaky breath and locked eyes with her before growling, 'Last night, last cocktail and final dinner under the palms, last of everything to do with our holiday.'

Last of that stupid ban on sex. Whoa, did that mean they could get up close and personal tomorrow? As soon as they landed back in Auckland could they go straight to his apartment? Or her house? He didn't care which as long as he could scratch this itch.

Olivia just laughed and picked up a pair of red shoes with heels that would be lethal if flung at a guy. 'Let's go enjoy ourselves.'

At least she had the sense not to hold his hand or slip her arm through his as they walked along the path to the restaurant. If she had Zac doubted his ability not to swing her up into his arms and run back to their bure. Last evening or not.

'We've been given the best table.' Olivia glanced around the outdoor dining area as she sank onto the chair being held out for her by their waiter. The table was set well back from everyone else with hibiscus growing on three sides, soft light from lanterns making it feel as though they were in a bubble. A very cosy bubble.

Zac blinked. Was he still trying to get his libido under control? 'Maybe it's our turn.'

Every other night honeymooners had sat here. She and Zac didn't have that qualification. 'I feel special.'

'What can I get you to drink?' the waiter asked.

Zac didn't ask her what she preferred, instead rattled off the name of the best champagne on the wine list. 'We're celebrating,' he told her when the young man had gone.

'Celebrating?'

'Anything and everything.' He leaned forward, those dark eyes suddenly serious. 'I haven't had such a wonderful holiday, ever. Thank you.'

Her eyes filled with unexpected tears. 'I didn't do anything.' *Except tease the hell out of you back in the bure.*

'Exactly. You were just you, and I'd never met that you before.'

A tear escaped. Then another. She quickly lifted her glass of water to her lips. What was with this crying stuff? She was usually stronger than that.

'You're supposed to reciprocate, tell me how you've discovered a superman.'

Then the champagne arrived. 'Compliments of management,' the waitress told them.

'This isn't anything to do with Josaia?' Zac asked.

A huge smile split the woman's face. 'Enjoy your evening.'

When Olivia had a glass in her hand she raised it to Zac. 'To us and our fabulous holiday.' This experience had loosened a lot of permanent knots inside her. She and Zac had gelled so well she was even wondering if it might be possible to have a life together in some way. She wanted to ask if they might continue seeing each other back in Auckland, but the old warning bells rattled in her skull, putting a dampener on that. *Just enjoy tonight and wait for tomorrow to unfold.* But she didn't do waiting to see what happened. That meant no control.

Zac tapped his glass on hers. 'We haven't finished yet. Our plane doesn't leave until ten in the morning.'

'Okay, to the rest of our stay in paradise.' Excitement shimmied down her spine. One more night. Dinner under the stars, maybe some dancing if the band of two turned out to be halfway decent, a stroll on the beach after ditching her heels, and then... Then she planned on seducing Zac into using that enormous bed for something other than spooning.

Those picks Olivia called shoes swung from one of her hands while she held onto him firmly with the other. 'There's something about walking on sand at night.' Her voice was a murmur, drifting on the warm, still air, encasing Zac in tenderness.

The need he'd barely been holding onto spilled through him, hissed out between them. It would not be contained any more. After days of bikinis and figure-hugging dresses, laughter and fun, he had to have Olivia—in his arms, under his body. He ached to fill her, to kiss her senseless. But there was that damned rule. He would not be the one to break it. He'd given his word. Never again was he going to make a promise. About anything. Tugging his hand free, Zac went for flippant. Only way to go. 'Who wouldn't love damp sand between their toes, scratchy and irritating? Wonderful stuff.'

Olivia's laughter was so carefree it tugged at his heart. She glanced down at their bare feet and dropped her shoes. 'Come on, then. Let's wash the sand off.' And in a flash her dress was being flung onto the sand beside those red picks. 'Coming?'

'You're such a tease, Olivia Coates-Clark,' Zac growled, even as he tore his shirt over his head. Talk about upping the ante. His failing self-control would never cope, and yet he followed her towards the sea, nearly falling flat on his face as he ran down the beach while trying to step out of his trousers at the same time.

Plunging into the warm water, he swam towards Olivia, who seemed to be treading water too far out. 'Hey,' he growled. 'Stop right there.'

'Or what?' She laughed and began swimming away.

Zac poured on the speed and quickly caught her, catching her around the waist and pulling her to him. 'Or I'll have to kiss you senseless.' She felt good. That compact, smooth body slip-sliding against his. Cranking up his lust. As if that was hard to do.

Salty lips covered his, and her tongue exploded into his mouth. Her hands gripped his head, holding him to her. This was no soft, sweet kiss. This was CC giving her all. This was what he needed. His hands were on her butt, lifting her higher up his body, across his reaction to her. Without breaking the kiss, she wound her legs around his waist and hovered over his throbbing need.

Twisting his mouth away from those lips, he croaked, 'No sex, babe.'

'Stupid rule. I'm breaking it.' Low and sexy laughter highlighted her intent.

Relief nearly dumped him underwater. Words dried in his mouth. So he went back to kissing while trying to hold Olivia and shove his boxers down his thighs all at once.

Suddenly a small hand pressed between them, her fingers splayed on his chest. 'Wait.'

'Wait?' His voice was hoarse with longing. If she'd changed her mind he'd lose his permanently.

'That massive bed. The bure. The Fijian experience. I want that.'

This time relief had Zac sinking into the water, taking Olivia with him, so that she sat over his point of desire. 'Since when have we been one-act-per-night types?'

Her answer was to slide over him, taking him deep within her, her head tipped back, her body quivering as she came fast. Four nights of restraining himself exploded in one deep thrust into her heat.

Dragging themselves up the beach, they scooped up their clothes and, holding hands, raced to the bure. *Except I'm not running.* Olivia grinned. *I'm skipping. I am over the moon with happiness.* 'What a goddamned waste. Four nights and we didn't do it. Are we idiots or what?'

Zac swung their hands high. 'There are plenty of words out there we could use, but I'd rather concentrate on getting you to beg me to make love to you in that bed we've been pretending we haven't shared.'

'Good answer.' Her shoes and dress slipped out of her hand at the doors leading inside. 'Let's hit the shower first. I don't usually season my sex with salt.'

'The outside shower.'

'Is there any other?' A quick sluice off and she dried Zac as he fumbled with a towel to do the same with her. Impatient, she tossed the towels aside and grabbed his hand, pulled him into the main room and leapt into the bed, taking him with her so that they tumbled into a heap of arms and legs. Not that Zac had needed any persuasion. He was already showing interest in her, in the way only men could.

Goddamn. She grinned and shook herself. This had to be the most wonderful, magical, fabulous way to end their stay on the island. Maybe waiting those long, tension-filled nights had been the way to go, had added to the tension and wound up the orgasmic relief. 'Zac,' she whispered. 'Long and slow.' As she trailed kisses over his chest she continued, 'We've got all night.'

'Yeah, babe, not leaving until ten tomorrow.'

Some time after four in the morning, as the sun began to lighten the bure around the edges, Olivia snuggled her exhausted body against Zac's and traced a line across his chest with a fingertip.

'This is unlike other times for us.'

'Yeah, you're talking too much, for one thing.'

'I feel different. I guess lying in bed together afterwards has something to do with that.' In fact, she was shocked at how much she was enjoying lying here with Zac, knowing neither of them would shortly leap out of bed and head home, or to work, or anywhere. 'This is taking it to a whole new level.' As if there was a depth to making out with Zac she'd never known before. She should be scared. She wasn't. Not right this moment, with Zac's body wrapped around hers and her muscles feeling deliciously sated.

The hands that had been working their magic on her back stopped moving. 'Regret not zapping that rule earlier?'

Locking gazes with him, her heart pounded at a ridiculous rate. He didn't look unhappy about what she'd said, more cautious. 'Not at all.' Having fun doing other things together had added more to their relationship. 'I have had the most amazing holiday with you.' *I want to have more of them.*

'Aw, shucks.' He pulled the sheet up to their necks. 'You say the nicest things. In case you're wondering, I've had a wonderful time doing some great things with you too. Now let's fall asleep in each other's arms for the last few hours of our holiday.'

Yep, soon reality would return in the form of Auckland, work and her mother. And in thinking where to go with this new relationship with Zac. Her eyelids drooped shut. She would not think about that now. Not when his strong arms held her as though she was delicate. Not when she could breathe in the scent of their lovemaking and Zac's aftershave. Not when… She drifted into a dream-laden sleep filled with images of the man sharing the bed.

Josaia and all his family were standing on the beach when Zac and Olivia turned up to board their float plane.

Olivia hugged Lauan. 'I'm so glad we met you and your family.'

Lauan was crying openly and shaking her head. 'No, it is us who are glad.'

'We'll be in touch very soon, I promise.' Leaving these wonderful people wasn't as easy as she'd expected. Zac nudged her out of the way to have his turn hugging Lauan. 'We'll schedule Josaia's surgeries as soon as possible.' He was repeating what they'd all discussed yesterday afternoon.

Donny stepped up and said, 'Josaia has something for you both.'

'Dr Zac, this is for you.' The boy handed over a bright blue *sulu* with all the gravity of a ceremony for royalty.

Zac took the carefully folded cotton cloth that Fijian men traditionally wore tied around their waists at special times.

Josaia stepped in front of Olivia. 'This is yours.'

She dropped to her knees and wrapped her arms around Josaia, a yellow *sulu* that could be wrapped around her body like a strapless dress in her hand. 'Thank you so much. I'll look after it, I promise.'

Once inside the plane Olivia leaned forward to wave goodbye. Suddenly the plane was racing and bumping across the sea and finally lifting into the sky.

She'd had the most amazing five days, and now she didn't know what was ahead. Hope rose, hope for a future they could share. The hope backed off. She couldn't make a full commitment to Zac. Her mother made sure of that. There just wasn't enough of herself to go round. She wasn't going to try to spread herself too thin. That's how people got hurt.

Zac lifted her hand and kissed her knuckles. 'Stop overthinking things.'

Did he know what was going on in her mind? Of course not. He didn't know the half of what went on in her life.

She gripped his hand and turned to stare outside, absorbing every last moment of Fiji.

Olivia shivered as she clambered out of the taxi outside her house. 'Why does the weather have to be wet and cold tonight of all nights?' she grumbled.

Zac only laughed. 'Bringing us back to earth with a thump, isn't it?'

Grabbing her case, she ran for the shelter of her covered veranda. That's when she noticed lights on inside. Then the steady beat of music reached her. And her stomach dived. *No. Not tonight. Not when I'm so happy.*

'You going to open that door?' Zac asked.

Not while you're here. She waved frantically at the taxi driver. He had to take Zac away. Now. Not after that coffee she'd suggested when they'd turned into her street. 'Wait,' she yelled.

'Too late,' Zac muttered. 'You don't want me coming in after all?'

'I've got a headache.'

Zac dropped his case and reached for her. 'That sudden? I'm picking it's because there's someone inside you don't want me to meet.' His hands were gentle on her upper arms, his thumbs rubbing back and forth in a coaxing manner. 'I thought we were better than that, had moved on from the quick visits to something more real.'

So did I, until reality slapped me around the ears. She'd been an idiot to think there was a way around the problem on the other side of her front door. 'I'm sorry.' She didn't want his sympathy—or worse, was afraid of seeing a look of horror in his eyes when he saw how far gone her mother would be.

The sound of her front door being unlocked sent a wave of panic through her. 'You have to go. Now.'

'Olivia, darling, there you are. I've been wondering where you'd got to and when you'd be back. They wouldn't tell me anything at the hospital.'

Olivia was a dab hand at interpreting the alcohol-laden slur. One glance at Zac and she knew he was also right up to speed on the situation. Anger—at her mother, at Zac for learning her truth—rolled up and spilled out. 'Mum, what are you doing here? You know I don't like you in my house when I'm away.'

A firm hand on her arm stopped her diatribe. 'Olivia, it's okay.'

'No, it's not. You don't get it. This is my mother, Cindy Coates-Clark. Mum, meet Zachary Wright, a friend—' No, damn it. 'Zac and I have been in Fiji together. We have had a wonderful time and now we'd like to wind down from our flight home. Alone.'

'Pleased to meet you, Zachary. Call me Cindy.' A wave of alcohol fumes wafted between them all.

Her mother stepped back and held the door wide, as though it was her place to do so. 'Do come in.'

'Thank you, Cindy.' Zac picked up the cases and nodded Olivia through in front of him. 'I'll leave mine just inside the door while we have that coffee.'

'You still want it?' When she locked her eyes with his, he nodded.

'Yes.' Like there was nothing out of the ordinary, being greeted by a scantily clad woman who was obviously plastered.

Heavy black smudges of mascara covered Cindy's cheeks, and bright red lipstick had run into the lines around her mouth. Her low-cut top revealed way too much cleavage, and her skirt...

Olivia gulped as anger and disappointment again boiled over. 'Mum, that was a new suit. I haven't even worn it.' And never would now that three-quarters of the skirt had been hacked off. She'd been thrilled when she'd found the emerald-coloured outfit at her favourite shop.

'It's far sexier now. You can be so old-fashioned with your clothes, darling.'

'I wonder why.' From the day she'd turned thirteen her mother had spent a fortune on buying her clothes that had made her feel uncomfortable even around the cat, let alone the kids she'd hung out with. Humiliating didn't begin to describe it.

Now Zac was seeing things she never wanted him to know about. 'Zac, about that coffee...'

'I'll make it, shall I?' He hid his disgust very well. 'Would you like a coffee, Cindy?'

'Coffee? I don't think so. Why don't you two join me with a gin? Zac, I know you'd like one. You're a real man. Not like—'

'Mum, stop it. Now. We are not having gin.' She stepped into the kitchen and crumpled. *Welcome home, Olivia. Welcome back to life as you really know it.* Empty bottles lay everywhere. Half-full takeout food containers covered the bench, dirty cutlery and glasses filled the spaces. 'How long have you been here?'

'I don't know. Days?' Mum sounded confused all of a sudden.

Strong arms wound around Olivia, held her from dropping in a heap. 'Hey, we'll get it sorted.' Zac's low voice was full of compassion and wove around her like the comfort blanket she'd taken everywhere with her as a toddler. 'You're not alone, okay?'

Yes, she was. Her mother was her problem. This had nothing to do with Zac, and never would. Despite the warmth that stole through her at his words. She stayed in the circle of his arms—just for one more minute. Her chin rested on his chest. One minute, then she'd toughen up and face the consequences of having gone away without telling her mother where she was.

Finally she stepped away, put space between her and Zac. 'You have to go.'

Frustration deepened his voice. 'No, Olivia, I don't. I'm with you, at your side, looking out for you.'

On her phone she found the taxi company number and stabbed the button. Forcing a toughness she didn't feel on her face, she snapped, 'I'm not asking, I'm telling you to go.' Someone from the taxi company answered and she rattled off directions, ended the call. 'They'll be five minutes.'

He gave no further argument, just kissed her softly. 'Good night, sweetheart. Talk to you in the morning.'

'No, Zac. Don't. It's over. We're done. Permanently.' It was the only way forward for her.

But when the front door had closed behind him Olivia leaned against the hall wall and felt her heart crack into pieces. It had taken this for her to realise her hope for the future with Zac was actually love for Zac. She wanted to be with him, to give him so much, to share a life. To openly show him her love. To try to be the woman she hadn't thought she could be. But that mess in her kitchen told her otherwise. Dreams were fairytales.

Sliding down the wall, she wrapped her arms around her legs, dropped her head on her knees, and let the tears come. She hadn't cried over her mother for so long but there was no stopping the torrent. For a brief time she'd let hope into her heart, had wanted more with Zac. How dumb could she get? This had always been going to happen. Therefore, the sooner the better. Now she could move on, without Zac, and do what she'd always done—survive and look out for her mother.

Zac stared at Olivia's house until the taxi turned the corner at the end of the street. His throat was dry, his heartbeat slow and his gut knotted tight. What a difference twenty-four hours made. From sexy and fun in that red dress to heartbroken at home, it was like Olivia had flipped from one person to another.

Now he understood so much. The control she constantly maintained over herself and everything around her was a coping mechanism.

There'd be no controlling her mother.

Olivia didn't want to be like her mother.

The glimpse of worry when he'd said that dress was so different from what he was used to seeing her in now made sense.

'Well, hello, you're nothing like your mum.' Despite having spent only a few minutes with Cindy and not knowing anything about her, he knew Olivia was the polar opposite from her mother.

But you didn't have to kick me out like I mean nothing to you.

When Olivia had mentioned her mother was an alcoholic he'd had no idea what that meant in real terms. Drunk and disorderly didn't cover it. Cindy whined like a spoilt brat, created chaos. She'd helped herself to her daughter's clothes, ruining them in the process. Helped herself to the house, the contents of the kitchen, and trashed it as only belligerent teenagers did. What had that woman done to Olivia's life? Her sense of belonging, her future?

The resignation in CC's eyes had hit him hard. She was responsible for that woman, and he knew all about responsibility. He'd learned it the hard way. Hopefully Olivia hadn't, but deep down he knew this situation went a long way to explaining why she ran solo.

You don't have to be alone any more.

Olivia wasn't made for that. She was loving, caring, sharing, and a whole load more.

The taxi pulled up in Quay Street. His apartment building loomed above, dark and unwelcoming. He'd rather be back at Olivia's house, no matter the mess inside. He wasn't thinking about the state of the kitchen.

But you sent me away, Olivia. Again.

As Zac rode the elevator to his floor a slow burn began in his belly. He'd been shoved out of Olivia's life for a second time. She hadn't given him a chance to stay, to talk about it, to do any damned thing except get out of her life. What had their holiday been about if not learning more about each other and getting closer?

Learning that I love you, Olivia. Do you know that? Do you know I've broken all my rules for you? That for the first time ever I'm seeing a future that's got people in it—you and our children.

The doors slid apart but Zac didn't move. The itch had gone.

The doors began closing. Sticking his foot in the gap so they opened again, Zac hoisted his bag and dragged his feet towards his apartment. He'd pour a whisky and try to fathom where to go from here.

How damned typical that when he'd finally fallen in love he wasn't wanted.

CHAPTER THIRTEEN

'DON'T HANG UP, OLIVIA.' Zac didn't give her time to say hello. 'This is about Josaia.'

'I'm listening.' Olivia could listen to him all day, but of course she'd spent the last ten days doing her damnedest to push him away, out of her head, her heart. She missed him so much it was unbelievable. It was like her heart and mind were stuck in Fiji mode with Zac, talking and laughing, while her real life was grinding along without any joy.

'Theatre's booked at the private hospital for Saturday morning. I've managed to inveigle a free bed for four nights so we're set to go.' Zac sounded upbeat and pleased with himself. As he should be. He'd been hassling everyone he knew to get Josaia's surgery organised. All the staff assisting were doing it gratis. No surprise there. When Zac wanted to he could charm the grumpiest of old men into putting his hand in his pocket and handing over his life savings.

'You should start a charity organisation for kids like Josaia,' Olivia acknowledged.

'*I* should? You're the one who knows how to pull at people's heartstrings. Look at how successful Andy's gala night turned out to be.'

Had she pulled Zac's heartstrings? Ever? Even a

teeny-weeny bit? Why was she wondering when a yes only added to her grief? Staying away from him was hard enough already. She only talked to him about Josaia's upcoming surgery, cutting him off the moment he started on about anything personal. 'I'll see you at the motel at five.' They'd decided between themselves to pay for a motel unit for the family close to the hospital. Zac was picking up Josaia and his family from the airport later in the day. Tomorrow they had a free day, and then it would be D-day.

'You could come with me.'

'I've got a clinic starting at two.'

Zac sighed, his upbeat mood gone. 'Promise me you'll be at the motel. It's important for Josaia.'

She didn't make promises. Her word was usually enough. 'I promise.' *I do?*

'Are you sure you're not a secret needleworker?' Zac asked from the other side of the operating table on Saturday. 'You're so patient, creating delicate stitches even where the outcome won't be visible to anyone.'

Olivia glanced up at him, her heart stuttering when his dark eyes locked on hers. 'I could've taken up knitting.'

'That'd be messy.' He grinned. She mightn't be able to see his mouth behind that mask but his eyes were light and sparkling.

Olivia concentrated on her patient. She'd reopened the wound that ran down the side of Josaia's face and removed tissue causing lumps where the previous stitches had been pulled too tight. Now she was painstakingly suturing layer after layer, careful with each and every stitch. While it was what everyone saw on the outside that upset Josaia, she could make it so much better by preparing the underneath muscle properly.

'You want to close the shoulder wound once I've worked on Josaia's shoulder?' Zac asked. 'We might as well go for broke and have everything looking as close to new as possible.'

'Make those kids want their friend back.'

Kay looked up from her monitors. 'I hope Josaia tells them where to go.'

'I suspect he might after this,' Zac told the anaesthetist. 'He's been different ever since we said we could operate. Hopeful, expectant. Which puts the pressure on us.'

Olivia clipped the end of her last suture and straightened her back. 'There you go, young man. As good as new.'

Zac swapped places with Olivia. It was his turn to set things right for Josaia. 'Let's hope I can do the same. At least no one gets to see what I do.' He picked up a scalpel.

'They will on the outside. It will be great to see Josaia with his confidence back, swimming and diving with the best of them.'

'I hope he finds some new friends. He doesn't need the old ones.' Olivia swabbed as Zac made incisions. 'But I guess Josaia doesn't have a lot of choice on the island.'

'It must be hell for his family, seeing how he's treated. No parent would want their child to suffer like that.' Zac exposed the collarbone, where it had been broken. 'Re-breaking this is kind of awful. The kid's going to be in pain for a while.'

'Think about how those pins you're going to put in will help him. One day he'll appreciate it.' The sooner the better if the boy was to make a full recovery with friends and school.

'Right, let's get this done.' He reached for the first pin.

As soon as the surgeries were completed and Josaia was wheeled away to Recovery, Olivia and Zac went to put the family at ease.

Then they headed for the car park and Zac suggested lunch downtown. 'We could go to the Viaduct.'

'Sorry, Zac, but I'm not hungry.' She'd eaten very little over the last couple of days, food making her feel nauseous.

'What's going on, Olivia? Don't give me the "nothing" reply. I won't believe you.'

The steel in his tone overwhelmed her. She could feel her body being pulled towards him. It would be so easy to lean in and let go of her problem for a while. The thing with that was that her mother wasn't going to go away; would be there causing havoc when she finally took up the reins again. Tightening her spine, she told him, 'I have an appointment in an hour, and before that I need to hit the supermarket.' Though why when she wasn't eating she had no idea. That had just dropped into her head when she was trying to sound convincing to Zac.

'An appointment with who?' Of course he went for the important part of her statement.

'A lawyer, a psychologist, and a cop,' she blurted, close to unravelling. Had to be why she'd answered with the truth. She needed to get away from Zac fast, before she became a blithering idiot and spilled her guts all over his classy leather jacket.

Where was her car key? Scrabbling around in the bottom of her bag didn't produce it. Tipping the contents onto the bonnet of her car, she couldn't believe it wasn't there. Great. Just great.

'This what you're looking for?' Zac swung a key from his finger.

Snatching it from him, she began throwing everything back in her bag. 'Where did you find it?'

'Where are you meeting these people?'

'At home.' She bent to pick up her wallet from where it had slipped onto the tarmac.

'I'll drive you. Come on.' He took her elbow.

She tugged free. 'I can drive myself. Anyway, I can't leave my car here.'

Zac's hand was back on her arm. 'You can and you will. I'm taking you home, Olivia.'

That got her. Slap bang in her heart. She didn't pull away. She couldn't. She needed Zac, and, as frightening as that was, she went with the desperate longing to have someone at her side. 'Next you'll be telling me you're coming to the meeting.' Geez, had she just said that with hope in her voice?

'I'll make the coffee.'

He did more than that. Even when she nodded at the door for him to leave he stayed and listened as the horrible facts about her mother were aired and discussion began on what to do about Cindy. The truth was that there wasn't a lot that could be done unless her mother committed to a programme and went into care. Her latest hideous deed, arrested for driving while drunk on Thursday, made Olivia's stomach churn, and when she lifted her eyes to Zac's she fully expected to see total disgust all over his face. But no. His hand engulfed her shaking ones, his thumb rubbed back and forth over her fingers, and his eyes were full of understanding.

Olivia *needed* to leap up and drag Zac to her front

door, push him out, and lock it behind him. She *wanted* him here with her, holding her hand as he was. Split right down the middle, her emotions were raw and out of control. She aimed to do what she always did when this happened and focus on her mother's current situation. But it wasn't working. The words were going in but they weren't registering as clearly as they should.

By the time the meeting was over she was as aware as ever that her mother was a ticking time bomb and unwilling to take charge of herself. It had been suggested Olivia walk away, make her mother face up to her situation, but she didn't think she could do that. It would go against everything she believed in. Even now, when she was fighting Zac's pull, fighting this deep, paralysing need to let him into her life, she had to hold on to the only way she knew how to cope with her mother—by standing strong, alone.

Shutting the front door behind the lawyer, she leaned back against it, closing her eyes. Did she even have the energy to make it to the kitchen where Zac was waiting? She had to tell him to leave. It was getting to be a habit.

'Hey,' Zac said from somewhere in front of her. 'You need to go to bed and get some shut-eye.'

'I have to check Josaia's doing okay.'

'I'm going to head in there shortly so I can let you know if there's anything you need to deal with. I spoke to the ward sister while you were showing that lot out and she says he's doing fine. The family are with him.' Zac draped an arm over her shoulders and led her down the hallway in the direction of her bedroom. 'When did you last sleep properly?'

'I have no idea.'

'Get into bed and I'll make you a hot chocolate.'

Olivia sank onto the edge of her bed. 'Hot chocolate? I haven't had one of those in years.' *Since I had measles and Dad looked after me.* Huh? Dad had done that? Yeah, he had, just as he'd once spent lots of time with her. Before he'd got jaded and bitter about Mum, and had made another life.

Zac pulled her to her feet again. 'No, you don't. Let's get you into your PJs first.' He began unbuttoning her shirt and it was nothing like last time when he'd made her body hot with need. This loving gesture filled her heart with gladness and relief.

'I'll manage.' Her fingers worked the zip on her trousers. When Zac reached her door she called, 'Hey, you. Thank you for…everything.'

He came back and kissed her on each cheek. 'Told you I was here for you.'

Scary. 'Zac, I don't do being looked after.' Deep, deep breath. 'You have to go. You have to stay gone this time. Please.' Her voice cracked over the lump of tears clogging her throat.

Zac shrugged. 'Here's the thing. I don't do walking away from someone I care about either.'

Had Zac just said he cared about her? No, he couldn't have. She must be asleep already, having a dream. At least it wasn't a nightmare.

Zac let himself out of Olivia's house and made sure the door locked behind him. With a bit of luck Olivia would sleep right through until tomorrow. One thing for certain was that she needed to.

It was about the only thing he was sure of, he thought as he climbed into his vehicle and slammed the door against the light rain. That, and the fact she wouldn't be letting him back into her house tomorrow morning.

Looking up the path to her house, he recalled some of the comments made by the lawyer, and wondered just what sort of childhood Olivia must've had with a mother so far off the rails. What woman wanted to dress up as her daughter's lookalike? Wanted to hang out with a bunch of giggly teens? One eyebrow rose. Olivia a giggly teen? Hard to imagine.

Slowly pulling away, he kept going over everything he'd heard about Cindy Coates-Clark. How cruel of Olivia's father to leave her to deal with her alcoholic mother, especially when she'd been so young.

Toot, toot. A quick glance in the rear-view mirror showed a truck up his boot. He waved. 'Sorry, mate.' And planted his foot, roaring away from the corner.

He'd go see Josaia, then head home for the night. Tomorrow morning he'd take breakfast to Olivia's house.

Think that's going to win you entrance to her lair, do you?

No, not a sod's chance, but he had to try, if only to show her he wasn't repelled by anything he'd heard today. If anything, he was more determined to be a part of her life. At the moment he'd take the crumbs, but he fully intended to win her over completely so they'd have a future together.

His hand clenched, banged the steering wheel. Damn—families could be such screw-ups. He and Olivia had got the pick of them. What was Mark like as a father? Did he show his boys he loved them? Would he blame them for everything or walk out of their lives when the going got tough? And if he did, who would be there for them?

I would. But he didn't know the boys. Not really. Only one way to rectify that. But he and Mark didn't get along. *So go fix that. Start at the beginning and get*

*to know your brother again, learn to put the angst be-
hind you and love him as you always did, always have.*

Olivia rolled over onto her back and stared up at the
ceiling. The sunlit ceiling.

'What time is it?'

Eight thirty-five, according to the screen on her
phone.

She'd missed a load of texts while in the land of nod,
starting last night.

Josaia says hi to Dr Olivia. He's doing fine and can't
wait to be up and running around, despite the pain.
Hope you're sleeping and don't get this till the morning. Hugs, Zac.

Thinking of you, and wishing we were back on Tokoriki
enjoying dinner under the palm trees. More hugs, Zac.

Hitting the sack now. See you in the morning.

*No, you won't. I've got a mother to sort out, and
wounds to lick.*

Outside your door with breakfast.

Had Zac knocking on the door been what had woken
her? Olivia leapt out of bed and headed down the hall.

*Wait up. You're going to let Zac in? Think about
this. Is it wise when you're going to walk away from
him again? It's not fair on him to be running hot and
cold all the time. Either let him into your life or cut all
ties—now.*

Her feet dragged as she turned for the kitchen and

the kettle. Strong coffee was needed. Her heart was so slow it was in danger of stopping. She didn't want Zac gone but what else could she do? She had nothing to offer him.

She loved Zac. She knew it bone deep. He was the one for her. *Sniff.* But she wasn't right for him. Never would be.

With two coffees on board and a hot shower having washed away the sleep sludge on her skin, Olivia headed out her front door to see Josaia, and tripped over a paper bag with a takeout logo on it. Breakfast. Gluggy cold pancakes, bacon, and maple syrup filled the container she opened. 'Oh, Zac, you're making this so hard for me.'

She dropped the bag into her rubbish bin and headed for her garage, only remembering when the door rolled open that her car was still in the hospital's car park. Back inside the house she changed her shoes. Walking to the hospital would help clear her head.

Maybe.

Josaia was arguing with Donny about getting out of bed when Olivia arrived at his room. 'I don't like staying in bed.'

'You have to wait until Dr Olivia's checked you over,' his grandfather growled.

'If Josaia's that keen to get up then there's no reason why he shouldn't,' Olivia told them.

Josaia grinned. 'See?' But when he moved pain filled his face and he stopped.

'Take it slowly.' Olivia spoke firmly. 'I need to look at your face first. Then you'd better be careful what you do until Dr Zac sees you.' She needed to get out of there before he turned up and started asking why she hadn't returned any of his messages.

'He came when I was asleep.' Josaia slowly sat up, his damaged cheek turned up to her. 'My face is better, isn't it?'

If he could think that with a line of stitches running down his cheek then he was well on the way to recovery. 'Lots better.'

'My friends are going to like me again.'

Thud. Olivia's heart sank. 'Josaia, you are still going to have a scar, just not as obvious and no more lumps and bumps.'

'My arm's going to work properly.'

'Soon, yes. You have to do a lot of work first, exercises that Dr Zac will show you.' But those friends? 'Let's take everything slowly, eh?' She sat down beside him and turned his head so that the overhead light shone on the wound. No redness or puffiness, just a neat line that would heal into a thin, flat scar that over time would fade to a pale mark on his skin. 'That's looking good.' Pride filled her. Hopefully she'd made this boy's life a little easier.

If only her mother was as easily pleased when she visited later.

'I am not going into one of those rehab places. They're full of pious do-gooders who think having a drink is a crime.'

Clocked driving at eighty-five Ks per hour in a residential area while drunk was a crime. 'You're lucky Judge Walters has given you another chance to fix your life. He's ordered you to go into a clinic. If you don't you'll appear before him again and this time he'll throw the book at you. You already have one drunk-driving conviction.' She drew in a breath. 'I've made you an appointment for tomorrow at the clinic in Remuera. I'll come with you.'

'Bet that man you went away with wouldn't do anything naughty, like having a drink too many.'

Olivia sighed at her mother's classic tactic of changing the subject. 'Leave Zac out of this.'

'Why? You got the hots for him?'

I don't want him sullied by you. 'We're friends, nothing more.' *Nothing less either. If only...*

'He's cocky, thinks he's every woman's gift.' Her mother looked smug as she raised her coffee to her lips, then put it down without a sip.

'No, Mum, he does not.' Confident, comfortable in his own skin, but not cocky.

'You watch. He'll get what he wants from you and walk away. He's not the settling-down type.'

Mum always aimed for the bull's-eye. Never missed either. 'You know an awful lot about Zac for having spent very little time with him.'

'He's going to hurt you, darling. Trust me, I know men and how they operate. You are fair game with this one.'

She snapped, 'Zac is not like you think. You're insulting him with your accusations.'

'Watch this space,' her mother drawled, before changing tactics again. 'Darling, I'm only thinking of you. I don't want to see you get hurt. I know what that's like, believe me.'

'Why are you doing this? You want to destroy everything I hold dear.'

'Ha, you care about him. Knew it. I worry about what happens to you. I'm your mother, I want you to be happy.' Her hands shook so badly coffee slopped onto the table.

Mum's frightened. Of what? She's been going on about Zac. Aha. Got it. She's afraid she'll have to share me. She's always done this. She drove Dad away, pushed friends out of my life, and I've gone along with it, believing I can't love two people at once, can't be there for anyone but her.

'Goddamn,' she said under her breath. *Have I been wrong?* 'Mum, I've got to go. I'll pick you up at ten tomorrow.'

'Come back, Olivia. I need to talk to you.'

'No, Mum, I'm done talking.'

She ran out to her car, leapt in, jerked the gearstick into drive, and sped away.

Cornwall Park was busy with families and their dogs, with joggers, walkers, and tourists heading up to the top of One Tree Hill. Olivia strode out under the massive trees, her hands stuffed in her jacket pockets, her chin down. And let it all in. Everything that had shaped her. Dad abandoning her. Her mother. Zac. *Her life.*

The answers for the future were elusive. *But I want to try. I love Zac. No denying it.* So now what? Race around to his apartment and tell him the good news? Leap into his arms and hang on for dear life?

Even as she spun around to return to her car and do just that, common sense prevailed.

Am I absolutely sure?

Hurting Zac was not on the agenda. There were a lot of things to think through, and she'd take her time, spend the next few days getting her head around the fact that she could be about to change her life for ever by giving her heart to Zac. By letting go of some of the control that had kept her on track most of her life.

Scary. Downright terrifying.

* * *

The days dragged. Sleep was elusive and work tedious. Her head was full of arguments for and against getting involved with Zac. *More involved.*

I love you, Zachary Wright. But I can't have a life with you, her old self told her. *I'll hurt you.*

Every day she got texts.

Hey, isn't Josaia doing well? He's like a new kid. Hugs, Zac.

Yep, their young patient had turned into a bright and bubbly boy desperate to get out and play.

CC, you want to have dinner at that new Italian place? Zac.

Absolutely, yes. But she didn't.

You okay? I'm here for you. Hugs, Zac.

No, I'm not okay. I'm missing you. So much it's like there's a hole where my heart used to be. She thought of those shoulders she liked to lean against, that strong body that made her feel safe and warm. And missed him even more.

Did your mother go into the clinic this week? More hugs, Zac.

Yes, surprisingly, Mum had.

Olivia didn't answer any of the texts. When she found a huge bunch of irises in gold and purple paper on her doorstep on Thursday night with a note saying,

'Love, Zac,' she wanted to cry. Oh, all right, she did cry. But she didn't ring to thank him. Or to acknowledge what his message might mean.

Friday night he sent photos of his nephews. 'Check these guys out. I'm mending bridges.' The cutest little boys hung off Uncle Zac's arms, beaming directly at the camera. Zac looked happy but wary. It wasn't hard to see him with his own kids hanging off him like that. Her heart rolled. She wanted that—with Zac. Children. She had no idea how to raise kids but with Zac at her side she'd learn.

Saturday morning her phone rang. She sighed when she saw the number. 'Hello, Mum.'

'Darling, come and get me. I hate it here. They treat me like a child. I can't have anything I want.'

'Where are you ringing from?' Patients weren't allowed any contact with family for the first few weeks.

'I'm at a coffee shop around the corner from the clinic. The coffee's terrible but the owner let me use the phone. Hurry, Olivia. I can't stand the place.'

'Mum, listen to me.' It hurt to breathe. 'I am not coming to get you. You have to go back and start getting better.'

'It's him, isn't it? He's told you to do this.'

'Don't blame Zac.' *I am finally opening my eyes and seeing that to be kind to you I have to be strong and hard.* '*I* want you to stop drinking.'

'Come and get me so we can talk about it,' her mother wheedled.

'Sorry, but I've got someone to see.' Why had she left it so long? Zac was her man.

'What about me?'

'Mum, I love you, but I am about to put me first.' *Me and Zac.* 'Don't bother coming around to my house. I won't be here. Please go back to the clinic. Do this for yourself.' She cut their conversation, then turned the phone off and put it in a drawer. She was on a mission and didn't want any interruptions.

In her bedroom she gazed into the wardrobe, trying to decide what to wear. That red dress stood out amongst the dark winter clothes. Reaching for it, she hesitated. Zac had lost his mind when she'd worn it in Fiji but this was early afternoon and it was very cold outside. The many trousers and blouses were too work-like. The green skirt she pulled out didn't excite her either. In the end she slipped into the designer skin-tight jeans and silk blouse she'd worn on the day of the gala when they'd caught up again at the hotel. Zipping up the knee-high boots, she did a twirl in front of her mirror. 'Not bad.' For the first time in days she could feel some control coming back, could feel her body tightening up. The thigh-length coat from that day completed the look, and made her smile briefly.

A quick check of her make-up and a swipe of her hair with the brush and she was on her way, not giving herself time to think about what she was doing. Laying her life on the line was what this was about.

Stop thinking, just concentrate on driving through the downtown traffic.

What if—?

No what-ifs, she told herself as she pressed the buzzer for Zac's apartment. *This is do or don't. And don't is no longer an option.*

'Hello?'

It's not too late to run. 'Zac, it's me.'

A soft buzzing and she was stepping into the elevator. She didn't hesitate but pressed the button for the penthouse floor and held herself ramrod straight, ready for anything, refusing to acknowledge the flapping sensations in her stomach.

Zac was standing outside the elevator door as it opened. His smile was friendly but cautious. 'Olivia.'

'Zac.' Suddenly the full import of what she'd come to say slammed into her like an avalanche. Her hand went out to the wall to steady herself.

He took her elbow. 'Come into the apartment.'

Through the thick layers of coat and silk blouse she felt heat spreading out from where his fingers touched her, filling her with courage. Reaching behind her, he said, 'Let me take your coat.'

As she shrugged out of the sleeves she breathed deeply, boosted her courage. Then she turned to face him. 'I'm sorry I haven't been returning your texts or thanking you for the flowers.'

'That's okay.'

'But it isn't. I was rude, and there is no excuse for that. Zac, I came to tell you I love you.' There. She'd done it.

That smile didn't change; didn't fade, neither did it widen or soften. 'I was hoping you might.'

'I think I always have, but I've been so busy trying to deny it that I've made a lot of mistakes.' This was hard, yet relief was catching at her. 'Is there a future for us?'

'What do you want, Olivia? Marriage? Children and a dog?

Too much too soon. She took a step back. 'Could we try living together first? See how that goes? I didn't have good role models growing up and I'd hate to make the mistakes my parents did.'

Zac closed the gap, standing directly in front of her. He ran a finger down her cheek and over her chin. 'No, sweetheart. It's all or nothing. I love you and I want the whole picture.'

He loved her. To hear those words did funny things to her heart. Wow. To hear Zac tell her he loved her was the most wonderful thing. She smiled at him, sure her face was all goofy-looking.

Then the rest of what he'd said hit her, and she shook her head. 'I know nothing about happy families. I don't even know if I can love you and kids and my mother. I've kept myself shut off from all that, only ever loved one person.'

His mouth softened and the kiss he placed on the corner of her mouth felt lighter than a butterfly landing. 'I'll help you. But I don't want a practice run. Let's get married, jump in boots and all, a full commitment to each other and our lives. I believe in you, Olivia. If you falter *we'll* work it out. Just as I expect you to do for me. My family history isn't any more encouraging than yours and yet I want to make it work with you.'

Hope began to unfurl at the bottom of her stomach. 'Really? You want all that with *me*?'

Now he gave her the full-blown grin she enjoyed so much. 'That's only the beginning, girl. There're the hot nights in bed, the lazy days lying in front of your fire and eating takeout food, the days when we're both working so hard the only contact we have is by text, but we'll always know we're there for each other.'

'What about the days my mother does her thing?' He'd seen what she could do.

'We support her and try to turn her back on track. We do not split up over her. We will be together, in love, war, and everything in between.' Those arms she'd been hankering for wound around her waist and drew her close so his eyes looked directly into hers. 'I love you,

Olivia, more than life itself. Please, say you'll marry me.' His mouth hovered close to hers, waiting.

'Okay. Yes, please. I will. Let's get married. Sooner rather than later.' Talk about jumping in at the deep end. But somehow she didn't think she was going to drown, not with Zac holding her. 'Did I mention I love you?'

'Not often enough for me to be absolutely sure,' he said just before claiming her mouth with his.

Minutes later Zac lifted his head. 'Now I know why I had the impulse to buy a bottle of your favourite bubbles. Come on, let's celebrate.'

'Just one glass.'

'CC, relax. You are not an alcoholic.'

'No, but I want to take you to bed and have my wicked way with your body, and too many glasses of champagne might spoil the fun.'

'Can't argue with that.' Zac grinned and hooked his arm through hers. 'Come on, we've got a cork to pop. And you can tell me why it took you so long to drop by.'

'Not tonight. Tonight's for us. But I'll fill you in soon enough. Promise.'

EPILOGUE

Fourteen months later

'HAPPY WEDDING ANNIVERSARY.' Zac sank onto the edge of their bed and placed a tray with breakfast on her knees. In the corner beside the small bowl of maple syrup for the pancakes and bacon was a tiny box.

Picking it up, she locked her eyes on the man she adored and who had been everything he'd promised and more since that night she'd told him she loved him. 'What's this?'

'Only one way to find out.'

When she flipped the lid a set of exquisite emerald earrings and a matching bracelet sparkled out at her. 'They're beautiful,' she squeaked.

'For a beautiful woman. Here.' He slid the bracelet over her hand. 'Perfect.'

She put the earrings in and then reached for the top drawer of her bedside table. 'Happy anniversary to you.' She placed a small, thin box in his outstretched hand and sat back to watch his reaction.

'What's this?' He gaped at the plastic stick he held up. 'Are we—?'

'Yes, we're pregnant. And I can hardly wait.' This past year had been wonderful, and not once had she faltered. Not even when Mum had run away from the clinic twice. With Zac there she could face anything. 'We're going to be parents, great parents.'

'Yeah, sweetheart, we are.' His kiss was made in heaven and had consequences that kept them busy for most of the morning and left the pancakes to go cold and gluggy on the plate.

Her hero for sure.

* * * * *

ONE LIFE-CHANGING NIGHT

LOUISA HEATON

For Sukidoo, the best friend I've never met. xx

CHAPTER ONE

SHE HADN'T EXPECTED to fall into the arms of a stunningly
handsome man on her first day at work. Or to have climbed
up a wobbly ladder in Welbeck Memorial's A&E department. But it was nearly the end of January and the Christmas decorations were *still* up.

Naomi had offered to take them down at the end of her
shift, which had been a long twelve hours, and her head
was buzzing with information and protocols and procedures. But she had nothing waiting for her at home—not
even a cat—and, quite frankly, putting off going back to
her little bedsit with its dingy second-hand furniture had
seemed like a good option. Starting a new life was one
thing, but starting it in a derelict, ought-to-be-bulldozed
ground-floor flat with a growing mould problem was another.

When she'd offered to take the decorations down, the
sister in charge had been very sweet. 'Oh, you don't have
to do that! We'll get one of the porters to do it. It's your
first day.'

But she'd insisted. 'Honestly, it's fine. Besides, it's bad
luck to keep them up this long. Bringing the old year into
the new.'

'Well, just be careful. There's a stepladder in my office you can use, but make sure you get someone to steady it for you, or you'll have Health and Safety on my back.'

Naomi smiled to herself, remembering the health and safety lecture she'd sat through that morning. She would be sensible and follow the rules. Just as she'd always done. She located the boxes for the Christmas decorations piled high in the sister's office and spent the first hour removing baubles and tinsel from the lower branches.

The old, artificial tree was almost bald in parts and she could see it was decades old, dragged out from its box year after year to try and brighten the place up. Her nose wrinkled as she leant too far into one of the branches and breathed in dust and the smell of Christmases past.

As she pulled her face free of the tree, another stench—this one of alcohol and body odour—mixed into the fray, sweeping over her like a wave. A scruffy-looking man with stained clothes staggered towards her. She turned to steady him as he passed by, hoping to steer him back in the direction of the waiting room, but the drunk angrily turned on her instead. 'Leave me alone! Shouldn't you be *working* instead of playing with that tree? I've been waiting to be seen for *ages* and you're out here messing around!'

They often saw people who were drunk in Accident and Emergency and Naomi knew they were mostly unthreatening. All she had to do was be non-confrontational and pleasant and they would be satisfied.

She smiled and led him back into the waiting room. 'You'll be seen soon, sir, don't worry.'

'Bloomin' patronising me! You should be working!' he slurred.

She saw no point in telling him she'd already worked a twelve-hour shift and that she ought to have been at home by now. He didn't want to hear that. He wanted to hear that he would be treated. 'I'm sure it won't be long now.'

Once he was settled back into his chair, she went back to the tree. To get the decorations down from the top she needed to go up the ladder. And that meant she needed someone to help steady it.

She headed back into the unit, looking for someone who was free, but everyone was so busy. And she didn't know anyone well enough yet to interrupt their work and ask them to help her. Because what was more important? Patient care, or an old tree?

Naomi looked down the long corridor at the stepladder. It wasn't that high. Just three steps. What harm would it do, if she was quick? Surely Matron wouldn't like her taking away a member of staff to hold a *ladder* when they could be *treating* someone.

Hmm. I'll be careful. These health and safety measures are always too cautious anyway.

She positioned the ladder where she needed it, noticing that it was a little uneven, and gave a quick look around to make sure no one was about to pounce and tell her off, and climbed up. She picked off the first few baubles and strings of tinsel and dropped them into the cardboard boxes beneath, hearing them plop into the decorations below. She worked quickly, steadying herself when she felt the ladder wobble a bit beneath her feet. The star on the top of the tree was just a tiny bit out of her reach and so she leant for it, stretching. The ladder wobbled even more so and she felt it start to move beneath her. 'Oh!'

She felt herself fall and braced herself for the impact and the hard, unforgiving floor. But instead, her fall was broken by a solid, reassuring pair of arms.

Stunned, she looked up to say thank you, but her voice somehow got stuck in her throat.

This man was nothing like the drunk that had accosted her a moment ago. *This* man had captivating eyes of cerulean blue, a strong jawline and he smelt just…heavenly! Masculine and invigorating.

'Whoa! Are you mad?' *That voice.* The most perfect accent she'd ever heard. Refined. Educated. Even if it was currently scolding her.

She blushed madly as she stared up into his eyes, her breath catching in her throat. She was embarrassed at having fallen. Ashamed at having been caught up the ladder when she'd been *told* to get someone to help her and desperately doing her level best to appear normal and not swoon like a heroine in a romance novel. She'd been determined to move to London and start life as a strong, confident, independent woman and yet here she was: it was only her first day at work and she was lying in a man's arms.

A very handsome man's arms! Her cheeks flamed with heat as he easily stood her upright, making sure she was steady before he let her go. When he did, she almost felt disappointed to be out of those arms, but…*oh!*

He was tall, almost a head taller than her, well past six foot, and he had the most startling blue eyes she'd ever seen. He was looking her over, assessing her, his gaze questioning.

She managed to find some words. 'Thank you, I… shouldn't have been up there.' She blushed again, brushing her hands down her clothes as if she were covered in dust and dirt. She wasn't. She just didn't know what else to do and she had to do *something*! Naomi had never been held in a man's arms like that. Cradled. Protected. Vincent had never held her that way. Not that that was his fault.

This man was probably used to women blushing in front of him. Women fawning at his feet, unable to string a sentence together.

He was dressed smartly in what had to be a tailored bespoke suit that fitted his finely toned body to perfection. This man knew how to dress and he dressed well, his clothes accentuating his best features. A red scarf slung casually around his neck highlighted the auburn tones in his hair.

Still, she wasn't going to let herself be blown away by a gorgeous man. She knew men like this usually came with health warnings.

Get involved at your own risk.

Look at what had happened to her mother, for instance.

She wasn't even sure who he was. She looked for the badge that all hospital employees wore, but couldn't see it.

'You must be new here?' She saw him glance at *her* name badge.

'Naomi.' She reached out her hand to shake his. 'Bloom. A&E nurse. First day.'

He looked at her hand briefly as if she were offering him a handful of sputum. Then he ignored it. 'Tom Williams. Clinical Lead and doctor. Almost *your* doctor for that stunt you just pulled.'

She faltered, her hand dropping away from him. This was her boss? She looked away, trying to think quickly, before returning her gaze to his. 'I'm sorry, I—'

'You had your induction this morning?' If this had been any other situation, she could have listened to his voice all day. It was rich and warm, classy. It was the sort of voice you heard from an English villain in an American movie.

Focus.

'I did, but—'

He smiled at her but the smile didn't reach his eyes. 'The health and safety briefing was covered?'

She nodded, feeling like a naughty child who was standing in front of a headmaster. 'Yes, but I didn't want to pull anyone away from their work, as they were all so busy, so I thought I'd do it myself.' The words burbled out of her quickly, showing her horror at having been caught so badly in the wrong.

She'd assumed she had been doing the right thing. Naomi had learnt the value of being able to do something for yourself. It was a pleasure denied to many people. A normality that they craved. To be able to do simple things like opening their own cupboard to reach for a mug, or taking themselves to the toilet. On their own. Without someone to help them.

He glanced at the tree. 'Well, luckily I managed to save you from a sprained ankle. Or something worse.' He shrugged his shoulders. 'A sprained neck wouldn't have gone down well on your first day. Nor would me having to fill in a three-page incident-report form after I've just spent twenty hours on non-stop duty.'

'I'm sorry, Dr Williams.'

Tom frowned, seeming concerned as he looked around them and over towards the waiting area. 'Who asked you to do this?'

She shrugged. 'I volunteered.'

'You volunteered?' He let out a short, impatient sigh. 'Well, if you're going to insist on doing this, I'd better stay and make sure you're safe.'

'Oh, you don't have to—'

'You might head back up that ladder. Besides, I was only on my way home.' He placed his folded coat down on top of his briefcase, removed his scarf and rolled up his sleeves.

He had beautiful forearms... Smooth. Strong.

If he hadn't just given her a dressing-down, she might have been tempted to appreciate them a bit more. 'Right. Erm…thanks.'

He looked the tree up and down. 'This old tree ought to have been passed through a chipper years ago.'

'I don't think they do that to fake trees.'

'No. Probably not.'

He started to take off some more of the decorations that he could reach just by standing there, which Naomi hadn't had a chance in hell of reaching, and then he passed them to her, so she could put them in their boxes a little more carefully than she'd been doing earlier. She hated feeling like a chastised child and wanted to get back on a more even keel, so she ventured some basic conversation. 'So you've worked here for a while, then?'

He glanced at her. 'Yes. What made you come to Welbeck?'

He didn't need to know her history. He probably didn't even want to know. He was just being polite. Or, at least, as polite as he could be.

She'd already vowed not to mention her past to anyone here. She didn't want pity or sympathy. She just wanted to get on with her life. If she told people she'd come out of a marriage where she'd been more of a carer than a wife, they tended to look at her with pity.

'I used to live in the East Midlands, originally, but I fancied a change of pace, so I got myself a cheap bedsit down here and hoped for the best.' This was better conversation, she thought. Much better than being told off.

'I thought I heard an accent.'

She smiled, never having thought of herself as someone with an accent. 'Really?'

'Yes. Bit of a northern twang. I'll go up the ladder and get the rest of them.'

'Be my guest.' She held it steady as he went up and together they made a quick, efficient team. The tree was soon naked of ornaments, broken down into its segments and boxed away for next year. Naomi quickly swept up the debris. It hadn't taken them more than fifteen minutes to get it sorted. 'Thanks for the help. It was really kind of you.'

'No problem.' He seemed to look at her for a moment longer than was comfortable, then suddenly shook his head at whatever thought he'd had and picked up his coat and briefcase. 'Let's try not to get hurt tomorrow, Nurse Bloom, hmm?'

'Course not.' She watched him walk away and let out a breath that she hadn't been aware she'd been holding.

Wow. What a bear!

And he was her boss! That was embarrassing. Her first day and she had already been caught breaking a rule, although thankfully not breaking anything else.

She determined to try and stay out of Dr Williams's way as much as possible. She would only let him notice her when she was being brilliant, providing outstanding nursing care.

She headed in the other direction and went to fetch her coat.

The weather was doing its best to let the people of London know that it was winter. There'd been snow a few days ago and, though there'd been nothing since, it was still on the ground, due to the freezing temperatures. The surrounding buildings looked grey, damp and cold and as Naomi came out of the hospital to head for home—a place she really didn't want to go, knowing it would be just as awful inside as it was out—she wrapped her knitted green scarf around her tightly and pulled on her gloves.

There were people standing outside the entrance to A&E puffing away on cigarettes, their hands cupped around them, as if somehow gaining a small measure of warmth. One of them was the drunk that had confronted Naomi earlier and he looked up, catching her gaze with vehemence. He came staggering back over to her, the overwhelming stench of body odour and stale alcohol almost overpowering. With one grimy finger he pushed her in the chest. '*You* lot kept me waiting.'

Naomi felt disconcerted. And a little afraid. She could handle this sort of aggression when she was at work. In the hospital. Then she had her uniform on and was surrounded by people who she knew would come to her aid. Violence against hospital staff wasn't tolerated and they had security guards, too. But out here, outside work, in her normal clothes, she felt more vulnerable.

'Look, sir—'

'You lot…kept me *waiting*!' He gave her another shove and she stumbled backwards, caught off balance, her heart pounding. What a first day she was having. She'd wound up her new boss and now she was being accosted by a member of the public. She held up her hands as if in surrender and backed away, afraid of what might happen, when suddenly a tall figure stepped between them.

It was Tom. He had stepped in, towering over the drunk like a menacing gladiator.

'Step away.' He dropped his briefcase to the floor without taking his eyes off the belligerent man and then slowly walked towards him.

Naomi watched, open-mouthed in shock. It had to be him! Rescuing her again!

What must he think of me?

'What *you* gonna do? Huh? I know my rights!' A small piece of spittle flew from the man's mouth, but his swagger and bravado soon dissipated as Tom continued to step towards him.

'If you *ever* touch a member of my staff again, you'll find yourself in a police cell quicker than you could ever imagine.'

The man staggered backwards, blinking. 'All right! All right! I'm going!' He looked most put out that his bullying tactics hadn't worked and he'd been knocked back by a better, stronger man. 'You lot are all the same!' He shuffled off, muttering, his cigarette smoke surrounding him like a dirty cloud.

Tom watched him go, his coat collar turned up around his neck. Only when he was convinced that the drunk was far enough away did he turn around to look at Naomi, his gaze checking her for any injury, concern in his eyes. 'Are you all right?' His voice held a note of the same concern.

She nodded quickly. Briefly. She was unable to believe how quickly the situation had escalated.

'Mick's a frequent flyer here. Often presents drunk. He's lonely, I think.' His voice had an odd tone, but whatever he'd been thinking disappeared from his face when he turned again to make sure Mick had truly gone.

'But still he has a go at the people trying to help him.'

He smiled, disarming her. 'It happens.'

'You can say that again.' She watched Mick from afar, glad that Tom had intervened. Although she felt she would have handled it, if she'd had to. She'd taken kick-boxing classes once, years ago. She had needed something intensely physical to do, seeing as it wasn't required in her marriage. At home, she'd had to be careful in everything she did, walking on eggshells, making sure she made no dramatic movements so as not to cause inadvertent injury. Being extra careful all of the time had just seemed to emphasise her natural clumsiness. By the end, her marriage had been a physical prison.

'Thanks again. It seems you've rescued me twice in one day.' She tried to break the tension she was feeling by making a joke. 'You really ought to be wearing shining armour and riding a white horse, or something.'

He just stared at her, his face impassive.

Not a lover of jokes either. Okay.

'Anyway. Thank you.'

'Will you get home all right?'

She nodded and pulled up the collar of her own coat. 'It's not far. Just around the corner, to be honest. St Bartholomew's Road.'

'Then I'll walk you home. Mick could still be a bother. I know him and he doesn't always do what's wise.'

She couldn't let him do that. He'd done enough for her today and, besides, she didn't need him witnessing the dump she was living in. That would be too embarrassing. By his expensive clothes, she could tell this was a man that probably lived in a penthouse apartment. He'd take one look at her bedsit and then what would he think of her? He probably already thought of her as incompetent and she didn't want him thinking of her as some sort of Cinderella figure.

'You don't have to.'

'I do.' He smiled. 'You've almost fallen once today. If you fell on the ice now, it would undo all of my previous hard work.'

Naomi smiled back, her grin almost freezing into place in the bitter wind.

Right. I just won't invite him in. Then he won't understand how bad it is. I can do this. He's not a complete ogre.

'Okay.'

They walked along at a pleasant pace. There was a large park by the hospital and, this late in the day, it was filled with people walking their dogs, or couples strolling hand in hand. Naomi always noticed people doing that. It had been something denied to her and Vincent. She'd always been pushing his wheelchair.

But today, instead, she caught herself sneaking looks at Tom and even though she tried to stop herself—sure that he would notice—she kept doing it.

He was so good-looking; tall and broad, yet slim. He frightened her. Not just because he was her boss and probably thought she was an incompetent nincompoop, but because he was without a doubt the most handsome man she had ever met. Handsome men, in her experience, caused trouble. They had certainly caused enough for her mother, who had brought back endless strings of attractive men. Fast-car driving, exquisitely clothed, silver-tongued individuals, so slick you'd have trouble distinguishing them from a vat of oil. Each man had caused their own problems. Borrowing money, never calling, one even taking his hand to her mother. Each and every one had been heartache and pain in a well-dressed suit. Each of them had broken her mother's easily led heart.

That was why Naomi had fallen so easily in love with Vincent. Why she had married him. He'd been none of those things. He'd been average-looking, physically disabled. She'd always known where she was with him. She'd always known the expectations. It had been simple. And there'd been no worry or risk of him running off, having an affair and breaking her heart.

'So how was your first day at Welbeck? *Scintillating* health and safety briefing aside?'

Naomi looked back at the road, busy with cars. 'It was good. Exhausting, but good. I'll be glad to get a decent night's sleep. You? Did you have a busy day?'

See? I can do this. Pretend this is normal. There's nothing more to it than one colleague walking another home, to ensure her safety. Having a normal conversation.

'Yes.'

'Why did you choose A&E as a discipline?'

'It's busy.'

She waited, assuming that he'd say more, but when he didn't, she didn't push him. They were both still strangers to each other. Perhaps he had personal reasons for his career that he didn't feel like sharing with someone he'd only just met. After all, she was keeping secrets, too. Holding things back. He was entitled to do the same.

Naomi adjusted her scarf. 'You know, it's not far now. You're probably coming out of your way to walk me home, so you can go, if you want to. I don't think I'm going to get mugged in the next fifty metres.'

He turned to her. 'You don't like people helping you, do you?'

She blew out a breath. 'I stand on my own two feet. I've got used to looking after myself and I like it. The independence. The freedom.' She couldn't tell him how much that meant to her. Being out in the world and doing her own thing without having to think of anyone else. She hadn't been able to do that for a very long time.

They continued to walk, turning into her road, and she felt twisting snakes of nervousness swirl around in her stomach the closer they got.

She knew what he would think. He would see the small front yard, littered with an old settee and someone's old fridge. The detritus and litter from what seemed like a million previous tenants—empty glass milk bottles, old cans, raggedy bits of clothing, dirtied by the weather and constant stream of car exhaust fumes. And if he got past her front door? Well, she'd tried her best to pretty the place up. She had done what she could, but it never seemed enough. The truth was, she couldn't afford anywhere better and it would have to do until she'd gathered some more savings for a small deposit elsewhere.

Naomi estimated she had another six months of being

here, before she could try and rent somewhere else. 'I hope you don't think I'm rude.'

He laughed to himself. 'I can cope with rude.'

'Well, I don't mean to be.' As they came to a halt outside her front garden she hesitated, sucking in a breath, her back turned to the property. 'Well, this is me. Unfortunately.'

Tom smiled and looked past her. The smile dropped from his glorious face in an instant. 'Did you leave your front door open?'

'Er…no. Why?' Naomi turned around and instantly saw the splintering down the door frame where someone had pried it open. She gasped and went to take a step forward, but Tom gripped her arm, holding her back.

'Stay here. Call the police.'

'You're not *going in*?' Whoever had broken in could still be in there! He had no idea what he would be walking into. There was splintered wood all over the place and goodness knew what they'd done to all her things inside. He could trip on anything, hurt himself. The burglars could be waiting with weapons. It was dangerous, and…

He's not Vincent. Tom can handle himself.

He'd certainly shown himself to be capable when he'd sent Mick away outside the hospital. He'd had no hesitation about stepping into the fray there.

'Just stay here.' He laid a comforting hand upon her arm and then he was gone, darting through the doorway like an avenger, keen to surprise whoever might still be inside.

Naomi pulled her phone from her coat pocket and stabbed at the buttons, dialling for the police. Once she'd reported the break-in, she stepped towards her flat, her legs trembling, her knees weak.

She'd heard no sounds from within. No sudden clashing of Titans, no battle, no fight for survival. Whoever had broken in must be long gone. Feeling sick, she peered through the doorway. 'Dr Williams?'

'It's okay. You can come in, there's no one here!'

She stepped forward, into the small hall and then through the doorway to her lounge-kitchen.

It was as if a typhoon had swept through it. Sofa cushions had been tossed around, her coffee table knocked over and broken, her books strewn all over the floor. The few pictures she'd found at a market—nothing special, just bright prints—were on the floor, their frames smashed, the glass cracked and broken.

All of her precious belongings had been tossed around, as if they were nothing but rubbish at a dump. The sense of loss and devastation was overwhelming. With her hand over her face, she began to feel a tremble overtake her body, until she was shuddering and shaking, sobs gasping from her body as if every intake of breath were a desperate struggle for survival.

Tom frowned from his place in the kitchen and stood awkwardly as she cried.

She had no idea how long she stood there like that, just crying. For the loss of her things, for the loss of her privacy, for the uncaring way in which her things had been used and tossed aside. She'd never claimed to be rich, or to have expensive objects that she treasured, but this had been her very first venture out into the world to stand on her own two feet alone. The items she'd gathered in that home might have been from car boot sales or markets or pound shops, but they'd been *hers*. They'd each been treasured and valued as they'd arrived in her home to take their place and make the hole that she was living in a beautiful, homely place to be. Or at least, an attempt at one.

That someone had forced their way in, breaking and trashing everything…well, it broke her heart. So she cried.

And she cried. Until suddenly she realised she wasn't crying any more and Tom had started trying to sort through her belongings. He'd been picking up books and ornaments, trying to straighten them, trying to return them to their rightful place.

She couldn't look him in the eye. Had she not embarrassed herself enough in front of this man, today? Falling from a ladder. Being rescued from a drunk. Being heard as she cried like a baby? That last had been the most horrifying. It was embarrassing. Crying always made other people feel incredibly awkward and she didn't need to look at him to know how much he wanted to leave, but was staying because he now felt obligated.

What am I putting this man through, today? The impression I'm making is terrible!

'It's okay, you can go. I'll wait here for the police. I'll deal with it. You must have things to do.'

'I'll stay.'

She found an old tissue in her pocket and she pulled it out to wipe her nose and then dab at her eyes. She must look a sight! Her eyes would be all puffy and her face all red...

'No, really, you don't have to...'

'I'll stay until you're done with the police. Then, you'll need someplace to go. I won't feel safe with you sleeping here on your own tonight. It won't be secure.'

'The police will fix the door.'

'With a sheet of *plyboard*. Hardly Fort Knox. I won't leave you here with that as your sole defence against the world in this neighbourhood.'

A short brief smile found its way onto her ravaged features. She was appreciative of his kindness. He clearly wasn't all gruffness. 'Thank you.'

'Now you ought to check to see if anything's missing.'

She nodded. He was right. There were only a few things that really meant anything to her. Her photos of her and Vincent. Her old wedding ring in her bedside table that she never wore to work, as jewellery wasn't allowed.

Alone in the bedroom, she made the grim discovery that the ring was gone, stolen. Along with some cheaper bits of jewellery that she'd bought and an old watch.

She felt strangely empty as she recounted what was missing to the police when they arrived.

Throughout it all, Tom was kind and attentive. He just sat there and listened to her ramble, making them both a cup of tea and heaping hers with sugar for the shock.

Although it had been caused by a terrible situation, Naomi found herself enjoying their conversation. Just sitting and talking to someone. Something she hadn't truly experienced since Vincent had passed. She missed him greatly, but she knew he was in a better place. No longer in pain. No longer a prisoner in his own body. No longer feeling guilty for what he'd done to her life.

So it was nice just to sit and talk. Even if it was only happening because she'd been burgled!

Her first day at work had gone fine. It was only the things that had happened *after* her shift that had been so awful! Now, after being berated by her boss and saved by him from physical assault, she was being comforted by him. He might not be the most smiley individual in the world, but he was being kind.

'You need to pack some clothes for an overnight stay.'

'Right.' He was right. Being practical would also help to take her mind off what had happened. She couldn't stay here. The place felt violated. Dirty. She didn't want to have to stay there a moment longer than she had to. 'You're right...'

'What is it?'

She bit her lip. 'I have nowhere to go.'

'You must have family?'

'They're all up north. A four-hour drive away.'

He frowned. 'Friends?'

'I've just moved here. I don't know anyone.'

'Of course not.' He let out a heavy sigh, his hands on his hips. 'A hotel?'

She winced at having to admit it. 'I couldn't afford it.'

'Right. I suppose you'll have to come to mine, then. For the night. I can take you to work in the morning, too.'

Naomi tried hard not to show how horrified she was by the thought of having to share a living space with the one man whom she'd humiliated herself in front of so much today.

She couldn't stay at his. They'd only just met and, yes, he was her boss, but he was also a prickly individual, standoffish and cool. He already clearly thought of her as incompetent and now he was offering to share his home with her...

Seriously...she couldn't accept his offer.

'That's very gracious of you, but—'

'Then it's settled. Pack your things and let's get going.'

Her mouth dropped open for a moment and when she became aware that she probably looked like a landed goldfish, she closed it again and headed to her bedroom.

I can't believe I'm doing this.

CHAPTER TWO

NAOMI WAS IN her bedroom, packing her clothes into a suitcase, as Tom sat on the torn-up sofa and stared into space.

Nurse Naomi Bloom.

What had happened?

He'd been his usual work-focused self. He'd been on call all night in the hospital and then he'd worked a full twelve-hour shift in A&E on top of that. He always did what was needed. Worked hard. He treated patients and kept his mind on work.

It was what worked for him. The work was a salve. A sticking plaster over the savage gash that was his heart. If he worked, if he took care of patients, if he investigated *their* ills, then he didn't have to focus on his own. His own pain. His own grief. Work kept the hurt firmly in its box where he never had to pay it any attention.

He'd been on his way home. Heading back for a shower, a change of clothes, maybe a quick four-hour nap. Then he'd planned on coming back to work.

But then he'd seen this woman climbing up a wobbly ladder, a ladder she should never have been up in the first place, on her own. He'd seen her reaching out for things that she hadn't got a chance in hell of reaching.

He'd seen how badly it had wobbled and he'd dropped his own briefcase and caught her, feeling the weight of her fall into his arms. He'd looked into her eyes up close, those pools of liquid brown, flecked with gold and green, and had felt a smack of something hard in his gut.

He'd intended to give her a dressing-down there and then. To yell at her for being so stupid and complacent, but in the fall her long hazelnut hair had come loose of its clip and lain over his arm, soft and silken, and it had taken a moment for him to realise that he'd been staring at her for much too long and that he really ought to let her go. The way you let go of a dangerous animal before it could bite or sting you.

She'd been unthinking in her actions. She'd assumed she would be okay, that somehow the rules didn't apply to her, and she'd been wrong.

Her beauty had thrown him briefly. There had been a second, maybe two, in which he'd momentarily been stunned by those chocolate eyes of hers, but then he'd cast those distracting thoughts to one side.

So she was attractive. So what? Beauty counted for nothing in his department. He needed solid workers. Excellent nurses. Team players. People who played by the rules. Not lone rangers who thought the whole world ought to revolve around them.

She'd blushed, looked embarrassed and had glanced down and away from him. His insides had twisted at her sweetness, flipping and tumbling like an acrobat in the Cirque du Soleil and the sensation had so startled him that he'd almost been unable to speak.

Offering to help her with the tree had seemed logical. Gentlemanly. A way for him to gather his thoughts and re-actions. To make sure she stayed safe. And give him time to put his own walls back up.

But it had been more than that. Exactly what, he

couldn't say. It had been a long time since a woman had disturbed him like that.

Not since Meredith...

He looked at the rest of Naomi's things dashed across the floor and started to pick them up again, trying to find places for them, trying to find order in the chaos.

He hadn't thought about Meredith for ages.

But that was a good thing surely. It meant he was moving on, didn't it? For too long, it had been a painful, persistent memory. When he'd thought of his wife, it had been about the days following the accident—sitting at her bedside in hospital, holding her hand, praying that she would wake, praying that she would recover. Holding out hope for her.

As the years had passed, the better memories of his time with Meredith had come to the fore. He was able to remember the good times they'd shared. Their happiness on their wedding day. Their love. The pain and grief was still inside would still torment him when he allowed it to, but it had taken on a different form recently.

His vow to never get involved with another woman, never to open his heart up to another, had held strong. He could never love another the way he'd loved his wife; it just wasn't possible.

Until now, he'd never had to doubt himself, or feel that that vow was threatened in any way.

Yet something about Naomi Bloom needled him. In the short time he'd known her, she'd practically demanded his attention, his protection, his help. He'd been forced to get involved. No decent man would have left her to fend for herself with Mick. No gentleman would have walked away from her after the burglary. When he'd found out she had nowhere to go, there'd been no other sensible option but to ask her to stay.

It would be difficult having her in his home. But he could stay out of her way. It would be all above board. She could have Meredith's old craft room that he'd turned into a spare bedroom during one mad weekend of decorating before he'd thought of what to do with his time and his life to cope with his grief.

One night to allow Naomi to get proper locks for her doors, better security. It was just about one colleague helping another. It was about being a decent human being.

One night only.

She opened her bedroom door and came out, lugging a heavy suitcase with her. He got up to take it from her and lifted it easily. 'A lot of clothes for one night!'

'I'd rather not leave anything here to be stolen. Just in case.'

'Is there anything else you want to take?'

'There was some paperwork, but I've packed that away. I'm ready to go.'

He nodded. 'I guess we'd better get going, then. Are you hungry? Would you like me to pick us up something to eat on the way home?'

'Oh! Well, only if you're eating, too. I don't want to get in your way or disrupt your routine any more than I already have.'

'You haven't disrupted me at all,' he said, picking up her case and heading for the front door, hoping she couldn't see the lie in his eyes.

They walked back to the hospital car park in silence. He put her suitcase in the boot of his car and then opened the passenger door for her. She looked surprised, smiled a thank you and then slid into the seat. He closed her door and walked round to his side, his mind going a mile a minute.

The only woman to have set foot in his home had been

Meredith and that was, of course, because she had lived there. Now he would be bringing home a stranger, a very attractive stranger, one who he hoped he could keep his distance from until she moved out. It ought to be easy, he thought. His penthouse flat was pretty large, and it was just one night.

If all else fails, I'll just put on my headphones and wear a blindfold.

Dr Williams's home was amazing. She'd never seen anything like it. She felt like Cinderella—going from her poor, ragamuffin lifestyle to this rich, sumptuous, stunning elegance that all seemed too much to take in.

His flat was on the top floor, not the bottom, like hers. The square footage must have been in the thousands and the space was open-plan, all glass windows, wooden floors and soft leather sofas. It had a minimalist element to it but looked nothing like what she'd expected from a single man. There were even fresh flowers on top of a grand piano in the corner of the living room.

He saw her notice them. 'My cleaner brings them in.'

She nodded, touching the long green stems. 'That's kind of her.'

'She insists. Tells me it brightens up the place. Makes it welcoming.' He didn't sound convinced.

'She's right.' Her fingers slid over the smooth black sheen of the piano. 'You play?'

He nodded. 'A little. You?'

She blew out a little puff of air. 'I could probably manage chopsticks if you reminded me how to do it.'

He smiled grimly, a darkness to his eyes. Was there pain there? Something… As if a part of him was missing. Or as if there was a part he was hiding, or at least trying to.

'You have a lovely home, Dr Williams.'

'Tom.'

She looked at him and smiled, feeling strange using his first name like that. 'Tom, okay.'

He looked about him as if seeing the flat for the first time. 'Let me show you to your room. Then you can settle, or I could make us something to eat. You must be hungry—it's been a long night.'

'You cook?'

'Yes.'

'From scratch?'

'Is there any other way?' He pulled up the handle on her suitcase and wheeled it across the floor behind him.

Naomi followed him down a corridor and through a door and suddenly she found herself standing in a bedroom that was as big as her whole flat. 'Wow. It's beautiful.'

'There's closet space…plenty of hangers. The bathroom is back through here; it's the door to your right.'

She followed him through the doorway into the bathroom and the light came on all by itself, controlled by a sensor. She smiled and glanced at her reflection in the mirror. She looked a mess! Her face was pale, yet blotchy and her hair all over the place, whereas Tom stood beside her, coolly detached, perfectly groomed.

Stepping out of the bathroom, she ran a hand through her hair in an effort to control it. 'I'll probably have a bath, if that's okay?'

'Sure.'

'Thank you, Tom. For everything. You've gone above and beyond today.' Her voice began to wobble as she spoke and she swallowed hard, forcing back the tears of gratitude. She hated crying when she didn't mean to, but sometimes it seemed like her body was just so overwhelmed by certain stressful situations that she couldn't stop herself.

But she would not cry in front of him again!

He simply smiled and backed away, most likely pleased to be escaping her tumultuous existence.

Naomi went back to the spare room and sank onto the bed, looking around her. What curious twist of fate had intervened in her life today? A new job. A burglary. And a soft place to fall. At least for tonight.

Sighing, she pulled off her coat and hung it up on the back of the door. She'd run herself a bath, maybe have a bite to eat and then hopefully she'd get a good night's sleep.

She didn't expect she would. It had been one heck of a day! And now she was suddenly living in her boss's home. That felt…odd. She didn't know him and the understanding he must have of her at this point was tenuous. He obviously didn't let people get too close. Everything about the man screamed 'keep away!' but he'd been generous and offered her a bed for the night when she'd had no other choice. That was good of him, right?

She was going to have to think of a way to thank him for this.

A huge thank you indeed.

Tom stood in his kitchen furiously whisking eggs for some omelettes. It felt strange knowing that he wasn't alone. That there was someone else in his home. A woman. A beautiful woman. And a work colleague, no less.

That would get the hospital grapevine going, no doubt. Especially if they arrived for work tomorrow together in his car. Perhaps he could let her get out at an earlier point?

He shook his head. Was he really that rude? Or worried about his reputation? Of course not. Everyone knew him at work. He was dedicated, honest, hard-working. No lad-about-town, causing outrageous rumours.

Besides, they might be lucky. No one might notice.

Naomi was in Merry's room. The room she had used

as a craft room, making cards, decoupage and that other thing she'd done…quilling? Or something like that. She'd been so talented at it. Sometimes he'd gone into that room to see what she was working on and had been amazed at this beautifully constructed hummingbird or peacock or mythical creature, all made out of coloured curls of paper. He remembered her smiling face looking up at him and saying, 'What do you think?'

And now Naomi was in there. Did she know? Could she sense it? He'd barely been able to stay in there and it had taken all his strength to redecorate it. To change it from what it had been. To take away the pain of the once pale blue walls.

They were a peach colour now. He'd not been in there since he'd painted it, except to change the bedding.

All the crafting stuff was gone, packed away. Some of it he'd given away. Instead, he'd installed a big wrought-iron bed in there along with bespoke beech furniture. It was all very plain. Simple. For guests. Not that he'd been expecting any guests. But if he gave the room a purpose, rather than it just lying empty, he could forget about his dreams for that room and what he'd once hoped it would turn out to be.

A nursery. Because one day, he and Merry would have tried to start a family. They'd talked about it anyway…

It would never be that now. And now it was Naomi's room. For one night anyway.

He tried to focus on the eggs, on grating cheese, on slicing courgettes and mushrooms, but his brain kept on torturing him with the image of her eyes, the way she'd looked up at him when he'd caught her falling from that ladder.

This was crazy! Why should it bother him what her eyes had looked like? Or that her skin had been smooth like porcelain, that her lips had looked full and soft? They were just work colleagues. Just associates. He was helping her out.

He whisked the eggs harder, trying not to think about her. He tried to focus on all the work he needed to get through tomorrow, but he could only envision her face and the way she'd felt in his arms...

Cursing, he put down the bowl of eggs and just stood still for a moment. Perhaps what he needed was a breather. A moment of mindfulness, to get himself back on track. He thought of the patients he'd seen that day. Their cases. The injuries. The treatments. The protocols.

Yes. That was working.

The door to the guest room opened and out walked Naomi in a thigh-length robe, with her hair all scooped up in a towel.

He quickly picked up the eggs and whisked them some more. 'Are you hungry?'

'I'm starving.'

'Good.' He tried not to breathe in all the aromas that she'd somehow brought out with her. There was a hint of lavender and something else sweet, warm and clean. She perched herself on a stool at his breakfast bar and he saw long, toned legs and dainty feet with pink-painted toenails. 'I'll make a start, then.'

'Can't wait.'

He swallowed hard and turned his back.

CHAPTER THREE

SHE WOKE WITH a start, a bad dream about smelly men in balaclavas still in her consciousness as she blinked quickly and looked about the strange room. Then she remembered. *Tom's.*

She glanced at the clock on the bedside table. Five-forty-two a.m. It was early. But she had to be at work at seven, ready for the shift handover at seven-fifteen, so there didn't seem much point in trying to go back to sleep. She'd be getting up in twenty minutes anyway. Throwing off the covers, she got up and quickly made her bed, before getting dressed.

She moved quietly, hoping not to disturb Tom. She'd already put him out enough yesterday, especially last night when her presence had meant he couldn't even relax in his own home. The last thing she wanted was to wake him early and disturb his sleep pattern.

He was a good man, she thought. Despite the prickly exterior. He'd opened his home to a complete stranger, giving her the space she'd needed to just settle and breathe and get over her stressful day.

After their omelettes last night—which, due to something magical he'd done with Tabasco sauce and tomatoes, had been the most incredible she had ever tasted—he had wished her goodnight and disappeared to his room. She had watched him go, silent and strong, his long, lean figure moving gracefully like a cat into the shadows.

She'd taken the opportunity to look around his living space and discovered that Dr Tom Williams seemed very much a solitary man. There was no room for sentiment here. Each piece of furniture or decor had been chosen for its aesthetic appeal, rather than being some old family heirloom. There were no pictures on the walls of family or loved ones, no photo albums. Every surface was clean and uncluttered and only his bookshelves showed some hint to his character—clearly work focused, as all his books had been medical texts.

Was work all he thought about? She saw no sign of any other interest. There were no knick-knacks lying around like those she'd had all over the place. No personal touches. There was just the piano and, even then, she wondered if that was for him to play, or just another element of style. The only homely touch—the flowers—had been brought in by his cleaner.

But Naomi was thankful that he was focused on his work. Because apart from that small chat they'd had whilst he'd been preparing food in the kitchen, he had left her alone. He'd given her space, stayed out of her way.

It was his home and he was hiding in it. Perhaps he wasn't that thrilled to have her here after all? Perhaps he had felt compelled to suggest that she stay with him because he thought it was the gentlemanly thing to do. Tom certainly seemed like a gentleman, from the little she knew of him.

Still, she felt safe getting up this early and having a few minutes to herself before he surfaced. Perhaps she could make him a coffee and some toast, or cereal. She had no idea if he would be a cereal type of man. A quick look in his kitchen would tell her what she wanted to know. But it would be good to do something nice *for him* to show her appreciation. After all, later today she would be out of his hair.

She opened her bedroom door and was surprised to find all the lights on and Tom already up and about in his kitchen. He looked over at her. 'Good morning. Sleep well?'

She wasn't used to being greeted like that in the mornings, even when she'd been married. Back then, she'd fall sleep, exhausted, after a long, physical day and when she woke and went into her husband's room, the first words out of his mouth would usually be to tell her what sort of a night he'd had. Whether he'd got any sleep at all. There had been no *hellos*. No *good mornings*.

'I slept very well, thank you. You?'

'Seven hours. Can I get you anything? Coffee? Breakfast?'

She stood on the opposite side of the breakfast bar. 'I was going to make *you* breakfast. I didn't think you'd be up yet.' She saw he must have been up for quite a while—his hair was still slightly damp from the shower, the auburn a deeper red whilst it was wet, and his jawline was freshly shaved.

'What would you like?'

'Just toast for me.'

'Anything on it? Jam? Honey? Marmalade?'

'You have all of those?' She smiled.

'I do.'

She liked watching him in the kitchen. He seemed at home in it. 'Marmalade will be lovely.'

He cut two fresh slices from a large bloomer and popped the bread in the toaster, then poured her a coffee from a cafetière and passed her the milk and sugar.

'You're very domesticated, Dr Williams.'

He paused briefly to consider her words. 'Because I can make toast and pour coffee?'

'Because you know how to make someone feel welcome. I can appreciate it must be hard to have a stranger in your home, but you've made me feel like it's okay to be here, so…thank you.'

His ocean-blue eyes met her mocha brown just for a brief second. He gave a quick glance of gratitude, of appreciation and then looked away again, busying himself with the breakfast. 'Any idea of what you're going to do about your flat?'

He was changing the subject. She wondered if she'd made him uncomfortable. 'I don't know. I've got work first, so I guess I'll have to sort it out later.'

'Everywhere will be closed later. Why don't you take the day off?'

'On my second day? No chance. No, I'll just have to hope for the best. Find someone to fix the door somewhere…'

He looked torn, as if he had something to say, but couldn't say it.

The toast popped up and he handed it over on a plate, piping hot, along with a choice of marmalades, one with bits and one without.

'Oh…er…thank you.'

'It's no problem.'

She hoped he was telling the truth.

'Josephine McDonald?'

Her first patient of the day had already been seen by the triage nurse, who had noted on her card that earlier that day Josephine had misused her father's nail gun and had a six-inch nail shot through the end of her index finger.

Naomi looked out across the waiting room and watched

as a young woman stood up, grimaced and then walked over to her, clutching at her left hand that was wrapped up in a tea towel.

It was an impressive-looking nail.

'Let's take a look at that, shall we?' Naomi walked Josephine back to a cubicle and sat her down, pulling the curtain closed. 'So, how did this happen?' She took hold of her patient's hand, slowly turning it this way and that, to see what damage had been caused.

'I was helping my dad out with a job. He's a carpenter and he was letting me use the nail gun. I got…distracted… and somehow my finger ended up getting pierced.'

Naomi could understand. She was the accidental type, too. 'What distracted you?'

Josephine blushed. 'A guy.'

Naomi smiled at her patient. 'Oh. I see. Was he worth it?'

Josephine nodded enthusiastically. 'Oh, yes! Definitely!' She sighed dramatically. 'What can I say? A girl gets her head turned by a handsome man and *always* gets hurt.'

Naomi smiled again and checked for capillary refill on the girl's nail, which was fine, and stroked her finger. 'Can you feel this? And this?'

'Yes.'

'Good. I don't think there's any nerve damage. Can you bend the finger?'

'Yes. But I can feel it pulling on the nail.'

'We'll need an X-ray to make sure it's not gone through the bone and if you get the all-clear we can pull it out. Have you had a tetanus shot recently?'

Josephine blanched. 'I think so. Just a year or two ago. Pull it out? Won't that hurt?'

'We'll do a nerve block beforehand and you can suck

on some gas and air if you need it. Is your father with you? Someone to hold your hand?'

'Dad's in the waiting area.'

'Didn't you bring the hot guy with you?'

'Er…no. Apparently he doesn't do well with blood.'

'Right.' She smiled.

'What can you do? You see a hot guy, you have to give him the old "come hither" look. I just wasn't coordinated enough to be alluring *and* shoot a nail.'

Naomi smiled, trying to picture herself giving anyone a 'come hither' look. But then she stopped herself. Why would she do that? She wasn't looking for a relationship. She was happy being single and independent for a while. This was her first foray into the world alone, without her mother sticking her oar in, or without having to consider her husband's needs. She was finally free to do as she pleased.

'It's not bleeding, so let's get you round to X-ray.' She turned in her chair, reaching for the X-ray referral card, and filled in the details. 'Take this—' she handed it over and reopened the cubicle curtain '—and head straight down, follow the red line on the floor, round to the right and past the second set of chairs. Put the card in the slot and they'll call you through when they're ready.'

'Thanks.'

She watched the patient walk away and then started to clean down the cubicle. They hadn't really used it, but she stripped the bed of its paper sheet, wiped it down with clinical cleansing wipes and redid the sheet. As she did so the cubicle curtain next to hers was whipped open. 'Dr Williams!'

Was her heart beating just a little faster than normal? It definitely felt that way. She took a steadying breath to calm herself and inwardly gave herself a dressing-down.

There was no need to get nervous with the man. He was her boss, yes, but that was all he was. She'd be moving out of his flat later.

'Nurse Bloom.'

He dismissed his patient, who hobbled away on newly acquired crutches, and then he turned back to smile at her. He looked very dashing today in his dark navy trousers and matching waistcoat against a crisp white shirt. She had to admit she did like a man that dressed well. Vincent had always worn quite loose-fitting clothes like tracksuit bottoms and T-shirts. They had been the easiest things to dress him in and he'd liked to feel comfortable whilst in his wheelchair. So to see a man who knew how to dress well, who took pride in his appearance, without being vain, was a nice thing to see and enjoy.

'The department looks decidedly less Christmassy today.'

She laughed good-naturedly. 'Yes. There should be hearts going up soon, in readiness for Valentine's.' She blushed slightly at the inference she'd made that it was time for hearts and romance. Her mind scrabbled to redirect their conversation. 'Or perhaps eggs for Easter? I'm sure the shops have them already.'

'You like to celebrate all the holidays?'

Naomi shrugged as she walked alongside him back to the central desk where a lot of the staff filled in paperwork or checked information on the computer. 'Well, I like the chocolate aspect. Is that wrong?'

'Absolutely not. In fact, I think it's almost law.' He sat down at the desk, opened his file and started writing his notes.

She noted his hands. He had fine hands, with long fingers, like a pianist's. So, perhaps he did play that beautiful instrument in his home. He wore a simple band on his middle finger, which might have been tungsten, or platinum. It looked as if it could be a wedding band, but it was on the wrong digit.

It's none of my business.

Irritated with her own response to that thought, Naomi picked up the next card from triage and glanced at it. It was a child with a head wound. As she went to leave she heard Tom's voice call her name.

'Nurse Bloom?'

Turning, she looked at him, admiring the strong line of his jaw, the flicker of muscle as he clenched and unclenched it, as if he were debating with himself. 'Yes?'

'When you have a moment…when you have a break, would you come and find me? There's something I'd like to run past you.'

Run past me?

'Have I done something wrong?' She frowned, not knowing what it could be and worried that she might be in trouble again already. Now her heart really *was* pounding in her chest.

'No. Just…something personal. That's all.'

'Oh. Okay.'

Something personal.

That's all.

She wondered what it could be. Maybe she'd done something she shouldn't have done back at his flat. Had she left something out of place? Not put the lid back on the toothpaste, or something? He might be picky about things like that. It had certainly been neat. Everything in its place…

Worried, she headed back to the waiting room and called her next patient.

After she'd seen the child with the head injury, Naomi dealt with an elderly lady with a bad chest infection, then a sprained wrist and after that a young man with a build-up of blood behind his fingernail that needed releasing. Whilst she treated them all, she worried about what it was that Tom was going to ask her.

Something personal.

If it had nothing to do with work, then what could it be? He knew nothing about her, really. She'd made her bed in the flat. She'd cleaned up after herself, and been the perfect guest, hopefully. As her break time arrived she let the sister know she was going and then she began to look for Tom, her stomach in knots, her mouth dry.

She did *not* need complications. She'd had enough of those to last a lifetime. This was the start of her *new* life. She'd moved away from her old one and had come here to London, to the city, to prove to herself that she was independent and strong and could live her own life, with her own rules. This was her chance to be free of routine and stress. To only have to worry about herself.

Maybe he was going to ask her to make sure she moved out by the end of the day. She hoped not. After a full day shift until four p.m., she'd be lucky to have time to get back to her flat on St Bartholomew's Road and then find someone to fix her door, or a locksmith to add locks. She also wondered how much it would all cost. She didn't have bags of money and the small amount of savings she did have was meant to go towards a deposit on a better place. It wasn't supposed to pay for repairs to an old flat she didn't even like!

Tom was at the doctors' desk when she finally found him.

'Tom. I'm on my break now.' She fidgeted with the pens in her top pocket and straightened her fob watch.

'Let's grab a coffee and a bite to eat.'

He walked her up to the cafeteria and bought both of

them a cappuccino. He ordered a grilled breakfast for himself and when he asked her what she wanted she just shook her head. 'You've got to have something.' He placed a yoghurt and a banana onto his tray and, once he'd paid for it, they settled down at a table.

'You're probably wondering what this is about?'

She smiled and watched him tuck into his food with gusto. It did smell delicious and she tried to ignore the gorgeous scent of bacon and what smelt like pork and leek sausage as she opened her peach yoghurt. 'You've got me curious.'

'I want to help you.'

She sat in the seat opposite, staring at him, waiting for the axe to fall. 'Okay.'

'In the interests of my wanting the department to run smoothly, I'd like you to feel you could stay at my place. For an extra day or two whilst you get your flat sorted.'

'Stay? I thought—'

'It's not ideal, I know, but I've been thinking about your situation and I would feel remiss if you felt that you had to leave when your circumstances aren't exactly sorted.'

She blushed. Wow. She had not been expecting that. 'That's very generous of you, Tom. Thank you.'

He sipped his coffee. 'Not generous. I'm just being practical.'

Practical. Right.

Tom saw her face change. The uncertainty and nervousness that had been there a moment before dissipated and surprise and relief manifested themselves instead.

He'd almost been as surprised about the offer himself. If someone had asked him yesterday whether he'd have taken in a waif or stray, he would have said no. If someone had asked him if he would then have offered that beautiful

young woman the chance to stay in his own home for a few
more days he would have said they were crazy.

Last night he'd felt uncomfortable with her being there.
He'd made as little interaction as he could get away with
without being rude. But he'd looked out for her, cooked for
her, talked to her a little and had found himself intrigued.
He was interested by this woman whom he'd suddenly acquired in his department and in his life.

Not that he was interested in her in *that way*. There was
no point in pursuing that. There was only ever one true
love, one true soulmate for a person, and he'd already met
his, even if she had been taken from him too soon. Meredith had been killed in a tragic accident that had taken
her from him before they'd even had their first full year
of marriage. His heart had truly belonged to her and now
he kept it locked away, safe and protected from the outside
world where cruel things happened and people in love were
tormented. No, there were going to be no more women for
Tom Williams.

They were off-limits. Even if last night he'd been
plagued with thoughts of Naomi in the next room. He'd lied
to her about getting that good night's sleep. He should have
had seven hours. But instead, he'd lain in his bed, thinking
about her, seeing those long legs that had emerged after her
bath, gazing into those eyes of hers that he couldn't bear to
look at for longer than a second in case she saw the *interest* in his own eyes. Oh, and the way that she laughed. The
way her whole face lit up with genuine joy when she did.

So he couldn't allow himself to think about Naomi. She
was everything that went against his self-imposed rules.
But he *could* help her with her living situation.

'This is so unexpected.'

He nodded. 'Yes. But expecting you to get your place
sorted in one night seems both impossible and imprac-

tical. St Bartholomew's Road? It's not a nice place. I'm sorry. I'm not normally judgemental, but you seem to deserve…better.'

'And I can stay at yours for the next few days?'

'Yes.'

'I can't believe it! That's so sweet of you. Are you sure? Don't you want to know more about me? I mean, I could be a crazy axe murderer, or something.'

'I know enough. And if you handled an axe on a regular basis, I'm sure you'd be missing a limb or something by now, from what I've seen so far. My place is big enough for us both to be able to do our own thing. We won't get in each other's way. And then, with a few days' grace, you can find a better flat. Something more suitable.'

'Less rough, you mean?'

'Less…challenging.' He smiled at her quickly, then looked away. He'd been thinking hard about this all morning. Did he really want to do this? Could he really open up his home to a stranger? It had already been odd having her there in Meredith's old room. It had been strange knowing she was there doing whatever it was that women did when they spent ages in the bathroom, but…he could arrange it for them so they had different shift patterns so that they wouldn't be running into each other all the time.

Naomi sat forward and this time sipped her drink, thinking carefully. 'Why do you want to help me?'

Because I can't get you out of my head and the idea of you living in that dump terrifies me.

'Because I think anyone would deserve better.' He couldn't tell her it was because he'd actually quite liked seeing her there this morning. He'd liked having someone to talk to, even if it was only briefly, over breakfast. Normally, once he was dressed, he'd head straight out to work, not talking to another soul until he arrived.

This morning had been different and he'd found he liked it. It had been like it had when Meredith was around.

Meredith.

Was he doing something wrong? No. No, he wasn't. But why then did he suddenly feel so guilty, when he was only trying to be kind?

The sooner the next few days were over, the better.

Living in Tom's flat was beyond her wildest dreams. She never would have imagined herself in a place such as this and yet here she was.

Naomi stroked her fingers along the kitchen surfaces, smiling in appreciation at the clean, smooth lines of the beech woodwork and the frosted etched glass in some of the cupboard doors. It was a dream home and she was living in it! If only for a little while.

Her suitcase, which she'd only partially unpacked the night before, was now empty, and all her things were hanging in the wardrobe.

Tom had given her a lift home and he was getting changed, whilst she'd offered to cook for them both. Not that she was a great cook. Or any cook at all, truth be told. Most things she cooked came out of tins or packets. 'Add an egg' recipes were the most adventurous she usually got. She looked through his cupboards to see what she could use.

In the fridge there was a large steak. She could cut that into two and maybe make some mashed potatoes and he had fine beans and broccoli. She started peeling and chopping and soon had a couple of pans on the boil, as Tom came out into the living area. 'You're cooking?'

'I am. Steak.'

'Sounds good.'

He *looked* good. He'd changed into some black jeans

and a soft white fitted T-shirt, which showed off his beautifully toned arms to perfection. Who knew a chiselled god
existed under the suit he normally wore at work?

'How do you like it?'

'Medium, please.'

She nodded. 'Good.' Now she was stuck. 'Er...how will
I know when it's medium?'

Tom's face cracked into a near smile. 'Hold out your
hand.'

Her hand? What did he want with her hand? She held it
out and then watched as he modelled, using his index finger to touch the fleshy pad beneath his thumb. 'The way
the pad of flesh under your thumb feels? That would be
what a raw steak feels like. Put your index and thumb together. Feel it now? That's well done.'

She watched him and focused, replicating his actions
with her own, marvelling at how the different parts felt.

'Now press your ring finger and thumb together. That
pad is now medium.'

Naomi did them all again. 'That's brilliant!'

'I'm glad you like it. Now you'll know.'

'Now I'll know,' she repeated, picking up the broccoli
and rinsing it under the tap. 'There is something I *don't*
know.'

'What's that?'

'How well you actually play that piano over there.' She
nodded in the direction of the piano and watched his face.

A strange mix of emotions passed over it and his eyes
clouded slightly. If she had blinked, she'd have missed it,
but she saw it happen. Something about playing the piano
had caused a bad memory.

'I haven't played for a long time.'

'No? Why not?' She knew she shouldn't press him, but

she was curious. Surely anyone who had such a beautiful instrument would play it as often as they could?

'Because I only ever played it for my wife.' Naomi watched as regret and grief filled his face and then he swept away from her and disappeared back to his room.

She stood in the kitchen, her hands pausing in their actions, her mouth slightly open. She hadn't known he was married.

But then…she remembered the ring on his finger. The wedding band.

I did know. I did! And now I've upset him.

She felt so foolish. It was only their second night together and she'd already ruined it. She'd upset her host, reminding him of a past he quite clearly didn't want to remember. Putting down the knife, she wiped her hands on a cloth and walked to his room, her knuckles raised ready to rap on the wood.

Only she paused.

Did she know him well enough to have an in-depth chat? Was it her place to pry into events he clearly didn't want to share? If he had wanted to talk to her about it, he wouldn't have gone to his room.

Clearly she shouldn't knock. Her hand lowered. Feeling redundant, she went back to the kitchen, her footsteps slow and heavy. Maybe he didn't want to discuss his wife and whatever might have happened there, but she could cook him an amazing steak and mash.

Well, I'll have a go anyway. Surely I can't get this wrong?

She turned on the small kitchen television and dropped the steaks into the sizzling oil.

Tom paced in his room. What the hell was he doing? Why had he reacted like that? What was he, twelve?

And what's that smell?

Feeling ridiculous, he yanked open the bedroom door, ready to apologise for his behaviour to Naomi, only to notice the kitchen area was filled with smoke and the smell of burning, his fire alarm suddenly squawking into life.

'What the...?' He rushed forward to see Naomi, gasping, flicking a towel at a burning pair of steaks, screaming every time she fanned the flames to even greater heights. 'Stop!' He pushed past her, turning off the gas, grabbed the tea towel and lowered it slowly over the flames, so that they were dowsed in an instant.

Naomi was coughing and spluttering. 'I'm so sorry! I don't know what happened.'

Tom grabbed another towel and began wafting it beneath the fire alarm, until he'd cleared away enough smoke for it to stop. Once silence reigned again and the alarm could only be heard as some sort of ghostly sound in their ears, he turned to her and raised his eyebrows in question.

'I'm so sorry, Tom. There was a cooking show on and they poured alcohol into the pan and tipped it somehow to...'

'Flambé?'

'Yes and it kind of worked.'

'Too well. How much alcohol did you put in there?'

'A splash.'

'Hmm.'

'I'm so sorry. I've never done it before and I so wanted to impress you with a good steak, after I upset you earlier...'

His face clouded over. 'It's okay. No one got hurt. Except the steaks.' He peered at the blackened bits of meat, so totally beyond rescue. To Naomi's surprise and disbelief pretty soon he was smiling, then laughing. She couldn't help but laugh, too, thrilled and delighted at how the expression lit up his entire face. It was as if he hadn't laughed properly in a long time.

When she got her breath back, she slumped onto one of the kitchen stools. 'You must think I'm a disaster area.'

He slid onto one of the stools beside her. 'A little. How on earth have you survived all these years?'

Her cheeks flamed. 'I became best friends with a microwave and meals where you only had to pierce lids before cooking.'

He smiled and shook his head. 'Has no one ever taught you to cook?'

She shook her head. 'My mother wasn't the best at passing on her skills. She didn't really have any, except for falling in love with the most unsuitable men she could find.'

He stared at her for a moment longer than was comfortable. Despite her hazardous skills in the kitchen and her total inability to not fall off ladders, he *liked* her. She was innocent and sweet and funny.

Don't.

Images of Meredith instantly flooded his mind and he felt guilty. Admiring another woman was wrong. He needed to think of something else. He shouldn't be thinking that it should be Merry standing with him in this kitchen, instead of Naomi. He pushed the guilty thoughts away. 'I'll teach you how to cook.'

'What?'

'I'll teach you.'

'But you've already saved me. Rehomed me. You don't have to turn me into a Michelin-starred chef, too.'

He picked up the pan with the charred remains and tipped it into the bin. 'Yes. I do. If we're going to survive this week.'

She sighed and smiled her thanks. 'Right. So…veg and mash?'

'There might be some fish fingers in the freezer.'

'I can manage those.'

He nodded in approval. 'Excellent. I'll await your culinary delights, forthwith.'

He laid the table and she brought over their steaming hot plates, laying one down in front of him.

It felt good to be serving someone a meal again. To sit down and just share that moment. They were simple pleasures. Even though she'd been looking forward to being free of all of that, to spending time alone, she suddenly found herself craving the company. 'I haven't done this in a long time.'

He looked up. 'Eaten fish fingers?'

She smiled. 'Shared a meal. It's good. You forget what that's like.'

He looked pensive, then he smiled back. 'Yeah.'

She pushed her broccoli around her plate, then patted the mash, sculpting it with her fork. She wanted to make him feel better, after she'd annoyed him earlier with that comment about his piano. Perhaps if he knew that she'd been through marriage and a loss, too, it would help. 'I was married, too, not so long ago.'

Tom took a drink of his water and met her gaze across the table.

'His name was Vincent and we were married for eight years.'

'Long time.'

'It was. Some days it seemed longer than that. Only afterwards, did I realise how short it actually was.'

Tom speared a piece of his broccoli. 'You don't have to tell me what happened, if you don't want to.'

But she did want to share it with him. If they were going to be sharing a flat, she saw no reason not to share with him part of her past. Besides, she thought he might be in-terested—in a medical sense. 'Fibrodysplasia ossificans progressiva happened.'

His fork stopped halfway to his mouth. 'Stone Man Syndrome? That's rare. Only about one person in every two million gets it.'

'Have you ever seen a case?'

'No.'

'Vincent had issues from a young age. It was noted when he was a baby that he had these deformed toes, but no one made the connection until later. At first it was bone growths in his neck and shoulders. When I met him, he was already in a wheelchair, confined to a sitting posi-tion, and he was in and out of hospital with pneumonia and lung infections.'

'It must have been difficult for you both.'

'It's hard to see someone you love become imprisoned within their own body, their own skeleton turning on them. The slightest injury caused another bone growth.'

Tom put down his knife and fork, totally focused on her story.

'I left work to become his full-time carer.'

'I'm sure he was an amazing man.'

She nodded. 'He was. Upbeat. Positive. As much as he could be until the end. He had his dark days, though.'

'Don't we all?' He looked down at the tablecloth. 'I'm sorry for your loss.'

She smiled and pushed away her plate. 'I managed not to burn the house down anyway. That was a bonus!' She picked up their plates and took them away into the kitchen, scraping the remains of the meal into the bin. It hadn't been the best thing she'd ever cooked, but it would do.

Tom came into the room and poured them both a glass

of wine. 'And what did you do to relax? When you weren't looking after your husband?'

She clinked her glass to his. 'Reading. Researching his disease. Looking for treatments, looking for medical trials. Anything that could help him.'

'And what did you do *for you*?'

'Me?' she asked, surprised by the question. 'I can't remember.'

He stared at her. Then he sipped his wine, thoughtfully.

CHAPTER FOUR

TOM FOUND THE next week difficult. It was harder than he'd imagined. He'd thought it would be a simple task of scheduling Naomi to work days and putting himself on late shifts or nights, so that he wouldn't be always in her space, or she in his, but somehow wherever he went, there were reminders—her perfume, her toothbrush in the bathroom, her little make-up bag sitting on the counter. And the times when they *did* find themselves at home or at work at the same time were even harder.

Once he came back to a darkened flat in the middle of the night, expecting her to be asleep. She had been. Only she'd fallen asleep on the sofa, with the television still playing, and he'd stood over her for a minute, just watching her sleep, her face so relaxed and peaceful. Then he'd felt guilty for watching her, aware she could have woken and found him standing there. So he'd hurried to his room and closed the door, lying on his bed and praying for sleep.

When he'd first met her, he'd been determined not to like her. But then he'd seen at work what a great nurse she was, what fabulous rapport she could achieve with even the most difficult of patients and at home…at home, she would make sandwiches for him and leave him notes pinned to the fridge, so he knew where to find them. She'd even attempted to bake some cookies one night and thankfully hadn't burned the place down in doing so. They'd been a little tough on the teeth, but he'd eaten them anyway, because she'd tried so hard.

She'd even made progress with getting her flat sorted. A few of their work colleagues knew people who knew other people and the plyboard door had been replaced with an old interior one. Her locks had been changed and she'd even had time to go over there and straighten the place up a bit.

Now, Tom had one more day with her before the 'few days' they'd talked about were up and he didn't know how he felt about that. For some reason he was a bit short-tempered with everyone. Irritable.

Tom and Naomi were both working in Resus, when an ambulance arrived with their first patient of the shift. She was an elderly woman, who was thin and frail with liver-spotted hands and patchy grey hair. Her pale pink nighty, edged with a thin line of lace, looked much too large for her tiny body.

The paramedic wheeled the patient into position. 'This is Una Barrow, eighty-nine years of age and a resident of Tall Oaks Care Home.' Tall Oaks was a residential home for patients with Alzheimer's. 'The care staff there grew concerned when she stopped eating and drinking yesterday and today she's got a temperature of thirty-eight point two, sats of ninety-three per cent and a blood pressure of ninety over sixty, which is usual for her. She wouldn't allow us to do a blood-sugar reading, she became combative and, due to her friable skin and past history of osteopenia, we didn't think it was worth the risk of injuring her. Hope that's okay, doc?'

Tom nodded. That was fine. They could get a blood-sugar reading for her here easily enough. 'Sure. Any other medical history?'

'Nothing of significance.'

'Family?'

'She has a daughter, but she lives over a hundred miles away. We got Tall Oaks to give her a ring and I believe she's on her way.'

Right. So it was best to try and get Una settled and sorted before the daughter arrived and then, hopefully, he would have good news to pass on.

'Okay, everyone, let's have a full top-to-toe assessment, please.'

He stood back, watching, listening, assessing, as his team, including Naomi, read out test results and observations. All obvious signs pointed to a urinary tract infection, but he'd need a urine sample to confirm the diagnosis.

Naomi was trying to get the blood sugar when suddenly Una clutched Naomi's hand.

'Rosie?' the elderly woman asked in a tremulous voice, staring off into the void.

'No, Una. I'm Naomi. A nurse. I'm here to look after you.' She gave the patient's hand a gentle squeeze, but Una tightened her grip and wouldn't let her go.

'Don't leave me, Rosie! They're trying to kill me!'

Tom watched as Naomi glanced back at him, signalling resignedly that she couldn't help with the assessments whilst the patient had a good firm hold of her hand.

He stepped forward. 'Una? I'm a doctor here and you're not in Tall Oaks any more. You're in hospital.'

Una blinked and focused on Tom's voice, her glazed eyes sliding from Naomi's face to his. 'Hospital?'

'That's right. You're safe. No one here will harm you, but you're not very well, Una. You've got a temperature and so we're going to make you feel better.'

She looked back to Naomi. 'Don't leave me here, Rosie.'

Tom glanced at Naomi and they shared a look. Alzheimer's was such a cruel disease, deftly taking away each and every day another small part of who someone was, often leaving them confused or frightened or, even worse, lucid, so that they had moments of knowing exactly what was happening to them. It was just as Naomi had faced with Vincent, those years and years of slowly losing someone.

Tom had also sat and watched Meredith slip away day by day. Luckily, she hadn't known what was happening to her.

But *he* had. He'd sat at the side of her bed, holding her lifeless hand, begging and praying that she would come back to him, and each day the doctors had reported a drop in her condition until those final, painful reports had indicated that she was to all intents and purposes brain-dead. By the end she'd only been kept alive by the ventilator. He and Meredith's parents had decided to turn off the machine keeping her alive, but it had been a horrible time, a horrible decision. Something he wouldn't wish on anyone. Just as he wouldn't wish Alzheimer's on anyone.

Tom caught Naomi's gaze, then spoke quietly. 'Let her think you're Rosie until the daughter gets here. It might make her feel better. Safer. We can get her blood sugar and urine sample from her if she's calm and relaxed.'

Naomi nodded, understanding. 'Okay. I'm here. It's all right.'

'Oh, my Rosie!' Una held Naomi's hand close to her chest and closed her eyes, seemingly more calm.

Naomi reached out to pull a plastic chair towards the side of the bed. Sinking into it, she smiled at Tom. 'She's got me held tight. I won't be escaping soon, I don't think.'

'That's okay. Hopefully the real Rosie will get here soon. Can you keep an eye on her? And note down her obs half-hourly?'

'Only because my writing hand is still free.' She

grabbed the patient's file, opening it and filling in what she could.

As Una's breathing deepened and she drifted off to sleep a male nurse, Stefan, came into Resus. 'Oh, Naomi…if only you'd hold *my* hand so intently!' Stefan was a dreadful flirt who, Tom knew, tried it on with most of the women in the hospital.

His skin prickled at the way he flirted so openly with Naomi.

Why should I let it bother me?

He stood over by the desk filling in his report at the computer station, keeping a subtle eye on them both.

Naomi simply smiled. 'I don't think it's your hand you want me to hold, Stefan,' she replied calmly, staring down at Una, keeping her voice regulated and not doing anything to disturb the sleeping patient.

Stefan laughed, collected the sterile pack he'd come in for and then headed back to the double doors. 'Ah, you know me too well, sweet girl. But I guess I can't compete with Dr Williams here. My pigeon chest can't outdo his six pack, can it? Must be nice seeing that in the morning, eh?'

As Stefan pushed through the doors, leaving them swinging back and forth, Tom looked to Naomi in shock.

Were they the subject of gossip already? How on earth had that happened? Naomi had been staying at his place for less than a week and *he* hadn't told anyone. He wondered if she had. Maybe they had simply been spotted leaving and arriving together on the few days they'd worked the same hours.

A surge of irritability flooded through him and he almost snapped his pen in half. He hated gossip. It distorted everything. The grapevine probably had blown the whole innocent affair out of proportion. God only knew what they were saying!

But what he really didn't like was the idea that his reputation was being run through the mud. Or Naomi's for that matter. They were just flatmates. Plain and simple. And it was only a temporary arrangement, which should be ending soon. Her old flat was practically sorted anyway and she would be able to start looking for a new place in earnest.

'Naomi…have you told anyone about our arrangement?'

She shook her head, looking just as shocked as he felt. 'No.'

'Two plus two is going to equal five unless we put a lid on this.'

'It's just gossip. They'll soon get bored.'

'Will they? I think you're more optimistic than I am.'

Tom looked at Naomi, her hand still in the patient's tight grasp. She had a simple beauty, an elegant face with regal features. Tom wondered if she knew she could probably be a model if she wanted to be. She didn't seem to be aware of her looks. Her long brown hair was always loosely gathered up into a clip and it never looked as if she'd spent hours styling it, but *still* it always looked amazing, soft and silken, deftly pulled this way and that, held in place by a pin or two. She wore no jewellery that he'd noticed, but she didn't need it. There was enough sparkle and colour in her eyes alone. Those deep chocolate pools captured him every time she looked at him. She had a very small beauty mark on her right cheek and soft, full pink lips. When she smiled, the effect it had on his insides was, simply put, devastating. He hated to admit it to himself but he was being pulled in by her lure.

Stefan and any of the other gossipmongers would have a field day with their idle rumours. It just wouldn't occur to them that the relationship he had with Naomi was completely innocent and above board. Surely anyone would take one look at Naomi's gorgeous good looks and assume that he would be trying to seduce her. They wouldn't assume anything else.

And I don't want to enforce their rumours.

He needed to try and create some space away from her and stop the rumour mill in its tracks. Asking her to stay had been a terrible decision.

'Any luck with flat-hunting?' He knew it was an abrupt change of subject and in direct contradiction of what he'd said to her the other day. Maybe he'd made a mistake. Maybe he shouldn't have encouraged her to get comfy and put her feet beneath his table. He really ought to be helping her to find a place to live. Then he could have his sanctuary back. His private place. His home. A place only for him and his memories.

'Um…no, nothing suitable yet.' She looked a little stunned by his change of topic and, although he felt guilty for making her feel that maybe she wasn't as welcome as she'd previously thought, he reminded himself that this was about self-preservation.

He didn't need complications in his life. Work was where he came to forget. It was the place where he thrived, where he felt safe, and if he couldn't feel that in the hospital, if it became yet another place where he felt uncomfortable, then he had no idea how he would survive.

'You might be needed in Majors, Nurse Bloom. Release yourself from the patient and go and check with them next door, please.' He knew he was being abrupt and he hated himself for it.

She looked up at him as if puzzled, but then she nodded and turned back to Una to see if she could slip her hand away, unnoticed.

She finally managed it. Stepping away, she quietly slid

Una's file into the space at the bottom of her bed. 'Who'll do her obs?'

'I will.'

'Okay. If you're sure.' When she disappeared through the doors, leaving him alone in Resus, he ran his fingers through his hair in exasperation and let out a heavy sigh.

What on earth was going on inside his head?

Majors had enough staff, but just as she was about to go back to Resus, Naomi saw a middle-aged woman walking through the department, looking lost and confused. 'Can I help you?' she asked.

The woman suddenly looked relieved to be able to share her burden. 'Yes! Please. I got called by my mother's care home to say she'd been brought here. Una Barrow? I asked at Reception and they sent me in here, but I think I've got a little lost.'

'It's a big department. It happens all the time. But follow me—I know where your mum is.'

'How is she?'

'Stable at the moment. We think she may have a urinary tract infection.'

'Oh, not again! But she's all right?'

'She's sleeping at the moment.' Naomi led the way into Resus, catching Tom's shocked expression at her returning so soon, but then his face registered relief when he saw she was with someone else. 'Tom? This is Una's daughter.'

'Rosie?' He came over to shake the woman's hand.

'Yes. Rosemary Sanders.'

'She's been asking for you.' He walked with her over to the patient and watched as she took her mother's hand. 'Your mother was brought into us with a high temperature, which we're slowly getting down. We've given her a paracetamol IV as well as a standard drip to keep her hydrated and to give the trimethoprim.'

'What's that?'

'It's an antibiotic. It works in about eighty per cent of these sorts of cases.'

'And what if that doesn't work?'

'We'll try a cephalosporin treatment.'

'Well, you sound like you know what you're doing.' She smiled at her mother. Una stirred and opened her eyes, spotting her daughter. 'Rosie…'

'Hello, Mum.'

Naomi stepped away to stand with Tom. 'Are you okay?'

He looked down, pulling a pen from his pocket and scribbling something on a scrap piece of paper. 'I'm fine. Why do you ask?'

She shrugged. 'You seem…upset.' She held his gaze and though he wished to tear his eyes away, he found, yet again, that he couldn't. 'If it's because I'm still at yours, it's just because I haven't found anywhere I can afford yet, and—'

'Would you check the stocks in the trolleys, please?' He could feel his heart pounding heavily in his chest and so he sat down to catch his breath. He suddenly wished she would move away from him, so he could think straight. He cursed himself for being horrible once again, but he didn't know what else he could do.

'Certainly. But only if you're all right.'

He laughed—a cynical, forced laugh. 'Why wouldn't I be all right?'

'I don't know.'

She looked at him, her face a mask of concern, and it was all he could do to ignore it. How did she have such an ability to affect him? It wasn't as if he'd been stranded in the desert, where there were no women, and she'd been the first one he'd seen when he got back to civilisation. He was surrounded by women all of the time. Why was *she* any different and how could *she* make him feel like his insides were all twisted? Like his blood were running hotter than normal? And those rumours... He couldn't stand people talking about him. He'd been the subject of gossip once before when Meredith had died and he'd come straight back into work the next day. People had gossiped then, whispering in corners, making judgements.

It irritated him. He was used to being calm and in control. Even when there was a dramatic event in Resus he could stay calm and focused.

But he couldn't with her around. Perhaps he could help her find somewhere. He could look a little harder. He'd really not done anything to help her find a new flat. Apart from providing a roof over her head whilst she looked. She'd had work to do and her old flat to sort out, so she could get her deposit back and...

He sighed. She was more in his space than he'd realised. And he wasn't ready for that. Not now. Not ever. He had to stop feeling this attraction to Naomi.

There couldn't be a future in it.

Naomi was in the staffroom on her morning break, feeling content. The days had flown by. She'd been living with Tom for a few weeks now, trying and failing to find her feet and a new flat. Although there'd been a few awkward moments between them since that day when Stefan had alerted them to the hospital gossip, it seemed to be going quite well. As colleagues, they'd worked together, mostly like a finely tuned engine. As flatmates, she had mostly felt welcome, and only on occasion had she got the feeling Tom was uncomfortable with her being there.

Valentine's Day, for instance, had been odd. With both

of them single, both of them trying not to reference the day, or the fact that they were both alone. She'd considered, briefly, sending him a joke card but common sense had told her that it wouldn't go down well, so they had both just worked as late as they could and grabbed a takeaway on the way home that night.

There were a few others in the staffroom, Stefan included, who sat chatting with his mates, laughing over a celebrity gossip magazine, whilst Naomi sat with a coffee and her new friend, Jackie.

Jackie was a healthcare assistant and they'd hit it off from day one. Naomi had immediately liked her because of her work ethic and ready smile. It seemed she knew everything about the department and she was always happy to point Naomi in the right direction if she needed it. But right now, Jackie was explaining to her about the Spring Ball.

'Are you going to go?'

Naomi shook her head. 'No.'

'You should. It's fabulous. Better than the Christmas party!'

'I wouldn't know. I probably won't go to that either.'

'Oh, you must go! It's fabulous. You get to dress up like a princess and dance with a handsome man. You could bring Dr Williams!'

Naomi tried to act confused. 'Why would I bring Dr Williams?'

'Because you're sleeping with him.'

What? 'No, I'm not! Is that what everyone's saying?' She felt her cheeks flame with heat.

Jackie leant in closer, lowering her voice. 'You've been leaving together. You arrive together. Everyone assumed—'

'They assumed wrong!' She got up and stormed over to the sink, unable to sit still for a moment longer. 'I got burgled. My place was trashed and Tom offered me a place to stay until I could arrange something else!'

Jackie held up her hands as if in surrender. 'Okay! I believe you! Whoa, calm down, woman. I'm only telling you what everyone is saying. We just thought…I mean, come on, he is delish!'

'He's a friend. A work colleague. My boss! Tom and I will be nothing more,' she said firmly and loudly, just as Tom walked in, holding his coffee mug.

He paused, glancing at her, his face impassive. He looked around at Jackie and the others all staring at him, waiting for him to say something, but he just went to the coffee pot and poured himself a refill and left again.

Naomi didn't realise she'd been holding her breath. She let it out, wondering how she would ever apologise to him for making them both the subject of so much gossip. Perhaps it would be wise to find a flat sooner, rather than later?

She sank down in the chair next to Jackie. 'Know anywhere I could live?'

Her friend stared back at her and shook her head. 'Sorry.'

She let out a sigh, wondering if everyone else's attempts at being strong and independent in the world came crashing down as badly as hers.

Tom stood outside the hospital clutching his mug of coffee and fighting the urge to march back into the staffroom.

He knew he wouldn't. He wasn't a violent man, or the confrontational type. But the urge to give everyone a piece of his mind had suddenly soared out of nowhere. Being the subject of idle gossip wasn't helping. He'd thought everyone had forgotten about all of that nonsense.

It was enough to make any man's blood boil.

I don't know why I'm getting so worked up about this!

She was just a work colleague. A tenant. A friend. An employee. Nothing more than that. And he didn't need her to be anything more than that, he reminded himself.

Naomi Bloom.

It all kept coming back to her! Nothing had been right in his life ever since she'd fallen from that stupid ladder into his arms.

Tom sat down on one of the benches and sipped his coffee. It wasn't too cold out. It was one of those rare February days when the sun shone brightly and there was no breeze, so it actually felt quite spring-like. Daffodils were coming up early and, above the light morning traffic, he could hear birdsong. It was almost a pleasant day, except…

It had been a day like this when Meredith had been hit by the car. The driver had been drinking and over the limit, but he'd also said the low sun had blinded him, blocking his view of another vehicle, causing him to swerve suddenly, mount the kerb and…hit Meredith.

She'd been jogging along the road, with her headphones in, music playing, and she'd not heard the rev of the engine, or the squeal of brakes before it was too late. Much too late.

He let out a heavy sigh. He had to be more vigilant. He couldn't involve himself with Naomi. Since her arrival in his life, he'd been disturbed, unable to concentrate, unable to sleep knowing that she was just in the next room. Now everyone was talking about them.

He didn't need that kind of reputation. He wanted everyone to think of him as a damned fine doctor and nothing else!

In the evening, Naomi was just starting to put together a quick meal. She'd put some pasta on to boil, had—admittedly—opened a carton of fresh tomato and basil sauce and was busy chopping up a fresh green salad. You couldn't burn salad. And she never went wrong with pasta. This was a good way to apologise to Tom for the day's events.

The radio was on and as she chopped she sang along to the music, not caring that she was off-key or didn't know half the words.

She had just reached for a handful of fresh herbs, when she noticed Tom had silently emerged from his room and was watching her dance and bop to the music. She blushed. 'Hi.'

Tom stood there, a slight smile of amusement on his face. 'Cooking again?'

Self-consciously, she patted her hair, realising the wispy loose bun was still held in place by the pencil she'd used earlier. She pulled it out, shaking her hair loose with her fingers as her cheeks coloured. She glanced down at the chopped salad leaves, the mix of rocket, radicchio and watercress. 'Erm, yes. But I'm certain we'll get through this one with the minimum amount of fuss.'

'No fire trucks?'

She laughed. 'No. Well… I hope not. Look, about today, Tom, I'm really sorry—'

'There's no need.' He held up his hands. 'It's fine. I should have known. I reacted badly to it, too. I was rude ignoring you and that was very wrong of me. I'm sorry.'

He looked it, too. She found herself feeling odd about it. Discomfited. When she'd had fallings-out with Vincent, they would apologise and she would hug him, gently, so as not to cause him injury. Injury only turned to more bone, but she had never stopped giving him hugs. She was that kind of person.

But to hug Tom? That wouldn't feel right. She didn't feel that she *had* the right to do that yet.

'I'm sorry, too. All you've done is look out for me

since you've known me and now I'm dragging your name through the mud.'

'I've been in worse. Mud is nothing, compared to some places you could be.'

She thought maybe he was referring to her experience with Vincent. Yes, that had been tough, watching someone die and not being able to do a thing about it. She'd felt the same sadness with the elderly patients with Alzheimer's. She understood how horrible it was to see a disease slowly picking away at a person, like a vulture, feeding on their soul, feeding on *who they were*. 'I agree.'

'I hope I haven't made you feel that you have to find another place sooner, rather than later.'

'I did feel that a little.'

'I'm sorry. But when Jackie implied today that we were…' he swallowed '…sleeping together, I just felt like they were all disregarding the feelings I had for my wife. I loved her so much and to lose her like that, in such a terrible accident… There should never be rumours like that about us. About me. I won't ever date. Not again.'

'Never?'

He shook his head. 'I've had my one true love. You don't get that a second time.'

She looked at him carefully. 'You believe there's only ever one true love for a person? That out of all the billions of people on this planet, we only ever have one person who could be our soulmate?'

He considered her words. 'It would be a miracle if there were another.'

'But in believing that, you're tying yourself to a lonely future. I loved Vincent, but I don't think he'll be my *only* love. I have to believe that there's more.'

'Maybe we're both right. But I won't have gossip about us. We have to set everyone straight.'

'All right.'

'And I'd like to help you look for a place. A *good* place. I can use my contacts.'

Clearly he still wanted to get rid of her. Disappointment filled her. 'I appreciate that, Tom.'

He looked as if he was going to say something else, but then he seemed to think better of it. Instead, he just smiled and went over to sit on the sofa.

The pasta was about to boil over. She caught it just in time and turned down the heat.

Disaster averted.

CHAPTER FIVE

THE DOORS FLEW open as the paramedics wheeled in their next patient. Tom, Naomi and the rest of the team all took a grip and helped transfer the patient from the trolley onto the flat bed.

Tom and Naomi had spent the last week or so flat-hunting but it hadn't gone well. Places had been either too small, or too far from work, bearing in mind that she would have to use buses or trains to get to Welbeck and the London traffic was notoriously bad.

They'd gotten into a routine. Work, eat, flat-hunt, sleep. It was a routine. A *safe* routine. Tom knew that just by concentrating on those few things, he could keep the topic of conversation away from the more dangerous areas. He didn't want to reveal too much of himself and he frequently felt that he was constantly warding Naomi off from asking personal questions.

The paramedic handed Tom the job notes.

'This is Derek, forty-two, he was involved in a car-versus-lamp-post incident approximately thirty minutes ago. The car was travelling at an estimated forty miles an hour and he swerved and hit the lamppost head-on. The airbag was deployed. Head to toe, he has a scalp laceration above his left eye, bruising and pain to the right shoulder and a query right broken wrist. Patient has admitted that he'd consumed a considerable amount of alcohol and police have done a breath test, which was positive.'

Tom glanced through the notes, keeping his face unreadable. This man had been drinking, another idiot who thought he could get behind the wheel of his car and drive? What would it take before these people realised how much they were endangering others as well as themselves?

'Was anyone else hurt at the scene?'

The paramedic shook his head. 'No. But he came close. Those kids were lucky their mother saw him coming and got them out of the way.'

Kids?

An anger began to simmer within him. He gave a quick nod of thanks to the ambulance team as they took their equipment and left.

His team were already working. Naomi was getting venous access, whilst another doctor was doing a fast scan of the patient's abdomen and another was taking blood-pressure readings.

The X-ray technicians arrived and took pictures of the man's chest and pelvis and Tom ordered pain medication whilst they waited for the results.

Derek had been lucky. Nothing was broken. His wrist was most probably sprained. The only attention he needed was to his scalp, where there was a wound that was deep enough to need stitches, not glue.

Naomi fetched Tom a suturing kit and some sterile gloves and set up a small station on a metal trolley, so that he could work. But first, she cleaned the patient's wound and irrigated it. There was still some airbag dust in and around the wound. At this moment in time, they had no idea how old the patient's car was. If it was an older vehicle, the dust would contain sodium azide, which they definitely didn't want to be embedded in a wound. It was better to be safe, rather than sorry.

'Is that okay?' Naomi asked Derek, noticing he was wincing slightly as she worked.

'It hurts. Can't I get some anaesthetic?'

'Dr Williams will do that for you.'

'How long's that going to take?'

'Do you need to be somewhere?'

'My brother's getting married.'

She put aside the used swabs and grabbed a fresh one to dry the patient's face and around his ear. 'What time?'

'Three o clock.'

'You've plenty of time.'

Tom washed his hands in the sink. It was his job, but dealing with people like Derek still angered him. He'd recklessly endangered others and Tom couldn't help but think that someone like this man had been responsible for killing the love of his life. Derek had been lucky today in more ways than one. He'd had a crash and avoided major injury to himself, but more importantly he hadn't hurt anyone else. Although it sounded like it had been close. It seemed that it was only down to a mother's due diligence that the children had not been hurt.

Would Derek be grumbling about time issues if he'd killed a child?

Tom wiped his hands dry on a paper towel and then turned to pick up the sterile gloves and put them on.

'Hey, Doc, give me the good stuff, yeah? I'm not good with pain.'

Tom wondered who was. He reckoned the physical pain this man was experiencing now was nothing compared to the kind of pain that Tom had gone through. He made no reply but picked up the vial of anaesthetic so he could draw it into the syringe.

He was aware that Naomi was frowning, watching him, confused by his silence, but he had no time to explain it all at this moment. And there was no way in hell he was going to explain it in front of this idiot!

Once he'd got the measurement right, he leaned over the patient to examine the now-cleaned wound and find the best place to insert the anaesthetic. 'This will sting,' he said, finding a tiny modicum of satisfaction when Derek winced and flinched.

'Whoa, Doc!'

He inserted the needle again in another spot and then another, before removing his gloves and going back to the sink to wash his hands. 'That will take a moment.' He looked at Naomi. 'I'll just add the meds to his notes.'

She followed him over to his desk. 'Are you okay? You seem...distracted. Is the gossip still bothering you?'

He looked at her askance. He hadn't given the gossip a moment's notice. 'No.'

'It's just that you don't seem...happy.'

'Well, why would I be?' He marched back over to the patient and washed his hands in the sink once again before putting on another pair of gloves. He didn't notice the odd look Naomi gave him before she left. All he could think about was how to keep his cool whilst dealing with this patient.

Naomi found Jackie in the sluice room, emptying a bedpan.

'Hey, Naomi. What's up?' Jackie was in her usual good mood today.

'Nothing.'

Jackie closed the lid to the machine that disposed of the cardboard pans and pressed the button to activate the mulcher. 'Tell your Aunty Jackie. Come on!'

Naomi shrugged and fiddled with the boxes of gloves

on the shelf beside her. 'Dr Williams is acting odd. More so than usual.'

'Lovers' tiff?' Jackie cackled at her own joke but, seeing her friend's reaction to it, stopped abruptly. 'Oh, yeah, that's right. You two are all "above board".' She wiggled her fingers to make quotation marks in the air.

'We *are*. Flatmates plain and simple.'

'It could be that latest case? The drunk driver?'

'Why would that bother him? We work in A&E; we see drunks all the time.'

Jackie shook her head. 'We do, that's true, but…well, you'd really need to ask him.'

'But I suppose everyone else knows about it?'

'Pretty much. I would have thought you'd know, you've lived with him for a month! Why don't you ask him? If you dare. He's been a lot more prickly lately. I'm not sure I'd want to poke that wasp hive.'

Naomi sank back against the racks. 'You're telling me.'

'I think you'd get away with it.'

She frowned. 'Why?'

Jackie washed her hands, then dried them. 'Because I've seen the way he looks at you.'

That evening, Tom gave her a lift home. He didn't say much in the car and she sensed he had a lot on his mind. Least of all the fact that he had a lodger that he'd never wanted in the first place.

But when they got to the flat and they both had changed, she watched as Tom came out of his room and went over to the piano, looking pensive. His fingertips touched the top of the sleek black instrument and he let them drift across the surface.

Was he thinking about his wife? He'd told Naomi he had

only ever played it for her. Was that case with the drunk driver today somehow connected? And if so, how?

She opened the fridge, looking for inspiration for their evening meal, but there was hardly anything in there. 'I think we need to go to the supermarket.'

Tom looked over to where she stood in the kitchen. 'I'm not sure I feel like that tonight.'

'I don't mind going. Tell me what you'd like and I'll fetch it,' she offered.

He stuck his hands in his pockets and came over to her. 'Do you like seafood?'

'Love it. Why?'

'Then I know a perfect little place.'

The Phoenix was a floating restaurant on the River Thames. It consisted of a beautiful wide yacht with a white hull, a phoenix rising from the ashes painted on the aft.

Naomi hadn't really known what to expect. Certainly, when Tom had suggested that he knew a restaurant they could go to, she'd expected somewhere on dry land. She hadn't known these sorts of things existed, and had had no idea how she ought to dress. In the end, she'd settled on a summery dress, mainly white but with small pink tea roses on it, and then a white shawl for her to wrap around her shoulders.

Tom had given her a nod of approval when she'd emerged from her room and she'd noted his dashing choice of simple black trousers and a tailored white shirt. He looked very handsome, so much so that her stomach had begun to flip and twirl with nervousness and her heart rate had gone up a few notches. She'd hoped she wasn't getting those ugly red blotches on her neck and chest, which was what usually happened when she got nervous, but if she had looked flushed, he didn't mention it.

He'd called a taxi to take them to the restaurant and when they arrived, she'd gasped in awe and surprise at the beautiful fairy lights that lit up the boat and along the gangplank.

Now, she felt Tom's hand at the small of her back as he guided her safely on board.

'Table for two. Williams.'

The maître d' checked his guest list, then escorted them to a table up on the top deck, under a canopy. Across the water, Naomi could see the Houses of Parliament all lit up and the London Eye and although there was a small chill in the air, she didn't feel it. All she felt was excitement.

She had never been somewhere like this. She had never been on a date like this! When she'd met Vincent, it had been in the hospital and she'd known from the beginning what she would be getting into. The only dates she and Vincent had been on were hospital appointments and the occasional drive to a local pub with disabled access. Certainly nothing like this!

She settled into her seat as they were handed the menu. There was a huge selection of seafood dishes: sea bass with lemon capers, a spicy salmon tikka, chilli prawns or a simpler, steamed fish served with vegetables. She decided to go for the prawn starter, the seafood kebab for her main and strawberry cheesecake for dessert.

'Excellent choice,' Tom said, before turning to the waiter. 'I'll have the same.'

The waiter bowed and then disappeared.

Naomi smiled. 'This seems lovely. Thank you for bringing me here.'

'Not at all. You've been cooking so much this week, it's about time you had an evening off.'

'To give the fire alarm a rest, you mean?'

He smiled back and took a sip of his water.

The wine that Tom had ordered, a nice Sauvignon Blanc, arrived. He tested it, giving his approval, and it was poured into both their glasses.

'Have you been here before?' Naomi asked. She wanted to know if he'd been here with his wife. If he had, she didn't think she would mind.

'No. I haven't. It was recommended to me by a colleague.'

'It was a difficult day, today, wasn't it?'

His gaze met hers. 'How do you mean?'

She hesitated, not wanting to spoil the evening right at the start, but also curious to know what had happened in his past. 'On a personal level. That drunk driver.'

Tom sipped his wine and looked out over the water. He seemed to be looking for something. After a moment or two, his gaze returned to her. 'I guess people at work have told you what happened to Meredith?'

She shook her head. 'No. They haven't.'

He seemed surprised, but before he could say any more their chilli prawns arrived. He thanked the waiter and, when he'd gone, he looked back into Naomi's eyes. 'She was killed. By a drunk driver.'

'Oh, no, I'm so sorry, Tom.' She reached out and laid her hand on his. This was the type of person she was. She touched people. She let them know that she understood. His hand under hers felt warm and she wrapped her fingers around his palm. 'If you'd rather I changed the subject...?'

He didn't pull his hand away. But she did see the way he stared down at their hands upon the table. He looked pained. 'It's fine.'

'Tell me about her. I'd like to know who she was.'

His lined brow grew less furrowed and a small light came into his eyes. 'We met at the hospital and she dazzled me from day one. She was this bright, breezy individual, a fantastic nurse, and we just hit it off. I'd rib her about how she'd eat junk food for breakfast on her way into work and she'd joke with me about being a health fanatic just because I'd eaten a banana or something.'

Naomi smiled.

'She called me the health freak, but she was the one who went jogging every day, no matter what the weather.'

'She sounds dedicated.'

'She was. She was jogging on the day she died. She used to wear headphones and listen to music. The driver mounted the kerb and hit her. She wouldn't have heard a thing. Or even have felt it. Or so the paramedics said.'

'I'm so sorry.' She truly meant it. She gave his hand another squeeze and he squeezed back, looking distant for a moment, then he smiled.

'Better eat your prawns, before they get cold.'

The prawns were beautiful. They were buttery and spicy, fat and plump with a hint of garlic and paprika. The freshly baked crusty bread was perfect to help mop up the juices and, when they'd finished, the waiter brought over some finger bowls so they could rinse their fingers.

'That was delicious, thank you,' she told the waiter, who smiled as he cleared their plates.

London at night, on the river, looked beautiful. Naomi had done all the essential touristy things when she'd first arrived, but that had been during the day. Going for a ride on the London Eye had been a treat and she'd looked out over the new city in which she would be living in awe. People came for miles to see this, to experience this. Now here she was seeing it all in a new light and with a great friend by her side.

Because Tom was her friend. She felt they had reached that point now. He was her boss too of course and her landlord, technically, but over time they'd grown quite close.

They'd been working together, living together, sharing meals, sharing a bathroom. She felt she understood him a bit better.

She remembered how when they'd first met, he'd been very standoffish. He'd been prickly and not friendly at all, but then he'd taken her in, making a grand gesture that she truly appreciated. She'd also watched him at work and seen him as the professional, caring, hardworking doctor. And at home he'd become her friend and her cooking instructor! In what seemed like very little time, she'd learnt so much from him in so many ways and now they were here, on this wonderful boat, and she wondered briefly if it was representative of their changing relationship.

She raised her glass for a toast. 'To Meredith.'

Surprise crossed Tom's face and then his expression changed to one of appreciation. He raised his glass and clinked it gently against hers. 'And to new friends.'

'New friends.' She sipped her wine, feeling the gentle fruity flavours wash away the heat of the spicy prawns. This was nice. She was enjoying being here with him. This side of Tom was much, much better than the first side that she'd seen.

The waiter arrived with their main course, which was seafood skewers of monkfish, scallop and salmon, drizzled in a cauliflower sauce, served with buttered carrots and broccoli florets.

They tucked in with gusto, relishing the way the sauce truly brought out the flavours of the fish, until all too soon both their plates were empty. Naomi laughed. 'Is this a sign that my cooking hasn't been as great as I've thought? Have you been secretly starving, Tom?'

He smiled back at her. 'Your food has been delicious.'

'Even the blackened bits?'

'Even those. I think these celebrity chefs are missing

a trick there. Carbonisation of food adds a certain *je ne sais quoi.*'

'Now I know you're lying!'

Tom laughed. 'Living with you has been an eye-opening experience.'

'Why, thank you!' She met his gaze and held it, seeing his eyes sparkling with amusement. 'So has living with you.'

'Oh?'

'I would never have pegged you for a cook.'

'Really? Why not?'

'You seem…' She tried to find the right words. 'You seem the kind of guy who would eat out every night. Restaurants, dinner parties, that sort of thing. Whereas I'm a microwave-meal-for-one kind of girl.'

Tom refilled their wine glasses. 'You mean you're a homebody?'

She nodded. 'Yes, I am. And I like being that. This is great, too, don't get me wrong, but I think there's a lot to be said for staying at home in your pyjamas and eating a bowl of popcorn in front of the television.'

'You're absolutely right. Homes are underrated.'

She looked at him. 'And your home? Do you enjoy being there?'

He pursed his lips momentarily and the action drew her focus. He had such a lovely mouth. A wide smile, good teeth. He didn't smile often enough, but when he did… It couldn't fail to make anyone smile with him. 'I do now.'

She swallowed. Did he mean that he enjoyed being there now that *she* was there? Perhaps she was no longer the interloper. No longer the unwanted tenant. 'Really?'

'Really. I think I'll miss you, when you leave.'

'It'll be quieter, you mean?' she suggested.

'It'll be…emptier.'

She sipped her wine and wondered what he meant by that.

The cheesecake arrived and, on a par with the previous courses, it was absolutely delicious, just as she'd expected. By the time they'd finished eating, Naomi was feeling comfortably full so they had coffee and then Tom suggested a walk along the river.

Naomi wrapped her shawl around her shoulders, glad that she'd brought it. It was a warm evening for early March but the air was slowly getting colder and her shawl wasn't enough. Tom proffered his jacket, wrapping it around her shoulders, and she snuggled into its warm depths. 'Thank you.'

'No problem.'

She smiled and looked up at him. Suddenly, it occurred to her that he seemed so alone. Not lonely. *Alone.* A man whose only companion was a grief that he'd carried with him for a long time. She wished she could make it better for him.

'You know…when I lost Vincent, it was expected. We'd known for months that the end was coming and we both hoped that it would be easier. You know? That we'd have had our chance to say goodbye to each other. Do you find that difficult, Tom? That you never had the opportunity or time to say goodbye? Is that why it still hurts you so much?'

He shrugged. 'Maybe. We'd had so little time together. I think it hurts because…well, because I'd had all these dreams for us—travelling, children—and that future has been taken away.'

She could understand. Her hopes and dreams for a future had been taken from her, too. 'Perhaps we've both got different futures awaiting us. And they may be different from the ones we were expecting, but perhaps they won't be as bad as we expect.'

He gave a grim laugh. 'For you, maybe. I'm not planning on getting involved with anyone again, remember? You still believe that there's another soulmate out there for you, so your future still shines bright with possibility.'

A couple walked towards them, looking so in love, so comfortable with each other. They had their arms around each other, the woman leaning her head against her partner's shoulder as he kissed the top of her hair. Naomi smiled at them as they walked past.

'I think there's someone out there for you, Tom. You've just got to look harder.'

She could feel his gaze upon her and she glanced up at him and smiled. She stopped walking for a moment and when he stilled and faced her, she tentatively reached for his hand and grasped it in her own. 'Promise me, Tom, that you'll look for her.'

'I—'

'I don't think you should be alone. Not for the rest of your life. That's a long time to be blind to the possibilities all around you.'

'You're very kind, Naomi.' He pushed back a loose strand of her hair, tucking it behind her ear. His eyes sparkled in the moonlight. Standing here, holding his hand by the riverside, seemed the right thing to be doing. Their relationship had changed so much and, where once she had been apprehensive around him, she now felt that she cared. That she wanted good things for him, and the idea that he would be alone for the rest of his life...

He was staring down at her, intently.

They were both standing so close to the other that she suddenly became aware of the small space between them, almost as if it were crackling with unseen electricity.

His eyes stared deep into her soul, and it was as if she

could feel him searching, see him looking for something within her that only he could find. And he took a step closer.

Naomi sucked in her breath, her lips parting as he came closer. Did she want Tom to kiss her?

Yes. Absolutely.

Suddenly the realisation of how much she wanted to kiss him slammed through her, making its presence felt. It felt as if this, the kiss that was about to happen, was the most obvious thing in the world. As if it were something she had always wanted and wondered about, only she hadn't allowed herself to think about it, or acknowledge it. Yet here it was and...

It was like everything was happening in slow motion.

Tom was moving closer. His head lowered to hers, their eyes closing as his lips approached hers.

Naomi held her breath, awaiting the touch of his lips, her heart pounding, her breathing fast and shallow. Could he hear her heart? Did he know how much she suddenly wanted this?

But where was the kiss?

She felt his hand pull free of hers and she opened her eyes to see him stand up straight again, wearing an agonised expression of pain and regret. 'I'm sorry...I can't...'

It was horrible. She wished she could give him what he needed and ease his pain. Make him feel that there was still a chance of happiness for him.

He began to walk again, waiting for her to follow alongside. 'I'm sorry, Naomi.'

'It doesn't matter,' she said, trying to make him feel better, but inside she felt crushed. She was bitterly disappointed.

It does matter!

Could she really have *kissed* Tom? She risked a quick glance at him. Yes, he was gorgeous and yes, she liked him.

In fact, she liked him a lot, but would kissing him really be wise? Perhaps it was a good thing that he'd paused and thought better of it.

He was her boss, her friend and her flatmate. Kissing him would have simply opened up a whole world of complication that she didn't need! When she thought about it sensibly, she knew it was probably a bad idea. After all, the man was obviously still in a quagmire of grief, wasn't he?

He was a man of deep feeling. She knew that. She saw proof of it on a daily basis. Now she had no doubt that if they were to kiss, then Tom would make her feel things that she had never felt before. Vincent, for all his sweetness and vulnerability, had never been an overtly passionate kisser. Their kisses had always been friendly. They had mostly been kisses of greeting, hello and goodbye. Vanilla kisses. Their whole relationship had been about being safe. About being careful and controlled. That was the reason why he'd been such a great husband, and one who she missed dearly.

But had she ever yearned for him? Had she ever been desperate for Vincent's touch?

No. That wasn't what their relationship had been based on.

So now? Being here with Tom, feeling the sudden desire to know what his kisses would be like, and where they might lead...

It was terrifying!

But it was also exciting. And a little bit dangerous. She could feel adrenaline zipping through her system like electrical shocks. She felt as if she could run. She felt as if she could achieve anything if she dared.

Except kiss him.

Just because she wanted to do it, it didn't make it right. Surely this was her worst nightmare. Getting involved with a handsome man, as she'd seen her mother do so many times, only to be used and cast aside later. Because wasn't that what they all did? Wasn't that what she had learned? The one thing she had decided upon from a young age was to never get involved with someone that dangerous.

And Tom was the worst kind of dangerous.

He wasn't free to be loved.

CHAPTER SIX

SHE'D SPENT MOST of last night lying in her bed thinking about the almost-kiss, and sleep had eluded her for a while. She'd expected to wake up feeling tired and awful, but to her surprise she didn't. Her new mindset had given her the energy and determination to make everything right again.

She'd decided as he'd driven her to work that she wouldn't mention it. Tom obviously regretted the moment and she didn't want him to feel embarrassed or awkward around her. Nor did she want to feel awkward around him. She wanted them to go back to the way they'd been before the almost-kiss. Good friends. Good flatmates. Boss and employee. Team players.

If she saw Tom today at the hospital, she would wish him good morning, smile and then get on with her day. If he raised the issue with her, then that would be different. But still, she'd listen and nod and smile and tell him it was all fine. She'd decided that she wouldn't put any pressure on him whatsoever. She would be strong and independent. She would not be clingy, or whiny or make him feel as if he'd almost kissed the wrong woman. She didn't want him to think she was someone who might turn into a weird stalker, desperate for his affections.

She put her coat into her locker, changed into her uniform and twisted her hair up into a clip. Then she headed to the staffroom to make herself a quick cup of coffee. She made drinks for Jackie, Stefan and Bobby too and settled down with her notepad and pen, waiting for the sister from the night shift to come in and do the handover.

Dr Thomas walked in, followed by a couple of health-care assistants, then another doctor.

She wondered where Tom was.

It doesn't matter, she told herself. *Be bright and breezy.*

And then...in he came. He was looking tall and delicious as always and his gaze found hers in an instant, before he quickly looked away.

Her smile froze on her face.

It was easy to tell yourself that you wouldn't let it matter. It was easy to *say* that you wouldn't show a reaction. But reality was just a little tougher and *doing* it was another matter entirely. Having him here so close to her made her entire body feel as if it were revving its engine, as if someone had pressed down on the accelerator, making the engine roar. She could feel her blood thrumming through her veins and could feel herself beginning to overheat.

It had been the same that morning, when Tom had driven her in to work. He'd barely said a word, but she'd been so aware of him next to her, just inches away. Every time he'd reached for the gear stick to change up or down, she'd sucked in a breath.

She didn't know why this was happening. She hadn't felt this way before he'd tried to kiss her. But now, after that moment, something had changed.

She dipped her head and sipped her coffee, aware of his every step, his every movement. He was making himself a drink and, although she wanted to watch him whilst his back was turned and try to gauge his mood or how he might feel about her, she kept staring straight ahead. He would be a perfect gentleman, of that she had no doubt.

Jackie said something to her and Naomi made a sound as if in agreement, but really she had no idea what her friend had just said.

She sipped her coffee again and stared at her notepad on the desk in front of her.

Just look at the notepad. Look at that and nothing else. Tom is just another person in the room. Don't look at him.

She looked at him. She took in the broad expanse of his back, the neatness of his small, trim waist. The way his hair neatly met the collar of his shirt, the soft curve of muscle beneath the material.

He'd tried to kiss her. He'd tried and so it *did* mean something! Because surely there had to be feelings behind that intention. Surely he must have felt an attraction to her.

She averted her gaze as he turned round to find a seat, intently aware of him moving round to sit next to Dr Thomas, out of her eyeline.

Thank you. At least now I'll be able to concentrate.

She took another sip of her coffee, willing herself to concentrate on something else.

Naomi was assigned to work in Minors. As was Tom. No matter, she thought. It didn't mean they were necessarily going to run into each other all day. It was a big enough department, with sixteen cubicles. As long as she kept busy, it should be fine. And A&E was *always* busy.

She had no patient already assigned to her, so she went to pick up the next patient card from triage.

Logan Reed, aged twenty, who had a cut on his leg.

She called him through, noting that he was a tall, young man, quite lanky in appearance, a little pale and weak-looking. She led him through to her cubicle and asked him to sit on the bed.

'So, Logan, what's brought you to A&E today?'

He answered her in a dull voice. 'I've cut my leg.'

'And how did you do that?'

He shrugged.

She sensed there was more to this, something he was afraid to say. 'Can you show me whereabouts on your leg the cut is?'

He stood up and unzipped his trousers, lowering them to his knees. He didn't look at her or make eye contact, but just waited whilst she took in the multitude of scars across the tops of his thighs. On one thigh there was a section covered with a gauze pad.

It was now clear Logan had been self-harming and her heart sank. What could be causing this boy so much pain that he felt he had to do this?

'Okay. Do you want to lie back for me? Then I'll have a look at this cut.'

He positioned himself on the bed and waited.

Naomi put on some gloves and removed the gauze pad. Whilst he'd obviously cut himself again, this gash was bigger than the others and quite possibly deeper. It was still bleeding, but it looked as if it had slowed.

'What did you use?' she asked, trying to keep her voice calm.

Logan shrugged. 'A craft blade.'

'Was it clean?'

He nodded.

She delicately replaced the gauze pad and removed her gloves. 'And what made you do this? Today? What happened to make you cut yourself worse than all the other times?'

His gaze met hers, briefly. 'A girl. You probably think I'm stupid.'

Naomi didn't. She knew people dealt with their pain in many different ways. Some just cried, whilst others buried themselves in work so that they didn't have to think.

Some people would exercise furiously and others would just wallow deep in depression. Then others, like Logan, self-harmed, perhaps preferring to feel physical pain, rather than the emotional one.

'No! No, I don't. Were you in a relationship with this girl?'

'I thought I was. I thought we were serious. Turns out she was just having fun.' He sounded bitter. She could understand his hurt.

'This might need stitches, Logan. I'll need to get a doctor to assess it properly in order to do that.'

'I know the drill. If it does need stitches, will I get an anaesthetic?'

Naomi thought that was an odd question. 'Of course you will. Why?'

'Last time I needed stitches I went to a hospital—not this one—and they said that if I could cut myself without anaesthetic, I could get stitched up without it, too.'

Naomi was horrified. 'What? That's awful!'

'In some places, when you self-harm, they treat you like you deserve it.'

'Well, we don't do that here! There are protocols in place. You won't be treated differently from anyone else.'

Logan nodded approvingly. 'Glad to hear it.'

'Are you receiving treatment for your self-harming, Logan? Are you seeing anyone?'

'I was. But I haven't for a while.'

'Then I'll refer you for another assessment. Is that all right?'

'Sure.'

She nodded. 'Are you in pain? From the cut?'

'A bit, but it's okay.'

'No. It's not okay. It's never okay to be in pain.'

She went in search of an available doctor, hoping to

maybe find Dr Thomas, or one of the others on duty. But they were already busy. The one doctor that had just finished with a patient and was about to see another was Tom.

Naomi relaxed her shoulders, letting out a low, long breath, and then she went over to him. She kept her manner businesslike. The epitome of professionalism. 'Tom, could I ask you to check my patient over, if you're free?'

He met her gaze and nodded. 'Of course. Who's the patient?'

'Logan Reed. He's self-harmed, and cut his leg. It needs an assessment and possibly stitches.'

'Has he got a current mental-health referral?'

'No, but he's had counselling before. I think he's fallen off the wagon somewhat, so I'm going to re-refer him.'

'Okay, let me take a look.'

They walked side by side to the cubicle, neither looking at the other, but each totally aware of how close they stood.

Naomi pulled open the cubicle curtain and introduced Logan to Tom, who put on some gloves and examined the wound. 'Can you feel me touching here? And here?' he asked Logan.

The young man nodded. 'Yes.'

'You can wiggle your toes and move your leg with no problems?'

'It's fine.'

'Good. I don't think it's too deep. It needs a clean and then I can stitch it. It's probably going to need at least three stitches. They'll be dissolvable, so there's no need to go to the doctor's to get them removed.'

Logan nodded again.

'What made you do this?' Tom asked, quietly.

Their patient let out a long sigh. 'This girl I was into. She was beautiful, you know? Popular. All the guys wanted to be with her and she picked me. I thought we had something special. This deep connection. But it turned out, she wasn't as into me as I was her.'

Naomi tried her hardest not to look at Tom's face. She'd thought Tom had sensed something between them, too. But she couldn't imagine what this poor young boy was feeling. To only be twenty years old, but to have more scars than years on his legs. She wondered what had gone wrong in his life, which compelled him to do such a thing in order to cope with emotional pain.

She thought of her own pain. The hurt and the grief she'd felt at the loss of her marriage. She'd dreamt of being married ever since she'd been a little girl. Her mother had raised her to believe that she could not be complete without a man, and that finding love was the ultimate goal. So as a child, she'd idolised marriage as the epitome of love. The way you would show the world how dedicated you were to another person. She'd drawn pictures of her ideal dress, imagined her perfect wedding day, dreamed about her perfect groom and how her life would be as a married woman.

But she'd had none of that. Meeting Vincent had changed it all. Suddenly she'd found a way to be married without leaving herself at risk of having that man walk out on her or cheat on her. She and Vincent might not have been able to have a physical relationship, but she'd told herself that didn't matter so much. So long as she was safe. And her heart was protected. She'd known that Vincent would die young and she would lose him quickly, but she'd felt that that was something she would deal with when the time came. She would still be able to tell the world, tell herself, that she had been married, had been in love and that she'd had a *good* marriage. That she'd not been desperate and unloved like her own mother, who had seemed like the loneliest woman on the planet.

Eight years she'd spent with Vincent. Eight years of being best friends with her husband: sharing the same jokes, sharing quiet times—reading books, having picnics, taking day trips to the beach or a country house. Eight years of doing the things couples did together. Of caring for him. Loving him.

Eight years of repressing her excitement, her joy, her passion for life.

We all deal with pain and suffering in different ways.

Her own suffering had turned her into a stronger woman. She felt sure of that. Now, she was single and strong and determined. She was free to live her life the way she wanted, without anything holding her back. She could have let her pain control her. She could have let her grief override her emotions, but she hadn't.

And look at Tom. He'd lost his wife. His suffering could have turned him into a bitter individual, angry at the world. But he was kind and considerate and friendly. What was it that made one person strong and determined not to be bowed down by tragedy, whilst others could barely cope?

Although, she knew better than anyone that sometimes grief and pain could still affect you, even when you thought you were over it. Tom had held back yesterday, for example. She'd seen the pain in his eyes, and it seemed Tom was still not over his wife's death. Maybe he still felt married. After all, he'd not chosen to end his marriage. His wife had been taken from him. Did he still have feelings for Meredith? Had he bowed his head to kiss Naomi and suddenly realised what he was doing?

Of course. Tom still loved his dead wife. He clearly felt like he had betrayed Meredith, by attempting to kiss Naomi.

If that were true, then it was definitely a good thing that he'd put the brakes on. He obviously wasn't in the right head space for her to get involved with him. She didn't want to be involved with a man who wasn't free. She didn't want to be involved with a man who still loved another woman.

She stood there, cleaning Logan's wound with saline, trying to be delicate, trying not to hurt him, until Tom could administer the anaesthetic.

All the while, she promised herself that from now on she would start looking harder for a flat. A place of her own. Tom clearly needed his space back. His life back.

The atmosphere between them needed lightening up. But how could she do that? Perhaps she should suggest they do something fun. Something that neither of them had ever done. Something that would get them both out of the flat, both out of that space where Tom's grim memories resided and back out into the world. Most of all, something that had nothing to do with relationships and kisses and heightened moments of tension.

They could still be friends. Good friends, even. But for her, flat-hunting was going to be a number-one priority from now on.

Tom was off-limits.

And so was she.

Tom watched Logan limp out of the department and went to write up the patient notes. He'd left Naomi clearing up the cubicle and suddenly felt a lot more relaxed than when he had been encased with her inside that small space.

His discomfort with her proximity hadn't stopped them from treating Logan to the best of their abilities. But he hoped and prayed that this current level of unease would soon pass. The last thing he wanted was for work to feel uncomfortable, just because of what had happened with Naomi.

He knew he had to forget the moment, but it was difficult. He'd loved Meredith. Of course he had. Their relationship had been built not just on love but friendship, too. But what about Naomi? That *need* to kiss her had just popped up out of nowhere, completely unexpected. He hadn't thought, *Well, this is a nice moonlit walk by the river, that's romantic, I'll kiss her.* It had just happened. They'd stood there, looking at each other, and suddenly Tom had just…*needed* her.

It had just seemed right. He'd felt comfortable with her. They'd been having a pleasant walk, enjoying a good conversation and she'd been so lovely, so beautiful, listening to everything he'd said, paying attention. She'd been funny and humble and such good company and he'd not been able to remember the last time he'd felt that good. Then he'd just felt the need to…

He sighed.

He'd almost kissed her and then had walked away without a word of explanation. She must have been angry with him and she must have had questions. And yet she hadn't asked him about it. She hadn't pressured him into talking. She was even being sweet today, her normal and professional self. There had been no unfriendly atmosphere between them, as he'd feared, especially after the drive that morning when she hadn't said a word. He'd been silent, too, waiting for her to say something. To receive a verbal assault, *anything*, but she'd remained calm and serene. And he truly appreciated that.

Maybe he was wrong. Maybe it hadn't meant as much to her as it had to him.

Tom looked up and saw Naomi walking towards him. Suddenly, he knew he had to apologise. Or at least he had to say something.

'Tom, can we talk?'

There were other members of staff milling around. Stefan was writing on a blood sample and Jackie was nearby, washing her hands in the sink.

'Of course. But it'll have to be at break.'

'I have a break at ten-thirty. Will you come and find me?'

He nodded. He watched her pick up another patient card and disappear to the waiting room.

Even after the way he'd treated her, she still acted with dignity, as if nothing had happened. He couldn't be more grateful.

When it got to ten-thirty, he found her dismissing her last patient. They both made a drink in the staffroom and sat opposite each other over the long table.

Naomi gave him a brief, polite smile, before she opened her mouth to speak. 'I've decided that what we both need is an evening of fun.'

Tom blinked. This wasn't what he'd been expecting. 'Okay.'

'We've both been through an awful lot of stress in our personal lives and everything has just been so intense. We need to break free of that and do something random and fun, to forget work and life's stresses and just enjoy *being*. What do you think?'

He gave a simple nod. 'I agree.' He liked the idea. She was right. 'Absolutely.' A smile crept across his face as he realised just how much he was beginning to really like this woman.

'Good. I've arranged something I've never done before and hopefully something you haven't done either. We'll have a laugh and enjoy ourselves and just let everything go. Okay?'

Tom nodded. 'Are you going to tell me what it is?'

She smiled at him. 'No. Not until we get there.'

'Right.'

She stood up. 'Right. I'll see you later.'

As she walked away he shook his head in disbelief. What had he done so right in his life that Naomi had been allowed to walk into it?

Then he laughed quietly to himself. He hadn't thought that when he'd first met her. He'd thought she was a clumsy rule-breaker, who had demanded his attention.

But now?

She was brightening up his life.

'We're doing *what*?' Tom looked at her as if she'd just suggested they go parachuting naked.

'A roller disco derby.'

'On skates?'

'Roller skates, yes. Don't worry, Tom. They give you helmets and everything.'

'But...*you*, on skates. Is that safe?'

She gave him a playful nudge and laughed. 'I'll stay upright and everything. Come on, it'll be fun. Eighties music, a bit of disco lighting and a whole room full of adults who all ought to know better. What could be more right?' She took hold of his hand and he allowed himself to be pulled forward, a grin on his face.

The large wooden-floored skating arena was filled with flashing disco lights and the heavy beat of loud bass-heavy music. Tom could almost feel the beat thrumming through his bones. Skaters—who'd obviously done this before—whizzed past him, whilst other people stumbled along carefully, as he was doing.

Naomi held his hand in hers and, laughing, pulled him onto the wooden floor.

'Hang on! Just let me grab this.' He reached for the side,

smiling broadly as his hand gripped the safety rail and he could suddenly stand fully upright once again.

Naomi stood by him smiling. 'We'll do this together!' she shouted. 'One step at a time, yes?'

He nodded and wondered what everyone at work would say if they could see him now. At the rate he was going, they might well see him, when he went to A&E later as a *patient* rather than a doctor, with a sprained ankle. But with a faltering lunge, he let go of the side and allowed Naomi to lead him.

The battle for his balance was an awkward one. He imagined he must look like a baby deer on stilts, all long legs and awkward wobbles, but Naomi was wobbling all over the place, too, so he didn't feel like a total idiot. There were lots of people struggling, but everyone was laughing and those that did fall down were soon picked up by those around them.

When had he *ever* had so much carefree fun?

He would never have thought to come and do this on his own. Nor would he have let any of his other colleagues even suggest it! But Naomi had managed to get him here, had managed to put wheels on his feet and make him move.

Another skater whizzed past quickly, sending Tom's arms whirling, and suddenly his feet had been lost from under him and he smacked down hard on his rump.

Naomi was bent double with laughter, but she shuffled over to give him a hand up. He was laughing so hard his sides were beginning to hurt. When he was at last back up on his 'feet' he clutched her hand and mouthed a 'thank you' as they began to skate again.

He had no idea how long they were on the arena floor, but pretty soon he started to get the hang of it and began to pick up speed. Naomi continued to stumble around behind him, so he doubled back and this time grabbed her hand.

'Come on!' he encouraged her, helping her to keep up with him.

Who would have thought it? Dr Tom Williams skating, and actually enjoying himself, at a roller derby! Happily, he surged forward, but then all of a sudden he felt Naomi start to wobble and he turned to catch her, doing it without thinking.

Suddenly she was in his arms again. Up close, he could see the sparkle in her eyes and he couldn't look away. She was *so* beautiful! And she felt so right in his embrace. Her smile faltered briefly as she saw him gaze at her mouth, but then it returned and Tom knew that *this time*, he *had* to kiss her.

Slowly, in the middle of the roller derby, with everyone dashing past with lights flashing and the music pounding, the rest of the world faded away. For just a moment, it was only the two of them, wrapped in a world of magic and wonder. He dipped his head and let his lips touch hers.

He closed his eyes.

Her lips were so soft, so warm. Her arms came up around his neck and he pulled her closer against him. She felt so good. So right.

He allowed himself to be lost in the kiss. To just enjoy it. He would worry about the consequences later. Right now, in this moment, it was just Naomi and him.

The kiss deepened and grew more intense. He felt hungry for her; he desired her, wanted her. How was it possible that he could lose himself so easily? So readily?

But he pushed that thought away.

Someone caught his arm as they raced past and it broke the intensity of the moment.

She stared back at him as they parted, surprise and desire in her eyes, and he moistened his lips, before smiling

uncertainly and taking her hand once again. They began
to skate, but now it felt different.

The kiss had changed everything between them. The
dynamics, the atmosphere…

And then it came.

The guilt. The pain. The flood of past memories, images of Meredith in the sunshine, laughing at him, calling
his name, reaching out to him.

But his hand was in Naomi's. And he couldn't let go.

He needed a break. A minute to breathe.

He headed over to the safety rail.

The next week passed in a blur. Tom threw himself into his
work once again, determined to get through every patient.
He took blood samples, he stitched cuts, he sent patients to
X-ray or CT. He was curt with everyone, no longer bothering to stop and chat, grabbing coffee on the go and not
taking his full break.

He saw Naomi everywhere, it seemed. She was in the
sluice, the drugs cupboard, holding patients' hands, tucking them in or helping them to walk, helping them to deal
with whatever health issue had brought them to A&E. He
tried his best to ignore her. He kept his head down and
walked past, keeping their interactions to a minimum.

But it was difficult. It pained him to do it. It was completely out of his character to treat a colleague like this.
He knew he was being rude. He noticed the reactions of
the other staff when he stormed past. He saw those questioning looks and the furtively raised eyebrows. He'd even
heard a few whispering, asking, 'What's got into Tom?'

He *had* changed. He sensed it. He heard it in his voice
when he spoke to people, felt it in his demeanour and
hated himself whenever he was terse with someone who
normally he would be cordial with.

It pained him to think what Naomi must think about his change in demeanour. She had to have noticed. But, of course, she was acting like the consummate professional she was. Always patient. Always kind and considerate. There was always a smile on her face for the patients. She interacted with him as little as was possible, but did so with extreme politeness. For example, there had been that last case, just an hour or so ago, the lady with the broken wrist. He'd confirmed the break to the patient and explained that she would need a cast whilst Naomi had just stood there, looking at her patient. When he had finished and had turned to go, she'd addressed him with a simple, 'Thank you, Dr Williams.' Then she'd turned back to her patient.

That was it.

He couldn't stand it. It all seemed so false. For him, there were plenty of emotions still simmering below the surface since the kiss they'd shared, but was it the same for her?

He knew he shouldn't let it bother him. That he needed to forget it. He knew getting involved with Naomi was the wrong thing to do.

Because despite the way he was acting, he wasn't indifferent to Naomi. That was the whole problem. He wasn't indifferent to her at all. And if she was suffering as well, because of him? Well, they both had to be adults enough to sort that out. He was damned if he was going to let it affect them any longer. Especially at work. Neither of them could afford to be distracted or to make any mistakes. Mistakes could cause serious danger to a patient.

He couldn't let that happen.

Naomi sank back against the toilet door, her eyes closed, as tears began to threaten to spill.

What on earth was going on? One minute they'd been

having fun, just letting off steam, trying to stay upright and the next moment she'd been in Tom's arms and things had started to get steamy!

How could a single kiss have such power to disturb two people?

Everything had changed the very second his lips had broken away from hers. She could see it in his eyes, the way his expression changed, as if he'd suddenly closed himself off from her, when all she wanted to do was talk about what had happened.

She needed to talk about that kiss! It had felt...monumental! Lip-tingling, body-scorching, heart-poundingly good! She'd never felt that before. Ever. Was this the type of passion she'd read about in love stories? Was this what it was meant to feel like? Because she had all these weird sensations and feelings whizzing through her system and she didn't know what she was supposed to do with them. Or how she was supposed to react to them. Her body felt alive, out of her control. Whenever she was with him, it was like her body was suddenly on alert, aware, and her heart would pound again, her mouth would go dry, her breathing would quicken. Yet Tom was acting weird and she didn't know what to do.

Did he regret their kiss?

She so badly wanted to ask him about it, but he was staying out of her way, not giving her the opportunity to talk about it. At home he either stayed in his room, or he went out. At work, he'd begun throwing himself into his cases again, acting cold as he'd been when she'd first met him. She felt like she was losing him.

Don't do this to me, Tom.

She needed to understand what was happening. Needed to make sense of it. For her, the kiss had been an experience that she would happily experience again and again.

She'd not known it was possible to feel that good. To feel that alive! And the fact that she'd felt that with Tom...

Tears began to run down her cheeks, but not from the hurt at being ignored. She was crying because she'd felt something so magical, something she'd never believed could have existed, and now it looked as if she would never experience that again.

She needed to talk to Tom.

They *both* needed to sort this out.

Naomi was returning the ECG machine to its proper place when Stefan strolled over to her.

'Hey, Naomi.'

She wished Tom would approach her just as easily. But the one man she wanted to talk to her was still avoiding her like crazy.

'Stefan.'

'I was wondering...have you heard of the Spring Ball? For the staff?'

'Err...I think I've seen the signs up for it on the notice boards, yes.' Naomi noticed Tom emerge from a cubicle and her gaze tracked him as he came over to the desk not far away and sat down, yet again, without making eye contact.

Stefan continued. 'I thought maybe you'd like to go with me? As my date?'

Naomi watched, but Tom continued to write, focused intently on his work. He probably hadn't heard what Stefan just said. He was so fixated on blocking out anything to do with her.

Going to the staff Spring Ball wasn't something she would normally be interested in, but hadn't she promised herself to be independent? She should be enjoying life. She should be trying out all these things she wouldn't normally do, now that she had the freedom to do them.

Letting Stefan take her wasn't what she wanted. She wanted Tom to take her. She wanted to walk in on his arm. To dance with him and enjoy a special night together. But he'd made it very clear that the kiss had been a terrible mistake. That she had been a terrible mistake. And that he wanted nothing to do with her in *that* way.

Well, fine!

She couldn't go to the ball alone and she couldn't see Tom taking her now, so… 'Sure. That'd be nice. Thank you.'

Stefan beamed. 'Great! That's fantastic! There's…something else actually. Jackie mentioned that you were looking for somewhere to live.'

She glanced at Tom, feeling her cheeks flame with heat, hating the way all of this was making her feel. It felt as if she might cry at any moment. She didn't want to move out. Not really. But she'd been forced into a corner by the whole situation and things were so difficult with Tom. It was probably best for her to leave. In fact, he'd likely be pleased to get rid of her. 'That's right.'

'I know of a place that's just come free in my block. I could get you a viewing, if you wanted? It has two bedrooms. Pretty decent. And the rent's not too high.'

'Oh…right. Erm…yes, sure, I'll take a look. Can't stay where I am forever, can I?'

Tom grabbed his notes and strode off, his eyes cold, his face impassive.

It was clear that he'd heard. Inside, Naomi felt devastated, but she wasn't sure what else she could have done. He wasn't even talking to her any more and his rejection of her hurt. She couldn't stay in his flat now. It had only been meant to be a temporary solution in the first place anyway and she'd been there fast approaching six weeks!

She was doing Tom a favour by moving. She was getting out of his hair, out of his life. It was what he was clearly asking for.

It was what he needed.

And if she was going to protect her heart…then it was what she needed, too.

CHAPTER SEVEN

EIGHT HOURS INTO his shift, Tom was standing in the waiting area of A&E watching his last patient hobble away on a new pair of crutches. Once his patient was safely through the double doors and on their way back home, he turned to hand some paperwork to the receptionist, but was suddenly tapped on the shoulder from behind.

'Excuse me, are you a doctor?'

Tom turned to see a tall man like himself, who was probably in his eighties, looking as grey as a ghost and sweating slightly. 'Are you all right, sir?'

'I don't feel very well, no,' the man replied.

His complexion, the sweating and the general look of confusion in the man's eyes told Tom that this was serious. His instinct went into overdrive and he grabbed the nearest wheelchair and manoeuvred the man into it gently. Then he turned around quickly and whisked the man through to Resus.

'What's your name, sir?' he asked as he pushed the man through the department, avoiding obstacles in his path and trying not to show the patient that he was close to a crash in more ways than one.

The patient didn't answer but just gazed about him as they passed through corridors and finally the double doors that led to the heart of A&E.

Tom would need assistance. He needed a nurse, some-one to help him with this patient and his assessment.

He saw Naomi coming out of the locker room, looking as beautiful as always, if a little paler than usual. His heart sank. He'd hoped he wouldn't have to ask her.

But he had to.

Patient care came first over personal issues.

'Naomi? Can you give me a hand?'

He saw the look of shock register on her face, then she resumed her professional air and smiled at the patient, be-fore hurrying along beside them.

He burst through the double doors into Resus and parked the patient in his chair next to an empty bed. Turn-ing to Naomi, he whispered, 'I think this guy's having a heart attack.'

He was too close. It reminded him of that kiss. Of feeling her there in his arms, breathing in her aroma, just *holding* her. And of the delight of her lips upon his. Abruptly—disturbed by the sudden outpouring of this memory—he turned away. 'Sir, can you get on this trol-ley for me?' There were no other patients in Resus. The department had their cases and all the other patients had been sent up to various wards or back home.

The old man stood on wobbly, weak legs, whilst Tom and Naomi held him steady as he turned to sit on the edge of the trolley.

'I'd better…take off…my shoes…' The man bent for-ward to remove his shoes and swayed dizzily.

They both grabbed him quickly, pushing him back against the bed and sweeping up the patient's legs. 'Your shoes are fine, sir. Up you go now.'

Tom quickly strode over to the ECG machine and dragged it across the floor. 'Can you remove your shirt for me?'

The man nodded slowly, as if he was hearing the instructions in slow motion. He seemed unable to focus on anything, with his head bobbing about like a boat at sea, as he slowly tried to coordinate his arms to lift off his jumper and shirt underneath.

It was taking too long. If this man was having a cardiac event, as Tom suspected, then losing all these precious seconds could have a fatal effect.

'Here, we'll help you.' He grabbed the hem of the jumper and shirt and pulled them over the man's head in one swift movement, so that Naomi could start attaching the leads to the patient's chest. Thankfully, the man wasn't too hairy, saving them a few more precious seconds that would have been wasted on shaving him to attach the electrodes. 'How long have you been feeling unwell, sir?'

'I don't... Was in the garden...' he mumbled, saying something further that Tom couldn't quite catch.

Naomi was just finishing attaching all the electrodes. She'd worked quickly and expertly, aware of the urgency, but not allowing it to overwhelm her. When she was done, she gave Tom a nod.

'Lie still for a moment, please, sir.'

Tom pressed the button to start the ECG recording the electrical impulses of the patient's heart. Whilst he waited for the trace to begin, Naomi wrapped a blood-pressure cuff around the man's arm and Tom put an oxygen mask over the patient's face and set it to full flow.

'Sir? Have you got any allergies? Anything I should know about?' Tom asked, leaning over the bed, his ear close to the patient's face so that he could hear an answer. Naomi grabbed the handset for the internal phone system and got through to Reception. 'Bleep Dr Thomas to Resus, please,' she instructed.

He glanced at the trace on the ECG machine. There was an acute ST elevation, indicating, along with his patient's other signs of confusion and waxy, pale skin, sure signs of a myocardial infarction.

He needed IV access and blood samples. He worked quickly, his mind buzzing, all his procedures and protocols running through his head like a military parade—in order, logical, precise.

This was what he loved doing. This was what he thrived on. Pressure, adrenaline, precision. Making decisions, reacting, recording, acting appropriately, *saving lives.*

'What's happening?' the patient mumbled through the mask, his head thrashing this way and that.

The double doors were pushed open as Dr Thomas arrived. The second he strode into the room, before the double doors had even swung closed again, the patient stopped moving and let out one long, heavy breath.

Naomi smacked the red emergency buzzer on the wall, calling for more assistance, and reached behind the trolley for the lever that would collapse it down flat.

Tom bent low over the patient, checking for breathing, watching for signs of his rising chest, but there was nothing. His fingers reached for the man's pulse.

Nothing.

In an instant, he stood and brought his fist down on the patient's chest.

Still nothing. The ECG showed ventricular tachycardia.

Tom hurriedly grabbed the defibrillator pads and placed them onto the man's chest, pressing the button and making the machine charge its joules ready for the shock. He looked around the patient's bed, making sure Dr Thomas, Naomi and the rapidly arriving team members were not touching the patient.

'Stand clear! Shocking!' He pressed the button again and the patient jerked slightly on the bed.

Naomi felt for a pulse and found one. 'We've got him back.'

Looks of relief were on the faces of everyone surrounding the bed as the patient slowly came to, blinking, before he promptly tore off the mask and vomited over the side railings.

When he'd recovered and been handed one of the cardboard bowls, the patient wiped his mouth and then looked around him at the mass of people. 'What happened?'

Tom stepped aside, avoiding the mess on the floor, and came to the other side of the patient's bed. 'What do you remember?'

'I was in my garden. I felt…odd. Thought I'd better come to A&E. I can't remember much more than that.'

Tom had seen that before. For some lucky people, the body prevented the mind from remembering something so traumatic and painful as a heart attack.

'You've had a heart attack, sir. What's your name?'

'Edward Stovey.'

'Well, Edward. You've been a very lucky man today.'

'Have I?'

Naomi reached for the man's hand and placed it in hers comfortingly. 'We nearly lost you there.'

Edward sighed. 'Wouldn't have really mattered if you had.'

Tom frowned. 'Of course it would. It would have mattered to us.' Losing any patient was something Tom didn't tolerate very well. To him, every loss was a failure. A failure to prevent the cruel twists and turns of fate that were sometimes visited upon good people.

'I… Thank you, Doctor. But in some ways, for me, it would have been a blessing.'

'In what way?'

Edward sucked in a gasp of oxygen from the mask before continuing. 'I've been alone for forty-seven years. Ever since my wife died.'

Tom looked away, feeling Edward's pain.

Naomi, watching him, realised he couldn't talk for a moment, so she answered the patient instead. 'I'm sorry to hear that. What happened?'

'Brain aneurysm. She was quite young when it happened. Only thirty-six. We'd not been married long. But she was my dream. My love. I could have met her again today.'

'You didn't remarry?' She stroked the patient's hand reassuringly with her thumb.

'No. My Betty was the only woman for me.'

Tom stared at the patient. They'd been in almost the same situation, widowed at a young age. But Edward Stovey had spent the majority of his life alone. Tom was still in the early stages of that path.

He wondered how Edward had coped. He felt suddenly full of questions he wanted to ask this man. But now was not the time. Their patient needed to be transferred up to the cardiac ward so that he could rest and be cared for properly.

He glanced at Naomi. 'I want half-hourly obs on Mr Stovey, please, Nurse.'

'Of course.'

Working with her in a desperate situation had been easy. They'd both known what had to be done. Their communication had been minimal, precise. Completely work related. But now their patient was in a better place and there wasn't the same kind of urgency, even though Mr Stovey's condition was still critical for the next twenty-four to forty-eight hours. The chances of another attack, maybe one even worse, were high. But now the immediate crisis was over, it was difficult to talk to Naomi again.

Tom couldn't be relaxed with her. It led to dangerous places, uncertain futures, pain and grief and guilt. Kissing her had been wrong. He knew it had been wrong, yet still it had been both amazing *and* terrifying.

He went over to the desk to quickly fill in his report on Mr Stovey so that a complete set of notes could travel up with the patient to the cardiac unit. He placed a quick call through to the ward that would take him and gave a potted history. Luckily they had a bed free and waiting. Once the notes were done, he would be able to call the porters to come and take Mr Stovey away.

Suddenly he sensed that Naomi was near him. He felt her rather than saw her there, and he turned to see her standing behind him, looking at him, as if contemplating whether to speak to him.

He bit the inside of his lip. 'Thank you for your help just then. I appreciate it.'

'No problem. It's what we're both here for.'

He couldn't drag his eyes away from her. It was like she had this magnetic pull over him.

What am I doing to myself? Putting myself through this torture?

He remembered that she'd agreed to go to the Spring Ball with Stefan. Unable to block out their conversation, he'd heard them arranging it. And the fact that there was a vacant flat in Stefan's block.

She's going to leave.

It had to be the best thing all round. Didn't it?

Tom turned away and went back to his paperwork. There was no point in going over it all. There was nothing he could do. Nothing he could offer her. At least, not what she deserved anyway. She was a wonderful person who deserved happiness and love. Two things he wasn't capable of giving her.

'I was thinking about what Mr Stovey said.' Her voice interrupted his train of thought.

'Oh?'

'Yes. About being alone for all those years.'

Tom signed his name on the paper, but didn't turn around. 'That's his choice.'

'Yes.' She came and stood by his side, laying her hand upon his to still the pen. He looked up into her stunning eyes. 'He *chose* that. I wonder if he was ever given another option.'

Then she walked back over to the patient's bed.

Tom watched her go, still feeling the intense heat upon his hand where she'd touched him and wondering what she'd meant. Had she been trying to imply something when she'd wondered if Mr Stovey had had another choice?

Was she implying that *he* had another choice?

Could she have been trying to say that, even though she'd agreed to go to the ball with Stefan, even though she was moving out, *they* still had another option as to how this could end?

He wasn't sure he could envision an alternative.

He returned to his paperwork, but he couldn't concentrate. He kept looking up at her, then at his patient. And back to her again.

Maybe she was right.

But what if she was wrong?

Two days later, Tom checked up on Edward in the cardiac unit. His patient was doing well, becoming more mobile and eating well.

The nurses informed him that Edward had had no visitors and no one had called to check on him either. That news had disturbed him the most.

He wondered how Edward was so alone. Surely a man in his eighties had friends or neighbours who would want to know how he was doing.

So he went to see the patient himself, waiting beside his bed for the older man to stir from his sleep. 'Good morning,' he said, when Edward blinked his eyes and pulled himself into an upright position.

'Morning. Dr Williams, isn't it?'

Tom nodded. 'How are you feeling?'

'I'm feeling good, I think. The doctors say I can go home soon.'

'That's excellent news. I'm really pleased to hear it.'

'Me too.'

'Yes? I'm glad. Do you have anyone that might help look after you when you get back?'

Edward shook his head. 'I look after myself.'

'No neighbours or family to check on you?'

'I'm on my own. I prefer it that way.'

'How long has it been that way?' Tom asked, genuinely interested.

'Ever since my wife died. She was all I ever needed in life. Since she passed, I've pretty much kept myself to myself.'

'Wasn't that lonely?'

'No. I had my work. I kept busy.'

'What did you do?'

'I was a taxi driver. Always with people, but, then again, always alone. But that was fine. It kept me busy and I could work for as long as I liked.'

Tom nodded uncomfortably, seeing too many similarities with his own life. Did he really want to be like Edward Stovey, working until his heart gave up? Then, what would happen when he *couldn't work*? Or when retirement loomed? How would he keep busy then? Tend a garden? Take up bingo?

'You never thought to remarry?'

Edward shook his head vehemently. 'There was only ever one woman for me. One true love. She was my soulmate, Doctor. You don't ever get to find another once you've lost them.'

He nodded. That was what he himself had always said. And he still believed that. How could he pursue something with Naomi when he knew it could never be the same as what he'd had with Meredith? Meredith had been his one true love, just as Betty had been Edward's.

Tom wondered if there was a chance they could be wrong. What if there was another person for you, as Naomi believed? What if that was true, but he didn't bother to look for her, or dare to take the risk? Would he be doomed to live like Edward? He shuddered at the thought of ending up in a hospital bed one day, with no one to care for him.

'How did you know Betty was your soulmate?'

Edward smiled. 'That's not an easy thing to answer. It's different for everyone. But for me, it was because Betty was in my thoughts all the time. She made me feel good. Alive. She made me laugh and she made me cry. When I wasn't loving her, I was worrying about her, or arguing with her, or laughing with her. I wanted to care for her. I wanted to be there for her. I wanted to take away her pain. I wanted to always see her smile. That's what it was like for me.' He looked at Tom. 'Do you have that with someone? Because if you do, then you should embrace it. Accept it. Love is a precious gift not always given to all.'

Tom sat back in his chair and thought hard. Yes, he'd had that with Meredith. All of it. But he was confused, because he'd also experienced it all with Naomi.

He didn't know how that was possible. Naomi was constantly in his thoughts, especially because he was trying his hardest *not* to think about her. She made him smile and laugh and he felt comfortable with her. Safe. Despite her clumsiness and her inability to climb ladders, cook safely or stay upright on four wheels. He cared for her and he didn't want to hurt her. But she was moving on. Agreeing to a date with Stefan. Looking for her own place to live.

By kissing her that night, by allowing himself that momentary weakness, hadn't Tom hurt her already? Their relationship had already been affected by that one act and he knew she had to be hurting because he was in pain, too. He'd kissed her and now he was enforcing this distance between them, because he thought that was the right thing to do. He'd thought that if he stayed away from Naomi, then he couldn't hurt her any more.

Because they couldn't have a future.

Could they?

No.

Tom shook his head and abruptly stood up. All this uncertainty, this toing and froing, was giving him a headache. He forced a smile and held out his hand to shake Edward's. 'Well, I just thought I'd come check on you. See how you were doing.'

'Well, I appreciate that, Doc.' Edward took his hand. 'Thanks for saving my life. You thank that pretty nurse for me, too.'

'No problem. Take care, Mr Stovey.' He started to walk away and just as he reached the ward entrance he heard Edward call out, 'Dr Williams?'

He turned. 'Yes?'

'I may be wrong, of course. There was someone I could have been with. *After* Betty. I liked her very much and we could have been happy.'

Tom stared at the man, not knowing what to say.

'I clung to my beliefs because I wasn't ready to let go of my wife. I knew that if I let her go, then I wouldn't have a direction. I wouldn't have a reason. I became so entrenched in my role as a grieving widower, I forgot that I could actually be someone else.'

Tom saw the meaningful look in his patient's eyes and understanding dawned on him. He also had two choices. One—take a chance on Naomi and challenge his theory about true love. Or two—remain as Meredith's widower for the rest of his life.

In one lay an opportunity for happiness, the other would lead to a life of loneliness and heartache.

'I saw the looks you were giving that nurse, but I also saw how she looked at you. There's love there, isn't there?' Mr Stovey smiled.

It seemed a simple choice.

Naomi watched as Tom walked straight past her without acknowledgement. Without a smile. He was fully focused, head down, reading a file as he walked, his brow lined in thought.

She missed him and she had no idea how that was even possible. They'd only been friends and flatmates for six weeks and yet she missed his smiles, the way he'd listen to her chat as they cooked together, the way he'd steal glances at her when he thought she wasn't looking.

The kiss they'd shared had been amazing. It had been the best kiss she'd experienced in her whole life and yet… she hated it. She hated it for taking Tom from her.

He'd retreated from her. They'd still shared a car into work and the same flat space, but that had been all. The conversations had gone, the caring had disappeared. In fact, any interaction between them had been non-existent.

Surely there had to be a way back for them. She'd meant for the roller derby to be fun, and at first it had been. They'd laughed *so* much. She could see him now, holding her hand, laughing, his eyes sparkling, as they'd both stumbled around.

How could she get that Tom back?

Naomi picked up the next patient file card and went to the waiting area to call her next patient through. 'Amy Smith?'

A middle-aged woman got up and smiled at her and she led her new patient through to a cubicle, pulling a curtain closed behind them.

'Take a seat. Right! Can you confirm your address and date of birth for me?'

Amy confirmed the details.

'Okay. So you've received an electric shock, is that right?'

Amy nodded emphatically. 'That's right.'

'Tell me what happened.'

She took a deep breath. 'Well! Lee has been renovating the house, but you know what men are like. They start a million jobs all at once instead of just doing one and doing it well. I'd been asking him to do the light switches for ages—we've barely had any proper electricity for a few weeks and he promised he'd do it, only he hadn't got round to it, so I had a go.'

'And what happened?' Naomi smiled through the explanation, cutting to the heart of the matter.

'I asked him to turn off the electricity and he said he would, but he disappeared off into the kitchen. So I thought he'd done it, only he hadn't, and when I went to touch the switch with my screwdriver I got this shock and got thrown back a bit.'

Naomi raised her eyebrows. 'Okay. Which hand received the shock?'

'My right, I suppose, but both hands were on the screwdriver.'

'Can I see?' She examined her patient's hand, but there were no burn signs or entry points to be seen, so that was good news. 'How far were you thrown back?'

'About a metre. I say "thrown"…it might just have been me staggering back, but I felt *something* and Libby who lives next door said I ought to come and get checked out in case the current passed through my heart or something.'

Electric shocks could be tricky. The effects weren't always immediately obvious and the more serious shocks could cause electroporation, where cell rupture caused tissue death.

In general, Amy seemed fine, but Naomi knew it was best to check her over just to make sure. 'I'll need to do an ECG, Amy. Have you had one before?' Her patient shook her head. 'It's a series of electrodes that I place mainly on your chest and it'll record an accurate trace of the electrical impulses in your heart. It'll just make sure everything's normal and it only takes a few seconds. In fact, it takes longer to set it up.'

'Right. That's fine. So you think I'm okay?'

'We'll do the trace just to make sure. Have you had any side effects? Nausea? Confusion? Pain?'

'Nothing.'

'You didn't pass out?'

'No. I've been fine.'

'We'll do the trace and make sure, then. Can you remove your top half for me?'

Amy began taking off her top. 'This is all Lee's fault. I swear, men are more trouble than they're worth! I don't see a ring on your finger, Nurse. I hope that means you're single?'

She nodded. 'I am.'

'Take my advice and stay that way. I wish I had. I would have been a lot happier. And my house wouldn't be such a mess either.'

'I...er...need to get the ECG machine. I'll be back in a tick.' Naomi slipped out of the cubicle and let out a deep breath. Maybe Amy was right. She should stay single and then she'd only have to worry about herself. Look at the mess she'd got into just because she'd kissed Tom. It hurt not being close to him any more and the pain was almost physical.

But that doesn't stop me wishing we had something more...

She pushed the machine back to the cubicle, closed the curtain once more and performed the trace. Amy's heart was fine. But she gave her an information sheet of things to look out for and sent her on her way.

'Thank you, Nurse. Let's see if I've got electricity when I get back!'

Naomi imagined that she would have. Amy might have complained about 'her Lee', but Naomi would still bet anything that she loved him. That she'd be heartbroken if there was something seriously wrong with him, or if he tried to leave her.

Or if he completely cut her off. The way Tom had done to her.

That's obviously what he wants. He's given me a clear message that he doesn't want anything to do with me any more.

Admitting that caused a pain in her chest and she had to stand there and rub at her breastbone for a moment, until it went away.

CHAPTER EIGHT

NAOMI SET OFF the next morning with more of a spring in her step, determinedly telling herself inwardly that what she was doing was the right thing. She'd spent a restless night tossing and turning, agonising over her decision. She knew she had to move out, find her own place and stand on her own two feet, as she'd promised herself she would.

Outside, it was slightly overcast as she walked purposefully to the bus stop and stood waiting, checking to make sure she had the right change. The sky darkened even as she stood there and she glanced up at it, worrying, realising she had misjudged the weather and hoping the downpour would hold off until later.

Her wish wasn't granted. As the bus took her to her destination the heavens opened and she knew that without an umbrella she was going to get soaked in just her small jacket.

Oh, well, she thought. She was only meeting a lettings agent after all.

She walked with her head down against the rain, as she headed for Echo Road where the flat was situated. From what she knew it was in a block of rather old flats. The flat she was looking at today had recently become empty after the tenant who had lived there for many years had passed away. The previous tenant had not decorated or touched the place since the seventies, the agent, Deanna, had said, but Naomi pushed that thought to one side. The important thing was that she could afford this flat. Decor could always be changed. Walls could be painted. As long as it was clean, she didn't mind.

By the time she got to the flats, her hair was plastered to her face and her clothes were soaked, her wet skirt constantly wrapping itself around her thighs.

Deanna was waiting for her and let her in exclaiming, 'Oh, look at you! You're like a drowned rat! At least you'll be able to dry off for a bit inside.'

Naomi managed a weak smile and followed her in.

The flat was dark with a weird orange wallpaper adorning the walls and she looked around disappointedly at the dark brown carpet and curtains. The kitchen was a melamine nightmare and the bathroom had an avocado-coloured suite and a discoloured linoleum floor. It smelt all musty, too. As if the place had been shut up for months, not weeks.

'It needs some modernisation, obviously,' Deanna said. 'But with a lick of paint and a bit of elbow grease, this place could be a stunning apartment. The sash windows are a real highlight and you could really make a feature of them. Maybe with some white voile and a bit of window cleaner.' Deanna laughed good-naturedly.

She was being optimistic, Naomi thought. The place needed a bit more than a lick of paint. The previous tenant had been a smoker, judging by the odd tinge of yellow to most things. However, she could see that with a bit of hard work and an awful lot of time she could probably make something of the place. Sadness washed over her as she pictured herself being here. She imagined her hair all tied up in a scarf to protect it, whilst she scrubbed and polished, with the windows open wide to air the place, to get rid of that stale smell.

It wasn't great. It wasn't what she wanted. But it would get her away from Tom and all the problems that came with living in his space. She had no choice. It was the middle of March now and she'd been living at Tom's for too long. If she were to live free of Tom and her feelings for him, then she'd have to move out of the beautiful flat she was in at the moment and take this place instead.

Sighing, she nodded to Deanna. 'I'll take it.'

The agent looked surprised. 'Great! I'll get everything in motion. The landlord will need a deposit and the first month's rent in advance.'

'Fine. I'll call you later and arrange it.'

'Fantastic!' She shook Naomi's hand. 'I'm sure you'll be very happy here!'

She smiled back at her. But it was forced. She could only hope that Deanna was right.

'This is Andi, sixteen years of age and, around two o' clock this afternoon, she took a heroin overdose. We've administered naloxone and given oxygen.' The paramedics gave them the rundown as they helped to slide the young girl onto the bed.

Naomi looked at her, feeling sympathy for the young girl. She wondered if the girl had meant to take the over-dose, or if she'd not truly known what she was doing. Whatever the case, the medication was just starting to take effect and she was coming round.

Blinking heavily, Andi looked around her and then she suddenly sat up and hauled herself over the side of the bed.

'Where do you think you're going, young lady?' Tom said as he managed to grab her, and Naomi lowered the rail so they could get their patient back onto the bed.

She was glad Tom was there, because she didn't think she would have physically handled the girl on her own. She was taller than Naomi and quite broad.

'Get off me! Don't touch me!' The girl yanked her arm away from Tom and he backed off, with his hands raised as if in surrender.

'Okay, okay...' He looked over at Naomi. 'I've got her parents' details here, I'm just going to give them a ring. Can you do her obs for me?'

'Sure.' This confirmed what Naomi had suspected, that Tom was happy to talk to her when they were working on cases, but that he stuck to the medical, through and through. She accepted it, but she also knew she had to tell him that she'd found a place to live and that she would be leaving at the weekend.

He was bound to be relieved. She couldn't imagine he would react in any other way, after the way he'd been acting lately.

She nodded and watched him walk over to the phone, but just when her back was turned the teenager bolted from the bed and shot through the double doors of the department.

'Tom!' she shouted as she ran after the girl. She knew she wouldn't get far. The drugs only had a temporary effect.

Andi blundered through A&E, pushing past staff as if she were running from an assassin, and then shot through the waiting room and out of the main door to freedom. It was impressive. Many people got lost in the maze of A&E corridors, but this girl had found her way out even half drugged.

Naomi ran through the doors leading to the outside world and blinked in the sunshine as she searched for Andi's figure. Then she spotted her, lying flat out on the grass by the waiting ambulances. She knelt down beside her.

Andi was out cold.

Tom caught up with Naomi and came to stand over them both. 'How is she?'

'Unconscious, but there's a strong pulse.'

'Let's get her back inside and she can sleep it off.' He signalled for help to a paramedic who was restocking his ambulance with oxygen and BVMs and together, using a trolley, they got the girl back inside. Once Andi had been parked in a bay and her obs had been done to make sure she was okay, Naomi turned to Tom and laid her hand on his arm before he could walk away.

'Tom?'

He stopped in his tracks and turned around reluctantly. 'Yes?'

'I've found a place to live. The flat in Stefan's block. I viewed it yesterday and I can move in on Saturday.'

'I see.'

She waited to see if he would give any other reaction. 'I thought maybe I could cook for you on the Friday night... One last dinner together?' It would mean a lot to her if they could part as friends. Perhaps he would even be more at ease in her company if he knew that she was going.

'I'll cook. My treat,' he added, although he didn't look as thrilled by the news as she'd imagined he would. She watched him walk away and wondered if it had really been sadness she'd seen in his eyes, or whether it had all been in her own imagination.

Was this really their last night together?

Naomi sat in her bedroom, deciding upon what to wear. Tom was already busy in the kitchen and the aromas drifting around the flat were mouth-wateringly good.

No fire alarms had gone off, of course, as he was cooking, but there were the dulcet tones of classical music playing from the speakers in the living room.

Naomi wanted to make their last night special. This was their goodbye to one another, after all that had happened after that first clumsy fall off the ladder. Had that really been six weeks ago? She had only meant to have stayed one night, and now a month and a half later…

It really was time for her to go! *Talk about outstaying your welcome…*

She perused the dresses in her wardrobe, allowing her fingers to fondly stroke the dress she'd worn to the Phoenix riverboat restaurant. No, she wouldn't wear that one. She wanted something different. Something a bit more… grown up.

She selected a dark green wrap-around dress, then sat in front of the mirror and took her hair up with a few pins and twists. She applied some mascara and lipstick and spritzed herself with her favourite perfume.

Then, taking a deep breath, she went back into the main living area to see what Tom was cooking.

He stood slicing vegetables, dressed in a beautifully white shirt with dark trousers. He looked up as he saw her approach, his eyes widening for a brief moment.

'You look…nice,' he said, after a moment.

She'd take nice. At least he was *being nice* to her, she supposed, but, then again, she was going to be moving out in the morning. 'Thank you. So do you.'

He began chopping some nuts.

'What's on the menu?'

'A cranberry-stuffed pork roast with seasonal vegetables and a classic lemon meringue for dessert.'

'Sounds wonderful.'

'It'll be about an hour. Can I pour you a drink?'

'I'll have whatever you're having.'

She wandered away from the kitchen area and found herself over by the piano. The cleaner had been yesterday and in the vase sat a beautiful bouquet of delicate pink roses. She stroked the top of the instrument, sad that she'd never managed to hear him play, and realised he'd spotted her doing so. He quickly looked away and busied himself in the kitchen again, pretending that he hadn't seen.

Moving away, she went over to the sofa and sank onto it, tucking her feet up beside her as Tom brought her over a glass of white wine. She thanked him.

'My pleasure,' he said. He was about to head back to the kitchen, when she reached forward and took his hand.

'Tom...'

His pained expression met her gaze and then he looked away, biting his lip. 'What is it?'

'Sit with me. Just for a moment.'

He seemed to think about it briefly, but then he did as she asked and she let go of his hand, allowing him to sit back and be relaxed. She didn't like being the cause of his pain.

'I wonder if we could forget the last week or so. The atmosphere between us...it's been...difficult. I'd really like our last night together to be an enjoyable one. For both of us. Could we do that?'

Tom looked at her and there was such a mix of emotion on his face. Pain. Regret. And something else that she just couldn't pinpoint.

This was all so strange for her. These strong emotions were so new. She'd never felt so pained before, except maybe for that day when Vincent had finally passed, but even then there had been a small measure of happiness in that moment because she'd been so relieved that he was finally free of his prison. His skeleton had betrayed him and had kept him a prisoner within a body that had no longer worked properly. He'd even been unable to talk towards the end and they'd spent their last few hours together just holding hands, waiting for the darkness to fill his eyes, and when it had... When it finally had, it had almost been a blessing.

But this... These emotions she was experiencing with Tom were so totally different. There was no skeleton keeping Tom prisoner. But his memories, his emotions, were doing the same thing. She really didn't want to make him feel as if he was betraying his wife's memory.

'Since the...what happened between us...I've felt...distanced from you and that's been hard for me. I felt like we were good friends before.'

'We are.'

'But since the kiss—'

'I'm sorry, Naomi. I'm sorry I made you feel like you weren't wanted, it's just...' Naomi could see he was struggling for the right words '...when I kissed you, I felt... different from how I'd expected to feel and I was overwhelmed with—'

'Guilt?'

He shook his head. 'No. Yes. I'd thought I was in control of my feelings. I'd told myself how my life was going to be and suddenly I was going against all of that. You were in my arms and I just *had* to kiss you, like I was drawn to you, like you were the air that I breathe.' He looked up at her and caught her gaze with his own.

She sucked in a breath, amazed at how wrong she'd been. He hadn't been feeling guilty about his wife at all. Instead, he'd felt guilt at a betrayal of himself. Guilt at losing control.

'I couldn't promise you a future. I was angry at myself for being weak and giving in to an impulsive urge.'

She laid her hand on his. 'Don't be hard on yourself. We were having fun. Laughing, skating, singing to the music—badly!' She smiled. 'We were close. Good friends. Sharing a good time.'

'It was more than that.'

She nodded. She'd been trying to make light of the situation, to let him off the hook, but he was being honest with her and she appreciated that.

'There's something about you, Naomi, that I can't resist, and that scares me.'

She stared back at him, feeling her heart pound and her blood race. She felt the same way about him, too. That was why his rejection of her had hurt so much. When he'd begun pushing her away, she'd found her mounting feelings for him hard to deal with. But if he had felt the same way, perhaps he'd been retreating from her for his own self-preservation... If he'd felt he could offer her nothing in the way of a future together, maybe he'd thought that it would just be better not to have been with her in the first place.

'I feel it, too,' she said softly.

'You do?'

She nodded.

'I've felt so bad over these past few days. It's been so hard to stay away from you.' He reached over and stroked her face and she had to fight the urge to turn and kiss his fingers. She *burned* for him. Despite everything that had happened. It was as if she'd been through a trial of separation. And now that they were close together again, on the same sofa, within touching distance, she was learning that her original desire was still there, if not stronger than before.

Absence makes the heart grow fonder.

Wasn't that right? Was her heart involved in all of this? Because if it was, then could this be the love that everyone talked about, sang about? That was a huge, scary prospect, because she'd never loved like this before. It was terrifying because, even if she loved him, she knew she couldn't have him. Tom had made that plain.

'We're together again now. For this last night. Let's make it perfect. Because I know that we both want each other to be happy.'

'I would never want to hurt you, Naomi.' He tucked a stray strand of hair behind her ear and she smiled, feeling tears prick her eyes.

'Then be my friend, if you can't be anything else.'

Tom wanted to take her in his arms there and then and kiss her until they were both falling into oblivion, but he didn't move. The power of his self-control surprised him, because he wanted more than anything to touch Naomi, hold her and kiss her.

Since their kiss he'd been tortured. He'd been almost sent crazy by his agonies of uncertainty, wanting to be with her, fighting against his mindset that he couldn't offer her anything. It had almost torn him apart.

He was starting to falter in his belief about there being only one true love for everyone. What if Naomi were right and there *was* another person out there who could be his soulmate? And what if Naomi was that person? And he was throwing their relationship away because he was so certain that it was only possible to love one person so much, so certain that all other relationships after Meredith would pale in comparison.

But who was to say that these 'paler' relationships were no good? That they weren't as valuable, weren't as enjoyable, weren't as *true*?

Because, damn, his feelings for Naomi felt strong! They felt as strong as anything he'd ever felt for Meredith and that scared the living daylights out of him. He still barely knew her! They'd lived together for the best part of a couple of months, but, really, that was nothing. What did that prove?

That I can't bear the idea of her moving out. That I can't stand this self-imposed prison I've created around myself.

He became aware that Naomi was staring at him, with eyes watery with tears, tears that *he'd* caused. He'd told her that he would never want to hurt her but he was still doing exactly that. And it was all because of his stupid rules!

I must be wrong, because Naomi feels so right!

She was *right there*. Right next to him. Within touching distance. He could wipe that tear from her cheek. He could wipe it away and kiss her again and throw away all those self-regulated chains that were holding him back. He could reach out to her and break free and—damn the rules!

He could make her feel better. Make *himself* feel better. He could be happy with Naomi if only he gave himself the opportunity.

He leaned forward and, closing his eyes, tenderly kissed away the tears on her cheek.

She sucked in a breath and he opened his eyes to look at her. They were just millimetres away, both of them holding back for just a second more, just a moment to make sure the other one wanted this as much as they did and then...

He pressed his lips to hers. His hands delved into her thick mane of hair, pulling it free of the pins and clips as it tumbled around her shoulders and down her back. Then suddenly he was tasting her and she tasted divine. She kissed him back fervently, her hands pulling him to her, pressing him against her as she lay back on the sofa and he enveloped her, his tongue exploring and his senses going into overdrive as he tasted, smelt, touched.

She groaned his name and reached for his shirt at his

waistband, pulling it up and free so that her hands could find his bare skin beneath.

He needed her. He needed her so badly and yet he had to be tender. She was so soft and delicate and he wanted to enjoy every sensation, every caress, to see her every delight, revel in her joy and her ecstasy.

Finding the knot of material at her waist, he tugged it free and began to remove her dress...

Naomi gloried in the delights befalling her body. Tom had an expert touch. He knew exactly where to touch her, where to taste, and his fingers played over her skin as if she were a finely tuned musical instrument.

Tom's mouth slowly tasted each breast, delicately licking and kissing her, trailing down over the gentle slope of her stomach, giving teasing little nips and licks, sending sensations of both shock and pleasure through her body, until finally his mouth came to settle between her thighs.

Arching her back, she groaned as he sought out her most delicate area. Grasping his hair in her hands, she gasped for breath, riding the waves of pleasure that sang their way through her nerve endings and sent her sensory system into overload, as her pleasure built and built until she was crying out his name, begging him to stop.

Was this what she had been missing all her life? This passion, this ardour? This frenzy of desire and want and need? She had dismissed such feelings as unimportant when she'd met and married Vincent, believing that the measured love she'd had for him would be enough to carry them through what was to come. She'd believed that her friendship with Vincent had been just as important as her love and that the heat, the fire, the intensity of all the feelings she was experiencing right now were something that she could live without.

She'd not known what she had been missing. Of course, she'd seen films where the two main characters got lost in a hot, scorching night, totally consumed by their passion for each other. But she'd dismissed them as *pretend*. They hadn't been real. Surely that wasn't what real people experienced. She'd thought it was impossible to find someone like that, someone who could make you go stir crazy in bed.

And so she'd continued to sit and watch the movies next to Vincent and had managed not to worry that she was missing out on something.

Now that she was experiencing it, she knew she couldn't live without it. If only she'd known...

Tom entered her and she closed her eyes in delight. This was *it*. This was the feeling that she'd read about, that she'd often wondered about, that she'd wanted to feel, but never had. This feeling of being consumed, of being filled, of being joined to another in such an intimate way. And it was wondrous! Being with Tom, knowing that he needed her as much as she needed him, made her feel so free. It was crazy, laugh-out-loud amazing.

She could feel Tom's ardour increasing as his movements got faster and harder. Gripping him to her, she gasped for air, feeling the hard strength of his taut body above her, riding her. His mouth found hers and then she lost herself yet again, allowing herself to fall into the wonderful chasm that was Tom's arms, letting go of everything about herself that she'd ever held back, encouraging him to do the same, until suddenly—wonderfully—he cried out, thrusting into her like his whole life depended upon it and then...then he stilled. Just for a moment. Then his mouth found hers once again, pressing his lips against hers. He continued kissing her, tasting her lips, her tongue, her neck, tracing her collarbone with his lips. His hot breath trailing along her skin made her tingle.

For a second, they just lay there, holding each other, still entwined.

Naomi revelled in this glorious sensation. She had found a new side of herself that she hadn't known existed. Never before had sex been anything like this. There'd been some drunken fumbling and Vincent had done his best to try and please her, but there'd been so many physical restrictions. With Vincent, the body had been something to fight against. For him to get angry at. He'd not been able to touch her the way she'd wanted. Not been able to excite her the way she'd really wanted.

It had always been a frustrating event and in the end something that they had stopped doing. Their marriage had become a friendship after that. It had been all about companionship and she'd lied and told herself that that was enough.

With Tom sex was something to be enjoyed. To be revelled in. She'd been made love to and she now knew it was wonderful. All her dreams about what it might be like, all her desires, had been fulfilled and she felt sated. She felt content.

And from somewhere, tears began to fall.

She couldn't help it. The tears came unbidden and poured from her like a bursting dam. Before she knew it, she was sobbing, curling in on herself. She felt her grief and her delight pummelling her alternately until she didn't know what she was crying about.

Tom looked at her, bewildered for a moment, but then he pulled her close, wrapping his arms around her, just holding her, waiting for whatever it was to pass.

'Hey, it's okay. Shh... Don't cry.' He stroked her arms, kissing her bare shoulders, then her cheeks and her eyelids.

He continued to be unbelievably kind as she lay there, until her tears were spent and dried upon her face. Then finally she lay still. She was afraid to look at him. Afraid of how he might react.

But he just held her, tightly, in his arms, her limbs still entwined with his. 'You okay?'

Naomi sniffed and nodded. 'Yes.'

'What was that all about?' he asked gently.

She stared at the wall, unable to look him in the eyes, but knowing she couldn't tell him what she was feeling. How she felt *loved*. She knew he wasn't ready to hear that. Not right now. 'I don't know.'

Tom frowned, but he kissed her one more time. 'Don't worry about it,' he said. He held her even closer, refusing to let go.

It was almost enough to make her cry again, but this time she was prepared. She was ready for the tears. They might have surprised her before, but she wasn't going to let that happen again.

She kissed his arm and laid her head against his chest, listening to his heart beat, falling in love with its rhythm. Falling in love with him.

She knew she was falling for him. She couldn't help it. Her emotions had always been quick to assert themselves. She'd always known that when she did, she would fall fast and hard. She was still wary. It had all gone so badly after they had only kissed. Now they'd made love. But maybe this was a good sign. She'd thought that Tom would be happy to get rid of her, but they had just made love in the most beautiful way...

Snuggling into his arm, she closed her eyes and imagined. She imagined a brilliant future for the both of them. Surely it had to go well from now on. Look at how well they fitted together. It felt *right*.

He kissed the top of her head and she turned to look at him. 'Okay?'

Tom smiled. 'I am. You know, I really ought to go and turn the food down. It's probably overcooked by now.'

Naomi laughed. He was even burning food like her. 'You should. But maybe you should bring some of it back here. I'm starving, suddenly.'

She saw his gaze travel to her lips and he kissed her once again. 'For food?'

'Amongst other things.'

He smiled. 'Well, maybe I could tempt you again with those...other things.'

Her hand slipped down his body. 'Tempt away.'

They made love once again and after, lying spent in each other's arms, their hunger for food overcame them. Naomi watched him walk away to the kitchen, tall and proud, admiring his broad back, neat waist, gorgeous bottom and long, powerful thighs. He was a beautiful man to look at but he was beautiful inside, too. He'd tried to stay away from her because he'd thought he had nothing to offer her, but he was wrong. He had everything to offer. She just hoped that he believed it now, too.

He came back into view with a towel around his waist and carrying a bedsheet for her. She took it, smiling, and stood up to wrap it around her body. 'Thank you.'

He smiled at her and dipped his head to kiss her again, his lips soft against hers. 'Can I get you anything? A drink? Something to eat?'

'Is dinner ruined?'

'It's rescuable. I think I might have carbonised the meat, though.' He gave a short laugh.

'As long as it's still edible, I could probably eat a horse.'

'Maybe we should get dressed, if we're going to eat?'

Naomi looked down at her bedsheet and his towel and grinned. 'Let's not.'

He laughed again and guided her over to the table. 'Take a seat. I'll serve.'

She sat patiently and waited, her olfactory senses suddenly going into overdrive at the aroma of the food, and her stomach rumbled.

When Tom brought dinner to the table, Naomi didn't think it looked burnt at all. The pork was perfect, with plenty of crackling, and the vegetables were soft and buttery just the way she liked. She'd always hated it when people served them al dente anyway.

It was a gorgeous meal, made better by the fact that she and Tom were at peace again. At least for the evening. Everything might change when she moved out. But hopefully, they were moving in the right direction. One with her and Tom together.

She raised her glass in a toast. 'To good food, good friends and love,' she said, impulsively.

He clinked his glass to hers. 'Good food, friends…and love.' He swallowed his mouthful of wine and gazed at her over the table thoughtfully.

Naomi had never expected the evening to go like this. They'd barely been speaking to each other at the start! But now they were close again and would hopefully remain that way. Even though she was moving out.

It was a grim thought, imagining the new flat. There was so much hard work she had yet to do in order to get it ready, to try and make it as wonderful as this. It was going to take a lot of time and she was going to miss living here. Tom had given her a truly wonderful gift by allowing her to share this beautiful space with him. By allowing her to share his life. His feelings. She glanced over at the piano and wondered. 'Tom…can I ask you a big favour?'

'Of course.'

'Before I go, would you…play for me? Play the piano?'

She saw him glance over at the instrument and take in a breath. He looked uncertain. He looked…doubtful. She wondered if she'd pushed him too far.

But he suddenly got up, brushed at his mouth with a napkin and walked over to the piano, staring down at it, as if he might be about to fight it. As if it were dangerous. But then he bent, pulled out the stool and lifted the lid as he settled onto the seat.

Naomi went over to him.

'What shall I play?'

'Whatever your heart tells you to.'

He glanced at her and nodded, raising his hands over the keys before finally, all of a sudden, he touched them and began to play.

The next morning, when Tom woke, he instantly looked to his side and saw Naomi sleeping. She looked so beautiful. Peaceful. With her face in gorgeous repose, her lips looked so soft and her naked body beneath the sheets was so tempting.

It had been a long time since he'd woken up with a woman beside him. The last time had been with Meredith and he'd never expected anyone to take her place, but suddenly there was…

Naomi Bloom.

What the hell do I do now?

Naomi had even mentioned love. It had just been a toast, but he wondered if she had read something into their relationship. He wasn't sure he was ready for that. It was a huge leap from friendship to love, and one he wasn't certain he could offer.

He wanted to give her everything. Very much so. But

love? He didn't know where he stood on that issue. And Naomi deserved to have someone who loved her and who could fully commit himself to her.

Could that person be him?

He had feelings for her, yes. There was no denying that. Making love to her had been amazing, deep and intense, but he wasn't sure he was ready to fully hitch his wagon to someone else just yet and give himself so completely. If he did that, if he could do that... He had no idea what would happen if he lost her. Would he be able to go through that turmoil again?

There must be an opportunity here to take things slowly. Naomi would be moving out later today, after her shift, and that would create some much-needed space between them. It would allow them both to get some perspective after living and working in each other's pockets over the last month or so. Judging by Naomi's tears, it wasn't just him who was feeling overwhelmed. He wasn't sure what to think about that. Although she hadn't seemed upset, so much as thoughtful. It didn't seem that the experience had been awful for her.

Their coming together had been something that neither of them had been able to resist. The moment had seemed primal, soulful. But in speaking those words in her toast, Naomi had imbued it with so much meaning. Did she think that Tom *loved* her? Because he couldn't promise her that.

He climbed out of bed, being careful not to wake her, and opened the door of his wardrobe. There, on the top shelf, was his one remaining photo of Meredith. It had been taken on their wedding day. She looked out at him from the frame, her head tilted slightly to one side, as if questioning him.

Why is there another woman in my place, Tom?

Her beautiful face amongst the flowers in her head-dress and veil was a vision in white. He'd known exactly what he was doing when he'd married Meredith and he'd known exactly what he could offer her. He had been certain. But with Naomi…

What have I done?

Tom closed the wardrobe door and sank his head against the wood. He'd made a dreadful mistake. What he'd done had not been fair to either of them. He'd allowed his physical urge to be with Naomi to override his logical thought processes. The ones that had told him to hold back, to keep a safe distance from her. He'd let Naomi think that there could be a future for them both and that simply wasn't fair.

He needed to tell her the truth. He owed her that much.

He went out into the living area and instantly his gaze fell to the piano. He'd even *played* for her. He was such a fool.

He knew they needed to talk. He needed her to wake up, so that he could tell her. So that he could let her know that this was something that would have to be taken slowly or not at all. That this wasn't love. Not yet. Even if she thought it was.

Tom sat on the sofa and waited.

Naomi woke and rose, grabbing a robe from the back of the bedroom door. All her clothes were in her room. This morning she felt good. Great, even. She and Tom had healed the rift between them and in the bargain she'd also discovered what it was in life that she had always been missing. Amazing passion, intensity, love.

It didn't matter that she was moving out today. The distance might even be a good thing, giving each of them their own space and putting the relationship on an equal footing. They would be able to date properly, Tom calling round to her, picking her up and taking her out. Their relationship would start just as any other one would. They would start separately, until that moment, when, if everything went right, they would come together and unite, be one.

She used Tom's small en-suite, splashing some water on her face and drying it before she headed out of the bathroom and into the living space. She smiled when she saw him, ready to wish him good morning.

Tom stood there, by the piano, and it seemed he had been waiting for her. He'd changed into his usual suit and still looked just as magnificent dressed as he did naked.

I'm a really lucky girl.

'I don't think we should do this any more.'

She was rocked to her very core. What? What did he mean? Had she missed something? Had something happened whilst she'd slept?

'You deserve someone who can offer you the world, Naomi. You deserve someone who can fully love you as you deserve to be loved. Until I know if I'm that man, I don't think we should…do that again.'

She wasn't sure what to say. She deserved love, yes, but so did he. She knew she could love him, and in fact, she knew she probably already did.

But he'd said he wasn't sure he could be the man for her. That he thought they needed to *wait* until he worked out whether he could be with her. Naomi wondered if this was some sort of a cruel joke. She didn't know what to think. She wouldn't put up with it; she wouldn't wait any longer. Not now she knew. Not now she knew what love could be like. The way it *felt*.

'And I'm supposed to just hang around until you work that out?'

'I think we might have rushed—'

'How dare you, Tom? How dare you? I've been nothing

but straight with you! I've held nothing back from you from the start and what…is that suddenly too much for you?'

He remained calm as he answered her, as if patiently explaining something to a child. 'We made love, yes, and that was great, but that didn't mean…I can't *love* you, Naomi, the way you expect me to. I just think we should hold back for a bit.'

'Do you?' she asked, suddenly furious! She couldn't believe he was doing this to her. Only last night, she'd been on cloud nine! How could he be so hot one moment and so cold the next?

'Well, hold back all you want, Tom, but I'm not going to. Life is for living and for being happy! I thought I was going to spend it with you, but if you're going to suddenly tell me to "hold your horses", then I'm getting off this ride. I've done the waiting game. I've been there, done that, and I'm not doing it again for anyone! You either love me or you don't.'

She waited for his response. She'd not meant to say it straight out like that. Although she didn't think it was that hard, to be honest. She knew how she felt, but if he didn't know, then…

Don't cry again.

She could feel the tears welling. She could feel them burning the backs of her eyes as she stood there, challenging him, but she refused to blink, holding them back.

When it became clear that Tom *couldn't* answer her, Naomi stormed into her room and slammed the door. Slumping onto her bed, she began to cry, pulling her pillow over her head so that Tom wouldn't hear.

CHAPTER NINE

NAOMI SAT HUDDLED in the staffroom. She'd checked the rota. She was on duty till four p.m. So was Tom. They had a whole day to spend together after last night. After their conversation that morning.

How can I look him in the eye?

She couldn't picture it. She couldn't imagine him wanting to spend even a tiny second alone with her, after what had happened. She wanted to be a million miles away.

How could she and Tom work together in A&E without it spilling over and affecting everyone else they worked with? What about their patients? She didn't know if it was possible.

She thought back to last night, to the moment where she'd cried in Tom's arms. He had made love to her as if she were the most amazing person he knew. As if she were precious and he never wanted to let her go. He'd made her feel special, important. As if she mattered. As if she were someone who deserved every moment of happiness he could give her.

And then that happiness had been crushed!

She sank her head into her hands and groaned out loud, just as Stefan came in with Jackie.

'Oh, dear! Rough night, was it? Need the hair of the dog?' Stefan joked.

She looked at him and sighed, shaking her head. 'No. It wasn't booze.'

'Right. Another man, then? Or did you get to the last episode of your favourite box set?'

She smiled and shook her head. It wasn't as if she could tell them what had happened. 'Something like that.'

'Well, you and Dr Williams must be watching the same box set, then, because his face doesn't look much better this morning, either!' As she spoke Jackie turned to put her coat in her locker, so she didn't see the look that crossed her friend's face.

Naomi wondered how bad Tom was feeling. She'd made her own way into work, so she hadn't seen him since she'd left this morning. She was still moving out this afternoon; everything was set.

She wondered if the atmosphere would be as bad as it had been after the kiss. Or worse. Then he'd just been standoffish. Distant. Polite. Terse. She fervently hoped that what they'd done last night wouldn't affect everyone else around them. They all had to work together. And a disrupted team in A&E did not bode well for the rest of the hospital.

But how could she face him after their confrontation this morning?

'Where is he?' she asked, trying to sound casual.

'Oh, talking to Matron, I think.'

She got up to look through the glass in the staffroom window and saw him talking to the matron across the department. He looked awful. He was a little pale and there were shadows under his eyes. A sickly heaviness weighed upon her, but then he turned and noticed her watching and he suddenly stood up taller. He finished his conversation with the matron and then he walked away, without looking back.

Her heart sank.

* * *

He'd wanted her. Pure and simple. It had been an agony to keep himself away from her, despite all his attempts to keep distance between them. Naomi Bloom had got under his skin. There was something about her that he just couldn't ignore.

Being with her last night had been... He sighed. There were no words to describe adequately the way he'd felt. And those moments afterwards, as they'd just lain in each other's arms, had been perfect until she'd cried...

Tom shook his head angrily. She'd got under his skin. And there was a chance she thought he *loved* her!

He couldn't let her believe that. He *couldn't*!

He couldn't let it be true.

Because if he let it be true, then he'd be going against his own vow. His promise to never love another because...

If I allow her in, if I let her get close and then I lose her, like I lost Meredith...

He rubbed at his eyes and sank back against the wall. He just couldn't do it. He'd taken things too far. He should never have slept with Naomi. Everything was complicated. He still had to see her every day at work, but now everything would be different.

That was one of the things he'd been afraid of from the very beginning. He should have made sure they stayed just friends. He should have rescued her from ladders and drunks and left it at that.

But he hadn't.

He'd got involved and, not only had he upset himself, but he'd also upset her. Had made Naomi feel things that she should have been protected from.

Tom sank down the wall until he was crouching and stared at the people that walked past, looking at him, concerned.

It had all gone so terribly wrong.

* * *

Naomi stood back as the paramedic wheeled in the young woman on the back board.

'This is Alison, twenty-one years of age, and the victim of a car-versus-cyclist incident. She was cycling along the main road, when a car swerved and hit her from the side. The vehicle was travelling at about thirty-five miles an hour. She was wearing this.' The paramedic showed them the cracked cycle helmet and Naomi winced at the damage, then her wince quickly turned to a frown as she noticed Tom enter Resus.

The paramedic continued, 'Head to toe, we have a scalp laceration in the right occipital region, neck pain with a score of seven, a suspected fracture of the right humerus and clavicle, a suspected fracture of the right femur and general cuts and scrapes down the right side. BP is one twenty over seventy, pulse is one ten and she has a BM of four point two. Pain relief was offered, but refused.'

Tom pulled on gloves and tied an apron around his waist. Studiously, he seemed to ignore her. 'Let's get her off the back board, please.'

They all worked together to roll the patient, sliding her out from the back board. Then the paramedics left and the team could continue monitoring the patient.

Naomi leaned over her, so Alison could see a friendly face. She looked scared and her long blonde hair was slightly matted with blood. 'Hi, Alison, I'm a nurse. I'm going to help look after you. Now you might hear a lot of noise, or feel some pushing or pulling, but we'll talk you through it all, okay?'

'Yes.' Alison tried to nod, but winced.

'Now, where do you hurt the most?'

'My leg and my arm.'

The paramedics had put both of her limbs into splints

and Naomi knew they'd have to wait for the X-rays before anything more could be done.

'Can you tell me where you are?'

'In hospital.'

'And what day is it?'

She told her.

'Okay. Are you allergic to anything, Alison?'

'No.'

Naomi proceeded to test Alison's blood pressure, whilst the rest of the team buzzed over her like bees, checking, testing, assessing. They got IV access and did a quick scan of her abdomen, whilst someone else checked her pupil dilation and tracking. Naomi couldn't help but notice old track marks on Alison's arms, indicating a history of drug abuse. But they were old, nothing recent. Perhaps that explained her reluctance to use the pain relief offered by the paramedics.

'Am I going to die?' Alison asked.

Naomi leant over her again. 'No, you're not going to die, Alison. It looks like you've maybe broken your arm and leg.'

Alison began to cry. 'He hit me. I can't believe he hit me!'

Naomi glanced at Tom, before she could stop herself. Here was a woman who had been hit by a car, who was clearly going to survive. Tom's wife had not been so lucky. She wondered what it did do to him every time a patient like this came into Resus. The memories of what had happened to Meredith must hit him hard each and every time. Did he resent the fact they'd not been able to save her? Had he been angry?

Tom's face was stony and impassive. It gave nothing away. 'Let's get her to CT.'

The computerised tomography suite would give them

a much better view of what was going on inside Alison's body without submitting her to a full MRI. It combined X-ray technology with a computer to create images of the structures within the body, not only including bone, but also organs and blood vessels.

Naomi went with them to the CT suite and stood to one side as the radiographers gave Alison her instructions to lie still.

She waited behind Tom, glancing at him, wondering what he was thinking behind his stony facade.

He glanced at her briefly, then turned back to look at the first pictures of the scan coming through on the computer screen.

He wasn't willing to talk just yet.

Obviously what had happened between them had shocked him. It had shocked Naomi, too. She would never have thought she would have reacted that way. She had never felt that way with a man before. What she'd experienced with Tom, she had felt certain was love, but he seemed to be denying that that was possible. It seemed that he'd promised himself he would never fall in love again and he was standing by that promise.

And what about me? I said I'd never get involved with a man again. But I did and now look at what's happened!

She had been weak to allow Tom in. She had been stupid, allowing a man to tangle up her emotions, after she'd sworn to always protect her heart. She should have known better.

Alison's CT results came through clear. There was a small fracture of the humerus, near the shoulder, a stable fracture of the clavicle and a hairline fracture of the leg. No other internal injuries could be seen and, as her blood pressure was stable and her pulse steady, the neck brace was removed and she was allowed to sit up to have her scalp stitched. She didn't need surgery. She'd been incredibly lucky.

Tom sat next to the patient, perched on a stool, with the suture kit ready in his hand. Naomi stood beside him, cleaning the wound and soon it was ready for him to stitch.

'I've been so lucky, haven't I?' Alison asked.

Naomi nodded. 'You have. Incredibly lucky.'

'This could have been so much worse.'

She said nothing. This seemed a natural reaction for people in A&E who had had accidents. They played the 'what if?' question too readily.

'The driver was hurt, too. Was he brought here? Is he all right?'

'He was drunk,' Tom said, starkly, his voice terse, his mood impenetrable. 'But fine.'

Alison breathed out an audible sigh of relief. 'Thank goodness.'

'Thank goodness? He was drunk driving; he broke your arm and leg.'

Alison glanced over at Tom. 'I can't judge. I don't know him. Perhaps he had a reason for being drunk at that time of the morning. Maybe he'd been trying to drown his sorrows, or he'd lost someone he loved. He might even have an addiction. So, I can't judge him. Not me.'

Naomi finished clearing away the blood around the wound and stood there shocked at Alison's kindness. She knew most people would blame the driver, would talk about suing him. But this patient wasn't doing any of those things. She didn't even seem angry. 'You have a good way of looking at life, Alison.'

'You have to think of it that way. You can't be bitter about things that aren't in your control.'

Naomi thought that perhaps Alison was right. Maybe what had happened between her and Tom had never been in their control. Meeting him that first time had certainly been a complete accident, when she'd fallen from that stupid ladder. And then her flat had been burgled... Living in an awful bedsit had been her only choice, because she'd wanted to live in London. That choice had led to this moment. But she'd had no control over these odd events.

She'd chosen to never get involved with another man again. But despite her choice, her determination, it seemed fate had intervened. And now...

'Do you need me for anything else?' she asked Tom. She was only referring to the patient's care, but suddenly she was all too aware that it sounded like she was asking about life in general.

'No. I'm fine here,' he replied.

She nodded. Of course.

Tom finished the stitching swiftly and they covered the injury with a gauze pad. Naomi smiled at Alison.

'Do you need me to call anyone for you?'

The patient shook her head. 'There's no one.'

'Are you sure?'

'I'm all alone. But that's okay. Because then, I only have to worry about me.'

Naomi frowned. She'd been so sure when she'd arrived in London that alone was the best way to live. It seemed she had been right all along. It was like Alison said. It gave you less to worry about. There was less to mess up and there was no chance of disappointing anyone.

'Would you like a cup of tea?' she asked.

Alison nodded. 'I'd love one.'

Naomi found Tom at the drink station in the staffroom, just as he scooped his tea bag out of his cup and dropped it into the bin.

'Sorry to disturb you,' she said. 'I was just going to make Alison a cup of tea.'

He nodded and stepped aside to make room for her, ardently stirring his drink.

'I'll move out the second I get back this afternoon. You won't have to see me.'

'Naomi—'

'No, Tom...I can see you're uncomfortable and so am I. But don't worry. I'm sorting it all out.' She picked up Alison's drink and left before he could say anything else.

There! she thought. *Simple. Decisive. To the point.*

If she'd kept her distance in the first place then it would never have been a problem. So, now if Tom didn't want to be committed to her, then fine. She didn't need him. She refused to want him.

There would be no more Tom.

There would be no more Naomi and Tom.

There would be no more of that heat and need and wanting and wishing and...

Naomi handed the drink to Alison, smiling grimly, lost in thought.

There would be no more feeling lost.

How had she misunderstood so badly? The way he'd touched her, kissed her, caressed her—it had been as if he'd been holding a rare treasure, as if he couldn't believe he was allowed to touch something so valuable. At least that was what his eyes had said. It had been there in his face, in his body, too. Every part of him treating her like a precious jewel.

Maybe she had imagined it all.

Perhaps Tom had been right when he'd been talking about them making love. Perhaps it was just sex, nothing more. Perhaps what they'd done hadn't been special. After all, she didn't have another point of reference.

No. She shook her head. *No, there was something else there.*

No matter what had happened, however, it had definitely grown far too complicated. Tom had made it absolutely clear that he wasn't in the market for a relationship and that he could never love another.

His relationship with Meredith must have been something truly special. She must have been an angel for him to fall so deeply in love that he couldn't tolerate the idea of loving someone else.

Naomi wasn't sure if she even knew what love was any more.

She'd been determined not to say anything more to him, and had decided to walk away with her head held high. But then she'd seen him, standing alone outside, taking a breather between patients, and before she had known what she was doing she had walked over to him. She was overcome with a desire to explain, to try and put into words what she'd felt when she'd sobbed with happiness in his arms.

He looked up, surprised, as she opened her mouth and the words poured out.

'Last night, Tom…it meant something to me. It meant more than just two people coming together to rid themselves of their frustrations. It meant…*more*. I can only speak for myself, when I say this, but I'm angry at myself for letting it happen. Angry because it ruined the friendship that we had and turned it into something else. Something uncomfortable. Something painful. I know you regret it. But at the same time, for me, it was something joyous, something mind-blowing. It meant that my eyes were opened to a possibility that I could only have dreamed of… That moment brought me you. And believe you me,

I didn't plan this. Like you, I told myself I would never fall in love again. I told myself that real, burning, passionate love caused too much pain, too much suffering for it to ever be worth it. But with you, I trusted that it wouldn't happen. That you wouldn't hurt me—'

'Naomi—'

'But you *have* hurt me, Tom. In a way I hadn't even known I should be protecting myself from. The way I felt in your arms was something I'd never experienced before and that was why I cried... It was overwhelming. Overwhelmingly beautiful.'

'I—'

'I need to step away from you. You said you can't give me what I need and I understand that, I do. I never even knew that I needed it myself! But I think I do now. I want to be loved, Tom, and I don't think that should be something to be feared. You're not ready,' she said, faltering, with tears flowing freely down her face. She didn't care what she looked like any longer. 'But I can't hang around and keep torturing myself with the thought of what might have been every time I look at your face.'

She turned, desperately, and began to walk away, her head too full to think.

Tom called her name, but the pain in her chest hurt too much to turn around and listen to anything he might have to say.

What could he tell her that she didn't already know?

He couldn't love her the way she wanted him to.

So that had to be the end.

Last night, Tom...

It was hours after Naomi had left the hospital and still he couldn't get her words out of his head. She was right. It *had* meant something. He hadn't let himself acknowledge it at the time and had been too overwhelmed by her emotional outpouring but now, when he considered how she'd made him feel... He knew that it really had meant something.

Naomi was truly special. And therein lay the problem. Because Tom didn't want her to mean something. He didn't *want* to care deeply for her. He didn't want to be falling in love. Love only hurt. He'd learnt the hard way that life got in the way and that terrible accidents happened. What if Naomi was taken from him just as Meredith had been? If he let himself care for Naomi, *love* Naomi, then he knew he wouldn't cope with losing her. His fear of that would ruin everything. He'd been there already. He wouldn't go through it again. Couldn't go through it again.

He'd relied on his work since Meredith had died and that had seen him through. It was his way of continuing to connect with people. He could still help them, if only for a short time. A&E had been perfect because he was able to step in and make their lives better, and then his patients could be on their way. No one had to develop feelings and no one would get hurt. Tom had thought that he would be able to live the rest of his life at an emotional distance from everybody.

It was all a form of self-preservation. Surely everyone was guilty of it in one way or another. Was it so bad of him to put up walls in this way? He was protecting himself. He was protecting Naomi. But of course, he knew, she couldn't see that, that he was doing this for them both.

Tom didn't know what to think, except that he needed this whole situation to change. He needed...*damn it!* He needed Naomi!

He would give anything to call her back, and take her in his arms. He wanted to talk to her, about something, *anything*. He wanted to just *be* with her.

But he couldn't be with her. He wouldn't allow himself to do so. What had happened was for the best. Yes, it still hurt, but surely it was best to make that clean break now, before the hurt turned to agony.

He headed back into the department. It was technically the end of his shift, but he didn't care. He needed to work. He couldn't face the thought of going back to the flat, and seeing her emptying it of her things. If he worked, he wouldn't think about her. Or, at least, he'd try not to.

The rest of the staff were thrilled to see him return. They were overrun with patients and, for a brief hour or two, he managed to forget about her completely. He didn't have time to think about what had happened that morning, or what she'd said. In those few precious hours, he didn't have to think about that look on her face when she'd run from him.

But then, when he was told to take a break, the thoughts came clamouring in. He pushed them to one side, telling himself over and over again that he was doing the right thing. He figured that if he told himself enough times, he might even start believing it was true.

Naomi packed up the last of her things. Most of her possessions were now in boxes, or the suitcase she'd taken from her old flat, but she'd just needed to return to Tom's flat to collect her toothbrush and make-up from the bathroom.

Moving here in the first place now seemed like such a mistake. She'd been sucked in by how beautiful it all was. After her experience with the bedsit, she'd been happy to escape to such luxury. And, of course, then there'd been Tom, who had been the most wonderful feature of the flat.

But this had never been meant for her. She'd come out of a lonely childhood, into a lonely, strangely solitary marriage where it had seemed she had spent the entire time *waiting.* She had always been waiting for something bad to happen, another bone to grow, another injury to occur, as Vincent had steadily grown worse. She remembered the big grandfather clock in the hallway of their home and suddenly its loud ticking had never meant so much. She'd been stuck on pause. Trapped in a place from which she'd had no escape, and so she had waited, patiently, for the end.

Vincent's condition had called all the shots in their marriage. It had governed everything and at the time, she hadn't minded. She'd enjoyed looking after him, had enjoyed that they were so close and had accepted everyone's praise of her, the way they'd said she was *being so brave.* At least, she'd escaped her childhood, always determined not to be like her mother, flitting from one relationship to another, always searching, always falling for the prettiest face and getting hurt.

She knew she'd chosen Vincent because he had been safe. She could admit that to herself now. He had been dedicated to her. Dedicated to their relationship.

He'd *needed* her.

And she'd revelled in that role as the dutiful wife, for their time together, playing it safe right to the end.

Then she'd made her big move to the capital. Finally she had been able to stand on her own two feet, throw caution to the wind and enjoy life. She had told herself that she would push her nursing skills to the limits, make new friends and live a whole new life. Naomi had been determined to move onwards and upwards, enjoying her freedom, just as she'd promised Vincent before he'd died that she would.

But she'd met Tom and had fallen for him. She'd been enticed by his good looks, given herself to him, and just like her mother she'd ended up alone and hurting.

But today I start again.

Naomi rallied herself. She would call the last few weeks a false start. They were just a minor blip in her plan. This time, she would stubbornly remain single, at least for a while.

As she gathered up her things Tom's toothbrush suddenly seemed lonely in its pot, now that she had removed her own, and she gazed at it wistfully. They had been so good in their brief time together. But now she had to put Tom from her mind.

Naomi zipped up her toiletries bag and left.

An hour or so later she looked around her new flat, trying to find some kind of optimism. Luxury and opulence were not part of her normal world. She had been spoilt for a little while. So she figured that, whilst the flat wasn't ideal *now*, it would get better. With time, with some hard work and an awful lot of deep cleaning, she would make it homely. She would paint the walls cream all over and get some fresh flowers to brighten up the rooms. If she got rid of that drab carpet, she could maybe hire a floor buffer and polish the wood underneath.

Naomi knew it could be beautiful. It just needed someone with a good eye for interior design and a bit of imagination. If she applied the same reasoning to her personal life, surely she could make that better, too. All she needed was some time, some space, and then maybe her heart might be ready for love. Naomi at least knew she wanted that now. Despite everything, Tom had still made her realise that she was worth being loved.

Her heart ached as she tried to push away the thought that the person loving her wouldn't be Tom. She had hoped that it would be. But he clearly wasn't ready. Whatever was going on in his head was preventing him from being with her. She had to put Tom and their brief relationship into a closed box. It had been wonderful whilst it had lasted. But she had to accept that their time together in the sun was over now.

At the hospital, Naomi had initially arranged to work opposite shifts to Tom. She had checked his schedule and if he was on days, she would agree to do nights. If he was on lates, she would do the early hours. But still, there were always those moments of handover, the occasional meeting in the locker room where he would look at her with sad eyes and seem to be on the verge of saying something. Except he always remained silent. She wasn't sure what to do. She didn't want to change jobs. She loved working in Welbeck's A&E, especially with all the staff, who had become good friends. But when the matron had mentioned there was an opportunity for one member of the staff to go out on a secondment with the paramedics, Naomi had leapt at the chance.

It was perfect. She'd be out of the department except for the times when they would have to bring in a patient. It would be good for her to get a new perspective on what it was like to be out on the road and on the front line.

She hadn't been in an ambulance since her days of training, when she'd spent a day as an observer. Back then, she'd felt useless and unsure. She'd stood back from the action in her neon-yellow jacket, carrying bags for the paramedics, or fetching and carrying whatever was needed from the truck.

This time, as she clambered on board with the two paramedics, Julia and Luke, she felt sure she would be better.

Stepping outside for a breath of fresh air, Tom saw Naomi clamber on board the ambulance. He paused, unable to tear his eyes away, then he promptly turned around and walked back inside, angry with himself.

His flat was so empty without her! Two weeks she'd been gone and he hadn't realised just how large it was until she'd left and he had been left alone again. He didn't know how he had managed living alone before. Because now when he came home from work, the silence was deafening. The space was endless.

On that first day she'd left, he'd come home from work late, sure that she would be gone, and had wandered into her room. He'd looked about—at the bed where she'd slept, at her empty wardrobe, at her empty drawers. For the time they'd been in his home they'd all been so full of her. The whole flat had been filled with her character, her smile, her laughter. She had managed to imbue the whole place with her spirit and energy and he wasn't sure that he'd ever be able to look at the kitchen again without thinking about her there. His mind had been full of memories of her madly cooking some crazy recipe, whilst singing to the radio, dropping spoons or turning on the blender after forgetting to put on the lid. He'd never forget her burning toast and giving his damn smoke detectors more work than they'd had in years.

He'd moved away from the kitchen and his gaze had fallen on the sofa where they'd made love…

I panicked.

His emotions had been all over the place after they'd made love and the fact that he'd been second-guessing himself hadn't helped matters. He had always been so sure of everything. Had always considered himself to be a clear, logical thinker. After all, with luck on his side, he could save a dying person—he could stem an arterial bleed; he could resuscitate someone. But now, he was flummoxed.

Because he couldn't figure out if he could know whether he was really in love.

It had been so clear-cut with Meredith. There'd been no hesitation there, no doubt. He'd just *known*. But with Naomi...it was like he couldn't think straight with her around. She scrambled his thoughts and toyed with his emotions and he didn't know whether he was coming or going!

Maybe that was love, too.

Maybe it was a different kind of love. Maybe he had been wrong about everything.

He shook his head, trying to clear his thoughts.

He certainly knew how it felt to see Naomi doing everything in her power to not come into contact with him. To see her choosing alternate shifts and volunteering to be with the paramedics. Julia and Luke were great and they'd look after her, he knew that, but...

His chest actually hurt, physically, like his heart was constantly aching with pain. His stomach was all over the place, his concentration was shot.

Perhaps separation was a good thing?

Naomi wandered around her new flat, opening windows, letting in the air before she started yet *another* marathon cleaning session in the flat. Then she turned on the radio, whilst she dusted and scrubbed and cleaned.

It was difficult. Some of the grime was really ingrained and it made her feel sick to look at the state of the dirty water in the bucket she was using. Not that it took much to make her feel sick these days.

She'd noticed it only recently. Her tiredness. Her exhaustion at the end of every day. And then there was the nausea that came whenever she prepared anything to eat. Last night, she'd gone to make herself a tuna sandwich and as soon as she'd opened the tin, the smell had made her heave into the kitchen sink. It was then she'd first wondered if it was something other than pure exhaustion.

She was late, too. She'd never been late. Ever.

She'd bought herself a pregnancy-testing kit, but she hadn't had the courage to use it yet. It had been three weeks since she had slept with Tom, but...

What would she do, if she were pregnant?

If Tom couldn't even love *her*, she didn't know how he would cope with a baby. Would he be able to love it? She hoped so, for the baby's sake. They might not be together as a couple, but she would want him to have a role in their child's life.

But then again, what would that be like for her? She knew immediately that it would be awful. Painful. She couldn't imagine going through a pregnancy, wanting someone to be there to hold her hand through all the scans and tests, not to mention labour and delivery, but knowing the father it wasn't an option.

She was getting carried away. She might not even be pregnant.

But a small part of her willed it to be true. She'd always wanted children, but she'd put that desire on hold during her marriage. Even though she'd known there wasn't a chance of conceiving, every month that had rolled around, bringing with it her next period, had made her feel desperately sad.

She decided she wouldn't take the test until she had cleaned the bathroom. The old avocado suite actually wasn't too bad, but there was mould on the grouting and limescale everywhere. There was no way she would use this bathroom for something so monumental as finding out if she was pregnant, without it being clean to her standards.

She emptied the bucket of water down the sink, swirled

it out with clean and then filled it once again. As she waited for the level to rise she took the pregnancy test out of her handbag and rested it on the sink.

First thing tomorrow you can tell me my future.

She woke suddenly, with trepidation. Amazingly, she'd slept quite well. The exhaustion she'd been feeling had hit her hard last night, after a whole afternoon spent cleaning and scrubbing.

Her stomach roiled as she sat up in bed. Could this be morning sickness? Naomi knew it was possible for a person to believe something with so much conviction that they could convince themselves that they had an illness. It was called psychosomatic disorder. Was it possible that she was wishing so hard that she was pregnant, that she was making herself feel sick?

More importantly, did she really want Tom's baby so badly?

She knew the answer was yes. She did want this baby. And she couldn't think of a better man to be the father. Tom was clever and kind and considerate. He would hopefully be a loving parent, even if he couldn't love Naomi. Even if there could never be any relationship between them as a couple, she couldn't imagine him turning his child away.

She stood up and headed for the bathroom. She knew what she needed to do, but she still read the instructions thoroughly, before following them exactly, and then she laid the test stick on the toilet cistern and waited.

Thirty seconds. She had thirty seconds to wait before she could find out if her life had changed. If it had, she felt sure she could turn it into a positive change. She would make this flat work for her. Make her job work for her, too, until she had to go on maternity leave. With this change, her life could be bright again. Being a single mother was nothing strange these days.

See? I can make myself believe I'll be happy.

Still, a small voice and a large ache in her heart told her that she would never be truly happy without Tom's love. She could tell herself as many times as she liked that this would turn out all right, but until that moment came she knew she would be miserable.

Be realistic, she thought. *Be honest. You want Tom, too.*

Yes, she admitted to herself. She did want him. Even now. Even after all this time that they'd spent apart, she was still haunted by the memory of him, of the way he'd kissed her, made her feel, made her laugh. The way he'd made her feel warm and safe inside.

She loved him. It was an inescapable fact. And whether she was carrying his child or not, she knew she could never have him.

Naomi picked up the test and stared at the result. It was positive. She was pregnant. With Tom's baby.

Never had she ever imagined that she wouldn't be thrilled at discovering she was pregnant. But with the news suddenly in front of her, she only sat there stunned, tears streaming down her face.

She stayed there for ages, just holding the stick in her hands and staring at it. Outside, she could hear the early-morning bustle of traffic—the honking of horns, the sounds of reversing lorries, people calling out in the street. For everyone else, life was carrying on as normal.

But for Naomi, it was as if time had stood still. She kept wondering how she would tell him. What the look on his face would be. He had told her he would never be able to love someone else.

Please, Tom. Be the man that I know that you are and tell me that you'll love our child.

* * *

It was now mid-April and Naomi knew she ought to be over the moon. Deep down inside, somewhere, she felt sure she was rejoicing. It was just that at the moment she felt numb, as if she was still in shock. She would have to tell Tom sooner or later. He had a right to know. Perhaps the best place would be at the Spring Ball in a few days' time? It would be neutral ground and they would be surrounded by people, so his reaction would have to be measured and controlled. They could discuss the issue calmly over a nice glass of champagne.

Oops—no. No alcohol for me.

Fruit juice, then. She picked up the phone and called her local GP surgery. She'd need to see the doctor, and organise getting some folic acid. The doctor would get her registered with a midwife and arrange the first visit once she had got past the first trimester.

She was relieved she hadn't forgotten everything about her maternity training. She could almost pretend that everything was well with the world.

She hoped Tom would take the news calmly and that he would be able to take responsibility and love their child. She didn't like to think about what it might mean if he wasn't able to. Maybe she didn't know him at all.

Surely she hadn't read him wrong. Tom couldn't fail to be a good father, surely. He was charming and dependable and caring. Caring for others was in his DNA. He was a doctor, for crying out loud, and a damned good one on top of that. He loved his work, making sure that others were okay.

An image of him cradling a child in his arms came unbidden to her and she felt an ache deep in the pit of her stomach. She allowed herself to imagine him looking at that child with such intense love.

She imagined him turning to her with the same look in his eyes, and drawing her towards him…

She dashed the image from her mind. She couldn't think of him in that way any more. She couldn't think of him in her arms. Holding her close.

It was all such a mess! She would wait until the evening of the ball and then she would tell him about the baby. She'd agreed to go with Stefan as a friend, not as a date, so she was sure she'd be able to slip away and find Tom.

That was assuming he was *going* to the ball!

CHAPTER TEN

IT WAS THE next weekend and Naomi had arranged to go shopping for her ball gown with Jackie. They went to a variety of stores on the busy London streets, searching for something that appealed. There were rack upon rack of lovely dresses in all colours, shapes and sizes, but still nothing had leapt out at Naomi.

She had been fighting off her exhaustion all morning, sipping from a carton of banana milkshake to stop the pangs of sickness from overwhelming her as they shopped. She didn't want Jackie to suspect she was pregnant, before she'd had a chance to tell Tom. It was only right that he found out first.

Jackie had managed to find her gown in the first store they went into. It was a beautiful off-the-shoulder scarlet dress, quite figure-hugging all the way to her knees, where it suddenly flowed outwards freely. The bodice was highlighted by small diamanté stones and it had looked gorgeous on her as she'd stood on the small podium and twirled in front of the mirror, so that Naomi could see it fully.

'It looks gorgeous on you, Jackie.'

'Oh, thanks. You know people have always said that red is my colour.'

Jackie had stepped down and wriggled back behind the curtain to get changed into her normal clothes.

'They're right. You looked great,' Naomi had added.

Her friend had peered around the curtain at her. 'Pity we can't say the same for you.'

'What?'

'What's going on between you and Tom? One minute you're flatmates, all nice and cosy, and the best of friends, the next you can barely tolerate breathing the same air as him.'

Naomi had briefly seen a vision of herself in Tom's arms, feeling cherished and adored and *loved*. Then she'd pushed the image away. He hadn't thought about it the same way. 'We had a difference in opinion.'

'What about?'

'I'd rather not talk about it. I've moved on.'

'You've moved flat! Stefan tells me you're in his block now. How's that working out for you?'

It's horrible, she'd thought. *I hate that flat. It's not home. It's not me!*

'Yeah, it's good.'

'It sounds like a lot of work from what Stefan tells me. You need a hand?'

'Er...maybe. Yeah. We could have one of those wallpaper-stripping parties.'

Jackie had swished the curtain open, dressed in her normal clothes once again. 'Please tell me you don't have a woodchip nightmare?'

Naomi had nodded and laughed when she'd seen the look of horror on her friend's face. 'I do.'

'Oh, shoot. That's such a delight to remove!'

Jackie had paid for her dress and, once it had been wrapped in tissue paper, boxed and bagged, they'd headed out of the shop.

Now they were trying yet another store, still searching for something for Naomi.

'How's A&E?' she asked as they wandered. 'What am I missing?'

'Not much. You should know—you bring in half the cases! How are you enjoying your time with the paramedics?'

'It's good. Interesting, but...'

'It's not A&E.'

'No.'

'Do you miss it?'

She nodded.

'You miss Tom, too, don't you?'

Naomi tried not to make eye contact with her friend, but Jackie was persistent. She stepped in front of her, forcing her to look at her. 'Naomi!'

'Yes! Yes, I do.'

'Even though you were *only* flatmates?'

She coloured.

'I *knew* it! I knew there was more to it than what you were letting on! What happened?'

'I don't really want to talk about it. It upsets me. Please, Jackie. Don't say anything to anyone. Least of all Stefan. He's such a gossip.'

Jackie threaded her arm through Naomi's. 'My lips are sealed. But, you know, I will say one thing.'

'What?'

'That that man cares for you beyond belief. He's miserable now; he's like a robot again. He's acting just the way he did after his wife died. I don't know what he's done to upset you, Naomi, but he loves you. You mark my words.'

She stared straight ahead.

No, he doesn't.

It didn't matter what Jackie said. Tom didn't love her.

He'd told her he was incapable of it. He'd said he didn't believe in a second chance at love.

You mark my words...he loves you...

She smiled sadly. If only that were true. It was nice of Jackie to say that, but Naomi didn't need to hear it. It only gave her false hope. But she wouldn't be able to cope if she went to him and told him that she loved *him* and he threw it back in her face. If it were true, and Jackie were right, then it needed to come from Tom. And Naomi already knew that would never happen.

Jackie said no more about Tom as they continued to shop. And eventually, Naomi found a wonderful dress in midnight blue. It was ankle-length, one-shouldered, and it had a beautiful black lace overlay around the waist. They found a gorgeous red clutch to contrast with it, which wasn't hugely expensive. Naomi decided this would be her last extravagance. All her future funds would have to go towards the flat and things for the baby. But this dress would be her swansong to being a single woman. After this, if all went well, she would be a single *mother*. She briefly wondered what Vincent would have said, if he could have seen her. She hoped that he would have been proud.

She was suddenly glad she was going to the ball. It was a fitting way to end this current chapter in her life.

'I've probably made a mistake in accepting Stefan's invite,' she confessed to Jackie.

'Stefan is full of himself. But he's a decent guy underneath all that rubbish he doles out.'

Naomi twirled in front of the mirror in her dress, eyeing the gown and trying to see if her pregnancy showed, which of course it didn't—it was still early days. Thank goodness. No one would guess her secret. No one would tell Tom until she'd had the chance to see him first.

CHAPTER ELEVEN

Tom was hard at work in A&E. Unable to cope with the maelstrom of thoughts in his head about Naomi, he'd sought solace the way he had used to do, treating the sick and injured.

So far that day he'd seen a cardiac arrest, a tree surgeon who had fallen over twenty feet onto his back, some victims from a bad road-traffic accident and a query stroke victim.

Work had been the only way he'd been able to make himself feel better after Meredith's death. And so he'd expected his work to have the same effect after everything that had happened with Naomi.

But it wasn't working. His head was still in a spin. He wasn't his normal calm, polite self. Instead, he was being terse. Curt. His temper felt extremely short and every time he caught himself snapping at someone, he would inwardly berate himself.

All he could think about was Naomi.

His neat, stable little world had crumpled in on itself. He could barely keep himself upright. He could barely keep putting one foot in front of the other, without thinking about her, wishing that he'd acted differently, wishing it all could have *ended* differently.

He'd sworn to himself after Meredith had died that he'd

never again go through that pain of losing someone that he loved. He'd promised never to expose himself to that all-consuming grief that he'd experienced once before.

But wasn't he suffering now anyway? He was certainly already in pain. And was that because he loved Naomi? Was he feeling this pain and uncertainty, all because he was denying himself the woman that he loved?

His brow rumpled in thought. If he admitted to himself that perhaps he did love Naomi, *then* what would happen? He didn't know if there was any point in telling her. He'd already messed her around once, upset her, so he doubted she'd want to listen to him now. It was too late. He'd already told her he couldn't love another.

He winced as he recalled his words.

If Naomi had any sense, she would run a mile. He'd used her. Unwittingly maybe. Naively, perhaps. But still, she'd said he had opened her eyes to possibilities in her life. That he'd made her realise a need for love that she'd closed the door on, just as he had. She'd just opened that door earlier than he had. She'd been ready to cope with it, ready to risk love again.

The question was…was he ready?

He was suffering so much now, because there was so much distance between them, when what he really wanted was the opposite. He'd imposed a self-built barrier of fear. And just as he'd done that, she too had tried to protect herself by moving away from him.

They'd both thought they had been protecting themselves, but in reality they hadn't. They'd only caused themselves more hurt, because they'd believed that the alternative could only lead to pain.

But what if I allowed myself to love again? What if Naomi gave me another chance and said yes?
Tom looked down at his paperwork. There was still so

much he needed to do. Yet the Spring Ball was just a few hours away and Naomi was going with Stefan. He was a decent nurse, but still… *Stefan*? The hospital Lothario? Tom couldn't bear the idea.

He glanced at the clock, trying to make his decision.

Suddenly he knew exactly where he had to go.

Tom knelt in front of the headstone and laid the bunch of calla lilies on Meredith's grave. Then he stood back and looked hard at the words and letters etched into the stone.

Meredith Williams
Beloved Wife

He cleared his throat.

'Meredith? I need to tell you…that I love you. That I will *always* love you and there will always be a treasured space for you in my heart, but…I've met someone. Her name's Naomi.'

His gaze drifted from his wife's name to her photograph embedded in the stone within a golden heart. He looked at that smiling face, the twinkle in her eyes, remembering her as she'd beamed at the camera on that day so long ago.

'You'd like her. She's a nurse, like you. Spirited. Funny. Passionate. Caring.' He sighed and his shoulders dropped as he looked up and past the other stones, across the empty field to the trees in the distance, gathering his thoughts. Gathering more words.

'She means an awful lot to me and that surprised me because I didn't think anyone could mean anything to me any more.' He reached out to touch the cold stone. 'I want to be with her. She may not want me, after the way I've treated her, but at least I'm thinking clearly now. I know what I want and I *know* that you, more than anyone else in the world, would want me to be happy. So I'm going to try.'

He stood there for a few more quiet moments, listening to the birds singing in the nearby trees, and spotted a squirrel scratching at the ground a few metres away. Even a rabbit had dared to venture out from the hedgerow, but it scurried away as soon as it noticed him.

Tom turned back to his wife's picture and sucked in a deep breath. This was it. His decision. He was moving forward now. He couldn't live his life the way he had for eight years. He'd been in limbo and it was all so clear to him now. Before Naomi had come into his life, and he'd just thought of himself as a widower, he had convinced himself that was it. That that was the way his life was going to be for the rest of his days. But he'd been wrong. He'd been so utterly wrong.

His feelings for Naomi had been so unexpected, so sudden. He had been like a man on death row who had been told that in actual fact he was being set free.

Naomi had set him free and he was no longer a prisoner. He'd done his time.

Tom gazed at Meredith's picture. He didn't feel sadness. He didn't feel regret.

He felt content. Right.

He felt *sure*.

'Goodbye, Meredith.' He touched his fingers to the stone one final time and closed his eyes, feeling the soft breeze on his face, and it was as if he knew she was telling him it was okay. A smile reached his face.

Opening his eyes, he began to walk away.

He didn't need to look back.

Naomi was getting ready for the ball. There was none of the excitement that she once would have had at the thought of such an event. Her dress was beautiful and Jackie had taken up her hair for her, which was now held in place by bejewelled pins. Looking in the mirror, as she finished her make-up, she felt she truly did look like the princess that Jackie had told her she would be.

But she didn't feel like one. She didn't feel the happiness she knew she ought to be feeling. After all, this was going to be her big goodbye, her first and last large event with the department. She'd decided that, after this, she would work out the months she had before she gave birth but then she would leave Welbeck. She would be the best mother to her child that she could be. She'd been given this opportunity, after all this time, and she was going to embrace it.

As she slipped on her heels and put on her bracelet and matching earrings, she tried to find the smile that had been missing from her face for so long.

She popped a small piece of ginger into her mouth. She'd been chewing on small pieces for a few days now. It seemed to help that awful sick feeling in her stomach that seemed to be there on a permanent basis. She took a deep breath.

When they arrived, she would plaster on that fake smile, be gracious and pleasant. She would greet people, all the while hating every minute, scanning the room, knowing that she had to talk to Tom.

Stefan arrived in his tuxedo, and she had to admit he looked rather charming, but she only felt sadness when she met him at the door. She felt it should have been Tom standing there.

There was a slight evening breeze, and the cool air danced around her bare arms and back as they went outside and climbed into the taxi. Stefan chatted amiably as they travelled and she tried to seem attentive. When they finally arrived at the hotel, she slowly made her way up the steps into the building and then suddenly, with her nerves racing, they entered the ballroom.

It was magnificent. It was as if they'd stepped inside a palace. Jackie had been right: the events team had really pulled out all the stops to make the place look magical. There were high vaulted ceilings lit by chandeliers and fluted lights lined the walls. Past all the porticoes and columns, Naomi could see a small orchestra in the corner, and could hear someone very talented playing the grand piano at its centre. Everyone was dressed in their finery—the men in tuxedoes and the women in beautiful ball gowns of every conceivable colour. Waiters covered the room like silent hummingbirds, offering drinks and canapés on silver trays as people clinked champagne glasses, laughing and chattering.

If only everything were different.

She wanted to be able to enjoy it. She could certainly appreciate all the hard work that had gone into the occasion. The fact that she couldn't be here with the one person she wanted the most made her sad, tearful almost.

There were already a few couples dancing in the centre of the floor. She would have loved to dance with Tom and be close to him again, the way they had been at the roller disco. The image came to her of being in his arms, laughing, pressed up close against his chest. She could almost feel his heart pounding away, her hands in his as they had stared deeply into each other's eyes…

She wiped away a small tear and offered Stefan a brave smile. 'It's gorgeous!' she exclaimed as she followed her date down the steps into the room.

It was warm and so many people were wearing perfumes or aftershave that the aroma started to make her feel queasy. Laying a hand upon her stomach, she took a glass from a passing waiter's tray and sipped at it to help wet her dry mouth.

Ugh. Alcohol.

She looked around for another drink, searching for something that looked like fruit juice, but as she turned away she lost sight of Stefan. Suddenly she was left in the middle of the ballroom all alone.

So this is what it feels like to be lonely in a crowd, she thought.

Jostled and bustled, she tried to make her way over to one side of the room where she could hide. There was a line of tables with a buffet selection. She wondered if she might find something there to help settle her stomach.

A few people she knew recognised her, greeting her with air kisses. Then she moved on again, telling herself that if she couldn't find Tom, she would only stay for an hour. She would make sure she'd said hello to everyone she knew, then she would make her excuses and go.

She felt a hand on her arm and she turned, expecting to find Stefan standing there.

Tom!

All of a sudden her stomach began churning wildly, her mouth grew dry and she almost couldn't speak. She couldn't believe how good it was to see him here! He looked absolutely dashing in his perfect tuxedo, staring at her, as if…as if he couldn't bear to look anywhere else.

'Tom?'

He was *here*. Which meant that she would be able to tell him about the baby. She'd been worried that he wouldn't turn up, and that she would have to find him at work. But now, the moment was here. She would have to stand in front of him and tell him that his world was about to change! That he was going to become a father. She would tell him that she would stay out of his way if that was what he wanted—even if it would kill her to do so—but she prayed that he would love and cherish their baby.

He would make a good dad, she felt sure of that. Perhaps he might be the one to teach their child to ride a bike? He would be patient, she knew; supportive, encouraging.

Tears were welling in her eyes again.

She blinked furiously, and dabbed at the corners of her eyes, hoping the tears wouldn't fall and betray her.

Tom gave her a small smile.

'Naomi. May I speak with you? Privately?' He seemed serious and Naomi wondered what this could be about. She wondered if he was going to discuss work with her. Maybe he wanted to talk about what would happen now that her secondment with the paramedics was coming to an end.

She didn't see the need for privacy if that was the case, but she was keen to get out of the crowd. She wanted to get away from the mixture of scents and the cacophony of too many people in one room.

'Sure,' she said.

'There's a small foyer over there.' Tom pointed and then took her arm as he escorted her through the crowds.

She tried not to think too hard about his arm tucked through hers. It was a too painful reminder of everything that she couldn't have. She wished he wouldn't touch her at all. That would be easier.

When they got to the foyer, he let go of her arm and closed the doors behind them, shutting out the noise of the chatter and the soft piano music. She breathed in deeply, relishing the fresher air coming in through the open windows.

Now that they were here, he stood in front of her, looking a little unsure of how to start.

'What's wrong?'

He licked his lips and stared at her for a moment. Then he spoke.

'Naomi? First off, I just want to say that I'm sorry. *Dreadfully* sorry for the way I reacted to you that night we were together.' He reached for her hands and held them in his as he faced her. 'That night was the most amazing thing in the world to me because it opened my eyes. No…not just my eyes. But my heart…my soul. I'd kept them locked away, determined that no one would ever have the chance to tear me apart again, but being with you…being with you made me realise that I *could* love again. That I could take that chance and risk my heart because I loved you.

'It scared me. It sent me into a whirlwind of confusion and shock. I hadn't known it was possible to care for someone that much for a second time and when you told me that I'd shown you that love was possible, I'll admit I was frightened. It was all too clear that you'd changed me in the same way and I wasn't ready to accept that it was okay. But I am ready now.'

She stared up at him, tears now openly falling down her cheeks as his words pierced her heart and the barriers she'd been putting up to protect herself. Those barriers were crumbling away, breaking into a million tiny pieces at every word he said.

'I know I hurt you—I'm sorry. I know I shut you out—I'm sorry. I can't say it enough to make amends for all the pain I caused you and I know that I have no right to expect you to forgive me. But I'm asking you to consider it. I'm asking you to find forgiveness in your heart; if not now, then maybe some time in the future, I don't know. I just need to tell you that I love you. And if you'll have me, then I'll be here for you until the end of time.'

Naomi sobbed, wanting to wipe the tears away, but at the same time unwilling to let go of his hands.

He *loved* her?

She laughed through her tears, knowing she must look a mess, but too happy to care.

'Oh, Tom! I do forgive you. I do. I'm sorry I put you through so much torment. And that I caused you this much pain in the first place! There you'd been, working your way through life, knowing exactly what you wanted from it, and I came along and turned it upside down.'

'I needed you to turn it upside down.'

'I needed *you*. You showed me what real love could be. It wasn't just the physical stuff, but also the incredible companionship, the time we spent together, having fun, taking risks—'

'The burnt dinners?'

She laughed. 'Yes! The burnt dinners…I told you what that all meant to me before you were ready to hear it. I knew what you'd been through, that you were uncertain, and yet I couldn't hold it back because I was so determined to be open and honest about how I felt. Because you know something? Even though I loved Vincent, I wasn't open and honest with him. I always kept my feelings about everything locked inside, because I didn't want to upset him, or worry him, because I thought he already had so much to deal with. But with you…' she squeezed his fingers in hers '…I was overwhelmed by my feelings. I spoke without thinking, but…I love you, too, Tom. You know that I do. It's torn my heart to pieces spending this time apart.'

'Me too.'

'I love you. I want to be with you.'

'I love you, Naomi.'

He dipped his head to kiss her, but she backed away and he looked at her, confused.

'What?'

'There's something else.'

'Oh?'

'*Someone* else.'

His eyes darkened and he glanced at the double doors leading to the ballroom. 'Stefan?'

She shook her head. 'No.'

Tom looked puzzled. 'Then who?' he asked, appearing to brace himself.

She smiled and blushed. 'I can't believe I get to tell you this and actually be happy about it.'

He stared at her, waiting for the axe to fall.

'I'm pregnant, Tom. With our baby.'

His mouth dropped open, then he gulped and glanced down at her abdomen, a smile slowly appearing on his face. 'You're pregnant?'

She nodded.

'Oh, Naomi!' He pulled her to him and kissed her.

Naomi was so filled with happiness to be in his arms again that she thought she might burst! She'd never expected this when she'd set out that evening, not even knowing whether Tom would be there. She'd pictured herself telling him about the baby, expecting it to be sombre and sad, with him dutifully promising to be involved. Her heart had almost broken there and then, imagining the scenario.

But here she was. Tom loved her. He wanted to be with her and he was thrilled about the baby!

They would raise their child *together*. As a *couple*. Not as single parents, as she'd been prepared to do.

His lips against hers were like magic. She tingled in every place that they touched. Her heart was singing. The dark clouds that had hovered over her earlier had dissipated and she felt like they were both standing in bright sunshine. They were together and strong. And together they would be able to tackle anything. Apart, they'd been broken and weak.

Not any longer.

Now the future looked bright. Optimistic. Full of promise and expectation.

Tom broke the kiss and smiled down at her, then he reached into his pocket and dropped to one knee.

Naomi gasped.

'Naomi Bloom. You fell into my arms the first day that we met and I want you to stay there until the day that we die. I love you more than life and you would make me the happiest man alive if you would do me the honour of marrying me.'

He opened the small box he was holding and she saw a beautiful diamond solitaire nestled in its bed of navy velvet.

'I will!'

Tom beamed as he took the ring from the box and gently slipped it onto her finger. Then he pulled her to him once again and kissed her.

Her body sang for him. Her heart soared.

This was the love she'd known was possible. *This* was what she'd dreamed about when she'd set off to London to find her own way in the world. Here was her chance to find love again. And the fact that it was with Tom, the most wonderful man she had ever known, made it more than perfect.

She couldn't be happier. It just wasn't possible.

The noise from beyond the double doors rose an octave, reminding them that the real world still awaited them. Including Naomi's date for the evening.

'What about Stefan?' she asked, smiling.

'He can be an usher.'

'I came here with him. I owe him an explanation.'

Tom held out his arm for her. 'Then we'll tell him together. I don't think even Stefan will stand in the way of true love.'

Naomi laid her head against his shoulder. 'We almost did,' she said, sucking in a breath as she realised what they'd almost lost.

'We found our way in the end.'

She looked up at him. 'I could never lose you again.'

He kissed her. 'You won't have to. We have eternity together.'

They both took in a deep breath and then they pushed open the double doors.

EPILOGUE

HE COULDN'T QUITE believe it. It was almost time. All these
months of waiting. Of watching Naomi's tummy grow, of
feeling those magical kicks through her skin and marvelling at the life beneath, wondering just *who* was in there.

Tom hadn't known he could be this happy. To think of
where he had been even a year ago, believing there was
nothing left in his life to be glad about…and yet here he
was, about to become a father.

Imminently.

'Come on, Naomi…*push*!' He gripped her hand, holding it against his chest, glancing from her scrunched-up
face to the midwife and then down to see if he could see
their baby's head yet.

'Baby's coming, Naomi. One huge push for me now!'
urged the midwife.

Naomi sucked in a deep breath and focused. She gave
this push her all, every tiny bit of strength that she had left.
Fourteen hours of labour were nearly at an end. She was
sweating. Her hair was plastered to her face.

Tom felt her squeeze his fingers as she groaned and
grimaced, before she let out her breath and then immediately sucked in another, ready to push again. The midwife stopped her.

'Here's the head! Just pant for me now...pant, pant, that's it. And just a tiny push for me.'

Tom looked down. They were nearly there. His baby's head and face were emerging. 'Look at all that hair!'

Naomi looked up at him and began to cry. 'Really?'

'Really.' He kissed her forehead. 'You're doing it. You're doing it! I love you so much!'

'Get ready, Dad. Are you going to cut the cord?'

Tom nodded, beaming at the midwife. 'Try and stop me.' He watched anxiously as the baby turned naturally and the midwife checked for a cord around the neck, but everything was fine.

'One last push and you'll have your baby in your arms.'

Naomi nodded and smiled, before giving one last almighty push, the effort of which caused her to cry out.

Their baby was finally fully born, crying, into the world and the midwife lifted the squirming bundle straight onto Naomi's stomach.

Tom wasn't sure when he had started crying. Had it been the moment he saw his beautiful baby? Or maybe when he'd seen Naomi's face, so full of love, as she cradled their child?

'Here you go, Daddy. Cut between these two clips.' The midwife handed him the scissors and Tom cut the cord in disbelief, tears streaming down his cheeks. 'Do you want to see what you have?' she asked.

Tom was almost afraid to touch the baby. It was so beautiful, so precious! But he rolled it gently onto its back to reveal the sex. 'We have a daughter!'

Naomi held her tightly, lifting up her top so that their daughter could nestle against her skin. 'A baby girl!'

The midwife smiled broadly. 'Do we have a name?'

Naomi looked up at Tom and smiled. 'We do.'

He laid his hand on his daughter's tiny head as he announced her name. 'Sophia Grace.'

He gazed down at his beautiful fiancée and his darling daughter, unable to believe that they were both his. That they were here with him. Safe. Together. Loved. He bent to gently kiss his daughter's cheek and marvelled how soft her skin was. 'I love you both so much,' he murmured softly. He looked up at Naomi and they kissed, their tears of happiness mingling, their joy immeasurable.

'I love you, too. I'm the luckiest woman in the world.'

He kissed her again, still in disbelief at what he'd just witnessed. He had a child! A beautiful, perfect baby girl, who he already loved so much and wanted to protect until the end of the earth. With love overflowing from his heart, he closed his eyes and kissed his daughter's head as he cradled both of them in his arms, unable to believe that all of this happiness, all of this joy, was his.

'Thank you,' he said, when the afterbirth had been delivered and the midwife had left them alone. 'For coming into my life. For falling into my arms and refusing to give up on me.'

She touched her forehead to his and smiled, tears of elation still on her cheeks. 'You're worth it.'

'Having so much…all this happiness, all this love…'

She laid her hand upon his cheek and brought his lips down to hers. 'We don't need to be afraid of it.'

'I know. I'll cherish every second I spend with you and Sophia.'

'And I'll cherish them, too.'

The midwife returned to take the baby to clean her up and check her APGAR score, then she handed Sophia back, placing her carefully into Tom's arms.

Sophia, swaddled and warm, blinked at the harsh lights in the room, then gazed up into her father's face.

Tom stroked his daughter's cheek, full of pride and love. Then he looked to the woman he loved just as much and reached out to hold her hand.

Together they were strong.

Together they could face anything.

* * * * *

THE DOCTOR'S FORBIDDEN FLING

KARIN BAINE

For Tammy. From one special snowflake to another.
Our field trip was epic! xx

Special thanks to my IT guru, Cherie,
who dragged this technophobe kicking and
screaming into the twenty-first century and
managed not to throat-punch me in the process!

As always, I couldn't have told this story without help.
A big hug to my editor, Laura, to Chellie, Susan
and Alison, and an extra squishy one for Amalie
for her author guidance too. xx

CHAPTER ONE

IN VIOLET DEMPSEY'S experience the family room in a hospital department was where good news and hope came to die. It was in one of these seemingly innocuous side rooms she'd learned of her mother's fate and now she was waiting to hear of her father's too. He was fighting for his life in the cardiac care unit down the corridor while she was staring at the wall waiting for that ominous knock at the door.

She knew how crucial the first few hours after a heart attack were and she'd spent them trying to organise a flight back to Northern Ireland from London. Even that relatively short drive from Belfast to the Silent Valley Hospital in County Down had seemed like an eternity when her father was so close to death.

Their relationship was strained to say the least, since she refused to conform to her role as the daughter of an earl, but that didn't mean she didn't care. After watching her mother's struggle to fit into society life, Violet had simply decided to take her own path rather than the one her father had paved for her. They'd barely spoken since.

The tap on the door still made her jump even though she'd been expecting it. This was the reckoning. Life or death. Her stomach clenched as the door opened and the harbinger of impending doom swooped in. Except this was no po-faced stranger invading the already claustrophobic space.

'Nate?'

He was taller, broader and better groomed than she remembered but she'd recognise that dimpled smile anywhere. The hardest thing she'd ever had to do was walk away from that handsome face twelve years ago. She had no clue what he was doing here but he'd always had that knack of knowing exactly when she'd needed him.

'Hello, Violet. Or should I say *Lady* Violet? It's been a while.' He closed the door behind him and took the seat opposite her. It was so like Nate to plonk himself in the middle of her problems without a formal invitation.

'It has, but as I recall you were never one to stand on ceremony. Violet is just fine.' She hoped he was teasing her rather than trying to rile her when he understood better than anyone how much she hated her title.

They hadn't parted on the best of terms, on any terms really since she'd left without a word of explanation. Although he would have just cause to turn his back on her after what had happened, or even want a showdown to confront her about her behaviour, she was counting on him cutting her some slack in the circumstances. The old Nate would always have put her needs first and it was odd enough trying to come to terms with the fully formed man version of her childhood companion without finding out he might've completely changed character since their last meet too. Especially as she was just as attracted to Nate the adult.

The dark blond floppy hair had been tamed into a dapper short back and sides, the boyish face now defined with a sleek jawline and dusted with enough stubble to be fashionable and sexy. The son of Strachmore Castle's domestic staff had apparently swapped his hard-wearing flannel shirts for more tailored, expensive attire. He could easily have moved in her family's circle of friends now. If either of them had ever wanted that. One impulsive teenage kiss had effectively ended their friendship and sent Violet scurrying off to London before she committed to something that could never have worked.

Nate cleared his throat and she realised she'd been staring longer than an old friend ought to. The heat started to build in her cheeks as she recalled their last meet when they had ventured into new realms of their relationship.

'So... I assume you're here at your father's behest? He told me he was the one who phoned for the ambulance.' She steered the conversation, and her mind, away from dangerous territory. There was nothing like the thought of disapproving parents to pour cold water on certain heated moments that should be left in the past.

Nate leaned forward in the chair, forcing Violet to meet those hazel eyes she'd forgotten were so easy to get lost in. 'It was Dad who found him, but that's not why I'm here. This chat is of a more...professional nature. I'm a doctor here. Your father's cardiologist, in fact.'

She opened her mouth to tell him to stop messing about, then closed it again when she saw how serious he was. There was a ghost of a memory of the sister in charge mentioning a Dr Taylor but she'd never imagined this scenario in her wildest dreams.

'I didn't even know you'd gone to medical school,' she blurted out before she realised how bad that sounded. Cold. As though the spoilt brat with the privileged upbringing had swanned off and never looked back. That their time together had meant nothing to her.

It wasn't that she hadn't cared, or thought about him, over the years. Quite the opposite. She'd been afraid she'd become *too* interested in the life and times of Nate Taylor. For the sake of her new independent life away from her family's estate, she'd deemed it necessary to sever all ties with the one person who could've convinced her to stay.

'I mean, I keep contact with home to a bare minimum.' She wanted to justify her ignorance of his success in her absence. Of course she wasn't vain enough to imagine he'd spent all this time tending the grounds with his father, waiting for her return. She simply hadn't thought of him as being so…ambitious.

'I decided medicine would be a better paid, more respected profession compared to following family tradition into service.' There was that same old chip on the shoulder that had dominated conversation between them for hours in the old boathouse. Obviously their determination to branch away from the routes their parents had chosen for them had shaped both of their lives. For the better.

'You've certainly done well for yourself.' Not that it made a difference to her. Nate was a good person at heart, no matter what salary he brought home. The very reason she'd needed to create some distance between them. He'd deserved better than getting mixed up in the hell that was society life when her main goal had been to escape it.

'I'm sure I've surprised a few people round here by working my way out of a minimum-wage lifestyle. Now, I hear you've gone into nursing yourself so I'm sure you'll understand the seriousness of your father's condition.' He was definitely pricklier than she remembered and not above shaming her by displaying greater knowledge of her achievements than she had of his.

Violet's inner teenager with the schoolgirl crush couldn't help but wonder if he'd specifically sought out that information about her, or if his mother had simply been bending his ear. As the housekeeper at Strachmore, Mrs Taylor liked to keep her finger on the pulse, and that extended even as far as London. Every now and then Violet fielded prying phone calls from her father's well-meaning employee and, although she tried to keep details of her new life to a minimum, snippets of her successes and failures tended to slip through. The failures mostly related to relationships when the purpose of these communications was primarily to see if Violet had found herself a husband yet. Not in this lifetime. To her, marriage meant giving up everything you were to make another person happy and she'd seen first-hand the damage that could do. The fact she was here without her mother was proof enough it didn't work.

'Mental health is more my area of expertise.' Violet had felt so powerless after her mother had taken her own life she'd wanted to train in an area where she could make a real difference. It could be a challenging role at times but one that brought its own rewards.

She was doing her best to emotionally save lives, if not physically like Nate.

That little nugget apparently was news to him, as his raised eyebrows finally gave an indication he felt something more than indifference to her.

'I guess that's…understandable and admirable.'

The compliment was hard won. Not that Violet had chosen her profession to gain brownie points from anyone, but Nate seemed reluctant to give her credit for getting off her backside to work instead of languishing in that house. It was another reminder they'd left those summer afternoons planning their escape far behind.

'Us kids done good.' For old times' sake she decided to praise them both for doing exactly what they'd said they would and breaking free from their parents' hold.

Although, her father would've been appalled by her murder of the English language after paying for her elocution lessons. That was exactly why she'd relished doing it so frequently during her adolescence. Credit where it was due though, those hours spent improving her pronunciation had probably made her transition to London easier than sounding like a Northern Irish Eliza Doolittle. Perhaps she owed the old man some credit even if it had felt as if he was trying to force her to be someone she wasn't at the time.

'And yet here we are…'

She knew he was trying to get her to focus back on what was happening here and now but the words held a different meaning for her. No matter how hard she tried, she would never be able to completely separate her world from her father's.

'Okay, give it to me straight. Is he going to make it?' At some point she was going to have to apologise for running out on him but that would mean having to explain why she'd done it. It wasn't the time or place for that intense personal conversation, given the reason they were both here.

The scowl marring Nate's brow was further indication that her father was as bad as she'd feared. 'As you know, your father has suffered a myocardial infarction—a heart attack. He was unresponsive when the paramedics arrived and they had to resuscitate him on scene.'

It was no wonder Mr Taylor's message had been so fragmented and frantic. Technically, her father had died. She really didn't know how to feel about that. Since her mother had passed away Violet had resented him—for the way he'd treated her and for not being the one to have gone in her place. Now she was faced with the possibility of losing him too, things didn't seem so clear-cut. When you stripped away the bad memories and anger, he was still her father. She was starting to understand why her mother hadn't been able to simply walk away when the going got too rough. Sometimes having a conscience could be a terrible thing.

'A heart attack,' she repeated. Even though she'd heard it from others, coming from Nate somehow made it more real.

He nodded. 'It's been confirmed by blood tests. The increased levels of cardiac enzymes have indicated the presence of damage to the heart muscle. We'll continue taking bloods every six to eight hours as well as running electrocardiograms, ECGs, to monitor his heart's electrical activity and make sure there are no further complications. The next twenty-four to forty-eight hours will be crucial. Our first line of treatment would usually be emergency angioplasty to widen the arteries and allow easier blood flow to the heart. Unfortunately your father has proved…opposed to that idea.'

Nate didn't sugar-coat it. He didn't need to. They both knew she preferred straight talking to well-meaning platitudes. That way she wouldn't get hurt by hidden truths further down the line. Such as finding out her mother's overdose hadn't been as accidental as she'd first been led to believe.

It was a typical response from her father to ignore advice and insist he knew better than everyone. This time it could cause his own death instead of someone else's.

She closed her eyes and took a deep breath, batting away those old feelings flooding back and that helplessness at not being able to shake her father into facing facts. It hadn't worked for her mother so her chances after all this time were slim.

'Do we know what caused it?' She knew nothing of his lifestyle these days but she doubted his love of whiskey and cigars had diminished since she'd last seen him. He was a man who did as he pleased and sod the consequences.

'There's no family history of heart disease that we know of and no current health problems, I understand. We'll know more after we run a few tests. For now, our priority is limiting the damage to the heart.'

'I'm sorry I couldn't give the nurses any more information.' She grimaced, imagining the low opinion the staff were already forming of the absent daughter who couldn't give them any insight into her own father.

'It's all right. I understand things have been…tricky

between you both. We've pieced together what we could in the meantime.'

No doubt the Taylors' close relationship with her father had played a part in gathering that information. Violet didn't begrudge the bond the families had, but it sometimes made her feel inadequate, superfluous to requirements. Indeed, no one had ever needed her until now. Even now she wasn't sure how her presence would be received by either side of the class divide.

'Can I see him?' No matter how fractured their relationship had been since her mother's death, or how frustrating he was, he was the only family she had left. Just because she wasn't the daughter he wanted didn't mean she'd stopped caring about him. It simply made it more difficult.

Nate bounced back up onto his feet. 'I might be able to pull a few strings and get you a couple of minutes with him.'

The way he'd been reacting to her she was surprised he was willing to do anything other than list the facts of her father's condition. She figured this one must be for old times' sake—the days before things had got complicated and she'd made him despise her.

Determined to make the most of this breakthrough, she followed him into CCU, bobbing up and down like a meerkat keeping watch for predators as she tried to locate the patient. Nate strode through the ward with an air of confidence and authority she'd never seen in him before. It suited him. She had a sense of pride in him as patients and staff alike sat up straighter as he walked by. Finally people other than her had realised his worth in this world.

She zoned out the blue flashes of nurses zipping by

and the hospital beds occupied by ill strangers to hone in on her father. He was in the top left-hand corner of the room, by the window. At least he'd only have one immediate neighbour to complain about when he was back to his grouchy self. The Earl Dempsey would not be happy to find himself on an NHS ward surrounded by the great unwashed when he woke instead of some private hospital he'd happily pay through the nose for. Tough. When all was said and done, Nate and his colleagues were all that was keeping him alive.

'He's a little out of it at the moment due to the morphine we've given him to reduce the pain.' Nate led her to the bedside and for the first time in her life Violet felt sorry for her father. The man who'd virtually driven her mother to death in the pursuit of gaining a higher status in society now looked like any other old man lying there in his hospital gown, his white hair matted to his head and tubes and wires covering every inch of him.

She couldn't miss the monitors charting his vital signs, the IVs pumping life-saving drugs into his system, or the oxygen mask keeping him breathing, but she didn't cry. Nate's shoulder was safe from her tears these days. That display of emotion was reserved for the privacy of her own home where no one could witness her weakness. There was no way she was going to end up like her vulnerable mother, letting others take advantage of her. She was stronger than that. She'd had to be.

'What are his chances?' Violet was so matter-of-fact, so devoid of emotion, Nate was concerned she might be in shock and he'd have to treat her too. Then this night really would be complete.

Until now, he'd only seen her act this coldly once before. He knew she hadn't visited home since leaving for university but this was still her father lying here on the brink of death. The girl he'd grown up with had years of fear and hurt built up inside her because of this man, whether she loved him or not. There ought to be some sort of reaction to finding he could die without ever resolving the past.

He'd held back from saying those things that had sprung to mind the minute he'd known she was in the building, all of them prefaced with 'why?'. He'd had no choice but to pick himself back up and get on with life after her disappearing act but that didn't mean he'd stopped asking himself what he'd done to drive her away.

Seeing her again brought conflicting emotions to the fore. That broken-hearted teenager who still haunted his relationships would probably always hold a candle for her but with that came the hurt of her abandonment and that dismissal of his feelings for her.

Instead of acknowledging his declaration of love for her, or reciprocating, she'd walked away and re-fused to see him again before she'd left for London. It had been the only time she hadn't turned to him for advice, or confided her plans. The only time she'd turned her back on him instead of leaning on him for support. Although her rejection had cut him deeply, he'd tried to turn it into a positive. If he'd carried on in that vein, as an emotional crutch for her, he would've remained stagnant at Strachmore in his parents' foot-steps. They'd given the best years of their lives to the running of the castle, sacrificing everything else in their loyalty to the Dempseys.

Despite his father's view that they owed the family some sort of non-existent debt that included tying the next generation of Taylors to the Earl's needs, Nate had sworn not to get drawn into that trap. His parents might have conceded some of their freedom to maintain their positions but he was pretty sure sacrificing their firstborn hadn't been included in the terms and conditions of their contracts. This was his life, and he'd had ambitions beyond the Strachmore estate.

Violet had been the one flaw in that plan. He'd probably have given up all of his hopes and dreams to be with her. It still hadn't been enough. *He* hadn't been enough. Her actions had been confirmation he needed to do something with his life beyond the estate and he owed her for giving him that final push. That was partly why he'd insisted on speaking to her himself tonight.

He'd often imagined the moment their paths would cross again. Every medical exam he'd taken and passed with flying colours had been his way of getting his own back, proof he had been worthy of her after all. He mightn't have been born into money but with hard work he'd earned it, along with a good reputation. She would've seen that for herself if she'd shown any faith in him and stuck around.

There were many points in his career where he'd been spurred on with the thought of being able to flaunt his success some day. As if she were a loser in a game show and he were showing her what she could have won. If money and status had been all that mattered to her when he'd only had love to give, he knew she'd be kicking herself to find out he had it all now.

He'd be lying if he said he wasn't curious as to how the years had treated her too. If her mother's death had changed her emotionally, life in London had certainly transformed her physically. Although she'd hate it, her noble heritage shone through in every step she took. The once waist-length raven hair was now styled in a sleek bob, and her skinny frame, although still slender, definitely had curves in all the right places. She was every inch the sophisticated woman about town even in her casual butt-hugging jeans and silky polka-dot blouse. However, her new look and altered attitude couldn't hide the real Violet from him. Those blue eyes, the colour of a stormy winter's night, were as troubled as ever and he couldn't bring himself to confront her about the past when she was already in such turmoil.

It could wait until they were both ready to talk and stop pretending seeing each other wasn't a big deal. She might've moved on, consigned everything they'd had together to the past, but he still needed an explanation as to why she'd turned her back on him so he could close that chapter. Violet's rejection had marked the one failure in his life and that wasn't something he found easy to live with.

Although he wanted answers, for now he'd have to put his personal feelings aside and treat her as he would any family member of a critical patient. In the old days he wouldn't have thought twice about throwing his arms around her and giving her a much-needed hug, but they weren't here together through choice. Neither were they angsty teenagers united in rebellion against their parents. They were adults, virtual strangers who knew nothing of each other's lives. He chose a clinical approach to appease this edgier version of the girl he once knew and try to maintain some sort of professional distance from the case.

After dealing with the Earl, he had a renewed appreciation for what Violet and her mother had contended with. The frustration at not being able to do his job and perform the angioplasty because of his patient's non-compliance had made him want to scream. In some ways he understood Violet's decision to leave him to his own devices; it was easier than standing by and watching him self-destruct. Even in the jaws of death he thought he thought he knew better than those around him. As if he imagined continued denial would somehow defy fate.

'He's not out of danger yet but he is in the best place. We've administered clot-busting drugs quite early so it should restore the blood flow and reduce the damage. In my experience, the earlier we treat the patient after a heart attack, the better chance of survival they have.' Although he performed this procedure day after day, it was never routine. Every patient was individual, reacted differently to medication, suffered varying degrees of muscle damage and experienced all sorts of complications on the road to recovery. All he could do was fight with all the drugs and technology he had available to him and the rest was up to fate, or the stubbornness of the patient.

'I don't wish him any harm, you know. Despite everything. I'm not heartless.' Violet leaned across the bed and for a split second Nate thought she was going to reach out to her father. At the last second she withdrew again.

'I know. I'm sure he knows it too.' He might have had his doubts about that when she'd abandoned her life here with him in it, but she'd proved that rumour wrong by simply being here. Clearly she still cared for her father, and Nate had no doubt somewhere deep down the feeling was mutual. The trouble was they were both too stubborn to make the first move on building that bridge. He'd seen how the loss of her mother had affected Violet and he dearly hoped there was still time for her to connect with her father, to get closure if nothing else.

Nate had had his own parental issues but he still checked in with them on a regular basis. He just made sure he kept enough distance to ensure they didn't interfere in his life and he didn't get roped into drama at Strachmore. Until now.

The steady blip of the monitors suddenly flatlined as the Earl's heart rate dropped. Nate swung into action as the alarm rang out to summon the crash team. A second arrest was always a possibility when patients were at their most vulnerable after the first. Especially when they'd refused life-saving treatment. In Nate's head he'd thought bringing Violet in could somehow prevent the worst from happening. Instead, she was here to witness it for herself.

'Violet, I'm going to have to ask you to leave.' He motioned for help to get her out of here. Saving a man's life wasn't as pretty as they made out in the movies and he certainly didn't want family members in the audience for the performance.

'Nate?' She didn't have to say anything else. The

trembling bottom lip caught between her teeth and wide eyes expressed her plea eloquently enough.

'I'll do everything I can. I promise.' He was forced to block out that haunting image of her silently begging him to save her father so he could focus on the job at hand. He didn't want to be the one to have to deliver that earth-shattering news to her for a second time.

Sweat beaded on his forehead as he charged the defibrillator that had been wheeled to the bedside.

'Stand clear.'

The first shock Nate administered to try and kick-start the heart again was for the Earl, and Violet, and a second chance for their father-daughter relationship. He started CPR, thinking of his own parents and their ties to this man with every chest compression.

So much for not wanting anyone relying on him. Now both of their families were depending on him to save the day. And a life.

CHAPTER TWO

NATE LEANING OVER the bed, pumping her father's chest, was the last thing Violet saw before the ward doors swung shut, closing her out of her father's struggle for life. A nurse steered her back towards the cell she'd vacated only minutes earlier for another interminable wait. With her pulse racing, her insides knotted, she didn't have it in her to resist a second incarceration.

There was nothing she could do but take a seat in her still-warm chair. Everything was in Nate's hands now. Literally. She trusted his word to do his utmost to save his patient; he'd never let her down before. It had been the other way around. When he'd kissed her, told her he loved her, she'd run away rather than confess she felt the same. It was the one thing she couldn't give him, dared not give him, when she'd watched love destroy her mother.

She admired Nate's professionalism after the way she'd left things with him. There was an aloofness about him she wasn't used to, but she guessed she'd been the one who'd created that by going to London without telling him why. Perhaps it was water under the bridge for him and not something he was keen to be reminded of. In fairness, she probably deserved a

lot worse than the cold shoulder and she didn't think
she'd be quite so civilised if the situation had been re-
versed. Whatever his thoughts on seeing her, she was
grateful to him for not calling her out on what had
happened. She didn't want to deal with any more emotional fallout today. For someone who did her best to
keep her feelings on lockdown, this had been a doozy
of a day already and she couldn't face any more demons from her past.

Yet, here she was relying on him the same way she
had every time her parents had fought, feeling sorry
for herself and wondering what the future held. This
time her thoughts were consumed with becoming an
orphan at the age of thirty instead of being married off
to another family who valued reputation above all else.

There was a tentative knock on the door and the
same nurse appeared with a tea tray. 'I thought you
could do with a cuppa.'

'Thanks.' Violet accepted the offering with a forced
smile. Despite the fact she hadn't eaten anything since
receiving that fateful telephone call, her stomach was
in too much turmoil for her to even face the plain bis-
cuits presented to her with the tea.

'You need something to keep your strength up.
You'll be no use to your father if you faint from hunger.'

Violet honestly didn't know what use she'd be to her
father whether she was conscious or not, but her new
shadow stood waiting and watching until she took a
nibble at a biscuit and a sip of tea. Only then, her care
of duty fulfilled, did the nurse leave her alone again.

The next time the door opened some time later, it
was Nate who entered. She told herself the little flip

her heart did was in anticipation of finding out her father's fate. It had absolutely nothing to do with the sight of Dr Taylor with his shirt sleeves rolled up and his perfectly groomed hair now ruffled and unkempt as if he'd just got out of bed. It was clear neither he nor her father had had an easy time of it.

'We got him back.' Nate immediately ended her suspense and she let go of the breath she'd been holding since he walked in.

'Thank you.' Her voice was nothing more than a whisper, her throat burning from the tears she couldn't shed. Until today she hadn't realised how much it meant to her to know she wasn't alone in the world.

'We'll keep him under close observation. A second arrest was always a possibility after the stress his heart has been under today but he's stable now.'

Nate's dedication was a blessing. Especially when her father had treated him with nothing but disdain when they were growing up. He thought associating with those below one's station was degrading and it had been to blame for Violet's 'rebellion'. In hindsight, she wondered if he'd seen how dangerously close they'd come to having a proper relationship and that had coloured his view of their friendship. Nate would never have lived up to her father's idea of a noble son-in-law to carry on his title. Not that he would've wanted it either. He hated Strachmore as much as she did. In the end the Earl's campaign to keep them separated had been a wasted exercise on his part. Violet had no intention of settling down with anyone, whether she loved them or not.

'Thanks for keeping me in the loop. I know you're probably needed elsewhere.' She was under no illusion that this particular cardiologist was assigned to her only. He'd undoubtedly done her a huge favour by personally informing her of her father's condition. For reasons known only to him when he'd made it clear he hadn't forgiven her for her sins.

'Do you need me to order you a taxi? Is there somewhere you need to be?' He eyed her small *I-left-in-a-hurry* luggage, probably keen to ship her out of his territory as soon as possible.

She'd barely packed enough for more than tonight, but that had been out of sheer panic rather than optimism.

'I'm fine here for the night if that's allowed? I can pull a couple of chairs together.' She hadn't thought beyond getting here before it was too late, never mind overnight accommodation. Since it was still touch and go, her personal discomfort didn't seem that important.

'You can't sleep here. I'm sure you're exhausted.'

There was a pause and a heavy sigh before he continued. 'I'll give you a lift back to Strachmore and get the keys from my mum to let you in.'

Nate sounded resigned to homing her for the night, as if she were a stray dog he'd picked up on the side of the road and was stuck with until help arrived. This was how things had always been between them—Nate finding solutions to problems of her own making. Except back then he'd always seemed to enjoy coming to her rescue.

'Honestly, I don't want to hold you back any longer. I'm sure you have other patients to see and this means I'm close if anything happens during the night.' If she was honest she wasn't sure her family home would be any more inviting than this windowless broom cupboard.

Nate dipped his head, looking decidedly sheepish. 'My shift finished hours ago. I'm all yours.'

A shiver played across her skin, teasing every tiny hair to attention. It was her guilt at keeping him at his post through some misplaced sense of loyalty manifesting. Definitely not a physical reaction to him offering herself up to her.

'I can't ask you to—'

'You didn't. I'm volunteering.' He was already grabbing her bag and robbing her of her refusal even though he made his offer sound as if he'd had no other choice.

He paused by the door and fixed her with those soul-reaching eyes. 'The night staff will phone you, and me, if there's any change. I'll get you back here in a flash if it comes to it.'

'Only if you're sure?' She'd finally run out of excuses not to go home.

Violet waited in the car while he paid his parents a visit. She hoped it was quick. The longer they were travelling companions with this elephant from the past, the more likely they were going to have to acknowledge it. She wasn't ready to face that, or the Taylors. Not that she held any ill will against the pair—after all, they were the ones who kept this place running—but she was tired and definitely not in the mood for grand reunions or lectures. Nate had left the engine running and the heater on so he clearly didn't intend to loiter either. He was probably every bit as eager as she was to put today behind them.

She shifted in the leather bucket seat, which was

marginally more comfortable than the hospital wait-ing chairs. The mode of transport she was being chauf-feured around the countryside in was still something of a shock to her system. To see the boy who'd spent his summers working umpteen jobs to save cash had splashed out on a bright red sports car was more sur-prising than if he'd turned up on an ancient motorbike and sidecar. It was almost as though he was sticking two fingers up at everyone who'd treated him as a sec-ond-class citizen in his youth and told him he'd never amount to anything beyond Strachmore. Ironically, the youngest member of the Dempsey family relied on public transport to get her from A to B. It was more practical for city life but it also had the added bonus of ticking off her father.

She watched Nate stride back to the car in the muted evening light. He could easily pass as the master of the big house now he'd swapped his ripped jeans for those tailored suits. Although, he would probably look good in anything. Or nothing.

Whoa!

Those teenage hormones she'd thought she'd left be-hind long ago had apparently resurfaced and mutated into adult ones. It had been a long, emotional day and clearly she was misinterpreting his reluctant kindness for something...sexier.

She cleared her throat as he opened the car door and climbed back into the driver's seat. If only she could clear her mind of the images she'd planted there as eas-ily. Her wayward thoughts weren't helped by the fact his tall frame was packed so tightly into the car, his thighs were almost touching hers.

'Mum's in a tizzy about not having the place cleaned

for your arrival. I assured her I'd roll the red carpet out for you myself but we'd best get out of here before we run into a cleaning mob brandishing mops and dusters.'

Violet ignored the barb, simply grateful he'd run interference for her, when Mrs Taylor was probably bursting with questions for her. 'I'm sure the house is as spotless as ever with your mother at the helm. I only wish I could clone her and take her back to London with me.'

Unlike Strachmore Castle, her poky flat was never going to make the cover of any magazines but she worked hard to pay the rent. That meant more to her than gleaming silver and polished marble floors ever would.

Nate threw the car into reverse and rested his arm along the back of her seat as he kept watch out of the back window. The smell of soap and hard-working doctor enveloped her and for a moment she was tempted to snuggle into his solid chest. He could give her comfort and a whole lot besides. Exactly why she should stick to the idea of him as only a friend, or her father's doctor, and not someone who'd taken the lead role in her first erotic imaginings.

'Do you know how long you'll be staying? I mean, is someone holding the fort for you while you're here?' He trained his eyes back on the dark road leading from the cottage up to the main house, so Violet couldn't tell if he was fishing for personal info or making polite conversation.

'I'll stay as long as I'm needed. I have a lot of personal leave I can use.' She preferred to keep busy with work rather than take duvet days where she had nothing to do but dwell on things beyond her control. It wasn't the first time her superiors had warned her of possible burnout if she didn't take a break from her caseload so they'd be only too happy for her to take some time off.

'If you need anything my parents will be here to help.'

He was leaving himself out of the equation but it was a long time since Violet had relied on anyone having her back. For good reason. She'd needed to learn to stand on her own two feet to make herself stronger than her mother had been.

'Thank you. I know you've gone out of your way to help me and I wouldn't want to get your other half offside by holding you hostage to my problems.' Okay, she *was* fishing. He'd been her first crush, her first kiss, it was only natural that this curious cat was wrestling a green-eyed monster at the thought of him going home to another woman. One who wasn't afraid to make compromises.

'There's no danger of that. I'm a confirmed bachelor.'

Those words had the same effect as if he'd thrown a bucket of ice-cold water over her as she jumped from one conclusion to another. She'd been so caught up in her feelings for him she'd never contemplated how much his could have changed for her, or for women in general. Suddenly his new grooming regime started to take on a whole new meaning. 'You're not—'

'No, I'm not gay, Violet. I thought you of all people would realise I'm attracted to women.' He turned and, though Violet couldn't see his face clearly in the dim interior, she imagined he was looking at her lips, remembering *that* kiss too.

She'd managed to block it out for over a decade but

here, so close to him again, it was all she could think about. That first tentative exploration of each other had soon given way to a raw passion she hadn't experienced since. These days she approached any romantic entanglements with a certain degree of cynicism and caution, which meant she was always holding back. In that moment with Nate's lips on hers she'd given no thought to consequence or complications that could arise. That had come later when she'd tried to imagine a future together and failed. He didn't belong in her world and vice versa. Ironically they seemed to have traded places anyway.

As the stately home loomed into view of the car headlights, the butterflies in her stomach turned kamikaze, dive-bombing her insides until there was a chance she might hurl over the expensive leather upholstery. At least it was wipe-clean.

'Home sweet home.' Nate's attempt at humour was a welcome distraction from the memories assaulting her from the second the stone pillars of the eighteenth-century house came into view.

Her father, spit forming at the corners of his mouth when she defied him by sneaking out to a concert with Nate.

Violet hiding in the old servants' quarters when she was supposed to be dining with the Montgomery family, whose son had been deemed a suitable match for her at the age of seventeen.

The empty pill bottle by her mother's bedside.

Dark humour was definitely the cure for dark memories.

'In case you can't see it, I'm giving you the death stare.'

Nate gave a hearty chuckle, letting the serious doctor mask slip for a glimpse of her old friend. 'Nostrils flaring, mouth puckered up like you've just licked a lemon, eyes narrowed to mere slits—I can picture it now.'

Violet flattened her lips back into a thin line with a huff. She could hear the smugness in his voice that he still knew her better than anyone even after all of this time.

They pulled up into the driveway and the sound of the handbrake meant there was no more stalling.

'Thanks for everything. I can let myself in.'

'No can do. I told you I'm under instruction to escort Lady Violet inside her ancestral home. Don't forget, under different circumstances I could've ended up as your official errand boy.'

He was being facetious. Violet knew he would never have played the skivvy any more than she would've been the boss lady. Still, it conjured up more interesting images if they'd chosen different paths.

She let out a long sigh and admitted defeat. Having a surly Nate here was infinitely more bearable than having Mrs Taylor fussing around her, or setting foot back inside alone. It was one thing going home to an empty flat at night but an entirely different game coming back here where the ghosts of her past roamed the hallways.

Nate really needed to work on that keeping-at-arm's-length ethos where relationships were concerned. He'd thought he'd built up a tolerance to all things Dempsey since his teenage heartbreak. One glimpse of those big blue eyes and he was taking on the duties of the whole domestic staff who'd once resided here—the chauffeur, the butler and housekeeper all rolled into one. He told himself his promise to light a fire and see her settled in was the only way to keep his parents at bay and Violet's discomfort to a minimum. They meant well, their subservient role so deeply ingrained in them the very thought of Lady Violet returning to a cold, empty house brought them out in a cold sweat. He knew this would be difficult enough for her without an audience and he still had a duty of care via her father.

Despite their history, or possibly because of the one they'd had pre-kiss, he still felt an obligation to help her. Perhaps he wasn't as far removed from his heritage as he liked to think. He'd really been the only one Violet had had to turn to when things had got rough and it would be callous for him to abandon her now for the sake of his own pride. He simply hadn't been able to leave her for the night in that waiting room, expecting her to bed down where she stood. In a fit of madness he'd even briefly contemplated taking her back to his house rather than expect her to face this place alone.

Ultimately he'd done enough damage to his relationship boundaries already. She was only back in the country five minutes and he'd already landed himself firmly in the friend zone. Not a position he wanted to be in with any beautiful woman. Especially one he already had an emotional history with. One who'd dumped him without a second thought. Then there was the double blow to his ego with the whole gay thing. He knew one teenage fumble probably hadn't made a long-lasting impact on her but he'd assumed it had been enough to define his sexuality.

Now he'd slipped back into a supporting role there was no way he was ever going to win top billing as Violet's leading man. If he'd once imagined taking her back into his arms and replacing that inexperienced make-out session with a more confident approach to recover his male pride, he'd stuffed up the minute he'd insisted on staying to talk to her about her father. Friends or lovers—there was no in between for him when it came to the women in his life. He didn't even want to peek inside people's personal baggage, never mind help them unpack it, and yet that was exactly what he was doing now. The pressure was on him more than ever to save his patient and return everyone back to their normal status quo. As soon as he'd done the gentlemanly thing and seen her settled in, he could walk away with a clear conscience. He'd proved the better person by not exacting revenge.

'You put the kettle on and I'll get the fire started.' He opened the heavy front door with a reverence the stately home deserved even if the current owner didn't. It was a beautiful building, full of history and wonder. Unfortunately it also held negative connotations for those entering it tonight. While Violet had been the princess held captive in the tower, he'd very much been the lowly serf kept in his place by his master. He'd dealt with a lot of those issues through hard work and determination but he couldn't help feeling Violet still had to face hers. Although he still had an axe of his own to grind with her, he wasn't totally unsympathetic. It was best he try to make this as normal as possible for her. As if they were walking into any other family home and not the country pile of her ancestors. Easier said than done when there was a huge chandelier dominating the space in front of them.

'We do have modern-day conveniences like central heating.' She was still resisting his attempts to phase her into her surroundings gradually with his assistance, but he was used to dealing with difficult patients and bolshie family members.

She was more defensive than he remembered. He guessed years of independent living had toughened her up. A definite plus given his aversion to needy people outside the workplace.

'And kettles?'

It amused him to watch her flounce away the way she used to when his teasing went too far. It was further proof her fiery spirit was very much alive. She was going to need it to see her through the next days, whatever they held.

'Milk, no sugar,' he called after her as he headed for the study.

It was the closest and smallest room on the ground floor, and easier to heat. The pale blue walls and ornate white ceiling of the entrance hall were pretty and in keeping with the period pieces dotted throughout but they didn't make the cool atmosphere any more inviting. Okay, they had no practical need for a fire but there was something homely about a real fire. It was cosy and welcoming, something this house was sadly lacking.

He could sense the disapproving stares of past earls staring down at him from the walls as he trespassed into the inner sanctum. They all had the same stern features of Samuel Dempsey. Nate wondered if not smiling was another one of the house rules Violet had deigned to disobey. Ruling with an iron fist might have worked in the olden days but, as far as he'd seen, all it had succeeded in doing in recent times was shatter the family.

'Is this where they found him?'

He hadn't heard Violet enter the room as he'd knelt to set the fire in the hearth. It wasn't until he turned around again that he understood why she'd sounded so pained.

Her father's papers littered the mahogany and brass writing desk and spilled onto the floor, his chair toppled over in the corner of the room with a whiskey tumbler lying next to it—the contents of which had seeped into the antique rug long ago.

'I'm so sorry, Violet. I had no idea. We can move into the drawing room and I'll get this tidied up.' Regardless of the painful history between them, he would never have purposely exposed her to this scene. He took the rattling cups and saucers from her shaking hands before she slopped the tea on the expensive furnishings too.

'It's all right. It was just a shock.' She righted the heavy chair and Nate set down the tea things so he could help.

They both bent down to reach for the upturned glass at the same time, Violet's bracelet clinking against it in the process. He reached for her wrist, curiosity getting the better of common sense.

'Is this the one I bought you?' It was only a cheap turquoise bead bracelet with a dainty seahorse charm hanging from it. So unlike the diamonds and pearls her mother had favoured on occasion. He was surprised it had stood the test of time, even more so to find she still wore it.

A trace of a smile lifted the corners of her mouth. 'Yes. From the day at the aquarium.'

The day things had changed between them for ever.

'You were fascinated by those damn seahorses.'

She'd stood for ages watching them as if she'd found her peace there and he'd wanted her to have a souvenir of that summer afternoon together. He hadn't known it would be their last.

'They're just so…serene. I envy the simplicity of their life. And, of course, it's the male who gives birth. The female seahorse has a much freer life than most women, she transfers her eggs and goes back to her own place—the onus isn't on her to carry on the family line.' It was a tragic narrative of Violet's childhood when she'd been jealous of a fragile species trapped in a tank. At least now she was free of some of her burden even if it had cost Nate a piece of his heart in the process.

He flicked the charm up with his thumb so it rested on his nail. So small, so inexpensive, so evocative. If that day had meant nothing to her, if he'd meant nothing to her, why would she still be attached to it now? He felt her pulse quicken beneath him, met her eyes with his, and they were back in that bubble where nothing mattered except the chemistry.

He didn't know who'd leaned closer to whom but suddenly they were no more than a breath away from kissing. Violet's eyes fluttered shut, her lips were parted and waiting for him. There was nothing he wanted more in that moment than to give into temptation. Despite how much she'd hurt him in the past, he'd wanted to do this the minute he'd seen her again but this was typical Violet behaviour. She couldn't drop him and pick him up when the mood took her. Not any more. Especially when she still hadn't done him the courtesy of an apology or an explanation, never mind simply acknowledging what she'd done to him.

Unfortunately physical attraction couldn't always override common sense. A kiss was much more than that when it was with your first love, the woman who'd broken your heart without a backward glance.

He let go of her wrist and stepped away from temptation. As he began to collect his thoughts away from her lips, the Earl's collection of antique clocks chimed the late hour and sounded the death knell for this… whatever the hell it was.

When he didn't swoop in and ravage her, Violet was afraid to open her eyes and face him. She'd done it again—gone with her heart instead of her head. Thank goodness one of them had been thinking clearly this time. She shuddered at how close she'd come to making another monumental mistake when she'd yet to address the last one she'd made with Nate. Her world was complicated enough now without resurrecting old emotions like zombies wandering through her life with no real purpose except causing eternal misery for everyone in their path. She needed to remember that every time she was tempted to lose herself in his embrace, that one place she was able to forget her troubles.

In her defence she'd been under a lot of pressure today and Nate had been her one source of comfort, the only familiar thing from home that didn't make her want to run screaming. Even in his current indifferent state. She blamed her faux pas entirely on stress. Apparently making moves on hot doctors was a side effect of tangled emotions no one had warned her about. They hadn't covered that in her course. Then again,

Nate was the professional—he should've known he was in danger simply by being in the room with her.

In fact, he seemed to have found the best treatment for her particular case by continuing to pick up the debris around them and ignoring the latest addition to the elephant herd now parading around the room.

'No wonder Mum was so frantic about getting this place tidied up before you set foot inside. I guess they just locked up the house once the ambulance left.' Nate in cleaning mode was as efficient as his mother and Violet decided to follow his lead. Time and distance hadn't made this any more feasible.

They worked quietly together, sifting her father's correspondence into manageable piles. The quicker they got this sorted, the easier it would make it for Nate to leave. She knew him well enough to know he'd see this out until the end, when he'd fulfilled his obligation to her and his parents.

'Violet?' After some time he drew her attention to a stack of letters headed with bold red lettering.

'Mmm?'

'These are all bills. Most of them final demands.'

'Let me see.' She snatched a few from his grasp and confirmed it. All correspondence, most of it threatening action against him, was leading to the conclusion her father was in dire financial trouble.

She collapsed into the chair with such force she almost toppled it over again. This was too much for her to handle on top of everything else today. Somehow she was going to have to fix this. She just had no idea how.

'You had no clue this was going on?' Nate spoke softly, as if he was afraid of spooking her even more.

The façade her father had presented to the world all these years had duped many into thinking their fortune was never ending. She'd known differently.

'The place has been leaking money for years but I didn't know things were this bad.' Her father's spending and refusal to admit they were in trouble had been the source of many an argument in the house before her mother died. The worry and uncertainty about the future had certainly contributed to her mother's fragile state of mind but he hadn't taken any responsibility then and he wasn't likely to do so now.

'What? There's no magical pot of gold hidden under the floorboards?' Nate pretended to be surprised the place didn't run by reputation and superiority complexes alone.

'Unfortunately not.' She lifted the stack of bills and slammed them back down on the table. This wasn't his problem. Hell, it wasn't even hers.

Whatever happened to her father, Violet knew she was going to have to be the one to sort this out. She should have known better than to come back. It had been inevitable that she'd get sucked back into her father's delusions of grandeur and the repercussions of stark reality. Perhaps she should have done as she was told at seventeen and agreed to marry Lord Montgomery's son. At least she might've been in a position now to help financially, possibly with her mother still around too.

This new discovery threatened to undo all the progress she'd made in her new life. Nothing had changed in her absence, she'd simply avoided dealing with it. She was back to being that frightened girl, lonely and overwhelmed by the burden her father had put upon her.

She wanted to confront him, scream and cry, and walk away for ever. Now she could do none of those things. She was stuck here. Again.

'I'll worry about these tomorrow, as soon as I know he's made it through the night. Then I might go up there and kill him myself.'

Nate arched an eyebrow at her with a smirk. 'Now, I know you don't mean that. I told you, there's help available. It's a shame you Dempseys are too damn stubborn for your own good. You don't have to do this on your own.'

Deep down she knew he was talking about his parents or some other official source of financial advice but it gave her more comfort to imagine he was still in her corner. 'You're the only person who was ever there for me, you know.'

Reuniting with Nate was the only light in this darkness and she wanted to run towards the safety she knew was there. For a little while she didn't want to think about tomorrow, or the next day, or the next. He could help her forget, take her to that happy place away from all of this mess. What was one more mistake when her life was crumbling around her? All she had to do was convince him, and herself, this wasn't the big deal it had been when they were teenagers.

Suddenly she was tired of being strong, of bearing the weight of Strachmore on her shoulders alone.

'Stay with me tonight, Nate.'

Nate's body reacted to the invitation before his brain kicked in and listed all the reasons this was a bad idea. He ignored all parts of him straining to make the decision for him, knowing Violet would regret this in the morning, as he would. For altogether different reasons. This was his chance to exorcise that painful rejection for good, but he knew her well enough to understand what this was really about. Her way of dealing with difficult matters had always been to divert her attention elsewhere, put off tackling the hard stuff for as long as possible. Violet was the Queen of Procrastination and he'd always been the Fool, keeping her entertained and distracting her from the hardships within the castle walls.

Not any more. He'd made certain he was King of his own castle since those days.

'I think it would be better if I went home.'

She'd let him know he wasn't good enough for her before and he wasn't going to be the consolation prize now.

She stood up so she was close enough to invade his personal space and trailed a fingertip down the front of his shirt. 'Don't tell me you haven't thought about this, about us—'

She didn't need to say any more. He was already picturing them together in bed, giving into that chemistry he'd never been able to forget.

He took a deep breath to purify his thoughts and make sense of hers. She'd taken an emotional battering today and he'd never take advantage of her when she was so vulnerable. Lord knew he wanted her and it was an ego boost to know it was reciprocated this time but it didn't change circumstances. *Friend or lover?* He reminded himself he couldn't be both and remain sane. He'd breached the professional boundary long ago and only friendship had remained before he'd ended up in no-man's land—a minefield he had to tiptoe through, full of the sort of explosive situations he'd happily avoided since he was nineteen.

'We're both adults, single, with no illusions this would be anything more than sex. I need the distraction.' It was confirmation of exactly where he stood with her and that wasn't any place of importance. She might as well have been hiring an escort for the evening for all the emotional significance she afforded him.

Normally that kind of detachment wasn't a problem. In fact he welcomed it. It stopped things becoming too messy. However Violet wasn't a faceless one-night stand. Uncomplicated sex should never involve the woman whose rejection had made you so cynical about relationships in the first place.

'Unfortunately, sharing a bed is not the modern-day equivalent of hanging out in the boathouse pretending real life isn't happening around us.' His heavy dose of honesty transformed Violet's coquettish eye-fluttering into a wide-eyed, open-mouthed, I've-just-been-slapped-in-the-face expression.

He was pretty sure he'd worn that same look once before and he took no satisfaction in being the one to cause it this time.

'You're right. I don't know what the hell I was thinking.'

He could see the shame clouding her eyes already. That wasn't what he wanted either.

'There's nothing I'd enjoy more than taking you to bed right now, but I think it would be a mistake. For both of us. Get some sleep and I'll see you in the morning.' He knew she didn't want to be alone, but he didn't

intend falling into that old pattern of being at her beck
and call again. He'd invested too much in that before
and paid the consequences.

'You always were the sensible one.' She gave him a
wobbly smile and Nate knew he had to get out of here
before the tears really did fall. When she finally did
give into the real emotions she was trying to hide from,
he knew he'd never be able to leave her.

'And you always were the impulsive one.' He'd lost
count of the number of times he'd had to talk her out of
doing something stupid—like running away or sabo-
taging her father's dinner parties with laxatives. It was
probably the reason she hadn't confided in him about
moving to London. She hadn't wanted to be talked
out of it.

This proposition was most likely a cry for help
rather than an unyielding need to have him in her bed,
but it didn't make it any easier to resist.

'Goodnight, Violet.'

He wondered if she'd ever regretted walking away
as much as he did now.

CHAPTER THREE

THE TROUBLE WITH the countryside was the quiet. There was no traffic noise to drown out Violet's thoughts and nowhere to go to escape her shame. She'd spent most of the night replaying the moment she'd made a complete fool of herself with Nate. Lord knew what he thought of her throwing herself at him like some nympho desperate for a quick lay. She shuddered, the cringe factor at an all-time high as she recalled the look of disgust on his face as he rejected her advances. All he'd done was show her some kindness, more than she deserved, and she'd implied she was only interested in his body. Nothing could be further from the truth. Well, okay, his body had been on her mind since she'd first seen him suited and booted but she'd needed him for so much more than that. She'd tried to use sex to get him to stay when she was really yearning for his company.

After one bombshell too many, her common sense had been blown to pieces. There was no other logical explanation for her behaviour last night. These past years of being so strong, so independent had skewed her idea of friendship until she'd seen it as a weakness. Until yesterday, when Nate had reminded her how good it was to have someone in your corner fighting your battles with you. In her messed-up head, sleeping with Nate had seemed like the only way to recapture that fantasy world they'd had when they were young but he'd called her on it. She had no right to expect anything from him when she'd been the one to burst that bubble in the first place. What had been the point of walking away then if she was simply going to drag him back into all Strachmore's problems now?

In the cold light of day Nate's refusal to stay had probably been the most sensible option but her ego was still a little bruised. Clearly he'd done what she'd ultimately wanted for him at the time and moved on from her. She should be happy about it. Not wondering what, apart from her badly executed proposition, had turned him off her. That one kiss had been so full of love and passion for her she hated to think she'd killed it stone dead with her actions, even though she'd acted in what she'd thought was in both of their interests.

At least *not* sleeping with Nate meant minimal embarrassment when she would inevitably run into him again. The good news this morning was that her father had made it through the night and was as well as could be expected for a man determined to be in control of his own destiny at any cost.

Now that the sun was up she was keen to get to the hospital and see him but her thoughts were as muddled as ever when it came to her father. Last night she'd been afraid for him, and herself, as far as his health and finances were concerned. Yet there was also that lingering resentment that he'd brought her back here, unintentionally or not. These rose-covered walls and four-poster bed might be the stuff of little girls' dreams but to her this had always been a prison, a place that had robbed her of her freedom. Even as an adult she was still trapped here.

She tossed off the covers and climbed out of bed, her bare feet sinking into the thick wool carpet reminding her she wasn't in Kansas any more. The wooden floors throughout her flat served a dual purpose— minimum cleaning and a stand against her old-fashioned upbringing.

She wandered down the halls trying to find the beauty in her opulent surroundings and failing. The shiny, gilded trinkets and ornate antiquities were exquisite but at what cost? She would've taken a childhood in a one-bedroom council flat if it had meant she could've had her mother back. Not so her father. Even when his wife had begged him to downsize to stem their outgoings, he'd refused to part with the family silver or make any concessions to give her peace of mind. If anything, he'd become more extravagant, throwing lavish parties to prevent the rumour mill churning with stories about the depleted family coffers. Her mother had been expected to be compliant in the façade, playing the glamorous, gracious hostess while quashing her anxiety with a cocktail of drugs.

Violet slid her hand over the smooth mahogany bannister leading down the staircase. It took her to a happier period when the house was her playground and this was her slide taking her from one floor to another. With few friends outside her preparatory school, she'd had to make her own entertainment when she'd been waiting for Nate to finish working in the grounds with his father. At least with him she'd never had to pretend to be something she wasn't. She shouldn't have tried to do that last night by making out she was some sort of good-time girl.

Perhaps he'd seen right through her façade the way he'd always been able to and realised she'd simply been acting out of fear. That thought was preferable to the one where he didn't find her attractive any more and enough to spur her on to get dressed and face the day ahead.

So many elements of what happened last night had been playing on Nate's mind. The most persistent one being Violet's indecent proposal and why he'd turned her down. He doubted she felt any more for him now than she had back then and surmised she'd been trying to use him as a sticking plaster over the wound coming back here had reopened. He knew he'd ultimately made the right decision. Going down that path again would only have led to that same dead end it had taken him years to navigate his way out of.

In hindsight her flight to London rather than take the next step with him had probably been for the best. Nothing had changed since then. Except they were no longer best friends and self-preservation was a higher priority for him now.

The discovery of the Earl's debts had added to his disturbed sleep; he was worried not only for Violet but for his family too. Regardless of his own thoughts on Strachmore, or the people who resided there, his parents were very much a part of it. Any financial problems would affect them too when it was their livelihood, and their affiliation was the only thing keeping a roof over their heads. The cottage was the only perk of the job as far as he could see and one that would certainly vanish along with the Dempseys. Strachmore's problems were also his now. He couldn't stand by and watch his parents lose their home simply because he and Violet had unresolved issues. They were all going to have to work together to find a solution. The future was going to have to be more important than the past.

He'd made Samuel Dempsey his first port of call on the ward rounds this morning to follow his progress. All had been quiet since the last dramatic intervention to restart his heart so Nate hoped this was the start of his recovery. There was no associated arrhythmia, with the heart beating too quickly, too slowly, or irregularly, which could sometimes occur after a heart attack. It would take a while to assess the full damage done to the heart and how much tissue would be able to recover but, for now, he was stable.

That was more than could be said for another one of his elderly patients, who'd suffered severe heart failure and had undergone stenting of his coronary arteries yesterday. The balloon catheter supposed to inflate/deflate timed by the patient's heartbeat and support the circulation hadn't been beneficial in this case. After examining him, Nate had had to concede that a large part of the heart muscle had died and nothing more could be done. A younger patient might have been a candidate for further surgery but it had been decided at the morning multi-disciplinary meeting not to pursue any further investigation. Already weak, the patient wouldn't have survived another round of intrusive surgery. It wasn't the outcome he wanted for any of his patients, no matter what their age or circumstance. He absorbed every loss as though it were personal, his failing. If anything happened to the Earl he'd never forgive himself for letting Violet or his parents down.

After seeing in-patients, outpatients and performing a pacemaker insertion, he'd come full circle back to CCU. Deep down he'd known Violet would be here.

'Hey, Dad.' Violet was glad to see he was a bit more with it and his pallor was a lot less grey today. She'd been sitting around for hours waiting for all the tests and scans to be completed before she got to see him. Making her own way to the hospital this morning had seemed like a better plan than car-sharing with the man who didn't want to sleep with her but it also meant no string-pulling visitor privileges.

'Violet? What are you doing here?' His eyes were flickering open and shut as though he wasn't sure whether or not to believe what he was seeing. It was no wonder when she'd spent so long out of the country, and his life.

'The doctors have told you what happened, right?' She didn't want the responsibility of breaking the news to him; he wasn't invincible. He'd probably call her a liar if she tried.

'A heart attack.' He nodded and closed his eyes again. She couldn't tell if he was tired, zoned out on drugs or annoyed she was here. Probably all three. She was the last person he'd want to see him weak and out of control.

'I wanted to make sure you were all right.' It was weird saying that when she'd barely let him enter her thoughts until recently. He'd been out of sight, out of mind, to enable her to move forward. Until one phone call had forced her to acknowledge he was still part of her life whether she liked it or not.

She stood by the bed, arms folded and doing her best to sound strong, as if admitting she'd been scared for him would somehow give him power back over her.

'I'm grand.'

And people wondered where she got her stubborn streak from. There was no point telling him how close to death he'd come. He knew. He simply wouldn't admit it to her or himself.

She waited for something more—a complaint about sharing a room with the general public, a request for water, an acknowledgement of what it meant for her to be here. Nothing. Not even an attempt to keep his eyes open.

Violet took deep breaths to try and quieten the urge to treat this as some sort of therapy session, unleashing years of unresolved issues in a verbal tirade while he was strapped down and forced to listen. He was still a sick man and she was living with enough guilt without having to shoulder the blame for his possible relapse. She'd waited this long, she could hold out a little longer to say her piece. Preferably when he and Strachmore were back on their feet and she'd bought a return ticket to London.

'And how are we doing today, Lord Dempsey? You were asleep when I came by earlier.' The sound of Nate's voice close to Violet's ear made her jump. Lost in her inner raging, she hadn't heard him approach, hadn't expected him to purposely come within five hundred yards of her after last night.

Even while she was trying to find the courage to face him her cheeks were burning. Looking him in the

eye after her epic seduction fail was akin to watching
your drunk antics at a wedding back on video. Except
she didn't have alcohol to blame for losing control of
her mind and there was definitely nobody getting married around here.

'I feel like I've been hit by a truck, Doctor.'

Violet could only shake her head in disgusted wonder as Rip Van Winkle bypassed her with the truth in
favour of the medical professional. It said everything
about their lack of communication and trust.

'Your body went through a lot yesterday so you are
going to be quite sore for a while. We'll give you some
more pain relief to make you more comfortable in the
meantime. I don't have a problem with you calling me
Nate if you prefer, Lord Dempsey.' He was smiling as
he reached for the chart at the end of the bed with no
obvious signs of long-lasting trauma after her little
display last night. Things could've been awkward but
he apparently wasn't going to make an issue of it. Not
in public at least.

'Why would I want to do that?' Her father was making an effort to sit up now, scowling as he did so.

Violet's stomach sank with the realisation he didn't
know who it was who had saved his life. Nate deserved
some sort of recognition. 'You remember Nate, Dad?
Bill and Margaret Taylor's son? He's a cardiologist
now.'

'For now we need you to rest but as soon as you're
feeling up to it we'll need to get you moving, even if
it's just to sit in the chair by the bed. It's important we
get the blood flowing around your body again.' Nate
ignored her attempts to big him up and went about his
doctory business.

Violet couldn't help the eye-rolling when she might as well be talking to the walls today for all the notice anyone was paying her. Perhaps she'd actually died of embarrassment when Nate had walked out last night and this was actually her ghost standing by the bedside whom no one could apparently see or hear.

'Nathaniel?' He was peering at Nate, his face screwed up in a sneer. Yeah, the penny had finally dropped.

Nate gave a curt nod. 'There appears to be some narrowing of your arteries, Lord Dempsey, and we will have to look into the possibility of a surgical intervention before they become blocked again.'

'You had a lucky escape this time, thanks to Nate.' She wanted to fend off the vitriol she could see was already building with his strength.

'I want to go home.' There was no thanks or recognition this man had saved his life, only demands.

Violet didn't know why that should surprise her. Owing his life to someone he'd looked down on for most of his life would mean admitting his stereotyping had been wrong. That chaos theory would rip his entire belief system apart. It was about time.

'I'm afraid you can't just yet. We need to build up your mobility gradually so you don't overdo it. Trust me, we want you recovered and out of here as soon as possible too. We need the bed.' Nate still managed to crack a joke even though it was probably killing him as much as her not to bite back.

'And when you do, you're going to have to cut back on the whiskey and cigars, Dad.' It was time he took responsibility for his own actions to save his own skin if no one else's.

'Just like your mother. Trying to tell me what to do. Who asked you to come back here anyway?' The old curmudgeon closed his eyes and lay back down. Conversation over as far as he was concerned.

Violet's blood was boiling. All anyone had tried to do was help him and all they ever got in return was verbal abuse. The olive branch she'd held out was being whacked around her head with every dismissive utterance.

'This is for your own good. If you don't want me here, if you don't want Nate involved, then start looking after yourself.' In all the years she'd spent with her own patients, she'd always been able to tread carefully and keep her temper in check in the toughest circumstances. Right now it was stretched to snapping point. There'd been a very good reason she'd left her personal baggage in a different country—it made her a different person. A weaker one.

He didn't bat an eyelid.

'This is something we can discuss once your father is up to it. Lifestyle will be something we'll cover during rehabilitation. I think we should let you rest now, Lord Dempsey.' Nate addressed her directly for the first time since he'd sneaked in and it was to undermine the stance she was trying to take here.

She swung around, hands on hips, and tried to communicate via the medium of dirty looks how ticked off she was with him. The patient gave a grunt next to them, which Violet knew amounted to another dismissal. The chance to get everything off her chest had passed and she wasn't best pleased about it.

Nate did his own spot of mime, nodding towards the door. She had no option but to follow when he turned on his heel and walked away from the volcanic eruption she was building up to. She didn't attempt to quieten the fast click of her footsteps out into the hallway after him.

'What?' She was mad at him, her father and, most of all, herself for ending up back in this situation.

He held one hand up in surrender, with the other resting on the door handle of that dreaded family room. 'Can we talk?'

'Not in there.' She was already on the edge without being forced to relive that nightmare again.

'That's right. It'll be safer for me if we go somewhere more…public.'

She heard the tease in his voice before she noticed the glint in his eye and the dimples blossoming in his cheeks. It was too hard to stay mad when he was giving her his best 'naughty puppy' look. Violet groaned in defeat. It had been too good to be true to think he would let last night's shenanigans sink without a trace.

'What can I say? I was clearly in the midst of some sort of breakdown. I promise not to try and jump your bones today. I'm sure there's some sort of medical ethics involved where you're not allowed to bring that up without my permission.' The only blessing about this continued humiliation was that, by turning it into a joke at her expense, they'd broken the ice before it had time to fully form between them.

She was loath to admit it but she needed him as a friend if nothing else. It was one thing being strong and independent when you were able to leave all of your troubles at work, quite another when they followed you home at night and invited their mates round to party. A familiar, if not overly friendly, face was the only thing stopping her from being completely overwhelmed and jumping on the first plane back.

'That really only applies if you're my patient...'

'I'm sure with the stress I'm under that's a definite possibility. So, if we can forget that ever happened... you wanted to talk?' If her father was going to continue playing dumb she was going to have to get back to Strachmore and make a start on that pretty red paper trail. She knew she wasn't going to like what she found at the end of it.

Nate gestured towards the empty plastic chairs in the corridor. It wasn't exactly the cosiest set-up for a heart-to-heart but there was every possibility she'd break her promise if they were holed up in that confined space again together. That white doctor coat suited him. It said he was in charge and that was irresistible to someone whose own confidence was floundering more with every second she spent back here.

'First off, I wasn't trying to interfere in there. I know you have a lot of things to sort out with your father but it's going to have to wait.'

She was so intent on watching his lips and imagining how differently things could've turned out last night, it took a few seconds for his words to register. 'Sorry. What?'

'We need to keep his stress levels to a minimum while he recovers. The lectures can wait until we get him through the other side of this. Trust me, we'll be giving a few of our own on his lifestyle before he leaves.' He rested his hand on top of hers, probably the way he offered his support to all family members who walked these hallways. Violet wondered if his touch had the same effect on them. The bolt of electricity shooting through her at the point of contact was powerful enough to make the heart defibrillators redundant.

She slid her hand out from his so she could think clearly. 'You're asking me to back off?'

'For now, yes.' He could just as well be talking about the inappropriate thoughts she kept having about him.

Back off. Stop picturing me wearing nothing but my stethoscope.

She reluctantly agreed. The strength of her willpower would surely be tested over the next few days. In both areas.

'Now, I don't want to tread on your toes any more than I already have but I was thinking about Strachmore.' His scowl seemed only natural. It pained Violet every time she thought of the place too.

'Did the nightmares keep you awake last night?' She thought he appeared a little more rugged this morning and had hoped that spurning her advances had kept him awake with regret.

Oh, wait. That had been her.

Nate gave her his version of the death stare. It didn't have the same menacing effect when he puckered his lips at her. She was simply tempted to help smooth them out again.

'I'm serious. I had a few ideas of what you could do to generate some income.'

'I'm listening.' So far her only plans had included selling up or torching the place for the insurance money. Both of which had her conscience screaming 'Cop out!' She'd probably find herself haunted by the ghosts of past earls for eternity if she surrendered their legacy so easily. Besides, she was none too fond of playing with matches. There was always a chance of getting burned.

'Okay, so, I was thinking more long-term financial stability. A way of making the estate self-sufficient. You have beautiful gardens, large banqueting areas and floors of empty bedrooms. It's the perfect wedding venue. Stately homes are all the rage these days and not only for receptions. You can apply for a licence to actually hold the ceremonies on site—' Nate had obviously given this a lot of thought in the space of a few hours. No doubt it was a ploy to get her out of the country quick smart before she put him in any more awkward situations.

'That sounds…complicated.' She rubbed her temples, the mere thought of tackling this bringing on another tension headache.

'Perhaps, at the beginning, but once everything is in place I'm pretty sure the bookings will come flooding in.' He made it sound so simple.

'Where do you even begin with that sort of thing?' It sounded like a lot of hard work that would keep her here far beyond a couple of weeks' paid leave. She didn't want to start something she'd be expected to see through to the end. Her idea of helping was to get the bills paid while her father was laid up, not take on a whole new set of problems on his behalf.

'You'll need public liability insurance for a start, and then the licences for alcohol, entertainment, et cetera. There'd have to be a fire-risk assessment, maybe some planning permission depending on how far you want to develop this.'

'I'm not sure I do. I'm not sticking around, remember?'

'I know. I'm just brainstorming ideas that will keep the place afloat so you don't have to come back.'

'Of course.' Violet took a direct hit in the feels. This wasn't Nate trying to ease her burden. He just didn't want her hanging around.

'You don't have to jump right in at the deep end. There's no reason why you couldn't test those waters first by opening the place up to the public. You could run tours of the house or hire out the gardens for photographic shoots. There's endless possibilities.'

And an infinite number of new headaches to deal with.

'I suppose it's worth looking into.' Especially if it meant she could absolve herself of further responsibilities or reasons to return. Coming back had only managed to upset the new life she'd created for herself and Nate had made it abundantly clear there was nothing left for her here. If only this weren't such a Herculean task to take on herself it could've proved the answer to all of their prayers.

'I've spoken to my parents and they're on board with whatever decision you make. After all, Strachmore is their home too. There's just one problem…'

'Of course there is. You're sure it's just the one?'

'Well, one particular obstacle which could shut the whole project down before it gets off the ground.' The way he was fidgeting with his tie gave away his sudden nerves, which didn't bode well for Violet. She thought he was supposed to be bringing her solutions, not more reasons to get wound up.

'Which is?' She sat on her hands so she didn't give into her instinct to stick her fingers in her ears. She had to hear this if she was to find some way out of this whole mess.

'Your father. We'll need his say-so on everything.'

Not even Nate's apologetic smile could salve that slap in the face.

The man who'd let the castle crumble around him was the only one who could save it. If he weren't so completely blinkered by his self-importance there might've been a chance that plan might've actually worked.

'That's the end of that, then.' Enough people had wasted their time and energy trying to wake him up to what was happening around him for Violet to know this was a lost cause.

'I get this isn't going to be easy but it'll be worth it in the end. You'll finally be able to leave Strachmore behind.'

She couldn't fault his logic. It was the lack of emotion she was having trouble dealing with. He apparently wanted this all neatly tidied up so he could wash his hands of everything she'd brought to his door.

'That's what we all want, I guess.' Unfortunately, even if she had been at her ass-kicking, emotionally detached, sleeping-at-night best, this was going to be a monumental task. If by some miracle she could engage her father in conversation long enough to convince him of the plan, the practicalities alone would cripple her.

She needed help. She needed Nate. All that was left to do was swallow her pride and admit it.

'I know you can do this, Violet.' He had more faith in her than she had in herself. Or perhaps it was wishful thinking on his part, pre-empting the words that were going to come out of her mouth next.

'I don't think I can do this on my own. Will you help me?' She almost choked on the words that went against everything she'd strived for in adulthood. This was the second time in less than twenty-four hours she'd showed him her weakness.

By asking Nate to sleep with her, now begging him to bail her out, she made her new life into a sham. She'd flown back into town as a city slicker, an independent career woman who hadn't relied on anyone to help her make it in the Big Smoke. Now she was back to being that simpering, frightened girl she'd done her best to escape.

A wave of nausea crested over her as she waited for what seemed like an eternity. He'd turned down her request last night and she wouldn't blame him for doing the same again. He didn't owe her anything and he certainly didn't need this clingy, emotional side of her any more than she did. She'd simply hoped Nate would be the one person who wouldn't hold the past against her.

'I'm sorry. I shouldn't have asked. You've done so much for us already and I know you're busy—' She tried to back out of this with her last scrap of dignity intact.

His brow was furrowed in contemplation and she could almost see his refusal making its way from his brain to his lips. This smart idea had been right up there with asking the man she'd unceremoniously dumped years before to jump into bed with her.

She got to her feet and scouted out the nearest toilets so she could have a good blub in private. It was her own fault she didn't have a friend in him now when she'd run out on him when he'd needed her the most.

'Wait!' Nate shot out a hand and grabbed her by the wrist, pressing against her bracelet and temporarily branding her skin with her seahorse charm. It was a reminder of everything she'd thrown away and apparently could never get back.

It was too late. The old Nate wouldn't have hesitated to offer his support.

'Don't worry about it, Nate. I've dumped my problems on you once too often. I'll put in a few phone calls myself tomorrow—the bank, Citizens Advice, the Samaritans…' She forced a smile past the lump in her throat and her trembling bottom lip. Even though she'd been content on her own for a long time, somehow the thought of not having him by her side now made her feel more alone than ever.

CHAPTER FOUR

'I'LL HELP. WE'LL FIGURE this out together if that's what you want?' Nate hadn't known what he was going to say until the words were out of his mouth. He hadn't known he was going to reach for her until she'd tried to walk away. Now it was too late to take any of it back. His conscience had got the better of him again when it became clear how desperate she was for him to stick around. Once upon a time he'd been in that very position, wishing she'd stay with him at any cost. Just because he'd been left in the cold it didn't mean he should do the same to Violet. He would never intentionally hurt her when her family had done such a sterling job of that throughout her entire life.

He'd hesitated with good reason. The 'no' had danced on his tongue where he couldn't quite catch it. This was everything he'd sworn to stay away from—Violet, Strachmore, and a commitment to be there for someone for more than purely physical reasons. It might've been easier to draw that line if they had slept together. But he couldn't bear to see that dejected look on her face again if he rejected her a second time.

Violet bit her lip and nodded her head. From everything he'd heard over the years, she'd had her life all figured out without assistance from anyone. He knew she must've been out of options to turn to him for help after all this time apart. A huge step backward for her. Lord knew he wasn't in a hurry to go back to the Dark Ages either, where everything revolved around her father's will, but he had to consider the long-term benefits. One pride-swallowing favour could render him guilt-free for the rest of his days from everyone who might expect something from him in the future. This would be a one-off.

He resigned himself to whatever fate had in store for him next as punishment for not learning his lesson the first time around. If he approached this new relationship with Violet with the logical side of his brain instead of that useless emotional one, he might just come out of this with what was left of his heart in one piece.

'Okay, then. First things first, we'll need to pay off the most pressing bills before applying for any licences. We can't have them cutting off the electric, or, God forbid, your father's champagne-of-the-month subscription before he gets home.'

Another nod. She was going to have to move from the back seat and take over some of the driving duties if his involvement here was to remain short-lived. He was assisting her in her hour of need, not enabling her to ignore the problem.

'How do you want to proceed with this, Violet?'

She was going to have to make decisions for herself and not get too comfortable with him being around. Once his idea was up and running, so was he. He'd thought he'd found his 'Get out of Jail Free' card by coming up with this venture in the first place. A pair of storm-coloured eyes had been his undoing yet again.

Perhaps he could persuade her to start wearing sunglasses and prevent any further forced promises being made in a hypnotic trance.

Violet inhaled a deep breath as though she was girding herself for the challenge ahead. The first good sign she was in this with him. 'We should sit down and go through the paperwork together to see exactly what we're dealing with.'

It was the logical first step and the proactive approach he wanted to see from her. However, it also meant spending more time together. Inevitable, he supposed, and also the main reason he'd initially resisted volunteering for being her second in command. He'd already proved how weak-willed he was when it came to Violet, barely surviving the last test of his strength.

'If you have everything with you now we could go through it in my office. I have some time before my cardiac clinic.' His attempt to avoid a repeat of their previous one-to-one at Strachmore earned him a raised eyebrow and a grin.

'I understand why you don't trust me not to rip your clothes off if we're left alone for too long, but I'm afraid I don't carry my father's shame around in my handbag. We'll have to come up with an alternative venue. Somewhere with a glass partition, perhaps, to protect you from unwarranted advances? Or would you prefer I was immobilised and trussed up *à la* Hannibal Lecter?'

It was his turn to give the dirty looks. He was simply taking necessary security measures to make sure this remained a platonic meeting.

'Let's not make this weird, Nate. I'm sure even you've been knocked back on occasion without being made to feel like a sex fiend by the other party.'

She was right. By shying away from being alone with her he was turning this into a bigger deal than it should be. There'd been instances where he'd turned down advances from patients and colleagues alike and he'd carried on without giving it a second thought. He shouldn't treat this, treat Violet, any different from anyone else. That was what had got him into trouble thus far.

'I can't say I've ever encountered that particular problem myself…'

He hit the jackpot with that one—a *'tut'* and an eye-roll combo.

'Well, Mr Smooth, I defer to your superiority in these matters. What shall it be? My place, yours, or somewhere neutral? Say, Belfast City Hall? It's a bit of a drive but there'll be plenty of people around to keep you safe.' This snarky Violet put him more at ease than the meek version even if she was making him the butt of her jokes.

If he was honest, he'd seen enough of Strachmore this last couple of days to last him another lifetime. The city hall was tempting but that merely compounded the theory he didn't trust her, or himself, not to act inappropriately. That only left one other option.

'My place it is. I can swing by after my shift to pick you and the paperwork up. Maybe even grab some takeaway to eat while we work?' He was going on the theory that at least if they were at his house they'd be playing by his rules. There was no chance of any last-minute sleepovers and absolutely no reminders of their shared past. He would set the boundaries and time limits on tonight's escapade.

'That would be great. I'll pop in and say goodbye

to Dad and head back to get things organised.' The smile back on her face was because of him. Her peace of mind came at the price of his but at least those eyes had their sparkle back.

'And I've got a waiting room full of patients to attend. Unless there's any emergencies I should be away around seven p.m.' He made a move to get back to Outpatients, where he was confident in his decision-making process.

'Thanks, Nate.'

Why did every pat on the head from Violet seem like a reward and a step back at the same time?

Violet couldn't sit still. She'd changed, twice, carefully applied, then removed, her make-up, and cooked a lasagne. All so she wouldn't come across to Nate as though she was trying too hard. This wasn't a date, it was an intervention of sorts. Yet the butterflies in her stomach were the same ones she'd had when she'd waited for him to take her to their fake prom.

Sure, she'd swapped her baby pink swing dress for jeans and the grey hoodie she usually wore for jogging, but it was the same sense of excitement making her fidgety at the prospect of spending the evening with him.

Until yesterday she'd forgotten the effect he had on her. It was entirely possible her subconscious had locked those memories away with the bad ones, fearing they were equally damaging to her equilibrium. Her London-based liaisons held no element of surprise when she was the one calling the shots. Having the upper hand enabled her to bail when things got too serious. Just as she had done with Nate. That had been a bigger step for her than leaving home, but one that had also given her the courage to protect herself first and foremost in her following relationships.

Now she was back to hanging around this big house waiting for Nate to rescue her. Except this time he was whisking her from a mountain of debt instead of the school dance she'd been dreading and taking her to his place instead of the old boathouse.

That had been the night her feelings for him had begun to change. He'd dressed in his best shirt and tie to escort her to their alternative prom. To this day no one knew she'd ditched the fancy hotel venue her classmates had attended for an evening in the draughty wooden shack. She'd been more comfortable there, safer, than in a room full of her peers.

Sweet sixteen and never been kissed but in his strong arms as they'd danced to the mix tape he'd made specially, she'd thought about it. He'd been the only one who'd taken her pleas that she hadn't wanted to go to her prom seriously but still wanted to make the night special for her. He'd always known what was best for her and it would be easy to sit back and let him make those judgement calls for her now, but deep down she realised those days were long gone.

She'd seen it in his reluctance to get involved, felt it when she'd had to ask for help rather than have him pre-empt it. It was down to her that things had changed between them and she hadn't regretted that decision until she'd had to come back and face him. It had been easier not to miss that close relationship when she wasn't seeing him every day.

She covered the lasagne dish with aluminium foil and put the salad ingredients into a portable container.

This way she was simply bringing dinner to a friend's house, leaving no room for misunderstanding when Nate wasn't paying for the food they'd eat together.

She'd been listening for a car horn to sound his arrival and hadn't expected him to ring the doorbell. Neither had she expected to see him waiting on her doorstep. All he'd needed were the bouquet of flowers and box of chocolates accessories and she'd found her dream date.

Not a date. Crisis management.

If she kept telling herself that they might both come out of this unscathed.

'Hey.' He scuffed his shoes on the stone steps the way he always had when they were kids, eager to get away from here as soon as she was ready before her father spotted him.

'Hey. I've just got to grab a few things and I'll meet you at the car.' She knew he was only standing here out of courtesy, being the gentleman her father had always told her she'd deserved.

After a quick dash inside to collect the makings of dinner, she joined him in the car.

'What's that?' He sniffed the air and peered at the mini tower of food containers on her knee as if she were using his vehicle to transfer toxic waste across the country.

'Dinner. Lasagne, to be more precise. I can't take credit for the salad but I made everything else from scratch.'

The car swerved as Nate turned to stare at her. 'Since when could you make more than burnt toast?'

Violet reached across to straighten the steering wheel so he didn't run them off the road. That split second of closeness made her heart beat a little faster. His breath was hot on the back of her neck, his frame strong around her and his spicy aftershave so enticing she wanted to sink back into him. She didn't.

'I know it was our secret snack of choice in the days of sneaking into the kitchen but the single life called for something more exciting and nutritious. The lack of a social life gives me plenty of time to experiment in the kitchen after work.' She was rambling now but since she was practically sprawled in his lap things could get awkward quickly if they let silence descend.

'I…er…think we're good now.' He gave her the nod to extricate herself from his side of the car.

Their brief encounter had given her more than a warm feeling inside. A tingling sensation had started at the top of her thighs and was steadily making its way south. It took a few seconds staring at the up-turned dish in her lap before she made the connection.

'Ack!' The bottom of her sweatshirt and her jeans were now coated in a hot tomato and minced beef marinade. Thankfully the pasta layers had remained intact between the foil and the dish so she was able to rescue it with a quick flip.

'What's wrong?'

'I spilled dinner. Don't worry, I caught most of it.' In her lap, which was now stinging beneath her denims. She tried not to make a scene and draw even more attention to her stupidity.

Hs curiosity deepened his forehead into a frown when he cast a glance in her direction. 'Are you all right?'

'Fine,' she said through gritted teeth as molten lasagne lava singed her flesh.

'We're here now anyway. I'll take a look once we're inside.'

They pulled up outside a very modern, very secluded two-storey glass building overlooking Dundrum Bay. Nothing like the city-based apartment she'd pictured him in.

'I had no idea you lived so close.' Even more surprising than this sophisticated bachelor pad with only the local wildlife for company was the fact Strachmore was merely a ten-minute drive away.

'Only for this last couple of years. I've worked all over Ireland but when the position opened up in Silent Valley, I decided to move back. It turned out I missed the peace and quiet out here. And it's still far enough away to deter my parents from dropping in when they feel like it.'

Violet imagined no one got beyond the gates without some sort of personal invitation. She tried not to think about those who had passed through here and took comfort in the fact she'd been personally chauffeured door-to-door by the owner.

Nate climbed out of the driver seat and walked around to her side of the car. He opened the door and took possession of their dinner remains in one hand. Even as he helped her out with his free hand, it was obvious he was assessing the extent of her injuries.

Violet groaned as the cool air made contact and increased her discomfort.

'That's it. Get inside and take your clothes off.' Nate opened the front door and practically shoved her inside.

'I bet you say that to all the ladies,' Violet snarked with a grimace.

In a different situation that line would've got her

hot and bothered for other reasons. Now she was simply cringing at the turn this night had taken already. It wasn't the civilised evening she'd planned.

'Only the ones who turn up on my doorstep with third-degree burns.' He chivvied her upstairs to the bathroom while he carried the source of tonight's humiliation to the kitchen.

Violet eased her jeans down to reveal angry red welts across her thighs. They were throbbing so badly now as she sat on the edge of the bath she wasn't sure how she'd ever put her clothes back on again.

She took a towel from the rail and ran it under the tap before draping it across her sensitive skin. The relief was only temporary as the heat from her burns began again in earnest.

There was a knock on the door. 'Violet? Are you okay in there?'

She wondered how it had come to sitting in her underwear in Nate's bathroom nursing a lasagne scalding.

'Umm…have you got any antiseptic cream I can use?' With any luck a dollop of cold cream and a few glasses of wine would help her forget this had ever happened.

'In the bathroom cabinet but I think I should take a look first. Can I come in?'

Her mortification was complete as Nate joined her, fully dressed, in the confined space.

'May I?' He hunkered down in front of her asking permission to see her mishap for himself.

She slowly lifted away the towel covering the last of her dignity. In keeping with her not-a-date mantra she'd forgone all sexy, lacy underwear in favour of the comfy cartoon knickers one of her friends had given her for Christmas. Her cheeks burned as much as her thighs.

'Ouch. It looks painful but you'll live. It mightn't feel like it now but it's pretty superficial. You won't require hospital treatment, although you should really keep those burns under running water for a few minutes.' He reached for the shower attachment over the bath and turned the tap on.

As Violet swung around to put her bare legs into the bath she was grateful he hadn't made her strip and get into his fancy-pants shower cubicle in the corner with more nozzles and buttons than she'd know what to do with.

Nate rolled his sleeves up as he administered the cooling jets of water to the burn site. After a few minutes of relative silence her teeth began to chatter from the cold.

'I think that should do for now.' He patted her dry with another towel then retrieved a tub of cream from the bathroom cabinet.

There was such a calm, gentle manner about him Violet could see what made him a great doctor. He applied the cream in soothing strokes, not batting an eyelid at her choice of underwear. It was unnerving having him so close, paying such attention to delicate parts of her. He was tender and considerate, and Violet was forced to clamp down on inappropriate thoughts as arousal took hold of her.

Nate was still intent on treating her burn, apparently oblivious to the erotic nature his touch had taken on in her corrupted mind. If his strong fingers massaged any further up her thigh she might spontaneously combust. And probably not very quietly.

As if reading her thoughts. Nate withdrew and got to his feet. 'We'll get you some painkillers but you should be fine. I wouldn't try and get your jeans on again though—they'll rub too much against the skin.'

'I'm not prancing around your house all night in my undies. Imagine the gossip.'

Nate looked as horrified by that suggestion as she was. Clearly all that electricity had been surging in one direction only.

Nate was having difficulty putting out of his mind that image of Violet wandering through his house in the altogether, not least because she was already half-naked in front of him. 'I'll go see if I can find you something to wear and throw those clothes in the washing machine before they stain.'

He needed space, and a reality check. Violet might not be his patient per se, but he definitely shouldn't be thinking about the softness of her skin while he was treating her. Not even her novelty underwear was helping to rein in his wayward libido. It reminded him he was one of the few who'd ever seen that fun side of her. A reminder there was more to her than glamour and pain.

He retreated to the sanctuary of his bedroom where there was nothing to stimulate his Violet fantasies any further. Except the huge bed with the black leather headboard dominating the room. He turned his back on his pride and joy and yanked the wardrobe open. He'd known nothing in here would ever fit her but he'd taken the time out to compose himself before more than his trousers became uncomfortable.

The rows of dry-cleaned shirts and trousers were

practical for a busy doctor but not much use for a slender burn victim who needed covering for both of their sakes. He paused flicking through the rails when he came to his lab coats and scrubs but apparently even they were too much for his over-sexed imagination to handle. He snatched a white shirt from the hanger. The sooner he covered her up, the sooner they could carry on with the real reason she was in his house.

It took a few seconds for his befuddled brain to clear so he could remember what that was.

She was still perched on the end of his bath where he'd left her, looking for all the world as if she were in that post-coital, comfortable-wearing-nothing stage. Except he hadn't had that pleasure and nothing about this was comfortable for him.

'Here. This should be long enough to wear as a dress with the bonus of letting the air around those burns.' He practically threw the shirt at her in his haste to get away. He even contemplated going back to the en-suite in his bedroom for his own cold shower.

When his stomach began to rumble it gave him a different body part to focus on. 'Just throw your clothes in the laundry and I'll see if I can rescue what's left of dinner.'

He reconstructed the layers of pasta as best he could and plated it up with the well-tossed salad. Violet reappeared in the doorway as he was setting it out on the dining table and diverted his appetite elsewhere.

The shirt skimmed the tops of her thighs, covering her curves and brightly coloured underwear, but it did nothing to hide those long, toned legs. He'd never be able to wear that shirt again without seeing her in it or smelling her sweet perfume.

He sat down at the table and took a long drink of water, trying to drown that persistent idea that this was how she'd look the next morning if she'd spent the night. All that could save him now was that folder of truth spelling out in great detail why he shouldn't get involved with the sexy heiress. She came with more than just overnight baggage.

Violet could see it written all over Nate's face that he wanted this night to be over. They ate dinner in virtual silence although she suspected neither of them had much of an appetite. Despite her efforts to make this a casual arrangement it had all the hallmarks of an awkward first date, or a really bad seduction attempt. After her last botched come-on, it wouldn't be beyond the realms of possibility for one to accuse her of faking a lasagne-related injury so she had an excuse to strip. If only she'd planned this. Or, Nate had been interested in her half-naked body.

'That was delicious. My compliments to the chef.' He cleared away the dishes in his obvious hurry to get down to the real business of the evening and send her on her way before she caused any more embarrassment.

'Thank you, and mine to the doctor.' Although she was still in some discomfort, the pain had considerably subsided, with only the occasional flare-up of mortification.

She hoped she'd recover sufficiently to put her own clothes back on, dirty or not. She didn't fancy doing the walk of shame home in Nate's shirt under false pretences. That was normally only a liberty taken after spending a night together. Naked.

'Let's see what the damage is.' He'd retrieved the folder of paperwork she'd left in the car so they were able to finally get the evening back on track and prevent her from forming any more ideas of how she could get him into bed.

Violet spread the bills and threatening letters over the table, glad she had him beside her to help get her through this.

'We've got household bills, unpaid credit cards, bank statements…'

They sorted the final demands into easier-to-handle piles. Her father would be apoplectic if he suspected they were going through his personal things but this was for his own good as well as hers. Perhaps one day he'd realise that.

'I'm sure some of these companies might be sympathetic and suspend payment for a while if you contact them and explain your father's current circumstances. I don't think they would deal with me since I'm not family.'

'I'll phone around first thing. It's worth a try.' It would help her if they could find some way to stagger the payments so she could work her way through these gradually.

Nate frowned as he gathered a handful of scarlet bills. 'Unfortunately, there are quite a few of these which require immediate payment before you find yourself cut off from civilisation.'

Electricity, telephone and rates bills were ones she couldn't afford to ignore even if her father had.

'And the credit cards are going to need at least minimum payment made on them. Not to mention the loans he's taken out with sky-high interest rates.' It took every scrap of courage inside her not to rip everything up and pretend she'd never seen it. Instead, she created a new 'red alert' pile to be dealt with in the morning.

'There's definitely no emergency fund anywhere to buy some time?' Nate's optimism had long outlived hers.

A thorough read of the bank statements confirmed her father had been living on a wing and a prayer for quite some time. No doubt his good name had given him more leeway than most but little else.

'I'm afraid his finances are as dire as my own.'

'Can I help?' Nate reached for the nightmare she was holding in her hand but she snatched it away from his grasp.

'No!' She'd put upon him enough, let him pry further into the family secrets than anyone, but she had to draw the line somewhere. Asking Nate for financial assistance would be the final insult to all involved. Her father would never forgive her and she didn't want Nate to feel even more used than he already did. If she could find any other way to bail out Strachmore than borrowing from him she would.

'It's only money, Violet. Something I can help with.'

It's only money.

How many times had she heard those words from her father? Enough to know it was never *'only money'*. It annoyed her more hearing it from someone who'd worked hard to make his fortune, not inherited and squandered it. It was more than money, it was a matter of pride.

'Thanks but I don't want to go down that road. I can cover a few of the smaller debts for now and I have an idea of how to raise the rest.' She didn't have much in the way of inheritance other than headaches and a useless title but there were a few things she could sell that her father had absolutely no say in.

'I don't like the sound of that.'

He had his arms folded across his chest, his pride probably wounded by her refusal of help, but Violet hadn't relinquished total control just yet. Nate was her support but it was important she didn't compromise her own principles to suit him. Otherwise, that made a mockery of everything she'd railed so hard against. She might as well be married in that case.

'Thanks to my mother I'm still a woman of certain means.'

'You can't—'

'I'm going to sell her necklace. It's only jewellery after all.' Suddenly the ball was firmly back in her court.

'I won't let you do that.' Nate couldn't stand back and watch her throw away the only thing of worth left from her mother. Not on behalf of someone who didn't appreciate her and certainly not when there was an alternative on offer.

Money he had, could give her easier than anything else when it held no emotional attachment for him. It could solve the problem and let him off the hook a hell of a lot quicker if she'd accept it.

'You won't *let* me? Who the hell do you think you are telling me what I can and can't do?' Violet leaned across the table to blast him as she battled for control. With that passion she could've been the CEO of her own company, defending her assets in the boardroom.

Assets he was getting a good view of every time she leaned over.

'Your friend. I know how much your mother's things mean to you.' He walked around the table beside her so this supposed *friend* wasn't getting excited with every glimpse of her white cotton bra.

'I have some of her other belongings, which don't represent the problems that kept her awake at night. Expensive jewellery was Dad's way of showing off money he didn't have, not an expression of love for my mother.' She had that defiant tilt to her chin she used to have when she was challenging her parents' authority.

Nate didn't want her to think she didn't have anyone in her corner. He was there, yelling advice from behind the ropes.

'I don't want you to give up something you love just to make a point to your father. You might come to regret it.'

'Been there, done that.' She was talking about him. He could see it in that wistful smile and he wanted to believe she'd loved him once. It meant everything to him to know she might've regretted leaving him. That he hadn't imagined the strength of their bond and he'd been more than part of the fixtures at Strachmore.

All of the anger he'd been holding against her for these past years seemed to fade and render his resistance to touching her futile. He reached out to tuck a wayward strand of hair behind her ear.

'How did we end up here, Vi?'

Things could've worked out so differently if she'd been brave then and given them a chance regardless of what anyone thought. He'd been so in love with her all she'd had to do was give him the word and he would've gone anywhere with her, done anything for her. Now he was a man on his own, too scarred to let anyone into his life.

'I don't know but sometimes I wish I could go back.'

With Violet standing here in his dining room wearing nothing more than his shirt and a smile, this was as far from those innocent days as they got. 'I can't say I'd rather be anywhere else.'

He leaned in to kiss her, reasoning twice in twelve years wasn't going to wreak too much havoc. He simply wanted to find out if her lips were as soft and sweet as he remembered. They were.

He should've left it at one gentle peck on the lips, enough to reconnect and erase the bad feeling left with her departure. When he opened his eyes and saw her lips parted for more, felt her hands slide around his neck in submission, he couldn't recall any reason to hold back. They both wanted this. In some ways they needed it to enable them to finally move on.

He slipped his arms around her waist and pulled her closer to deepen the kiss he'd waited too long to repeat. As Violet pressed her body against his it soon became clear this was more than one innocent smooch. His erection grew ever stronger with every flick of her tongue against his, every breathy moan of acceptance.

With his hands at her waist he lifted her off the floor and set her on the edge of the table. Violet gave a yelp against his mouth in surprise but wrapped her legs around him to keep him in place. With one sweep of his arm he cleared the papers from the table to the floor so he could lay her down. He went with her, kissing the exposed skin at the open V of his shirt. She was a feast he intended to enjoy guilt-free.

Violet's limbs had turned to jelly with that first

brush of his lips on hers and made her forget they were in the middle of an argument. Her thoughts were hazy with desire but she'd known he'd only been trying to help as always. She'd been the one to let emotions get in the way by almost letting slip the extent of her feelings for him in the past and lighting the touch paper for this chemistry that had been bubbling between them since she'd come home. If she was honest it had always been there and it had been a long, hard fight to keep it at bay, and not always a successful one.

That second kiss had nothing to do with the past. This time around they were acting on pure carnal instinct. Having sex on a dining table was as animalistic and far from emotional entanglement as she could hope for.

As if to illustrate her point, Nate was reaching beneath her shirt to remove her panties and making her wet with want for him. Her skin was so sensitive every brush of his fingers sent a shudder rippling through her in anticipation. She couldn't distinguish her scald marks from the rest of her skin burning up with his every touch.

He stepped back and tossed her underwear over his shoulder with a grin, leaving Violet squirming on the hard wood surface. She didn't care how uncomfortable this was, all that mattered was the ache he'd created inside her and how soon he was going to cure it.

Not any time soon, it seemed, as he began a torturously slow ascent along her thigh using his mouth and tongue. Her body was on high alert—her nipples hardening, her arousal heading to meet him—as he teased her with a sample of everything he could do for her. To her.

Violet braced her hands on the table, fighting off the too early waves of ecstasy trying to drag her into oblivion. She wanted this to last as long as humanly possible because in all likelihood it could be their first and last surrender to temptation.

Somewhere in the distance she heard a faint buzzing sound. She hadn't figured Nate to be into anything kinky but, spread-eagled before him, it wouldn't be right to start getting prudish now. She heard Nate groan and bit back one of her own. He was certainly taking his time. If he was into that tantric nonsense she was going to have to take matters into her own hands pretty soon.

'I'm really sorry, Violet.' The sound of his voice and the cold air hitting her where his hot lips had once been pulled her sharply back from the brink.

'Hmm?' She was struggling to sit up, her body limp with desire and Nate-tending.

'I have to go. I'm needed at the hospital.' He waved a battery-powered device at her, which was unfortunately ending their evening, not getting it off to an exciting start.

'You've been paged?' She came close to banging her head on the table in frustration.

''Fraid so.' The bulge in his trousers and his sad eyes said he was as disappointed as she was that this was over before it had begun.

Violet scrabbled to sit up, her hands sliding on the remnants of the bills scattered around. Her guilt receptors kicked in immediately. Putting her own needs first had saved her sanity in the past, but in this case she'd lost sight of what was most important. They were supposed to be working on helping her father, taking steps to make sure she could escape at the end of all of this. Getting jiggy with Nate certainly wasn't doing anything to fast-track those plans.

He was integral to all aspects of her life here and she didn't want to jeopardise any of that. She should be doing everything she could to try and get her father back in his rightful place instead of finding reasons to keep her around.

'It's probably for the best. You're my dad's cardiologist…you're helping me with Strachmore…that has to be more important than this…us.'

Nate was left breathless with the full impact of Violet's comment. It was bad enough that he'd been physically pained at having to call a halt to this moment of madness but Violet's reaction had body-slammed him and stolen what was left of those feel-good endorphins.

He was acceptable in his professional capacity treating her father, helpful in his role as financial advisor, but, when she'd stopped to think about it, not good enough even as a temporary bed partner.

Of course, hooking up with Violet hadn't been a good idea; he'd known that from the first time they'd almost done this. He'd simply got carried away with the revelation she might've loved him at some point. If he'd been thinking with his head he might've realised that had made her even more callous for leaving him.

'I have to go straight into surgery so I'm afraid I won't have time to take you home. I'll leave money for a taxi. Make sure you lock the door on your way out.' This time he wasn't going to sit around brooding about why she didn't want him. He had a job and a life outside Lady Dempsey's whim.

CHAPTER FIVE

VIOLET HAD KEPT herself as busy as possible in the days following Lasagne-Gate. She'd managed to sell her mother's diamond necklace back to the jewellers her father had originally bought it from, for probably a fraction of what he'd paid for it, but it had eased some of the financial burden heaped on her shoulders. For the best part of forty-eight hours she'd had the phone attached to her ear, fending off the bailiffs before they descended on the castle to seize the family silver. It had taken a lot of time, talking and money but she'd managed to pacify most of the creditors chasing her father. For now. Unfortunately none of it had managed to keep Nate from her thoughts for long.

If the hospital hadn't paged him she had no doubt they would've rocked that dining table all night long. That call had given her the clarity to remember how much sleeping together could complicate things. Even he seemed to have had a change of heart since then, reverting to that aloof Nate she'd encountered on that first night. There'd been no mention of the fact they'd almost done the deed at his house, neither had there been an invitation to finish what they'd started. It was a shame her body wouldn't let her forget the sizzling after-dinner entertainment.

She and Nate had kept interaction about Strachmore matters in strictly public areas since that night but it didn't prevent her from thinking about what they'd done in private. His talk of fire-risk assessments could have well been about the physical effect he had on her. A five-minute chat these days was enough to leave her hot and bothered when she could still feel his lips inching along her inner thigh. It wasn't fair only one of them appeared to be suffering, and it was confidence-crushing to find he had no lingering desire to see that night to a conclusion. Even if her conscience had played a part in bringing matters to an end.

Unresolved sexual tension aside, this past couple of nights had been tough. It didn't cost her a second thought to come home every night to her London flat but Strachmore seemed to amplify her loneliness. The chimes of antique clocks echoing through the empty house taunted her, reminded her of the time that had passed between her and everyone here. She couldn't get it back and some day her lone occupancy of the castle would be permanent.

When she was with Nate there wasn't a moment to dwell on the past, or the future. With him, it was all about the present. She missed his company at night, especially when she had absolutely nothing to come home to. He was part of the reason she was spending longer at the hospital. It certainly wasn't all about being in her father's presence. She was as sympathetic as anyone could be for everything he'd gone through but his self-pity was exhausting.

He was still in some pain and Violet knew a lot of

his bad temper was down to fear and frustration. It didn't make it any easier for her to come here two or three times a day and bear the brunt of his complaints. Especially when she was working so hard behind the scenes to make his life as uncomplicated as possible when he got home. That revelation was another headache waiting to happen. She knew he would explode when he found out and she would have to justify the fact she'd cared enough to try and alleviate some of his stress. Samuel Dempsey never asked for help and he certainly wouldn't appreciate it.

Even now Violet could see a commotion around him at the nurses' station. Over the past couple of days he'd progressed to bathing on his own and taking short walks around the room. She suspected they'd come to rue their encouragement of his mobility. Now they'd all be in the line of fire.

'Dad? Is everything okay?'

She fought the urge to turn on her heel and let someone else deal with him. That selfish attitude was probably part of the reason Strachmore was in the mess it was. She'd had to put herself first at eighteen but that meant the Earl and his bloody-mindedness had been left unchecked for too long. He hadn't been accountable to anyone in her absence and it was a big ask to expect him to take on any advice now. They were both going to have to shoulder some responsibility for the current state of affairs and take steps to rectify the damage. As much as she longed to have this all neatly wrapped up so she could get back to her own life, Violet wasn't convinced she was strong enough to make a difference.

'I'm fed up with being poked and prodded every day

in this...this torture chamber. How am I supposed to rest when I'm woken every five minutes for scans and tests? There's absolutely no respect for me here and I've had enough. I want to go home.' He slammed his fist down on the desk and Violet jumped, along with several of the nurses.

If her prayers were answered she'd disappear into the bowels of the earth any second now and not have to face these people as her father spat abuse at them. It was different when she was the one subjected to his tirades—she was family, had grown up listening to them—but these people should be exempt.

'The doctors and nurses have worked tirelessly to get you well again. You've got to understand these tests are necessary—they're not done out of spite.' Sometimes it was like talking to a petulant child when she tried to reason with him. When he was in one of his rages there was no logic involved, only emotion. The overriding one usually being anger. In these circumstances it was liable to kill him.

'I was explaining to your father that we want to move him onto a main ward to continue his recovery. We would prefer to continue the ECG monitoring for a few more days there before he goes home.'

She hadn't seen Nate standing in the melee until her father had turned to glare at her impudence. But there he was, standing toe to toe with him and trying to run interference for her. Even when he seemed to be avoiding her his chivalry still shone through.

'Do you know who I am?'

Violet cringed as he played the nobility card. The one that had done nothing but bring her embarrassment over the years.

'Yes, Lord Dempsey, and I assure you you'll receive the same standard of treatment as all of our patients.' Social status had never held any sway with Nate either. It wouldn't need to, given his professional approach to his work. Violet was certain every one of his patients was treated with the utmost respect no matter what their background, perhaps even despite it in cases such as this.

'That's what I'm afraid of. Thanks but no, thanks. I want to go home to a clean bed where the staff are paid more than the minimum wage to take care of me.'

'Dad! That's completely out of order.' Not to mention factually incorrect. It showed how delusional her father was when he was under the impression his staff were being paid more than a qualified cardiologist.

'I appreciate this is a difficult time for you but we need to take precautions for the good of your own health. Your physical activity needs to be increased gradually and we would like to make sure you attend cardiac rehabilitation.'

It could've been another run-in between the pair when Nate was nothing more than a schoolboy, given the manner in which her father continued to speak to him. Not once had Nate been forced to raise his voice to make his point even though he was surely wounded by the insults flying around. Violet had never seen anyone stand their ground with the Earl in full flow. Even when she'd mounted her great rebellion she'd done it over the telephone rather than face to face.

'I'm sure those are matters which my own doctor can facilitate. He's a man with over forty years of experience. I trust *him*.' Another dig at Nate, both personally and professionally.

Not that her father would've taken any more notice of a different staff member, Violet was sure, but this continual slight against Nate was very hard even for her to stomach. By denying his achievements he somehow rendered her own unremarkable. The great Earl would never admit he'd been wrong in trying to force them into their society pigeonholes or congratulate them on their successes. Until now Violet hadn't realised she'd been waiting for his approval.

Nate had dealt with his fair share of obstinate patients over the years. People had different coping mechanisms when it came to facing their own mortality and sometimes that manifested itself against the very staff treating them. Usually he took it in his stride. After all, who was to say he wouldn't lash out if he were the one on the other end of the stethoscope? Today he was finding new limits to his tolerance he didn't know he was capable of.

In the space of ten minutes his integrity and his professionalism had been called into question by someone who'd known him since he'd been a child. That was the problem, he supposed. His parents' employer was still judging him on the nonconforming teen he imagined had robbed him of his daughter. It was ironic that Nate hadn't gained anything from that loss except the successful career that was now being maligned. Regardless of how hard he tried, those from Strachmore would never see him as anything but the next generation of domestic staff. The only difference was the Dempseys weren't paying him to take this abuse.

He'd even had to battle his own family to pursue his chosen career. In their eyes by going to medical school he'd thrown away the honour of working for the aristocracy. As if their allegiance meant he should've sacrificed his prospects too. They hadn't understood his resistance to doing manual labour so a privileged family could sit comfortably on their pedestals. There'd been no support, financially or otherwise, as they'd seen him as some sort of traitor.

That attitude had created a distance between Nate and his parents. He'd hated them at times for their blind devotion to the Earl when they'd effectively disowned their own son for the sin of ambition. In a roundabout way they had been part of his success when his anger had driven him to reach the pinnacle of his career. These days he accepted them for who they were in the hope they would some day do the same for him. He'd learned it wasn't healthy to hold on to grudges or look for answers where there was none, and taken back control of his life by simply accepting circumstances beyond his control. No matter how much it jarred.

'In that case all I can do is ask you to wait until we have your discharge papers ready. We need to have it in writing that you are going against our recommendations by leaving before your treatment here is complete. There's also the matter of arranging your medication before you leave.' If it was merely a case of one stubborn patient showing he was still in control of his own fate, Nate would sign off and move on to the next patient who actually wanted his help. That was practically impossible when Violet was standing opposite worrying her bottom lip with her teeth.

'I will not linger here a second longer than is absolutely necessary.' The Earl continued to bluster, his cheeks reddening as he pointed a knobbly finger at

Nate as though he were holding him to ransom. It was the other way around. As tempted as Nate was to have Security bundle him out of the door, he couldn't bear to be responsible for anything happening to Violet's only surviving family member.

'That's entirely your prerogative, but it would be in your best interests to wait for the reasons I've stated. I would also ask you would do so quietly to prevent any further disruption to your fellow patients on the ward.'

His thoughts were also for Violet, who was standing with her arms wrapped around her waist in a self-comforting gesture being completely blanked by her father. The more distressed he could see her becoming, the harder it was for Nate to keep his own temper in check.

'How dare—?'

'Dad! He said he'll sort it. Go and lie down before you do yourself any more damage.' Violet cut him off as he launched into another rant, her hands now planted on her hips.

The strength of her bravery was belied by her trembling bottom lip, which only Nate seemed to notice. The Earl, whether exhausted by his own ire or his daughter's, finally returned to his bed with a grumble.

Violet visibly relaxed when the argument was brought to a close. Nate had never been privy to the rows she must've witnessed at Strachmore and, although he'd been dismayed at times by his own parents' behaviour, he'd never been afraid in his own home. He had seen the fear in her eyes as she'd confronted her father about his attitude and Nate had just witnessed how vile this man could be. Although he'd tried to back off before he and Violet acted out any more erotic scenes on his furniture, he couldn't seem to stay away.

If he'd truly meant to keep his distance he could've transferred Samuel Dempsey's care elsewhere and reduced the chances of running into his daughter, but Nate was very much a part of this dysfunctional relationship. Despite the constant reminders he would never be a suitable match for Violet, it had been hell trying to put that night at his place out of his mind. The handprints left on his table were a frustrating reminder they were physically compatible, combustible even, if not couple material.

Now today's drama was over they were left staring at each other pretending there wasn't a conflict of interests going on. He had history with Violet, and her father, which he was doing his best not to let cloud his judgement. Unfortunately whatever happened with this patient was always going to affect his personal life too.

'You can't let him leave.' Violet was imploring him to intervene with those big expressive eyes. He preferred the dark glittering sapphires when she was in the throes of passion to the all too familiar worried baby blues.

'Now *you're* trying to tell *me* what's for the best?'

She'd almost bitten his head off for daring to do the same over the matter of her mother's jewellery. A matter that he still wasn't happy to lay to rest.

'I'm serious, Nate. You said yourself he should stay here. He's not ready to go home.' Everything in her tense body language said she wasn't ready for it either. If he could've chained her father to the bed rather than subject her to any more of his outbursts, he would've found a way to do it. They both knew her father's return to Strachmore would throw everything they'd been working towards into chaos.

'My hands are tied, I'm afraid. He's an adult, of, allegedly, sound mind. I can only advise him to remain under my care, not force him. This is clearly also an extremely volatile environment for him and staying won't benefit him or the other patients around him.' He hated himself for doing this to her. While she was doing her best to be strong, Nate had seen enough of her telltale signs to see she was struggling.

'What am I going to do with him? I'm a mental-health nurse, I'm not qualified for cardiac care.' Violet kept glancing across to his bed, where he was still grumbling and slamming his things around. It was impossible to tell which of them was more stressed here.

'I'll get in touch with his GP, see if he can't persuade him to stay where he is. Failing that, between me, you and my parents, we'll have to muddle through.' Another commitment he'd made just so he could put that smile back on Violet's face. There was also that niggle about not being able to perform the angioplasty making him uneasy. It was the first time he'd been unable to complete his duty of care to the full.

'You'll come and check on him?'

'We'll probably have to find some covert way of doing it but I won't let you take this on alone.' At least then he could keep an eye on the Earl's recovery and watch for any complications arising from his refusal of conventional treatment.

'You won't *let* me, huh?'

'Well, I thought on this occasion you might concede a small piece of that iron will.'

They exchanged wry smiles over the private joke. The origin of which was rooted in that night at his house. Not long after they'd argued over Violet's stance on selling her mother's jewellery, they'd ended up locking tongues, and almost a lot more besides, on his dining room table.

He began to regret his decision to wear a tie today as the air seemed to dissipate and leave him struggling to breathe. It made no difference if they were alone or in a ward full of people when it came to chemistry. Violet was staring at his lips and he could tell she was recalling the last time she'd yielded to him.

The silence that fell between them crackled with tension and unfinished business. It didn't matter to his libido that both members of the Dempsey family had judged him and found him wanting. He was programmed to enjoy the benefits of a physical relationship without any emotional messiness and he shouldn't start changing the rules now. It was his pride keeping him awake at night imagining what could've been instead of living it.

'Dr Taylor, you're needed in Room One.'

Nate was reminded he was supposed to be working, not trying to figure out a way he could sleep with Violet without compromising his principles. He gave the nurse a nod of acknowledgement.

'I'd best get on and do what I'm paid for. Don't worry, Violet, I'll make sure your father has the best care whether it's here or at home.' The promises tripped off his tongue as easy as denial and insults flowed from Samuel Dempsey's. They were both trapped in a pattern of self-destructive behaviour that could jeopardise their future if they weren't careful. Sooner or later they were going to have to make changes in order to survive. For Nate that would entail cutting out more than whiskey and cigars.

True to his word Nate had sent in a crack team of physiotherapists and dieticians to speak to the Earl. Neither Violet nor the forest's worth of advice leaflets had been enough to convince him to stay put. As usual, they'd all had to bend to his will and accept he was going home. He'd offended so many people along the way, there was a certain amount of relief mixed with Violet's trepidation.

Regardless of their lengthy estrangement she still felt the need to apologise to everyone he came into contact with for his abrupt manner. She should have been firmer with him, tried harder to make him modify his behaviour, but the truth was she was still intimidated by him herself. If he objected to her interference and really cut loose on her, she wasn't sure she would turn out to be any stronger than her mother.

She'd given up any right to tell him what to do when she'd left home at eighteen and vice versa. There was no way she would've accepted him swanning back into her life and trying to run it for her after all this time either. The difference was, she wasn't putting other people's livelihoods in jeopardy with a blinkered approach to her finances. She'd made damn sure she had no dependants for that very reason, when it had cost her so much to simply take responsibility for herself.

It was late afternoon before they were ready to leave, much to her father's continued agitation. He didn't seem to grasp the fact that a crotchety old man going against medical advice wasn't the top priority on a ward full of seriously ill patients.

Not even the whistling porter who came to escort him from CCU escaped his wrath.

'I'm not a cripple,' he said and kicked the wheel of the wheelchair in disgust.

'It's only to take you to the door, Dad. Bill's picking us up outside. The physio said gentle exercise only, remember? You don't want to end up exhausted before you leave the grounds.' She imagined by this stage they were all glad to see the back of him from the department.

He was already out of breath with the effort it had taken to get dressed but he eventually got into the chair with a huff.

'A lot of fuss about nothing, if you ask me.'

She hadn't asked him, because that had the potential for her to lose her temper and demand to know why it was impossible for him to thank Nate for saving his life. They might get into hostile territory sooner than anticipated and run the risk of shattering the fragile remains of their father-daughter relationship, dooming Strachmore for ever.

As they made their way through the corridors she hoped to catch a glimpse of Nate, but he undoubtedly had his hands full with clinics and surgery. His skill in his field still astounded her, and she appreciated the time he'd dedicated to helping her even if her father didn't. He'd borne the brunt of her parent's rudeness through no fault of his own.

She wondered how much of that bitterness was actually apportioned to her. Her father had always associated her belligerent attitude with Nate's influence rather than his own tyranny. There was the possibility he blamed him for encouraging her to break out on her own. In which case she was going to have to set the record straight with a few home truths.

She'd never stopped to consider how her new start in London might have impacted on those she'd left behind. It had been easier to believe they'd all carried on as normal instead of adding more ballast to her burden of guilt. Only now were the consequences of her actions, her cowardice, becoming clear.

The next step was for all those who'd messed up to hold their hands up and admit their mistakes so they could start to move on from past transgressions. Even Nate, who appeared to have his life together, hadn't managed to let go of all responsibility to Strachmore. She owed it to him to enable that final break but just not yet. She had an inkling she was going to need his support more than ever now she was faced with living under her father's rule once more.

The Taylors did enough fussing over her father to enable her to take a back seat for a short while. When they were fawning over him his level of churlishness significantly decreased and gave Violet a reprieve from her 'tightly coiled spring' act every time he opened his mouth.

Bill had kindly arranged for his bed to be moved down to the ground floor to save him from having to take the stairs and Margaret had prepared a light dinner following his new dietary regime. It was only when the couple went home that the interminable silence fell at the dining table.

Of course he'd refused to take a dinner tray on his

lap, insisted on keeping things 'normal' with the formal dining, regardless of how ludicrous it was with only the two of them seated around the massive mahogany table. She suspected this charade was more for his benefit than hers. He looked like the king of his castle perched at the head of the table even if he mightn't feel it.

'I've missed Mrs Taylor's cooking,' she said to break the tense atmosphere spoiling her appetite.

'There was nothing stopping you coming back if you missed it that much.' He didn't miss a beat as he scored a point against her in between spoonfuls of soup.

There was nothing to be gained by getting into a fight now, when he was still wearing a hospital band around his wrist. They could get into the whys and wherefores of their non-relationship when he was fully recovered and she wasn't afraid of causing him to relapse.

'I've been so busy with work I haven't had much time for holidays.' It wasn't completely untrue. She'd simply omitted to tell him he was the reason she didn't take any.

'For twelve years?' He paused mid-slurp to raise a bushy white eyebrow.

She'd never been a particularly good liar.

'I didn't think I'd be very welcome.' She wasn't even sure she was now. At the minute his attitude towards her labelled her as more of an uninvited guest rather than the prodigal daughter returned to the loving arms of her father.

'I never asked you to leave in the first place.'

This was exactly the sort of backwards-and-forwards blame game she'd hoped to avoid.

'Well, I'm here now. I have some time off to take while you recuperate.' The way her nerves were stretched she might very well need some extra time to recover herself when this was all over.

'Why the sudden interest in me now? Or did you only come back to claim your inheritance? I'm sorry if I ruined your plans but it seems I'm going to stick around a while longer.' He resumed sipping as though he hadn't completely ripped her good intentions to pieces.

Violet could barely find the words to refute his allegations. She'd never expected to have to justify caring for him. 'I… I… That's not fair. I only came back for you. To make sure you were all right.'

'Unfortunately for you, and me, I'm fine.'

She was sure her frown matched her father's as she struggled to work out what the hell he meant. Were things so bad that he didn't want to be here any more? Was that the reason he'd refused treatment and insisted on leaving hospital too early? A chill blasted through her at the thought of losing another parent to the jaws of that black dog that had hounded her mother to her death.

'You're not fine. You're recovering from a heart attack and you're drowning in a sea of debt. All I want to do is help you.' Her voice hitched as she held out that olive branch. Despite everything, he had to be her main priority now or she would end up truly alone for ever.

He very carefully set his spoon down and fixed her with that withering stare that made Violet want to hide under the table. 'What do you know about my personal affairs?'

Only now, faced with the prospect of telling him what she'd been up to over the past few days, did she realise how intrusive he'd find her actions. She gulped. 'We found the bills and final demands when we were tidying up. It wasn't as if we were snooping.'

'What do you mean "we"? Who else has been prying into my private business?' He was red in the face, building up to one of his eruptions, and Violet braced herself to take the full force of it.

'Nate. He has some really good ideas about what we could do here—'

The fist came down hard on the table, rattling the dishes and the cutlery in its wake. Even Violet was shaking from the impact.

'Who the hell do you think you are coming back here and rifling through my things? Nothing at Strachmore is any of your business. You made that clear when you ran away, Violet. And it certainly has nothing to do with *him*.'

'I understand why you're angry at me. I stayed away too long, I realise that, but why do you hate Nate so much? He saved your life.'

'I didn't ask him to.'

There it was again, the unmistakable sound of a man who'd grown tired of living. She'd dealt with enough suicidal teens in her time to take his comments seriously and not simply dismiss them as attention-seeking. Lord Dempsey would never willingly admit defeat unless there was something seriously wrong.

'Dad—'

The doorbell chimed before she could query his

state of mind any further or tell him how selfish that kind of thinking was.

'You'd better get that. Or do you expect me to struggle all the way to the front door and back?' Apparently the invalid card was only valid if it involved her guilt.

Violet made her way to the door on somewhat shaky limbs. Trying to get her father to open up would be like death by a thousand paper cuts—slow, with each new wound more painful than the last. Whoever was on the other side of this door, be it the Taylors or a door-to-door salesman, she intended to drag them inside to interrupt the direction the conversation with her father was taking. Neither of them were ready to tackle that head-on without building up their strength first.

'Hi. I thought I should pop over and see how the ground lay. Should I get my flak jacket from the car now or have you laced his tea with sedatives already?' Nate greeted Violet with a joke in an attempt to hide the nerves that had kept him from knocking on the door for the past ten minutes.

He'd stayed in the car with the engine running, contemplating whether or not to get involved in the Dempseys' domestics. He'd had no doubt the two of them under the same roof was causing friction when it was in their nature to rub each other up the wrong way. The reservations had come when he'd pictured himself in the middle of it. In the end, his conscience had rapped on the door for him. He couldn't leave Violet to manage his patient and his moods alone. Not when he kept promising her otherwise.

'Oh, Nate. You're a sight for sore eyes.'

He had no room for preening when he saw Violet

was visibly shaken and as pale as the alabaster statues in the entrance hall behind her.

'What's happened?' The whole idea had been to make this a casual visit but he was well versed in emergencies too.

'He's angry about me being here...about our meddling in his affairs...and he's saying such morbid things. It's as if he's upset he's still here.' Violet was hanging on to his arm as she rambled. There was absolutely no danger of him leaving now.

'Okay. We knew he wasn't going to react well when he found out we'd been digging into his financial status. As for the rest, depression or anxiety isn't uncommon in heart-attack survivors. He'll be feeling weak and vulnerable. Something which your father definitely won't be used to. He might need to start a course of anti-depressants. I'll have a chat with him and see if I can get a handle on his mental state.' Another reason Nate would've preferred he'd prolonged his hospital stay. There were so many possible after-effects, and not all of them physical, aftercare was a vital part of recovery. He'd been denied giving that and Violet was the one suffering as a consequence.

'That would usually be where I come in.' Violet sighed as she stepped aside to let him in, looking as dejected as she was describing her father.

'Hey, it's not your fault. You're too close to see this objectively and you're doing your bit simply by being here.' He hooked a finger under her chin to lift her head up and was tempted to kiss her worried mouth to bring them both some comfort.

It seemed an age since they'd last done that, their night together almost nothing more than an erotic fantasy now. He'd wanted that intimacy again, even for the briefest moment, to remind him it had been real, that she'd wanted him once as more than someone to bail her out when the going got tough.

'Who is it?' The dulcet tones of a crotchety Earl soon put paid to any romantic notions, reminding Nate of his professional responsibilities.

The medical stuff was within the remit of his normal day-to-day life. Whatever this was with Violet certainly wasn't. He let his hand fall down to his side again and took a deep breath. 'I guess it's time to face the music.'

Violet led the way towards the dining room with no real urgency in her step and he could see her steeling herself before she went in. It had never been the homely environment he'd been lucky to have even before his strained relationship with his parents, but the atmosphere here was so tense and thick with resentment it wasn't conducive to anyone's health.

'Hello, Lord Dempsey. I was just down visiting my parents and I thought I'd see how you were settling in.' It was a little white lie to soften the idea of his trespassing where he wasn't wanted. In all these years he'd never just 'popped in' for a visit, even when he'd been only a stone's throw away.

Samuel Dempsey eyed the offer of a handshake with a suspicious glare. 'I don't need to settle in. *I* live here.'

'I know Violet has been very worried about you—'

All concerns were brushed aside with an ungentlemanly snort.

'Worried about her inheritance more like. Is that why you're *really* here? Violet tells me you've both been helping yourselves to things while I've been fighting for my life.' He leaned back in his chair, arms folded across his chest, giving the impression he was enjoying this power play. It was as though he saw this as a game, where they were competing for the title of top dog and there could only be one winner. Nothing could be further from the truth. Nate wanted them to work together to make sure he was still fit to rule his kingdom.

'That's not what I said. We were simply trying to get things organised for you coming home.' Violet made a futile attempt to clear their names. Futile because her father wouldn't even look at her while she was talking, keeping his beady eyes firmly tableside on Nate.

'I've got your number. You're teaming up to snatch this place from under me. I see you riding around in your fancy car pretending you are somebody. Well, let me tell you, class isn't something you can buy.' The blue veins were pulsing beneath his flushed skin as he raged against his imagined foes.

Nate had to count to ten in his head to keep his own temper in check. It wasn't his place to make this any more personal than it already was by pointing out the Earl's faults in turn. Class didn't always equate to decency and it was entirely possible to have one without the other.

'Please don't do this again, Dad.' Violet's small plea was so full of fear it instantly made Nate think of her caught in the middle of her parents' battles. He didn't want to put her in that position again and he certainly didn't want to inflame the situation any further.

'It's okay, Violet. Your father's entitled to say how he feels in his own home.' It was a shame he'd never let his daughter do the same. Still, it wasn't his family, or his battle.

'Damn right I am. Just as I'm entitled to some privacy. I shouldn't have to put my personal correspondence under lock and key every time I leave the house.' For a man so predisposed to dramatic outbursts, he was doing a good job of making his near-death experience sound like a trip to the shops. Painting Nate and Violet as a pair of opportunistic burglars in the process.

'Perhaps I should leave.' Nate made eye contact with Violet. Her father wasn't showing any signs of having given up on life, at least not to him. If anything he seemed to be fighting to hang on to everything he had.

'Good idea. I've been perfectly capable of taking care of myself for the past I-don't-know-how-long. I don't need anybody's help now.' The Earl was clinging desperately to his independence.

Nate could sympathise to some extent with his stubborn stance against them. They were essentially trespassers who'd taken it upon themselves to get involved in his affairs. But he could also see that Violet was simply doing what she thought was best for him. This had moved so far beyond the professional excuses he'd made for coming here tonight he was in danger of having his say on the matter. Something that probably wouldn't please either side and would only drag him in deeper.

'Everyone in this room knows that's not true. You have no money coming in and nothing to cover the debts you already have. I've managed to cover a few of the most urgent bills but you need to generate some sort of income.' Whether it was because she'd found strength in numbers or she was so exasperated, Violet was starting to find her voice. She didn't need him; she hadn't done for some time. Nate imagined it was a case of reverting back to type because she had so much unfinished business with her father. And him.

'I didn't ask you to pay for anything. I suppose the money came from Dr Flash here? Well, the Dempseys don't need anyone's charity. Especially not from domestic staff.'

'I paid with my own money. I sold Mum's necklace, if you must know. One of us had to get our priorities straight.'

Nate could only stand and watch as Violet threw herself under the bus to save him from further abuse. Now she had her father's full attention.

'How could you?' He visibly paled and sat up straighter in his chair with her full disclosure, acting as though it were a betrayal rather than the huge sacrifice Nate knew it had been for her.

'What's the alternative? Wait for the bailiffs to seize it anyway in lieu of payment? Or do you have a Swiss bank account somewhere you've forgotten to mention?'

Violet was in full flow now. There was no reason for Nate to intervene when she was managing so beautifully without back up. She needed to have her say. It had been a long time coming.

'Does her memory mean so little to you that you can sell it for a few pieces of silver?'

'If you knew Mum at all you'd realise she hated those gaudy baubles you insisted on buying her. It was sentimental things like the clay bead bracelet I made at primary school she wore every day, not expensive statement jewellery.'

Not unlike the bracelet she'd worn on her own wrist for over a decade. There was a flutter of something he didn't want to recognise in his chest at the thought he'd held the same special place in her thoughts. It felt a lot like hope.

'Your mother was a good woman. She deserved the best.'

'But at what price, Dad? She knew you couldn't afford that kind of expense and worried herself to death over it. I think she'd be only too happy at the idea of using it to make a difference here.'

It was the first time Nate had witnessed something approaching shame on the Earl's face before he hung his head. 'I know you blame me, Violet, but your mother was a sick woman. I can't change what happened in the past.'

Violet dropped to her knees and reached for her father's hand. 'But you can do something about the future. We can open Strachmore to the public and bring enough money in to cover all your outgoings here. Nate's been looking into the idea of hiring part of the place out as a wedding venue.'

Just when it seemed as though they were making progress, Samuel Dempsey got to his feet, almost knocking his daughter to the floor in the process.

'Over my dead body! This is my home. It's not for sale or rent and neither is my pride.'

Nate immediately went to Violet's aid and helped her up to a more dignified position. It was too much of an insult against her good intentions to simply let him get away with this one. He turned, fully prepared to wade in and add his voice to Violet's cause, only to find the Earl had his eyes closed, refusing to entertain further discussion. He truly was the most infuriating man to try and get through to.

Then Nate noticed his hand move to his chest, then

grab his left arm before he fell to the floor with a sickening thud.

'Dad!'

His expletive was drowned out by Violet's shout.

Along with the Earl's sickly pallor and clammy skin, all the signs pointed to another cardiac arrest. Nate should've seen this coming but he'd been too caught up in other people's emotions to keep his doctor head in the game.

Although the Earl had dropped like a stone he'd thankfully avoided hitting the table on the way down and there was no indication of any head injuries. Nate loosened the shirt around his neck and tilted his head back to check his breathing. Nothing.

'He's not breathing. Phone 999.' He delegated phone duties to prompt Violet into moving. He couldn't afford to have her in shock too. Far from helping, his meddling had simply caused more catastrophe. He should've left well alone and they might all have carried on down their own paths they'd chosen a dozen years back. Oblivious to each other's emotional dysfunction.

If he hadn't still been hung up on Violet and insisted on getting involved in her father's treatment in the first place this could've turned out differently. The Earl might've accepted help easier or sooner without all of this added stress.

Leaving the past unresolved now seemed a better option than being directly responsible for his death. If the worst happened there was no chance Violet would ever forgive him, never mind love him.

CHAPTER SIX

VIOLET STAMMERED OUT the address and the details of what had happened to the switchboard operator. It was difficult to focus on what was being said on the other end of the phone when she was watching Nate pump life back into her father's chest for a second time. The difference now was there was no defibrillator to shock the heart back into rhythm. He was literally the only thing standing between her father and certain death.

'The ambulance is on its way.' Sooner rather than later, she hoped. Every second counted now in bringing her father back.

Violet was helpless in the fight, watching her father's body jerk with every violent chest compression needed to keep the blood circulating around his body. It was her fault they were all in this situation. If she hadn't come back in the first place, or dragged Nate into their family politics, her father might still be recovering in his hospital bed. Not lying here on his dining-room floor literally heartbroken because of the accusations she'd thrown at him. This was what happened when she finally stood up to him.

He'd never forgive her for this. If he made it through. She'd never forgive herself if he didn't.

'Did they say how long on that ambulance?' Nate was breathing heavily, sweat beading on his upper lip, with the continued effort of CPR. It was easy to forget how physical a task it was doing the heart's job when it was out of commission.

'Five minutes. Apparently there's one not too far from here.'

Nate nodded and turned his attention back to his patient.

Watching him work, his hair falling over his forehead as he tried to prolong life, was impressive and mesmerising. She, on the other hand, was standing here like a spare part with no active role in saving her father's life.

'Do you want me to take over for a while?' Her mouth was dry at the mere thought of undertaking such a crucial task but Nate needed a break and she needed to do something useful.

'Are you sure?' His serious face told her he wasn't going to leave his post unless she was confident she could do this.

'Yes.' She knelt down beside him on the floor, not giving her brain time to start overanalysing everything that could go wrong.

'Remember, you need to be forceful to be effective. Ready?' He scooted over so she could move closer for the transfer.

'Yes.' No.

She'd never performed CPR on an *actual* person, only synthetic dummies whose fate didn't affect anyone. If she screwed this up she'd have her father's death on her conscience for ever as well as Strachmore's fate.

She locked out her arms and linked her fingers in

preparation, throwing her weight into the first compression when she took over.

'One, two, three…' She counted out each chest pump to keep the timing regular and her brain occupied.

'That's good. Nice and steady.' Nate laid a hand on her back to support her and used the other to grab his phone from his pocket.

Her father's skin was cold beneath her fingers and she tried desperately not to convince herself it was already too late but Nate wouldn't give up and neither would she.

'Come on. We can do this,' she told him in the hope he would suddenly bat her away and tell her he could do this on his own. This was the first time she'd actually been in a position to help him and she prayed it wouldn't be the last.

'Apparently the ambulance is coming up the drive. I'll go out and direct them here if that's okay with you?'

'Sure. Hurry.'

Her arms were beginning to tire with the tension and repetitive movements but adrenaline was keeping them moving. She could hear the sirens, see the shadows of the ambulance lights dancing through the windows, but she didn't relax until Nate returned with the crew, giving them the lowdown on events to date.

'We can take over from here.' Nate gave her a reprieve and took over the compressions while the paramedics set to work with the oxygen and defibrillator.

'Stand clear.'

This time Violet was there to witness the shocks as they were delivered in between Nate's chest compressions as everyone crowded around to save her father's life. They had him hooked up to so many machines and life-saving equipment he might as well have been in the hospital.

After the second shock was administered there was a renewed flurry of activity.

'We've got a pulse.'

'Lord Dempsey, can you hear us?'

'Open your eyes for us, Samuel.'

'Dad?' Violet held her breath, waiting for confirmation there was still a chance he could make it. Nate came to her and put her mind at ease with a squeeze of her hand.

'He's breathing on his own again. You did an excellent job, Nurse Dempsey.'

'We made a good team, Dr Taylor.' Her limbs were shaking as the tension began to ebb from her body, only to be replaced with shock at what she'd just undertaken. They were a long way from celebrating just yet but they'd done their bit to get him this far.

'I'll ride with you in the ambulance in case there are any complications. We might have to operate this time to prevent this from happening again.' Not even Nate's warmth could prevent the cold chill that ran down her spine. They were right back at square one, with the stakes higher than ever. This time she was directly responsible for putting her father in hospital and it was down to Nate again to save the day.

Nate had been more forceful about the need to perform emergency angioplasty as soon as they reached the hospital to prevent any more attacks. This latest episode had obviously shaken the Earl as he'd agreed without much of a fight this time. Now Nate's blue scrubs were sticking to the sweat on his back. He performed this procedure as a matter of routine but not usually on people who thought he'd somehow forged his qualifications, and not with old girlfriends sitting outside waiting for news.

With the Earl awake and aware of everything going on around him, Nate was under pressure more than ever to prove himself. He'd never been more aware of the small risks involved in this minimally invasive treatment, or his responsibilities during it, as he stood over Violet's father.

'Okay, Lord Dempsey, you'll be awake during the procedure but you shouldn't feel anything with the local anaesthetic we've given you. You can even watch what's happening on the monitor beside you.' He usually tried to make his patients more at ease by remaining on first-name terms but he didn't want to antagonise his patient before they started.

'Thanks.'

They'd administered a mild sedative along with a local anaesthetic but Nate was still pleasantly surprised at how co-operative the patient was being, considering his earlier mood. Well, at least less combative than he'd expected. He'd had visions of having to strap him down to stop him taking a swing at him for bringing him back to the hospital.

'We're just going to insert a catheter into the small incision we've made in your wrist. That will allow us to inject X-ray dye into the arteries so we can get a clear picture of what's going on in there.' He could make a better assessment of how to proceed when he could see the problem for himself instead of guessing.

Once he had the nod, Nate carried on as he would

normally do. There was nothing out of the ordinary about this case if he could set personal history aside and stop thinking about how much was riding on this being a success. Potentially this was his chance of winning the Earl's approval, essential in making his and Violet's lives a little easier. It mattered to him to be accepted when he was spending so much time at Strachmore. With Violet. There was also the matter of professional pride when this was his patient who'd been readmitted only a matter of hours after leaving.

With the help of the monitors, he concentrated on feeding the thin, flexible tube through the blood vessels until it reached the coronary arteries on the heart. It was an intricate process, one which he'd honed over the years. Hence, his continued irritation when people dismissed the skills he'd worked hard to perfect.

'You can see on the screen that your right coronary artery is almost completely blocked, preventing blood flowing to that particular section of the heart.' It was clear now exactly what was causing the problem and, providing there were no objections, he could repair it.

'What's next, Doctor?'

If the Earl's co-operation had taken him by surprise, being referred to respectfully in his professional capacity was nearly enough to knock him off his feet.

'The best thing to open the artery is to insert a tiny balloon and inflate it to let the blood flow. I think in your case we'll also need to use a stent too. It's a small mesh tube that helps support the inner wall of the artery to make sure it remains open once we remove the balloon.'

'Whatever you think's for the best.' He deferred to

Nate with his eyes closed, either too tired to argue or too squeamish to watch.

It enabled Nate to relax a tad without being scrutinised as he threaded the guide wire into the affected artery. The balloon was inflated to widen the artery and squash fatty deposits against the artery wall, the stent expanding with it. Once the stent was open, he was able to deflate the balloon and remove it.

'And that's us finished.' The whole thing had taken just over an hour, a typical time for the procedure but, under the gaze of Lord Dempsey, it had felt like a never-ending test of his abilities.

'Already?' Lord Dempsey was straining to make sure he'd been true to his word.

'Yes. We'll send you back to CCU to monitor you overnight but with any luck you should be back home again tomorrow.' He removed the catheter and the lab nurse applied pressure to the site to prevent any bleeding. Job done with a great degree of satisfaction and relief.

'Thank you, Nathaniel.' The Earl reached out to shake his hand and Nate stood a little taller in his comfy Theatre shoes.

'I think you need to thank your daughter too. She was very much part of the team keeping you alive until you got here.' She deserved some positive recognition from him for once too.

'Violet?'

'She helped me perform CPR until the ambulance reached you. That is one lady determined to keep you around for a while longer.' Nate wanted to put to bed the ridiculous idea that she wanted him out of the way.

No devious gold-digger would have worked so hard to bring him back from the dead.

'I'll talk to her.'

'I think it's about time you did but, please, hear her out this time. She only wants the best for you, and the estate.' He'd held his counsel too long and in his eyes both he and Violet had proved their true intentions over the course of the evening. Despite their resistance to Strachmore and all it stood for, they'd both made a commitment to them in their own way.

He stripped off the lead apron that he'd worn to protect against the X-rays and tossed his surgical gown aside, keen to report back to Violet and share this feeling of after-surgery euphoria with someone for once.

Violet was biting what was left of her fingernails. She inspected her once-beautiful nails, now raggedy, the candyfloss-pink varnish starting to flake. It was funny how quickly frivolous things such as her weekly manicure became insignificant in the grand scheme of things. Nate had reassured her that her father's was a relatively straightforward procedure and she had every faith in him, but her father's health was so precarious she couldn't relax until she saw them both coming out of Theatre.

'Did everything go okay?' Her father was awake, Nate was smiling, but she wanted confirmation all had gone to plan.

'Like clockwork. We're just taking your father back to CCU, if you want to come with us?'

He was so handsome in his scrubs, made even more so with his amazing life-saving skills, Violet was liable to follow him anywhere. Overcome with relief and gratitude, she launched herself at him for a hug. She found solace in the smell of sweat and soap, which told her everything about how hard he'd worked over the course of the last hours. Now the drama was over she wished they were able to take time out in one of their old haunts to decompress and simply enjoy each other's company. Somewhere she wasn't constantly faced with reasons she shouldn't want to be with him.

From the corner of her eye she saw her father struggle to sit up. She instantly let go of her hold around Nate's neck and stepped away from the hunky cardiologist. Even though she was proud of him, it was her natural response to back off, knowing her father would never approve of such a public display no matter what the circumstances and especially with someone he deemed beneath him.

'How are you feeling, Dad?'

'Sore.'

If she'd expected Nate to flick on her father's humility switch while he was in there, she was sadly mistaken. She couldn't bear for him to take umbrage against Nate for any residual pain after all his hard work.

'I'm sure Nate did everything he could—'

'I didn't dispute that. From what I saw in there Nathaniel is a very, very skilled physician but I think I'm entitled to express my discomfort after everything I've been through. Now, if you don't mind, I need some rest.'

Violet could only stand open-mouthed as he was wheeled away.

When she finally regained control of her paralysed body parts she turned to stare at Wonder Doc. 'Did

I imagine that or did my father just pay you a back-handed compliment?'

If so, it was a breakthrough of epic proportions. She'd never heard him praise anyone for anything. It was probably the closest thing to an apology they'd ever hear from him. Violet was pleased on Nate's behalf that he was finally being recognised for his achievements even if she wasn't likely to receive that honour herself.

Nate gave her a wry smile to warm her frozen limbs. 'I told you I was good at what I do.'

'Yes, yes, you are.' That brought all things non-medical to Violet's corrupted mind, forcing her to break eye contact before he saw her lustful thoughts for himself. She knew how good he was at everything he did—she'd had a sample for herself. That taster had only made her crave more.

Nate gave a nervous cough and she got the impression those wayward thoughts hadn't been confined only to her head.

'It's late but you can go to CCU and say goodnight before you leave if you want.' Apparently he'd decided to go with the relatively safe ground of dealing with her father compared to that minefield of their relationship and the boundaries they'd come close to redrawing.

'I'm not sure that's such a good idea. I don't want to push my luck and end up in another row with him after that bombshell. I don't want a repeat of what happened at the house.' Their cosy chats didn't have a great track record. For all the good she'd done so far trying to help, she was tempted to simply let his world collapse around him rather than take any more responsibility for his ill health.

'You saw him for yourself. He's quite mellow at the minute. For him. Although, it might be wise not to mention Strachmore. At all.'

'Message received loud and clear.' Violet pondered his advice. There'd been enough excitement for one day, but surely five minutes spent bedside saying goodnight couldn't hurt? It might even put her mind at ease to see him settled at the end of such a traumatic twenty-four hours. Then she might stand a chance of a decent night's sleep.

She set off after the porter towards the coronary care unit safe in the knowledge Nate had fallen into step next to her. She was getting too used to having a sidekick with her during her trials and tribulations. When she finally went back to London she was probably going to have to get a dog or something to pour out her troubles to even though it would be a poor substitute for this man, who knew her better than she knew herself at times.

'I'm just popping in to make sure you're comfortable before I head home.' Violet approached her father's bed with as much caution as ever. There never was any warning of what mood he'd be in from one minute to the next, and he was bound to be tired and cranky after the evening he'd had. This wasn't the time or place to start pointing out his flaws and mistakes again. With any luck he'd begin to realise them for himself some day.

'I know you would rather I'd died instead of your mother. I do too.'

It was such an out-of-the-blue statement coming from him it stunned Violet into silence. Not so long ago it would've been true, she'd have preferred to have lived without him instead of her mother, but she'd moved past that. Nobody could change the past and it had been her mother's decision to leave them when all was said and done.

The greatest surprise, other than her father considering anyone else's feelings, was that he'd expressed something approaching remorse. She guessed facing his own mortality had finally awoken his conscience from its long slumber.

'Why would you say that now when we've done everything we could to keep you here tonight?'

He'd never shown any emotion over her mother's death, not even in the immediate aftermath. He'd done what he'd always done: pretended the bad stuff wasn't happening around him and carried on as usual. That had included hiding the truth from her about the overdose, leaving it to others to break that news to her. Hearing him express a wish to swap places with his dead wife at any point was unexpected, out of character, and made him more human. It went some way to softening the hard stance she'd taken against him because of his apparent indifference to her great loss, but he should be celebrating the fact he was still here tonight.

She eyed Nate, hoping he knew where the hell that had come from. Perhaps he'd done some counselling alongside the heart repairs—a full mind and body MOT.

'Lord Dempsey, are you feeling okay?' Nate's frown didn't tally with insider knowledge of his patient's sudden attack of conscience. Now he'd witnessed that morbid decline for himself he might be able to prescribe something to lift his mood.

'I know you only came home through a sense of duty, Violet. I've barely heard from you in over a decade, for goodness' sake. I could've died tonight without us ever clearing the air and I think it's time we had this talk before it's really too late. You've made it pretty clear you thought I was responsible for you losing your mother but do you honestly think I ever wanted to be here without her? I blame myself for her death as much as you do but I can't change what happened. Lord knows, I wish I could.' He bypassed Nate's question to continue his train of disturbing thoughts, his eyes red with stubborn unshed tears.

Nate pulled the curtains around the bed, giving them some privacy. It merely added to Violet's sense of emotional suffocation.

It was the first time her father had taken any responsibility for her mother's death, everything Violet had wanted since losing her. Seeing his distress as he did so didn't bring her the peace she'd always imagined. Quite the opposite. It was distressing to discover he'd been hurting all this time on his own too. Perhaps if he'd been this open with her back then she wouldn't have been so desperate to leave and they could've used their combined grief as a base to evolve their relationship instead of leaving it to stagnate.

'All you had to do was love us.' Her voice became smaller as the tragedy of her loss got bigger.

'I did. I still do. I never meant to hurt you or your mother but I always wanted to do the best for Strachmore too. Generations of my family kept the castle through war and unrest. I couldn't be the one to let it all slip away. I didn't realise it was your mother I'd truly failed until it was too late.'

'Why couldn't you have said this at the time to your teenage daughter who thought she'd lost the only parent who cared for her?' Until now she'd only ever seen the dark side of him and had run from it at the first opportunity. This guilt, this expression of actual emotion had come too late for her mother, perhaps even for her. Everything she'd thought she'd known about her father and her parents' marriage had coloured her view on every relationship she'd ever had. It had even cost her one with Nate.

'I dealt with things the only way I knew how—with a stiff upper lip. I was devastated, but what use would I have been to you if I'd fallen apart too? I might have gone about things the wrong way but I was the one who had to be strong. I've come close to death too many times this week to take anything for granted. I don't want to die with you still hating me. It's difficult enough knowing your mother went feeling that way about me. I'd do anything to change places with her. I've wanted that since she passed but I can't undo the past. Nathaniel has given me a second chance to at least try and make amends with you.'

Silence fell in the small cubicle, heavy with unspoken apology. She wouldn't have expected him to break down and beg for forgiveness but seeing him contrite like this was unnerving in itself. It was a bittersweet moment. This was the conversation he should've had with her mother, explaining his actions and exhibiting signs of humanity—capable of making mistakes and now owning up to them.

The logical part of her brain knew her mother must've had mental-health problems beyond her father's churlish ways to do what she'd done. Violet had chosen to ignore that fact and diverted all the anger she felt as a result of her mother's actions towards her father. It wasn't going to be easy to shift her perception of her father overnight and she needed time to process everything. With his roundabout apology she wasn't certain what he expected from her in return either.

'I don't hate you and I'll be here for as long as you need me. We'll discuss this again when you're feeling better. Now get some rest.' She was desperately fighting her own tears, her breath catching on the lump of emotion wedged in her throat. She didn't want to cause him any more pain than he was obviously already in.

She leaned over and placed a kiss on his cheek. An act she'd never carried out without being prompted. He wanted her forgiveness, and she would willingly give it if she thought they could move on, but she couldn't help feeling as though she was walking into another trap.

'Are you going to be okay?' Nate had snatched his keys from the dining-room floor where they'd fallen from his pocket during the fight to save the Earl and now he was saying his goodbyes on Strachmore's marble steps.

He and Violet had taken a taxi back together, since he had to get his car, but she'd been non-communicative during the journey home. She was entitled to some quiet after another fraught day. He'd inadvertently intruded on her heart-to-heart with her father and been as shocked by the outcome as she was. However, he didn't want her to sit brooding all night, feeling guilty about what had happened, or dwelling on her father's state of mind. None of this was her fault.

'I never saw that coming,' she said, staring off into

the distance. 'He was grieving in his own way, still is, and I left him alone. I'm supposed to be a mental-health expert and I didn't even consider that a possibility.'

'You couldn't have known when you were in a different country. I would say he's been very good at keeping his feelings to himself when my parents didn't pick up on it either and they see him every day. Hell, he's my patient, if you want to start pointing fingers at people who should have seen he was having trouble coping with his grief.' Perhaps if Nate hadn't known the background to their estrangement he might've picked up on other reasons for the Earl's mood swings besides his relationship with Violet. Blame wasn't going to solve the problem, only more of the plain talking he'd witnessed tonight.

'That's the point, I wasn't here. I was feeling sorry for myself in London, learning to treat people with mental issues when my own father was mourning the loss of his wife. Hating him all this time makes me the awful person I thought he was.' Her eyes rested on him again, two oceans of blue crashing with waves of sorrow.

He grabbed her by the shoulders, desperate to still those troubled waters. 'Stop this. It's obvious he wants you to stay here—that's why he's telling you all of this. He's trying to leave whatever has gone on between you behind so you can now both start to look forward. You've both suffered and I'm sure you've both said things you've regretted but now's the time to let the healing begin. These plans for Strachmore could mean a clean slate and a chance for you two to start building bridges if we can get him on board.'

A strengthening of Violet's relationship with her father would not only bring them some peace of mind, it could also give Nate some space from the happenings at the Dempsey household. He was already in way over his head and if he could hand over the reins so much the better. When all was said and done he wasn't going to be part of Strachmore's legacy any more than he was going to be a permanent fixture in Violet's life. These were all simply temporary arrangements due to circumstance. Not even his first love took priority over his sense of self-preservation. At least, not long-term.

'And I want that but not at the price I suspect I'll have to pay. What if I'm simply swapping one prison for another? I ran away so he wouldn't be able to force me to marry and keep me tied to this place. After that emotional outpouring I'll be the bad guy again if I leave again. I don't want him under the illusion I'm staying indefinitely. Whether he chooses to go along with this wedding idea or not, I've still got a job and a home in London I have every intention of returning to.'

Her torment was pretty much the same as his own. Somehow they had to find a way to fulfil their promises but still maintain their hold on their lives preheart attack. Ones which hadn't included Strachmore or each other.

'Everything's still raw at the minute. You can clarify the situation tomorrow and discuss what you both expect to come from this.' When everyone had had a good night's sleep and some time to think about exactly what they'd committed to.

'I don't know how to do that without disappointing him again. I want Strachmore to succeed but I'm not sacrificing everything else for it.'

'Tell him you're glad he got everything off his chest

but your personal circumstances haven't changed as a result. Set very clear boundaries so you remain in control. If you don't have a firm date for going back to work, make one and don't break it.' That would prevent them both from falling any deeper into this quagmire of guilt and responsibility they'd unwittingly stumbled into. With an end date they'd be able to claw their way back out at some point and carry on as though this had never happened.

'He's always been such a dominant force I don't think I can cope if he starts talking about dying again. I'm afraid I'll let him guilt-trip me into staying permanently. I'm so weak.'

He could feel her shoulders sag under the weight of her burden. Nothing tonight seemed to have eased it for her. He gave her a gentle shake in an attempt to awaken that fighting spirit he'd seen in her earlier.

'Emotionally and physically exhausted perhaps, but you're certainly not weak. You took over CPR tonight without hesitation when I began to tire, pumping your father's heart as though it was your own life depending on it. Does that sound like a woman who can't handle a crisis to you?'

That raised a faint smile. 'I did surprise myself.'

'You didn't surprise me. I've always known how amazing you are.' He let go of his grip on her shoulders to cradle her face in his hands. With only the shine of the moon lighting the darkness, bathing Violet's heart-shaped features in its silvery glow, she'd never looked so beautiful.

With adrenaline and pride still coursing through his veins post-op, he leaned in for a kiss. He'd gained some respect tonight and it was enough to bolster his ego. Although he might never find total acceptance, her soft lips against his would be sufficient reward.

Violet accepted his tongue into her warm mouth, met him with her own. Somehow she tasted sweeter now he knew there'd be no complications in getting involved. She didn't want to stay at Strachmore any longer than was necessary or any more than he did. They could both walk away at the end of her stay without any ill feeling or recriminations this time.

They wanted each other—that much had never really been in doubt. Everything preventing this attraction reaching its natural conclusion was an obstacle constructed by his own pride.

'Are we really going to do this?' Violet already knew the answer but they'd both changed their minds so often she didn't want either of them to end up disappointed. Her head was so full of every word spoken, every life-changing decision that had been made over the course of the evening, she needed to be free of her thoughts for a while.

Nate was encouraging her to leave as soon as feasibly possible, removing that last obstacle before they got naked with each other. They were going into this with their eyes open and their hearts closed this time around. Neither would expect more than the other was prepared to give, avoiding any guilt or misunderstandings. Exactly how she preferred to conduct her love life.

'I guess so.' Nate interrupted her inner conciliation with what she was doing with his husky breath in her ear. It instantly revitalised her weary body, awakening every nerve ending and hitting each erogenous zone simultaneously.

Why was she still waiting?

'Shall we take this inside?' She was breathless; the cold night air and Nate's trail of kisses over the sensitive skin at her neck conspiring to make her shiver.

'Only if we can skip the acrobatics on the fixtures and fittings and go straight to bed. I've been on my feet all night.' Nate grinned as he backed her over the doorstep and kicked the door shut with his foot.

'You're just full of brilliant ideas, Nathaniel Taylor.' She wasn't about to object to some tenderness after the day she'd had. A night lying in each other's arms sounded perfect to her.

'I think this is one of my best ones yet.' He growled and grabbed her backside. She flung her arms around his neck as he kissed her again, keeping them locked together as he hoisted her up around his waist.

'I thought you said no acrobatics?' It did a girl's ego good to be picked up so effortlessly and carried upstairs as though she weighed nothing. Even more when she could feel the hard evidence of her seducer's arousal pressing into her.

'I'm simply making sure I have you where I want you. The door is shut, my phone's off, and I'm not due back to work until tomorrow. No more interruptions. Tonight is ours. I'm reclaiming it.' He fastened his mouth to hers, sealing that promise he would do everything to drive her demons away for a while at least.

'Well, in that case, giddy up, Taylor.' She dropped her hand to slap him on the ass, giggling at the surprise on his face.

'Oh, it's like that, is it, Dempsey? You think you're the one calling the shots here?' He halted their journey at the top of the stairs, pushing her up against the wall and rendering her limbs useless.

'Uh-huh,' she mumbled, daring him to prove her wrong.

Now he had her pinned between the hardness of his body and the brickwork, his hands were free to do just that. He slid the sleeve of her white peasant blouse off her shoulder, exposing her skin to more soft kisses. Her insides turned to mush while everything on the outside stood up and begged for more.

'You sure about that?' he asked with a devilish grin that caught her breath as she waited to see what else he had in store.

'Hmm, mmm.' She nodded, temporarily struck dumb as he slipped his hand inside her bra.

Her nipples were as hard as diamonds now at the very idea he was claiming her body for the night as he palmed her breast with an authority to make her gasp. She could afford to relinquish a little control if it meant feeling this good.

He teased her at first with a flick of the tongue over her puckered pink flesh, only increasing the pressure, and the enjoyment, when she bucked against him demanding more. There were no more thoughts buzzing in her head except those of the carnal kind as Nate drew her nipple into his mouth, sucking her towards oblivion. She was caught between a moan and a gasp as he took her to the crossroads between pain and pleasure.

She'd been right not to let this happen when they were young. If she'd known this would be how it felt to be in his bed she might never have left home. At least here and now she was free to savour this for what it was without trying to predict what happened next. She'd take an orgasm and one hell of a memory to keep her warm in her old age over a doomed relationship any day.

'You're a stubborn so-and-so. I guess we'll just have to take our turn at going on top.' He peeled her back off the wall and carried her towards the bedroom. It was just as well when she knew her trembling legs would never have carried her there on their own.

He dropped her gently onto the bed and proceeded to strip her clothes away, leaving her panties to the very last. If sexy was a handsome cardiologist tugging your underwear down with his teeth she'd hit the jackpot. It was like watching her wildest, most erotic dream play out for real. Except someone had censored out the best bit.

She teased her fingers along the ridge in his trousers, making it his turn to moan. And strip. He stood strong and proud, meeting all of her expectations as he sprang free from his confinement.

'What about contraception? I don't have any with me.' The pained expression as he made the confession said he'd put an end to this now, regardless of his own discomfort, if protection was an issue.

'It's okay, I'm covered.' She might've been offended he was so frightened of somehow getting trapped if she hadn't been on the pill since her first real boyfriend for the very same reason. A pregnancy didn't go together with her independent woman stance.

Nate's relief was there in his smile, and every other part of his body she could see was willing this to happen. There didn't seem a valid argument for holding back any more when they were clearly ready to take the next step. One they'd both waited a long time for.

He joined her on the bed, covering her lips and body with his. She rubbed herself against his erection, her softness yielding to his long length until they were joined together in one quick thrust. He exhaled a shaky breath in her ear as she settled around him. The sound of his contentment echoed the same sense of satisfaction travelling from her well-tended lips to her curled toes. This moment was everything she'd expected it to be, everything she'd feared it could be.

He was kissing her again, tending her lips at a leisurely pace, reminding her they had all night to indulge this fantasy when her body was craving everything he had now. She trembled with need, her urgency to reach that final peak increasing every time he drove into her. Her mind drifted between this plane and the next, only the pinch of Nate's fingers on her flesh keeping her anchored in the present for now.

As their bodies slammed together she made the mistake of looking into his eyes. Regardless of the fact this was supposed to be a one-time-only deal, those eyes were shifting from brown to green, reflecting emotions that weren't included in the terms and conditions. They should've made some sort of 'no kissing on the lips' rule, like Julia Roberts in *Pretty Woman*, to prevent this from being any more than sex. Except they weren't strangers who'd hooked up on the sidewalk and the kissing damage had been done a long time ago.

She tightened her hold on Nate internally and externally, hitching her legs around his waist and clenching around him. They needed to start treating this like hot, dirty sex, not childhood sweethearts who'd finally consummated their feelings for one another.

She clung to him, dug her nails into his back, picking up the pace and trying to stop this from turning into something it wasn't. His irises were now only full of desire, dark with lust and need, his breathing erratic as she pushed him towards surrender. This was all about one thing now—sexual release—and that was exactly how she preferred it.

Nate's entire body shuddered against her as he cried out. Finally Violet was able to give herself completely over to the moment as their bodies rocked together one last time. All of the tension and stress she'd been carrying inside flowed away as she threw herself into that welcoming abyss.

She didn't even know she was crying until Nate wiped her tears away.

'Hey. Was it really that bad?' Not once had he seen her break down during everything she'd faced since coming back here. Although she'd come close to cracking at times, she'd held it together with every new challenge her father's illness had brought her. To see her break now pained him when they'd shared something amazing together. Society ranking had meant nothing when they were rocking each other's world and he hoped these weren't tears of regret. Not when he expected her to be soaring up on the clouds with him after what they'd experienced together.

'No. It was really that good. You made me forget all the bad stuff.' She gave him a watery smile.

'My reputation remains intact.' He lay back, hands behind his head, his ego as satisfied as the rest of him.

'Definitely. I guess it all caught up with me for a

moment.' She turned her face away from him as though she was embarrassed she'd let him see her cry.

Nate turned on his side and pulled her close. There was no reason for her to feel ashamed when lesser mortals would have struggled long before now. Still, he didn't want to draw any more attention to her tears when she was uncomfortable about it.

'In that case it's my duty to keep you occupied—body and soul. I do believe it's your turn to go on top.' He rolled over, taking Violet with him so she could feel as though she was back in control for a while.

He'd spent a long time imagining this time with her and he didn't want anything to spoil it for either of them. They'd already shared the lows of today, they were entitled to enjoy a few highs too. Tomorrow they'd have to face all of those same problems keeping them tied to the estate, but tonight was still theirs.

CHAPTER SEVEN

THE RIGOROUS BEDROOM workout might have taken Violet's mind off everything except what Nate was doing to her body, but it hadn't helped her sleep any easier. She sat up watching his broad chest rise and fall in peaceful slumber as the sun rose.

He had a body made to help a girl forget—those perfect pecs, lickable abs, and…damn she needed him gone. Lying here naked together wasn't going to help matters one iota. Bedding him once had been exciting, eye-opening, leaving her curiosity and body satiated, but ringing the bell for round two was only asking for trouble. It had been easier to tell herself this would be a one-off before she'd known how good they were together.

This wasn't her usual casual affair where no feelings above the waist came into play. Never mind he was involved in everything going on between her and her father, now he'd seen her cry, for goodness' sake. She never cried, not in front of anyone, and certainly not during sex. It was a wonder he hadn't bolted out of the door at the sight of the first tear. In fact, it was kind of disturbing he hadn't. If this was purely sex, why was he still here?

Nate rolled over, the sheet falling lower to display that sexy 'V' of his torso leading to the danger zone. She dragged her eyes away with more discipline than she'd known she possessed. Good sex was like any other addiction—hard to resist when it could make your troubles fade away so easily and leave you feeling invincible. It was the side effects you had to watch out for. Emotional attachment had a way of sneaking into temporary 'fixes'.

She sneaked another peek at Sleeping Beauty, who was definitely beginning to stir beneath the covers. There was absolutely no chance of going cold turkey when she was going to be exposed to said addictive substance every day here. Only the sound of the front door opening stopped her from falling off the wagon before she'd even got on it and taking one last hit of that Nate Taylor good stuff.

'Cooee!' It was closely followed by the morning call of the lesser-spotted housekeeper.

Violet had forgotten the Taylors had more than one set of keys between them. They always rose with the larks to start their duties and let themselves in so as not to disturb the Earl before he was ready to wake. Apparently those same rules didn't apply to her. She wasn't used to having to answer to anyone except herself these days.

'It's only me!' Mrs Taylor called again, louder this time, as though she was getting closer.

There'd be no way of passing this off as anything casual if Nate's mother caught them in bed. They'd never hear the end of it. Although her father had begun to warm towards Nate, if he found out about this all hell would break loose.

'Wake up!' she whispered and shook her bed partner awake.

'Hmm?' His eyes fluttered open with a moan that almost made her care less about getting busted. Almost.

She scrabbled around the floor for her discarded clothes and hastily threw them on. She might think more clearly if she wasn't naked. Or lying next to Nate's impressive morning glory.

'Your mother's here.'

That woke him up and killed his libido quicker than a bucket of ice-cold water.

'What?' He bounced up, wide-eyed now and with that same look of panic he'd had when she'd once caught him skinny dipping in the lake. Unfortunately Violet hadn't had as clear a view of his assets then as she did now as he hopped around the room trying to get dressed.

'Violet? I wanted to make sure everything was all right. Have you seen Nathaniel this morning? I see his car's still parked outside—' Mrs Taylor voiced her concerns from somewhere on the stairs.

Nate muttered all the expletives running through Violet's head at the same time. The first rule of secret liaisons was to be discreet. History should have told them privacy wasn't an option around here.

'How the hell are we going to get out of this one?' He jammed his feet into his shoes, the muscles in his back flexing with tension. He'd always been a completely different person when he was around his parents than when he was with her. In this case his frustration was most likely directed at himself and her for letting this happen.

'I've got an idea. Stay here.'

He was so straight-shooting he might well stomp out and announce what they'd done to shock his mother and get her to back off. Violet didn't want them making this into a big deal simply because they'd been interrupted.

She stepped out of the room before he could grab her and tiptoed to the top of the stairs. 'Hello, Mrs Taylor. Nate stayed over in the west wing last night. It was late when we got back from the hospital and he'd left his car here. I thought it would be better for him to stay than drive home when he was so exhausted. I'll give him a call and perhaps you could make us something to eat in the meantime?' She hated using her position here to suit her agenda, the lies made her sick to the stomach, but in this instance she deemed them necessary, for everybody's sake.

'Of course, dear.' Mrs Taylor beamed, no doubt thrilled at the idea of resuming her duties to the family in the Earl's absence. Violet couldn't imagine one without the other any more, nor did she want to. The Taylors were part of Strachmore and would hopefully take the reins when she was no longer here.

Violet waited until Mrs Taylor scurried off towards the kitchen before she turned back. Nate was fully dressed now and standing by the door with a scowl to sour the milk his mother was probably pouring on their cornflakes. She suddenly found the need to justify her actions. After all, this was his family she was bossing about.

'I thought it would buy us some time.'

'Sure. There's nothing Mum loves more than playing the faithful servant. I guess I'll see you downstairs for breakfast in five.'

It was her turn to be dismissed and she didn't enjoy it one bit. The fairy tale was well and truly over and now they were back to that upstairs-downstairs divide that had always dominated their lives.

Nate doubted there was anything more cringeworthy than a post-coital breakfast with an ex and your mother. When had his life got so messy? Oh, yes, the second Violet Dempsey had walked back into it wearing skin-tight jeans and a worried smile.

'I'm so glad things went to plan with your father at the hospital. I hardly slept a wink last night.'

Nate declined a second cup of tea. He'd only agreed to this charade so his mother's suspicion was kept to a minimum and he wouldn't be expected to pay penance for defiling the Earl's daughter.

'Neither did I, Mrs Taylor.' Violet's reply was innocent enough for his mother's ears. To his, it was a reference to something definitely inappropriate for the breakfast table. Something that was now reminding him of everything they'd done last night instead of sleeping, in all its X-rated glory.

'Speaking of which, I'm going to have to nip home and change before I go into work and check on him.' He drained the last of his tea and took a big enough bite of toast to reassure his mother he'd eaten. Her fussing wasn't confined solely to the Dempseys' welfare but he didn't have to pay for the privilege.

It hadn't sat well with him when Violet had requested she make breakfast for them. Deep down he knew it had been a ploy to save their blushes, but it had succeeded in also reminding him of his place too in the scheme of things. Although he still couldn't quite believe they'd finally slept together, he wouldn't let his ego get too inflated. He was always going to be the son of the hired help, no matter how big his pay packet.

'Thanks for everything you did last night.' This time he knew she was deliberately trying to make mischief as she fixed him with those ever-darkening sapphire eyes.

She pursed her lips together to blow the steam from her china cup and Nate's mind immediately connected her actions to scenes of a sexual nature. He jumped up from the table, lucky it was only his knee banging against the table in the process.

'You're welcome. Any time.' They hadn't discussed what happened next with regard to this new development in their relationship, but something told him it was going to take a great deal of willpower to prevent it happening again. That something was going to require a long cold shower to get rid of.

At least she hadn't seen him off to work with a packed lunch and a kiss in that we've-slept-together-so-let's-set-the-wedding-date fashion some were fond of after one night in bed. He'd met enough of those to recognise the hope of commitment even with a promise of none. He should be happy Violet didn't have it, not lingering on his Dempsey-induced inferiority complex. It left the bedroom door open for another casual hook-up with no expectations beyond those four walls. If she was agreeable, continuing the more physical side of their relationship for the time she had left at Strachmore could be the ideal way to work out their residual issues and finally get closure.

Today's status update: *Lover*.

* * *

It had all but killed Violet sitting so close to Nate this morning, pretending they hadn't spent the entire night getting to know each other more intimately than ever before. While they'd swapped their private thoughts and feelings in their younger days, it was nothing compared to what they'd shared together in bed. Sex with Nate had been the only positive experience she'd had since coming home, and the most fun.

She didn't know what new discoveries she'd make regarding her father from one day to the next but so far they'd all taken an emotional toll. Her time with Nate had been cathartic, a chance to wind down and remember how it was to be a young, carefree woman. She could do with more of that. More of him.

His mother's interruption this morning had prevented them from analysing their actions and discussing where they went from here. With her body still zinging from their tryst, she hoped he was on the same page she was as far as letting this thing run its course. The only commitment she'd intended making was to her job back in London with a phone call today.

Although her father's altered attitude was a revelation, she'd discovered for herself it hadn't made him Dad of the Year overnight. His old, grouchy self was very much alive and kicking when she'd been to see him this morning. She'd left him talking to the rehabilitation team and come back to make a start on making Strachmore accessible to the public in the hope he'd agree to give the idea a chance. The first step was a deep clean of the areas she thought might appeal to history buffs. Mrs Taylor ensured the main house was spick and span but it had been some time since anyone had paid any attention to the old servant quarters.

This part of the house where her ancestors had housed their domestic staff had always intrigued her and she'd used it as a hiding place at times, safe in the knowledge her parents would never venture there. The major flaw in the architecture here was the lack of ventilation. She stripped off the denim shirt she'd found in her closet so she was cooler in her strappy white singlet as she worked, moving from room to room with her duster and mop.

It was like being in a time warp once you set foot on those stone steps. The period pieces of furniture and personal effects left from days gone by were still in good condition under their thick layer of dust. From the huge wooden table in the servant hall where the staff would've congregated for their meals, to the sparsely furnished bedrooms, they'd all played an important part in Strachmore's history.

She was cleaning down the worktops in the room where the butler used to polish the household's shoes and boots when she thought she heard footsteps. The idea of seeing past residents had never frightened her, but she held her breath as the steps grew closer and louder.

'Thank goodness, it's you.' She let out a relieved sigh when Nate stepped into view, but her heart didn't beat any slower. He was the quintessential gentleman today, again dressed in his dapper charcoal-grey fitted waistcoat and trousers. Although, she preferred him wearing only a sheet. Or not.

'Everyone seems so happy to see me today. It makes a

change. Even your father managed to be civil.' He joined her in the small space, stealing more of her oxygen.

She bustled away to the farthest side of the room to clean the sink so she could breathe again. 'You saw my father?'

'I did. I can't lie and say trying to discuss treatment was a fertile exercise, but he has agreed to see a grief counsellor.' He skirted around the leather-covered bench in the centre of the room to come towards her.

She scrubbed the sink a little harder and tried to avoid his gaze. Her morning had been productive but less than glamorous. If she was to convince him another tumble in the sheets was a good idea she wasn't going to do it covered in dirt and sweat.

'That's great. I really appreciate you doing that for him. It will help him move on.' And her, if they could start some dialogue over what had happened to her mother without blaming each other.

'I really do think he's beginning to soften, though, and it shouldn't be too long before you can persuade him about the benefits of Project Wedding Venue.' He slipped his hands around her waist and made her drop her scrubbing brush.

Was he simply more tactile because he was celebrating their future liberation from Strachmore, or making a move? She wasn't sure if her now supercharged libido was interpreting his actions to suit her needs.

'I…uh…can't wait. That's partly why I'm down here. I thought if we got this cleaned up we could do house tours to break us in gently.'

'You are rocking this domestic goddess thing you've got going on.'

Her mouth was dry now and it wasn't down to the dusty atmosphere. He was nuzzling her neck, holding her tight and giving her the unmistakable sign now that he was interested in picking up from where they'd left off last night. Every step she took with Nate, as much as she wanted it, was also a test of her courage. It was a step further from her comfort zone, and one closer to keeping her here.

'There's so much to do to get the place ready. The paint's peeling everywhere, it'll all need to be redone. Then there's the structural repairs if we don't want to be sued by people getting hit by pieces of loose masonry.' All things that could be remedied easily but suddenly seemed so important to excuse her current state.

'Don't worry—I'll help. We'll all chip in when and where we can while we're waiting for approval from up above.' He spun her around to face him and she forgot why she cared so much about her appearance when he so clearly appreciated it.

He was kissing her neck, grazing her earlobe with his teeth and generally turning her into a puddle of hormones.

'I didn't think I'd see you today. I thought you'd be busy with work.' She was sure he'd be able to feel her pulse throbbing violently beneath his lips.

'I've no patients scheduled for the next few hours. I thought we could take the time to discuss our new *arrangement*.' He dropped a feather-light kiss on her lips.

'What's that?' Violet was burning so hot for him all these wooden fixtures and fittings were becoming a serious fire hazard, but she wasn't going to be the one to make the rules. After the way things had ended the last time between them she wanted this to be his call.

'We had such a good time last night, I don't see any reason to keep us from doing it again. I'd go as far to say we should do it every night before you leave.'

Before you leave. They were the crucial words she wanted to hear. That way there was no room for misunderstandings when her time here was done.

'Every night, huh?'

'Maybe every day too if we feel the need.' He would definitely have the need for her in his arms, night and day, now he'd established a clear time frame. His commitment would end the minute she was on a flight back to London and that was an even bigger aphrodisiac than seeing Violet get her hands dirty.

He'd spent the morning flitting between arousal and annoyance every time he'd thought about last night and this morning. So much so he'd been in danger of becoming distracted. For the sake of his patients, and his sanity, he'd needed to come and see her here. He hadn't known what action he should take regarding their tryst, whether it was better to draw a line under it or repeat it. One look at Violet had made it a no-brainer. Literally. That wasn't the part of his body doing his thinking any more.

'It might make my time here more bearable, I suppose...' She was teasing him now. He could see through that flimsy shirt she was as turned on as he was.

'I think I'll make that my new tagline on my business cards. Dr Nathaniel Taylor—making life more bearable for over thirty years.' He hadn't come here with sex on his mind, only a desire to see her, but the time limit they'd just set meant he didn't want to waste any more time talking.

He planted his lips on Violet's with an urgency he'd never felt with anyone but her. It was an all-consuming need to be part of her, have her be part of him, which he could indulge now he knew there'd be no consequences or regret.

They were a flurry of hands and clothes as they tore at each other's clothes. The waistcoat had been a spur-of-the-moment decision this morning, one he was now cursing for its many, many buttons.

'Sod it.' He tore it open, the damnable buttons pinging around the room in the process.

'Shouldn't it be my clothes you're tearing off?' Violet helped him undo those of his shirt in double-quick time so he was topless, and halfway to where he wanted to be.

'Don't worry, you're next.' He whipped off her shirt in one swift move to find she'd gone commando, her perky breasts greeting him without restraint.

Violet writhed beneath him as he buried his head in her cleavage, revelling in her softness. She was opening his belt, unzipping his fly and letting his trousers pool around his feet. When she gripped his erection in her surprisingly strong hand he had to grab hold of the bench behind him before the instant rush of blood from his head caused him to black out. When she knelt and took him in her mouth there were fireworks in the darkness behind his eyelids.

With her hands gripping his hips, his hands pulling her hair, she took him to the edge of oblivion and back time and time again.

'Come here.' He urged her up beside him to make

this afternoon delight last longer than he was currently anticipating. She kicked off her own jeans and underwear and pressed her naked form against his fevered flesh.

'You know, we're not the first people to make out in here. Rumour has it this was the favourite spot for one of the most notorious butlers who worked here. He had a reputation for seducing the kitchen maids and he carved his initials wherever he made his conquests. They're all over the house. See?' She traced her finger over a set of initials scratched into the leather-covered bench.

He could see where this was going. 'You got a penknife on you?'

'There's an old kitchen knife on the window sill.'

He hurriedly carved a crude NT into the wooden cabinets on the wall. 'Now we're making history too.'

'There? Really?'

He pulled her over beside him. 'Well, the randy butler's already claimed the bench and we've done the furniture thing already...'

As much fun as it was marking his territory, he wanted to finish what they'd started. He braced himself against the cupboard doors, caging Violet against the cupboards. His beautiful sex monkey hooked herself around him, permitting their bodies to forge together with ease.

They were so in tune with each other she met his every thrust, kept pace with him until they reached that glorious peak together. Their combined cries of ecstasy were loud enough to wake the dead and Nate was glad they were far enough from the main house to be heard. He didn't often get carried away in such a fashion where anyone, including his mother, could catch him *in flagrante*. His reputation was his livelihood but when he was with Violet nothing else seemed to matter. A dangerous game to play in real life but thankfully this was nothing more than a holiday fling, giving them the excuse to take a walk on the wild side for a week or two.

Once they got their breath back and their clothes back on, Violet returned to the scene of the crime to inspect the graffiti.

'He must've had a lot of fun during his time here. I've seen these initials in the wine cellar, the laundry room and the stone archway at the back of the house.' She studied the carving, lost in thought, as though she somehow envied the freedom of a paid servant.

Nate didn't want her to relate this moment between them to feelings of regret when that was the very thing they were trying to avoid.

'I reckon we could give the horny butler a run for his money. Let's set ourselves a challenge to reclaim every nook and cranny where he's made his mark with one of our own. It shouldn't be Strachmore subordinates only who get to have all the fun. I think it's time the lady of the house got to play too.'

This became more like an illicit romance between servant and mistress with every clandestine meeting in the big house. He could live with that as long as they kept treating this as an exciting fling with a definite deadline. There was no better way to do that than to make love in every room of the house, erasing every bad memory associated with the place in the process. It was therapy on an enjoyable level for both parties, ensuring they chased the pain away with lots of plea-sure. A way of closing out the past and opening up their hearts for the future. One that couldn't include each other.

CHAPTER EIGHT

VIOLET DIDN'T KNOW much about *BH* but he'd certainly been a busy boy and *NT* had been doing his best to rival him. Of course, they'd been discreet in recording their exploits for posterity, careful not to vandalise valuable historical artefacts, and they'd had fun along the way. In all, these last two weeks exploring, and supposedly renovating, the forgotten rooms at Strachmore had been some of the best days of her life.

Her father was growing stronger every day, thanks to his work with the physiotherapists and Mrs Taylor's close attention to his diet. Violet had made it clear she'd be returning to her job at the end of the month and that had been sufficient to prompt him into sitting down with her and Nate to discuss the ideas they had to make the estate self-sufficient. He'd eventually agreed in principle to their suggestions and put his signature to the required paperwork for now.

Nate's cool, calm explanation of the proposed changes and the expected benefits had been a crucial part of negotiations. Having him as a third party helped prevent a lot of the emotional obstacles from getting in the way. In the end her father had even offered to sell a few of the paintings he had in storage so she could hire an events manager and whoever else it took to make this thing work in her absence. She might even come home every now and then, now there were a few more attractions, and a few places still left for *NT* to conquer.

There hadn't been a conversation between her and Nate about the possibility of her coming back, or reconnecting if she did. It didn't seem such a stretch to carry on with what they had going on. She wouldn't be a permanent fixture in his life, expecting any more than she did now—great sex. It would be a shame to end things completely when they were having such a good time together. Spending more time with Nate would give her something to look forward to other than TV and pizza at the end of the working week.

She watched him now, schmoozing with the wedding party and the photographer in the grounds, and listened in fascination as he recounted her family's history to the bride and groom. Despite his resistance, he was as much a part of Strachmore as she was. More than ever given their recent antics. She couldn't imagine coming home and not seeing him here.

He waved her over, not ready to leave his post as today's host just yet. The bride and groom were his colleagues from the hospital here to use Strachmore as the backdrop for their wedding photographs. It was a favour both to his friends, and Violet. They got free use of the grounds and it was the first step to gently break her father into the idea of sharing his family home with strangers.

Violet watched the newly-weds smiling for the camera capturing their love for eternity. She wanted to be sick.

'I'd be crying too if I'd been condemned to a life of misery.' She sidled up to Nate, making sure she was out of earshot of the over-emotional couple now dabbing their eyes and hugging. She didn't want to ruin their day but marriage had a lot to do with the misery that had surrounded her ancestral home for so long. Her father's confession of his love for her mother had only served to confuse her views on matrimony further. It had all seemed so black and white when she'd thought her mother's love for her father had never been recip-rocated and had cost her her life. The fear of giving everything and receiving nothing in return had kept Violet from falling into that marriage trap.

Now she knew how much her father had loved her and how lost he was without her, it made her question if refusing to admit your feelings was equally destruc-tive. Apparently once love had you in its clutches it was game over, either way, and no amount of pretending or running could prevent it.

'Not a fan of the bride, or the groom?' Nate cocked his head at her as though she were some anomaly of nature for not getting sentimental over the proceedings.

'Marriage in general. You saw what it did to my family. It's all flowers and romance now but she's prob-ably given up all her hopes and dreams to play wifey.' She clung on to that belief her mother had been the only casualty in the marriage—the only one with feel-ings to consider. The alternative was to admit both of her parents had been at fault and their marriage had been a partnership rather than a dictatorship, with each of them responsible for their own actions. That idea of free will, even as part of a couple, called into question every excuse Violet had ever made for being on her own.

'It's not the eighteen hundreds any more, you know. Women get married, have children and still work if they choose.' He was being surprisingly pro-commitment for someone who'd taken great care to make sure they didn't have one.

Violet's stomach flip-flopped. Perhaps it was only her he didn't want around long-term. She hadn't contemplated having to see him with someone else any time she came home, someone he might want to settle down with.

'You didn't strike me as the marrying kind.' At least not since they were teenage sweethearts when the intensity of his feelings for her, and hers for him, had sent her running.

'I'm not. It seems to work for some people, though. My parents would be an example of that, I guess. For the record, I have no problem with the honeymoon part. It's being tied down I take issue with.' Nate confirmed his place alongside Violet on the dark side, enabling her to breathe a little easier.

'I don't know who's in your little black book but I'm sure you could find someone who *isn't* into bondage.' Not that she was encouraging him to start hooking up with anyone else. She'd prefer he did that when she was long gone. If he really had to.

Nate snorted. '*That* I can handle. It's this notion that love can solve problems that galls me when, ultimately, it only creates more. All this nonsense is fine for sentimental types whose only aspirations in life are a semi-detached house and two-point-four children but you're right, some of us have bigger dreams.'

She should've been relieved to hear his matrimonial views were in sync with her own but hearing he was as cynical as she was chilled her insides. He was so changed in his views since a teen and she knew she'd been the cause. She must have hurt him more than he ever would admit. Her selfish actions might well have cost him the happy family she'd always thought he'd deserved. The Dempsey curse had struck again.

For a split second she'd zoned out, light-headed and unsteady in her high heels. Her conscience had clearly taken news of his commitment phobia badly, manifesting her guilt physically. They moved with the wedding party through the gardens and she slipped off to take a seat on the carved stone bench under the eucalyptus tree. She stripped a couple of the long blue-green leaves and crushed them in her fingers. The smell of menthol and pine instantly filled the air. She took a deep breath, hoping it would help quell her rolling stomach.

It was coming up to that time of the month too, which probably wasn't helping this feeling of nausea. She did a quick mental calculation—she'd been here for three weeks, her last period had been before she'd taken time off work… She frowned. That couldn't be right. She was as regular as clockwork, every four weeks. Her calculations made it more than five. She did another tot-up of the dates. It was still longer than she'd ever gone. It had to be down to the stress.

Another cramp doubled her over, surely a clear sign all was as it should be. What was the alternative? She hadn't eaten anything other than Mrs Taylor's nutritious meals, same as her father, so it wasn't food poisoning. That left one glaring possibility. She couldn't be pregnant, she just couldn't.

Nate chose that moment to come and sit beside her. 'Are you okay? You look a little pale.'

He put his hand on her forehead, her skin suddenly clammy now. Her own health hadn't been of any significance when her father had been so critical. Now it meant everything. With horror she recalled the fraught night waiting for news of her father and that whole debacle with Nate at the house. Her routine had gone completely out of the window and she'd been a day late taking her pill. In the circumstances she hadn't thought in a million years she would have to take extra precautions. Sex with Nate had never seemed an option. Her recklessness had apparently come at a price after all.

How would she ever make her escape from Strachmore now if she was pregnant? She didn't have the support in London needed to look after a baby and work at the same time and she certainly wouldn't be able to afford childcare on her wages. Nate hadn't asked for this either, when she'd promised him this would be nothing more than a fling. She couldn't expect him to take two of them on when he'd made it clear he didn't even want a plus one. Hell, she didn't even want one.

Parenthood had never been in her future plans. It had been too much for her mother to cope with and not enough for her to stick around. Violet didn't want that level of change, or responsibility, causing chaos in the new life she'd made for herself. Her quiet, organised life, where loving anyone except herself was simply out of the question. It was part of the reason she'd been keen to get back to it, knowing she'd be safe from her feelings for Nate there. Now she was in double trouble.

All she could do was throw herself at her father's mercy now, if the worst had indeed happened, and beg him to take in his pregnant, unmarried daughter. Her life was never going to be the same.

'I think I'm gonna be sick.'

Nate had tried to go after Violet when she'd taken suddenly ill, but she'd shooed him back to the wedding party, insisting someone should be taking an active role in the day's events. He'd had no option but to return to the gathered guests when Strachmore's reputation would soon depend on good word of mouth. Someone had to escort them around the grounds and smile in all the right places. Even if he had been desperate to go check on her.

He'd spent most of his waking moments outside work with her these past weeks, and all of his sleeping ones too. If there was something wrong he wanted to be with her, looking after her the way he always did. He guessed that sense of duty towards the Dempseys was simply born into him. That was the only acceptable explanation for why he cared so much.

Once he'd seen the wedding party off to continue their celebrations elsewhere, he sprinted back to the house. He bounded up the stairs calling her name but she didn't answer. Eventually he found her in her bedroom, changed out of the dress she'd bought specially for today back into her casual jeans and grey hoodie. She seemed even paler now she'd removed her makeup, looking lost perched on the end of her princess bed. He was sorry he'd left her alone for so long.

When he saw her suitcase lying open on the bed, clothes strewn all around, he went into full panic mode.

'What's wrong? Is it that bad? Do you need me to take you to the hospital?'

'I'm fine. Actually, I'm not. I'm far from it but I don't need to go to the hospital. I need to go home.'

She wasn't making any sense and was starting to freak him out.

He knelt on the floor and took her hand. If he'd known she'd react so strongly against the idea of marriage he'd never have suggested bringing his friends here. Her commitment issues were clearly greater than his. In a moment of sentimentality he'd even contemplated how Violet would have looked in a wedding dress. Beautiful and elegant as always, he supposed. If she hadn't run away, breaking his heart, or he'd been enough for her to contemplate staying, they might have had this one day for themselves. It was a shame their parents' actions had skewed their view on marriage for ever when people like his co-workers today seemed to find their happiness in it.

'You don't need to go anywhere. The condemned couple has left the building. We are officially bridal-party free. If it's an allergy to weddings you have, perhaps we can go hang out in the divorce courts to counteract the toxins.' Usually his naff jokes were enough to make her smile, but not today.

'It's not that. Thank you for setting that up today,— they really seemed to enjoy it. It's just…it's just… I can't do this.' She dropped her head into her hands and sobbed her heart out.

This was it—she was going to run again before he was ready to accept it was over. He was supposed to have two more weeks with her. Now she was cutting their time together short he was left with that same sick, empty feeling inside as before. He needed some warning before he was back to his 'work, eat, sleep' routine with none of the fun in between and no one to come home to at the end of the day.

'Do you need me to get you anything?'

'A pregnancy test?' Violet gave a forced laugh, but there was nothing funny about it.

'Don't joke about something like that.'

'I'm not. I'm late.'

Nate dropped her hand to steady himself before he fell over. This couldn't be happening. 'But you're on the pill, right?'

'I think I missed one the night I flew in from London.' Her grimace sucker-punched him in the gut.

'You've been under a lot of stress too though.' He slowly got to his feet, still trying to come up with alternative theories. Ones that wouldn't tie them together for the rest of their days.

'I've been queasy and light-headed today. We both know if there's a possibility the worst could happen, it will. I should have known things were going too well.' The tears started again and it was obvious she didn't want this any more than he did. Neither of them had signed on for parenthood; they hadn't even been able to commit to each other for longer than a month, for heaven's sake.

'We'll get through this. Somehow.' The sickness was spreading to him now, his stomach twisting into a tight knot of anxiety.

A baby, their baby, was going to affect so many—him, Violet, his parents, the Earl... Nobody was going to take the news well. Why should they? He'd messed up big style. He should've taken extra precautions to prevent this happening, but he'd been too lost in his own desires to consider the consequences. Now he'd ruined Violet's future, the one she'd worked so hard to ensure didn't include him.

'I don't expect you to take this on. That's why I'm leaving. This was my mistake. I'll deal with it on my own.' She wouldn't look at him and turned her attention back to throwing her clothes haphazardly into her case.

A vice gripped his heart and squeezed. If there *was* a baby he wanted to be part of its life, wanted to be included in any decisions concerning *their* child. He didn't want Violet to deal with this on her own, regardless of how she did or didn't feel about him. A child needed two supportive parents to have the best possible start in life. To make sure it wouldn't ever feel abandoned, as he had when he'd attempted to improve his lot in life.

'Let's not jump too far ahead of ourselves. First things first—we get a test.' If their lives were about to change for ever they should really find out for sure. The delay would also give him a chance to figure out how to get her to stay. Indefinitely.

The sight of Violet packing to leave had crushed him almost as much as finding her room empty had when she'd first gone to London without an explanation. This was much, much worse. That had been puppy love, a childish infatuation. Now he knew how powerful real love was. The kind that was ripping him apart from the inside out at the thought of her leaving again. She was taking an even bigger part of him with her this time. Literally.

This baby might not have been planned but that didn't mean he didn't want it or wouldn't take responsibility for it. All of those steps he'd taken to avoid emotional attachments had led to the biggest one of all—fatherhood. He got chills every time he thought about it. Twelve years ago this would've been everything he'd wanted. Violet's rejection had changed all that, clouded his view on relationships even more. He'd dodged commitment as if it were some deadly disease when all along he'd still been devoted to Violet. She was the only woman he'd ever imagined spending his life with. Still was.

Unfortunately, the last time he'd confessed his feelings for her she'd skipped the country. He doubted ruining her life with an unplanned pregnancy was going to do anything to improve his chances of her loving him back. She'd only just begun making progress with her father and this news could set them back at loggerheads. Nate knew the Earl's reputation was everything to him and he would never want to sully Violet's name because of his selfish mistake.

The journey in the car to the chemist for the pregnancy test had given him the space and clarity to decide what to do.

'Marry me, Violet.' He loved her. No matter how much he tried to deny it, in the midst of this chaos, the strength of his feelings for her were abundantly clear. Until now he'd refused to admit it and run the risk of repeating the past. Although he'd never be the great love of her life he'd hoped to be, he'd always supported her. He'd always been afraid of marriage but now it seemed the best solution for all three of them. They needed each other.

'Don't be stupid.' A marriage proposal wasn't help-ing her dizziness as she glared at Nate and back at the screen. She knew it was a knee-jerk reaction to the reading when he'd told her what an awful idea he thought marriage was only hours ago. He didn't love her and she doubted he'd even entertained spending the rest of his days with her until they'd sat on the edge of her bed watching the digital screen spell out their future.

Pregnant
2-3

There was no mistaking her symptoms now, the damage apparently done at the beginning of their sup-posed fun fling. She gave a strangled laugh. It was ei-ther see the irony of that or start crying again.

'I mean it. This baby needs a father and I know how you feel about marriage but you need a husband. Hear me out—' He put a hand up to stop her as she bristled. 'It can be in name only, or you know we can keep the physical side going since we've both enjoyed it. What I'm saying is, love doesn't have to enter the equation. I don't expect it to. But I have a house you and the baby can live in, I can provide for you, and your reputation remains intact.' He looked so pleased with himself as he shredded her heart into tiny irreparable pieces.

The man she'd apparently never stopped loving, the father of her unborn child, was offering her a marriage of convenience. It somehow seemed worse than the ar-ranged marriages her father had proposed to maintain his social status. Probably because she knew she was in love with Nate and she'd ruined her chances of him ever feeling the same way about her. It was the reason she'd made certain she would leave the country again for London, a place she'd hoped to be able to forget him. Now she would have a permanent reminder.

Nate would always do the right thing, that was who he was, and it was the only reason he *would* want to marry her. She'd wreaked havoc in his life once too often and it wasn't fair to lumber him with a wife and child he'd never wanted. Neither did she want to give up her job to fake a happy marriage, following in her mother's tragic footsteps after all.

In an ideal world her baby would have two doting parents, madly in love with each other, providing the happy, family environment she'd never had. Marrying Nate would simply be perpetuating that myth that money and good name were all that mattered. She would rather raise this baby alone than with a father who was only there out of a sense of duty. The next generation of Dempseys deserved more after the trouble she'd caused to emancipate herself from society rules in the first place.

'It wouldn't work, Nate. We'd only end up making each other miserable. Marriage isn't for us. It's for people who love each other and are willing to give up everything to be together. Forget about me, forget about the baby, and just pretend I never came back. That this never happened.'

The vertigo was back, her head spinning with snapshots of these weeks they'd spent together and memories of her parents' tumultuous relationship. Neither of them should have to compromise who they were simply because they'd made a mistake. In her case, it was falling in love with a man who could never love her back after everything she'd done to him.

'That's impossible.' Nate rested his hand gently on her stomach, staking a claim on the life growing inside her.

She slapped it away. It would be easier for him to walk away now before this was about more than a bunch of cells. 'Not if I'm in a different country. I don't want you in my life, Nate. That wasn't the deal.'

She was shaking with nerves as the lie left her lips, hoping he couldn't see through it, or if he did he'd realise this was her way of letting him off the hook. She wanted Nate in her life more than anything but not through a sense of responsibility. This was her way of trying to protect him, sacrificing her desires again and putting him first before her own needs. No matter how much it hurt.

Violet had taken a sledgehammer to what was left of his heart and pounded it until it was nothing but a big red stain he would never be able to scrub away. He was willing to give himself to her body and soul, something he'd never thought he would do, something he'd never imagined he would *want* to do. Everything he had worked to achieve seemed to have been building up to this moment and asking Violet to share it with him and their baby. Yet, she still didn't want him. The house, the job, the car—none of it was enough to convince her to be with him. None of it seemed to matter without her.

'I know this wasn't what either of us had planned but I'm simply trying to make the best of the situation.' He was doing his damnedest not to get too emotional and make her even more skittish than she was. She didn't respond well to intense personal discussion, as he'd found out to his cost. Her default setting was to run and hide rather than confront the truth; he'd seen it so many times before. She'd disappeared for twelve years after one kiss between them and he knew if she went back this time he'd lose her for ever.

'I just want you to go, Nate.' She sounded tired, resigned to life as a single parent already and he was being forced into the role of absent father. He didn't want to make things even more difficult for Violet than they already were by arguing with her, even though he was dying inside with every push further away. Neither could he, in good conscience, simply walk away after getting her into this condition in the first place.

He wanted to be there as she blossomed during her pregnancy, see their baby on the screen as it happened, not in some grainy printout he'd been sent as an afterthought. That role of a supportive father was important to him. It was something neither of them had really had growing up. Violet's father had been more concerned with his place in society than her feelings and Nate's parents' priority had always been Strachmore.

His childhood hadn't been carefree either, but an endless round of chores and lectures on being respectful. He'd practically had to make himself invisible so as not to offend the Earl. That wasn't conducive to making a child feel wanted or loved. More like an unpaid, unappreciated skivvy. Perhaps if they'd both been accepted for who they were by their own families they wouldn't have the problems they had connecting now.

If Violet didn't want him in her life there wasn't much he could do, but he had to at least try to be a

part of their child's. That wasn't going to work long
distance and he was willing to make sacrifices to get
her to stay if it prevented their baby becoming another
statistic of a broken relationship.

'I'll go and I promise not to come back unless you
want me to. On the condition you stay at Strachmore
until you're due back at work. I want you to be one hundred per cent sure that this is what you want.' His feet
were blocks of wood, heavy and clumsy, as he reluctantly made his way to the door. He'd thought knowing
she was leaving would be easier than finding out after
she'd gone. He was wrong. However, whenever it happened, Violet walking out of his life was always going
to be the worst thing that would ever happen to him.

'I am.' She threw one last knife into his back and
killed the last dregs of hope stone dead.

CHAPTER NINE

'I'M SURE IT won't be much longer now.' Violet tried to pacify her father, who'd already picked up and set down the one magazine sitting on the waiting-room table. She understood how difficult it was to manage time when dealing with emotional patients, but she also knew how much of a short fuse her father had when he was kept waiting for an appointment. Especially when grief counselling wasn't something he was totally on board with.

He checked the clock again and gave a huff but at least nothing had been thrown in the interim. It was progress but she was still tense sitting here in the hospital with him. Her heart picked up the pace again as the thought of bumping into Nate came to mind. It had been over a week since she'd seen him at the house. He'd kept to his word to stay away as she'd known he would, enabling her to spend her last few days at Strachmore trying to figure out her next move.

'I haven't seen Nathaniel for a while. Did something happen between you two?' Her father picked up on the very subject matter making her unhappy.

Although she was glad he'd chosen conversation over berating the staff to fill the time, every time she thought of telling him about the baby her heart fluttered in her chest and she felt as though she might pass out.

'He's a busy man and we've probably taken up too much of his time at Strachmore.' She had no wish to take up any more of it by making him pay for her mistake. Whether she stayed at home or went back to London, she had to plan the rest of her life without him in it. The thought alone made her light-headed.

'I'm not blind, Violet, nor am I stupid. That boy has been in love with you for years and vice versa, unless I'm very much mistaken. He's hardly been away from Strachmore these past weeks and I doubt that's solely because of me. Now, he's suddenly incommunicado. Something clearly happened between the two of you and, whatever it is, I don't want it to affect your decisions about coming home in the future. I know I drove you away in the past but I really want you to at least visit.'

It was a huge step for him to admit his past behaviour towards her and let her know he wanted her to be part of his life again but, oh, how she wished he were right about Nate's feelings for her. He might have been in love with her when they were kids but time and distance, not to mention her actions, had changed that. She fidgeted with the sleeve of her shirt, knowing she in turn should be honest with him, regardless of how petrified she was at the prospect of having to tell him she was pregnant. He might have mellowed slightly since his heart attack and subsequent procedures but that didn't mean his principles had changed.

The Earl's daughter was pregnant by the son of the housekeeper and it didn't get much more scandalous than that when it came to society gossip. This would be a real test of his priorities but she couldn't put it off much longer. Her condition would soon become apparent if she did come back in the future. It wouldn't be fair on her father to disappear again without telling him why.

She took a deep breath. And another. 'I'm pregnant.'

She braced herself for the backlash—shouting, screaming, crashing furniture—all of his typical reactions to such news would be justified this time. Most of them she'd done herself since sending Nate away.

'And he's not stepping up to his responsibilities?' Only when he'd jumped to the wrong conclusion did his face take on that red hue of impending rage.

'No. It's not that…he even offered to marry me.' She was quick to defend Nate; he'd done everything right. Except love her.

'What's the problem, then?'

'I don't want to get married because it's the right thing to do. I'm sorry, but I'd rather be on my own than in a cold marriage put on for appearances' sake.' Her reasons for turning Nate down might seem a tad insensitive in light of the present situation but it was the truth. Perhaps if there'd been a bit more of that between her parents, or between her and Nate, things could've turned out much differently. If she'd been honest with him about the strength of her feelings for him in the first place they might've actually stood a chance together.

Her father's frown turned into a half-smile. 'Marriage always was your sticking point. That doesn't mean you can't still be together. Times have changed, so you keep telling me.'

She was surprised he'd paid any heed to her word against that of his ingrained sense of tradition. An illegitimate child would have devastated him not so long ago but he was clearly working hard on keeping their relationship alive.

'I can't be with someone who doesn't love me. It wouldn't be fair on me, or the baby.' She rubbed her hand over her still flat-belly, wishing only happiness for the life growing inside her.

'I don't believe that for one minute. Only a man in love would put up with your irritable father and do everything he has to secure Strachmore's future. I think it's *you* who doesn't want to commit.'

'Well, he's never said it,' she huffed, upset at the accusation she was the one at fault here. As far as she was concerned she'd done everything right to ensure Nate had been treated fairly. Not many women would've given him the green light to walk away. Especially when they were head over heels about him and carrying his child.

'Have *you*? You know, if I could change things I'd make sure your mother and I had really talked about how we felt. I'd make damn sure I listened. Don't throw something special away because you're scared to face the truth. You'll spend the rest of your life regretting it.' His teary blue eyes were a reflection of her own but she feared they'd both left it too late. She'd pushed Nate away, said some horrible things to ensure he'd stay out of her life. Unfortunately, given his silence since, she seemed to have succeeded in her quest.

'You're not mad at me? About the baby?' She was going to need at least one person to be there holding her hand when this bundle of trouble arrived and turned everything upside down. If she had her father's support it would ease some of her stress and help her enjoy this pregnancy more. So far it had been all tension and sickness and she was still waiting for the so-called blossoming to start.

He sighed.

'It's not what I wanted for you but it's not the end of the world. I just want you to be happy.' He reached over and gave her hand a squeeze, the only loving gesture she could ever remember getting from him. She cursed her hormones as the tears tipped over the edge of her lashes. She wasn't sure she'd ever be truly happy again.

'Lord Dempsey?' The receptionist called him for his appointment, drawing them both out of their heart-to-heart and on their feet.

'Whoa.' Violet had to sit down again as all the blood in her body seemed to rush to her head at once.

The receptionist rushed over to check on her. 'Are you all right?'

'She's pregnant,' her father answered for her, rubbing her back, already playing the role of protective grandfather.

'Just a little dizzy. My heart's racing a little but that's been happening a lot recently.' She didn't want to make a fuss and somehow have Nate get wind of it, but she was a bit breathless and seriously feeling as if she was about to faint.

'At least you're in the right place. I'll put in a call and get them to check you out in A and E.'

Violet could only nod as she struggled to stay conscious.

It wasn't long before she found herself stretched out on a bed with electrodes stuck all over her body, hooked up to an ECG machine. They'd gone over her medical history, and taken blood samples. She didn't know what they were expecting to find but the longer she lay here worrying what was happening, the faster her heart rate seemed to get. It was beating so hard she could easily have just finished running a marathon rather than simply have had an intense conversation with her father. She rested her hands on her invisible bump. It was still early days into her pregnancy and she was trying not to freak out about the fact she was already in hospital.

The doctor studied the printout of her test with a frown, which wasn't helping her relax at all. 'Your heart rate is higher than we would like. At the minute it's beating so fast the heart muscle can't relax between contractions and the lack of oxygen is what's causing the dizzy spells.'

'Will it harm the baby?' That was all that mattered right now. She mightn't have planned on this baby but neither did she want anything to happen to it. It was all she had left of Nate now.

He shook his head. 'There's nothing to worry about. We do want to send you to CCU, though, so they can keep a close eye on you during treatment.'

If she didn't laugh at the irony she'd cry. It was the one department in the building she was virtually guaranteed to see the man she'd been trying to avoid. There was no way her baby daddy was going to remain a silent partner once she and junior rocked up on his turf. He was going to have plenty to say about looking after herself and his child. Fate was going to make sure they had one last showdown before she left for London this time.

London. It had been her salvation, her road to independence, but now going back to her empty apartment felt like a punishment for her mistake. She had family here, and friends. And Nate. All she had in London was her job. She'd been so busy building walls to protect her heart she'd isolated herself emotionally and physically from anyone who'd tried to get close. It wasn't the ideal set-up for a woman raising a child on her own. What if there were any more complications during the pregnancy? She had no one to lean on there because that was the way she'd wanted it. Impending motherhood had since changed her views on complete independence.

These past weeks had reminded her how good it felt to have companionship, to be loved, to be *in* love. Even having her father waiting patiently outside for news she and the baby were safe was a turning point in their relationship, an insight into the family life she could have had here. Returning to a one-bedroom flat, pregnant and broken-hearted, wasn't something she was looking forward to. She was going to miss Strachmore and everyone associated with it.

Nate was on his way to do the rounds on the coronary care unit, having just finished fitting a pacemaker for one of his patients. It was best to keep busy to stop him from running up to Strachmore to see if Violet was still there. He'd given her his word he wouldn't go near her to give her space to think, but the distinct lack of communication indicated his plan to get her to stick around had backfired. As she'd told him in no uncertain terms, she didn't want, or need, him in her life. He didn't even know if she was still in the country. This time he wasn't simply going to accept her decision. He would follow her to London if it meant he could at least see their child grow and flourish. Without Violet and the baby here he wasn't sure what was keeping him here anyway. The house he'd been so proud of owning now seemed too big for a single man, too empty. The rooms should be full of toys and plans for the future, not a reminder of everything he'd lost. He didn't know how he was ever going to get over her this time, knowing what they could have...*should* have had together. Too bad his peasant status had let him down again. It was a stigma he would never be able to overcome to become worthy of the Earl's daughter. Or perhaps he'd simply have to face the fact that she'd never loved him anyway and he'd been the one using his upbringing as an excuse. Either way she didn't want him, and he was lost without her.

If only it were as easy to fix his broken heart as those of his patients. He'd gladly volunteer as a guinea pig for any new research looking into replacing emotionally battered hearts if it meant an end to this misery. He hadn't even been able to share the pain of losing the woman he loved and his baby when no one had known they'd existed, including his family. This was only supposed to have been a meaningless fling; there'd been no reason to broadcast the fact they were together. He'd had no way of knowing this would change him for ever. Somehow he was going to have to break the news to his parents they were soon to become grandparents and they might never see their first, and possibly only, grandchild.

Thoughts of Violet and the baby had tormented him for days; he'd been wondering if some day another man would take over *his* role as husband and father.

He knew without doubt he could never replace what he'd lost, but that didn't mean Violet wouldn't love someone else, someone acceptable. If she didn't relent about seeing him again to at least discuss future arrangements, he might have to move away too. He didn't think he could face Strachmore again or hearing any stories coming out of it. He'd been here before, knew the pain he'd go through to come out the other side and the only thing to get him through was hard work.

In fact he was obsessing over his personal life so much it was encroaching on his professional one. He would've sworn he'd seen the Earl walk past when the CCU doors had flashed open at the end of the corridor. Impossible. He would've known if his patient had been readmitted. Still, it would put his mind at rest to check with the senior nurse in charge.

'Has Samuel Dempsey been admitted again, by any chance?'

'No, but he's here with his daughter. She came in yesterday.'

'What? Why didn't anyone tell me?' In the fearful haze clouding his brain he'd forgotten this had been a secret affair. His colleagues had no idea this woman in jeopardy was everything to him.

The nurse frowned. 'She said she didn't want us to contact anyone. We've put her in Room One—'

Nate didn't wait to hear any more. He was already haring off to find Violet, regardless of whether she wanted to see him or not. People weren't admitted to CCU on a whim, especially pregnant women. If Violet, or the baby, were in danger he was going to be there for them regardless of her objections.

He burst into the side room and, while he was glad

to see her again, the sight of her lying in the hospital bed, small and pale, was almost his undoing. The heart monitors that were part of his everyday job now took on a sinister new meaning as they charted her progress.

'Nate!'

Perhaps he should have given her some warning before crashing in here as he watched her heart rate spike on the screen. He reached for her charts to find out exactly what was going on. 'Are you and the baby okay?'

'We're fine. I didn't sleep very well last night so they moved me in here for a little more peace and quiet.' Despite the circumstances and how they'd left things the last time they'd seen each other, she actually looked pleased to see him.

'Why didn't you phone me?' He directed his question at her father, sitting by the bedside, not a figment of his imagination at all. It was more of an accusation that he'd been purposely kept out of the loop. Probably by the man who'd made it his life's work to interfere in hers. So much for the new leaf they'd supposed he'd turned over.

'I told him not to. I've caused you enough grief over the years. It's not fair to keep involving you in my problems.' Violet's admission saved him from beginning a new battle with her father even though it was completely without foundation. He'd never backed away when she'd needed him.

'Why not? This is my baby too. I *want* to be involved.' A second too late he realised he'd blown the big secret. She might not have wanted her father to know her predicament before she'd gone back to London and now Nate would have his reaction on his conscience too.

'As I told her you should be. Now, I think it's about time you two had a serious talk about your future, about this baby.' The Earl's lack of punch-throwing and willingness to walk out of the room, leaving him alone with his daughter, led Nate to believe Violet had already broken the news of the addition to the family.

'You told him?'

'I didn't think I'd be able to hide it much longer. He took it better than I could ever have dreamed of.'

'Clearly. I'm still standing.' It would've been a different story twelve years ago, pre medical school, if he'd knocked up the Earl's daughter. The long road to cardiology had been worth it to be accepted on some level, if not as part of the family.

'Actually, he didn't seem that surprised. I guess we weren't as discreet as we thought we'd been.' That twinkle in her eye took Nate back to a time and a place he was already having trouble letting go of.

'Okay. Let's see what we have here.' He resisted running over and kissing her when he knew for sure she wasn't in immediate danger. It might be pushing his luck too far.

SVT, supraventricular tachycardia, was something he'd had plenty of experience with in his patients, including pregnant women. The complications that could arise were often due to the presence of heart disease, a cause for concern given her father's recent history. Thankfully her ultrasounds and ECGs had ruled this out. She had, however, been admitted with a very high tachycardia rate, reaching between one hundred and eighty and two hundred and forty beats per minute.

'I'm fine, honestly.' Violet tried to convince him

there was no need for him to worry, or be here, but he could see her arrhythmia had not yet abated.

'We still need to get that heart rate stable again before you leave.' There was no way she was going home until he knew all was well. A beta blocker had already been administered to no avail. There was always a small chance the administered drugs could cross the placental barrier so it wasn't something he wanted for her long term when there were no obvious benefits in her case. The alternative wasn't something he relished for the mother of his unborn child either.

'They said they might have to take me to Theatre?' There was a slight tremor in her voice belying her nerves even though she was insisting on her indestructability.

Since she hadn't bawled at him to get out of the room he dared to get closer to the bedside. 'If your heart rate doesn't regulate they are planning electrical cardioversion. Essentially this will be delivering a mild electric shock to jolt the heart back into a normal rhythm.'

'The same thing you did to Dad?'

'Something similar. Except without the drama. And you're a much prettier patient.' He couldn't stop himself from reaching out and stroking her hair back from her forehead. This could be the last time he'd see her if she chose life in London alone over one with him. The last chance he had to tell her how he really felt in the hope it could somehow make a difference.

She closed her eyes. 'Nate—'

'You scared me, you know. When they told me you were here I nearly flipped my lid. I know you don't want to hear it but I want to marry you. I want to raise our baby together. I don't want to find out what's happening to you via a third party.' There were eight months left of this pregnancy, never mind the next eighteen years of their baby's life.

'I appreciate the sentiment but a marriage of convenience isn't what I want. It never has been. Forcing you to marry someone you don't love makes me no better than my father when he was trying to pair me off for the greater good. I don't expect you to make compromises in your life to suit me, nor am I willing to do that for anyone. I saw what that did to my mother.'

'I'm not asking you to make compromises. I'm simply asking you to be with me. And what's this nonsense about not loving you? I've loved you since our private prom night in the boathouse and I doubt I'll ever stop loving you. You're the one who keeps running out on me.' He wasn't about to take responsibility for her fleeing the country again when he was the one trying to get her to stay. If she was insisting on leaving because the thought of being with him was so abhorrent, he wanted to hear her say it. It was the only way he was ever going to be able to accept it.

'But…but…you made it sound as though you felt an obligation to marry me. You never mentioned the L word.' Violet held her breath, the impact of what he was saying too great to comprehend in her current state. He was basically killing her argument for getting on a plane back to London stone dead.

'The last time I did that you disappeared for over a decade. I was trying to prevent another vanishing-woman act. Listen, I know I didn't measure up then and no amount of certificates will make me a qualified member of the aristocracy, but I will look after you and our child. I don't want you to change. I'm not asking anything from you except to give us a chance.'

She thought her heart was going to burst through her chest, it felt so full. Nate loved her; even after everything, he loved her.

'I was scared, that's why I left the first time, why I was leaving now. I thought it was best for you. I watched my parents' love turn to hate with the pressures of society. I didn't want that for you, or us. The strength of my feelings for you was never in question but I didn't want it to be at the cost of anyone's freedom. You didn't sign up for a baby, or a grumpy Earl, or a run-down country estate.' It said a lot that he was still here now she'd reminded him of all the baggage she was lugging with her.

Nate sat on the edge of the bed and took her hand in his. 'I love you. Everything else we can deal with.'

She didn't think she'd ever get tired of hearing him say those words. 'You mean it?'

'I mean every word. I want to marry you because I love you. A baby is just the icing on the cake. I'll move to London with you, leave my job and be a stay-at-home dad, whatever it takes for us to be together because that's what I want more than anything else in the world.' He leaned over and placed a gentle kiss on her lips.

As soon as he touched her the tension left her body, a sense of peace finally descending and releasing her from the burdens of the past. This was everything she'd been waiting for.

After a long, satisfying smooch, Nate got up from the bed. 'I don't believe it.'

'What?'

He was staring at the heart monitor and she automatically feared the worst. No matter who tried to reassure her, having electrodes stuck to her body to conduct electricity to her organs wasn't how a first-time mum wanted to begin her pregnancy. She'd take morning sickness or a craving for pickles over that scenario any day.

'Your heart rate is stabilising on its own.'

Violet followed his gaze. Sure enough the figures were dropping, evening out to where they were supposed to be. Finding Nate *actually* wanted to marry her had been enough to shock her heart into working properly again. Although, she might have to insist he keep his distance for a while longer. If he kept kissing her and things got steamy there was every chance he'd send her pulse sky-high again.

'In that case I guess we can start making plans for the future. We've got a baby to think about.'

She didn't want to spend any more time looking back. Not when she had so much to look forward to. Her life was going to change for ever, probably bring more challenges along the way, but with Nate at her side she knew she could face them head-on.

After all, one kiss from him had been enough to heal her heart.

EPILOGUE

VIOLET WATCHED FROM her bedroom window as the wedding guests filed around the side of the house to the Victorian conservatory. This was it, the day she'd fought against for most of her life in the very place she'd run from as a teenager and she couldn't have been happier. In less than an hour's time she'd be marrying Nate.

With Strachmore now fully licensed to hold weddings, it seemed fitting that theirs would be the first. They'd agreed upon a small affair with only close family and friends in attendance, simple and discreet with none of the palaver she'd always associated with society weddings. Today was about celebrating their love and nothing else. Everything was perfect.

She stroked her small baby bump concealed under her white lace bridal gown. It wouldn't be long before the three of them would become a family. The past four months had been a whirlwind of activity. After a great deal of thought she'd decided she wanted to move back to Northern Ireland, with both families nearby when the baby arrived. Nate had gone with her back to London to help her pack her things for moving in with him while she worked out her notice. With all of their pre-planning she hoped the rest of her pregnancy was going to be more relaxing.

Once the baby was born she would go back to work at a local level and share the childminding with Nate and the excited grandparents anxiously awaiting the new arrival. Everything was slotting into place. She just wished she had her mother here to share it.

A knock on the door interrupted her maudlin thoughts before they could fully develop and taint the happiest day of her life.

'I just wanted to see how my beautiful bride was holding up.' Nate, devastatingly handsome in his wedding tuxedo, stepped into the room and immediately lifted her spirits again. She couldn't help but wonder if he wore one of those mood rings she'd had as a kid, which had some way of telling him when she needed him most.

'I'm fine, but isn't it bad luck for us to see each other before the wedding?' She really didn't want to tempt fate when it had taken so long for them to reach this point.

'I thought we'd broken free of tradition and superstition by now? These days we make our own luck.' He crossed the room in three strides to reach her and slip his hands around her waist. It was all she needed to feel complete again.

'You're right. I'm sure there's a million women out there who'd want to swap places with me at this moment.' She was the luckiest woman alive to be marrying this man today and she wasn't going to let any imagined curses get in the way of that a second time.

'Have I told you how stunning you are yet? I have to keep pinching myself as a reminder that this is actually happening.' He deflected her comment with one of his own, standing back to admire her vintage-style dress.

'This is *actually* happening. We're minutes away from taking our vows in front of all those people out there.' The nerves started to creep back in at the thought of leaving this lovely cosy cocoon with Nate and proclaiming their love in public.

'Well, we've got a little while yet...' He had that twinkle in his eye that said *NT* wanted to make his mark one last time as a single man.

'Do you know how long it took for me to squeeze into this dress? There's no way I'm taking it off again.' The knowledge he still found her irresistible despite her changing body was enough to send shivers of need skating across her skin and make her want to fast forward to their wedding night.

'Who said anything about getting you naked? Honestly, the way your hormones are raging I'm wondering if I'm going to make it back from the honeymoon alive.' His fake outrage widened Violet's smile even further. She couldn't promise him that when they were going to spend the next two weeks alone on a tropical island. They were still making up for lost time.

'So if you're not going to seduce me, what are you doing in my bedroom, Mr Taylor?'

'I have a present for you, soon-to-be Mrs Taylor.' Nate reached into his pocket and pulled out a small velvet jewellery box. He opened it to reveal a delicate silver necklace.

'It's beautiful.' Violet fingered the tiny diamond-encrusted entwined seahorses dangling from the end of the chain he was now fastening around her neck.

She'd taken off her bracelet today and had felt naked without it, as if a piece of her were missing.

'I'm afraid I couldn't get your mother's necklace back for you, but I thought you could do with an upgrade from my last gift of jewellery.'

'Thank you.' She knew this was his way of marking the start of their new life together and fading out the past.

'I thought we could have our first dance here too. Without anyone else.' He placed her hands around his neck and took her in his arms. She closed her eyes and relaxed into his embrace, remembering their faux prom where they'd danced in secret and fallen in love for the first time. Nate was all she'd ever needed.

As they held each other tight, their bodies swaying together with nothing but the beat of their hearts keeping time, Violet knew there was nowhere else she'd rather be. She'd finally come home.

* * * * *

COMING SOON!

We really hope you enjoyed reading this book. If you're looking for more romance, be sure to head to the shops when new books are available on

Thursday 11th July

LET'S TALK
Romance

For exclusive extracts, competitions
and special offers, find us online:

MILLS & BOON

MODERN

Power and Passion

Prepare to be swept off your feet by sophisticated, sexy and seductive heroes, in some of the world's most glamourous and romantic locations, where power and passion collide.